THE
PENWYTH CURSE

Titles by Catherine Coulter

The Bride Series
THE SHERBROOKE BRIDE
THE HELLION BRIDE
THE HEIRESS BRIDE
THE SCOTTISH BRIDE
PENDRAGON
MAD JACK
THE COURTSHIP

The Legacy Trilogy
THE WYNDHAM LEGACY
THE NIGHTINGALE LEGACY
THE VALENTINE LEGACY

The Baron Novels
THE WILD BARON
THE OFFER
THE DECEPTION

The Viking Novels
LORD OF HAWKFELL ISLAND
LORD OF RAVEN'S PEAK
LORD OF FALCON RIDGE
SEASON OF THE SUN

The Song Novels
WARRIOR'S SONG
FIRE SONG
EARTH SONG
SECRET SONG
ROSEHAVEN
THE PENWYTH CURSE

The Magic Trilogy
MIDSUMMER MAGIC
CALYPSO MAGIC
MOONSPUN MAGIC

The Star Series
EVENING STAR
MIDNIGHT STAR
WILD STAR
JADE STAR

Other Regency Historical Romances
THE COUNTESS
THE REBEL BRIDE
THE HEIR
THE DUKE
LORD HARRY

Devil's Duology
DEVIL'S EMBRACE
DEVIL'S DAUGHTER

Contemporary Romantic Thrillers
FALSE PRETENSES
IMPULSE
BEYOND EDEN

FBI Suspense Thrillers
THE COVE
THE MAZE
THE TARGET
THE EDGE
RIPTIDE
HEMLOCK BAY
ELEVENTH HOUR

T H E
PENWYTH CURSE

Catherine Coulter

Doubleday Large Print Home Library Edition

JOVE BOOKS, NEW YORK

THE PENWYTH CURSE

A Jove Book / published by arrangement with
the author

Copyright © 2003 by Catherine Coulter
Cover art and design by Brad Springer

All rights reserved.
This book, or parts thereof, may not be reproduced
in any form without permission.
For information address: The Berkley Publishing Group,
a division of Penguin Putnam Inc.,
375 Hudson Street, New York, New York 10014.

ISBN: 0-7394-3146-3

**This Large Print Book carries the
Seal of Approval of N.A.V.H.**

A JOVE BOOK®
Jove Books are published by The Berkley Publishing
Group, a division of Penguin Putnam Inc.,
375 Hudson Street, New York, New York 10014.
JOVE and the "J" design
are trademarks belonging to Penguin Putnam Inc.

PRINTED IN THE UNITED STATES OF AMERICA

To Karla Peterson

*You're beautiful, smart, talented,
and have great taste in books.
I wish you the very best in the years to come.*

—CATHERINE COULTER

Dear Reader,

How would you like to be eighteen and four times a widow? If you live with a curse, sometimes things like this happen. And so they did.

We have two sets of heroes/heroines; one set is in the present (1278 A.D.) and the other set is, quite simply, sometime else. We have both over- and underlapping stories, a dynamic mystery, lovers underfoot (visit with Dienwald and Philippa in *Earth Song*) and mega-doses of magic and mayhem.

Come back to the present, and maybe even further back than that. I hope you have lots of fun, and smile until your jaws lock.

Do write me at P.O. Box 17, Mill Valley, CA 94942 or e-mail me at ReadMoi@AOL.com. I hope all of you visit my website at www.catherinecoulter.com and check out my newsletter.

Catherine Coulter

Catherine Coulter

1

Four Years Earlier . . .
Penwyth Castle
Cornwall, England
May 14, 1274

Sir Arlan de Frome pulled up his destrier and raised his mailed hand to halt the thirty-two men behind him, experienced and hard, mercenaries all. Horses whinnied, dust swirled, and Sir Arlan smelled fear. Maybe it was churned up in all that dust, or maybe it was in the very air itself. Sir Arlan was familiar with this smell and he liked it, particularly when it poured off a man who had something Sir Arlan wanted.

Sir Arlan saw it in the faces of the men who lined the ramparts of Penwyth Castle, the tidy hold that would soon be his. The town of Penwyth, nestled in the shadow of the stone walls of the keep, quickly became deserted when the people saw him coming. He hadn't let his men stop to loot. After all, it would become his village soon. The keep itself stood solid as the granite of Cornwall's cliffs, atop a rise that looked toward the sea off Land's End, a barren hunk of land that stood between Penwyth and enemies from the sea come to attack England. It was a keep of great strategic value, and Sir Arlan knew in his bones that King Edward would be delighted to make him the heir, once, naturally, he already had Penwyth in his grasp.

Penwyth Castle—would be his by conqueror's right. Once the girl was his wife— what was her name? Something strange. Lady Merryn, that was it, a silly name, romantic, a name the bards would doubtless sing ringing verses about. Once he married the girl, it would be another encouragement for the king to make him the Penwyth heir. There would be none to gainsay his ownership. He would take the title of Lord de Gay of Penwyth. And why not? His own name, given to him by a bastard father who'd hated him, held no prestige, no power. But Arlan de Gay—it was a good solid name, with at least four generations of steadfast reputation backing it up. It sat well. Sir Arlan smiled. The old lord wouldn't be alive that much longer, now would he? He wouldn't really want to stay around, would he, now that the next generation had arrived?

He had no intention of razing Penwyth, since it would soon belong to him. He didn't want to kill the soldiers or the servants or the serfs who worked within the keep walls, only as many as it took to make the others believe that he was indeed now their master and they owed him their lives.

He looked around the fertile green land, at the flourishing crops, and smiled.

Sir Arlan hoped the old buzzard who was sitting in the lord's chair had a lot of gold hidden away. Those men whom he couldn't entice to remain with him, he would have to reward or kill. He wanted no looting, no excessive violence.

Aye, there was naught but an old man, an

old woman, and a young girl. Fourteen was the age he'd heard, an excellent age for marriage, ripe enough for the marriage bed, young enough that after a couple of clouts to the head she wouldn't ever think to flout him or his wishes. It was good.

He looked up to see a score of faces lined up along the ramparts, staring down at him. He'd heard rumors about all the soldiers here at Penwyth, but he'd discounted them. He would soon see.

He motioned for his lieutenant, Darrik, to ride forward to present his terms. Darrik had a magnificent voice, hard and deep, and it would carry all the way to the sea beyond Land's End.

Arlan nodded to him.

Darrik called out: "Lord of Penwyth, soldiers of Penwyth, tenants one and all. There is no heir to Penwyth. Sir Arlan de Frome agrees to wed with Lady Merryn de Gay and to entrust unto himself, as heir, the welfare and safety of all Penwyth lands until such time as Lord Vellan de Gay dies. Then Sir Arlan will become Lord of Penwyth.

"No one will be harmed if the drawbridge is lowered and we are allowed to enter in peace."

"Well done, Darrik," Arlan said, even as he smiled at all the outraged shouts, the loud murmurings, men leaving the ramparts, doubtless to run down to tell Lord Vellan that there was a lion at the gate.

A bit of time passed—not much, but Sir Arlan was an impatient man. His destrier fidgeted as his master grew more agitated.

He spoke to Darrik in a low voice.

Darrik shouted, "Open the drawbridge or your blood will be forfeit!"

Another bit of time passed, and then came the loud winching of the wrist-thick chains as the drawbridge slowly lowered over the brackish water, deep and stagnant, and a good dozen feet wide. It was happening, just as he'd wanted it to. It was a sign from God.

Never was a keep taken so easily. Sir Arlan led his men over the wide wooden bridge, looking upward at the portcullis that, in times of war, could drop down, its pointed iron bars embedding deeply into the earth, or spearing into an enemy. They rode through the outer court, narrow and thick-walled, through a double set of open gates into the inner bailey. Scores of people had gathered there, all of them still, staring at him and his men, children clutched to parents' sides, animals quiet and wary, heads raised, as if scenting the danger. Everything was normal, it seemed to Arlan, except for the silence. Well, silence wasn't a bad thing—it showed respect to the new lord.

There wasn't much dust for the horses to kick up in the inner bailey. Arlan smiled when he saw Lord Vellan de Gay standing on the bottom stone stair of the keep. His granddaughter stood behind him, nearly out of sight, but he glimpsed her peeking around her grandfather to see the man who had so easily taken their keep. Her soon-to-be husband. Aye, it was good.

Lord Vellan didn't look away from the big man, covered in chain mail, who was riding straight at him. At the last moment, Sir Arlan pulled his powerful destrier to a halt not six feet from Lord Vellan.

"My lord, I am Sir Arlan de Frome of Keswick. I am here to save you from marauders who would raze your keep and kill all your people."

There was a frozen moment of silence, then, "Doubtless I am blessed that you came to save me," said Lord Vellan.

An impertinence, but Sir Arlan let it pass.

He was an old man and old men had their pride, even when they had nothing else. Sir Arlan said, "You have need of an heir, my lord, and your granddaughter has need of a husband. You now have both standing before you."

"My son died but a fortnight ago," said Lord Vellan. "You made good speed to get here."

"Aye, I did. I wanted what was mine. Where is my future wife?"

Lord Vellan said, "Before you see my granddaughter, Sir Arlan, before you announce that you are here to become my heir, I feel it only fair that I warn you."

Sir Arlan laughed. "Warn me? Warn me about what?"

Lord Vellan said, his voice lowered just a bit, "For hundreds of years, this land, all the different fortresses that have stood here, all have been protected by a curse fashioned by the ancient Celtic Druids. These Druid priests held the honor and safety of this land dear. Never in the hundred years that this Penwyth fortress has stood have these lands been invaded and taken. Indeed, none of the fortresses that existed on this site in the past fell to an enemy. They weathered and fell on their own over the centuries. But no man brought them down, because this place was protected by the ancient Druid curse."

"The Celtic Druids? Those blood-covered monsters died out hundreds of years ago, old man. I have no fear of any Druid priests or their prophecies. You only claim that none of the fortresses built on this site were conquered. You have no proof that this is the case. Aye, I think you are lying, old man, and it angers me."

"I am not lying, nor am I speaking of an ancient prophecy. I am speaking of a curse. There is no curse more potent than a Druid curse."

Sir Arlan heard some movement behind him, nervous movement by some of his men, the superstitious fools. He said, his voice loud and laced with scorn, "I have heard of no such curse. A curse from the Celtic Druids? That is nonsense, and you know it. I will not be frightened away by this stupid tale."

"Few have heard of the curse, that is true," said Lord Vellan. "But that doesn't make it any less real. Would you like to hear the curse? It has come down whole and pure through countless centuries of strife and chaos."

Sir Arlan dismounted and handed the reins to one of his men. "No, I don't wish to hear any blasphemy. I care not about a curse that doesn't exist save in your ancient brain. We will come inside, I would inspect my new great hall. I would meet your priest, for I wish to be married before the sun sets. Where is the girl?"

A skinny child, dressed in boy's trousers, a loose woolen shirt, hair scraped back in tight, thick braids, stepped around Lord de Gay. The old man grabbed her arm, as if to hold her back, but she shook him off and stood straight and tall in front of Sir Arlan.

"I am Merryn de Gay."

"And I will be your husband come night-fall," he said, reminding himself that she was still a child, and surely she would improve with age. He walked up the steps and looked at her more closely.

She wasn't at all appetizing. But as long as he could fit himself between her skinny legs and breach her maidenhead, nothing else mattered. Sir Arlan didn't have any problem at all with this scrap of humanity becoming his bride. He doubted a gown would make her any more toothsome, since she had no breasts or hips to draw attention, not a single curve on her small child's body. On the bright side, he didn't think she could get any worse.

"Aye," he said, after looking at her, "I will be your husband by eventide. You may address me as 'Sir Arlan' or 'my lord.' "

"I will not address you as anything. You are an intruder. If we hadn't let you in, you would have been perfectly satisfied to kill everyone. You are here to claim what was my father's and is now mine. Go away or the curse will kill you. The Druid priests who placed the curse owed a great deal to my ancestors."

Sir Arlan heard his men speaking quietly behind him. He said, "I care not about such nonsense. There is no curse, or if there is, it is as meaningless as a goblet of wine that disappears quickly down a man's gullet."

She said very softly, leaning toward him so that she wasn't more than an inch or two from his face, "It is really a very simple curse, Sir Arlan. *If you don't leave, you will die.*"

"Ah, so, long ago Druid priests knew of

you, Lady Merryn? Mayhap they saw you in the dead eyes of one of their sacrifices?"

"Mayhap," Merryn said.

Lord Vellan grabbed her hand and nearly threw her behind him. He had rich white hair and an even more luxuriant white beard that cascaded down his chest to come to a point just above his wide leather belt. He yelled, "Listen, all of you. Sir Arlan may dismiss the ancient curse, but it is quite real. The Witches of Byrne, who are descendants of the Druids, have blessed it. They have claimed this land to be held apart from violence and strife. Aye, for hundreds upon hundreds of years Penwyth has been protected by forces mightier than a few paltry men astride horses."

Lord Vellan heard a man ask, "What is the curse?"

Lord Vellan shouted, "You see my granddaughter, her red hair, her green eyes? She is the image of an ancient priestess who once lived on this site hundreds upon hundreds of years ago. The story goes that an enemy came to that ancient Penwyth and claimed both her and the fortress. The Druid priests collected here, outside the wooden fortress walls, and pronounced the curse. The enemy died a dreadful death, Sir Arlan."

More murmuring voices. "What death? What happened?"

"The enemy fell into a cesspit and strangled to death on waste and rot, all his men looking on."

"You weave a ridiculous tale, Lord Vellan! A cesspit with his men not aiding him? There is no damned curse!"

Lord Vellan smiled. "Listen, all of you!

"The enemy will die who comes by sea.
The enemy by land will cease to be.
The enemy will fail who uses the key.
Doubt this not,
This land is blessed for eternity."

"What key? What key is there to use? What is this, old man?"

Lord Vellan shrugged. "I simply recite the ancient curse to you. If there is a key, its meaning is long forgotten. But you come by land, Sir Arlan, and that means you will die if you do not leave peacefully."

Before Sir Arlan could spit, Lord Vellan called to the men grouped behind him, "I do not know how he will die because no one has ever before taken Penwyth, but Sir Arlan will die unless he leads all of you away from here at once. Will the rest of you die as well? I don't know."

Sir Arlan didn't spit. He knew his men were frightened; perhaps he felt a niggling bit of fear himself, but it didn't matter, and so he threw back his head and laughed, loud and deep. "That's it, old man? That's the stupid curse? I heard nothing about your precious granddaughter in the curse."

Lord Vellan shouted, "This is the rest of the curse. Look at my granddaughter, and know it is true!

"Maiden's heart pure as fire
Maiden's eyes, green as desire
Maiden's hair, a wicked red
Any who force her will soon be dead."

There was utter silence. Lord Vellan saw that Sir Arlan's men were afraid. Good. He said, "It is simple and straightforward, Sir Arlan. Two parts to it. What more need you?"

Merryn said, "A curse should be simple because men are required to understand it."

Sir Arlan raised his mailed hand, his fingers closed into a fist to strike that insolent child's face. No, he would hold to his control. He smoothed out his hand. He was the one with the power. Aye, he had the strength, the might of his men, all loyal to him—or they'd better be. "I see," he said. "And you pretend that you are a witch, Lady Merryn? You believe that this curse was prepared especially for you? Or all green-eyed witches with red hair throughout the years?"

The girl shrugged and looked at him as if he were dirt beneath her boy's boots.

Merryn said, "There is a girl in every generation who has red hair and green eyes, going back to the beginning of time."

He said, "Nonsense. You have no way of knowing that."

Lord Vellan said, "It is true that none of it is written down. The curse has passed down over the years until at last my grandfather wrote it down so it would never be lost. Had it been lost, why, then you would have done what you have done, and died, without due warning."

Sir Arlan laughed again. He stood very close to Lord Vellan de Gay, on the same step. They were the same height and that surprised him. Lord Vellan was an old man, shoulders rounded, thin as a snake, aye, even scraggly he was, despite all that thick white hair, and he should be bowed over, no taller than Sir Arlan's armpit. But no, the old man was staring him in the eye.

Sir Arlan said, "I am now your heir, Lord Vellan. I am not your enemy to take Penwyth from you. Will that please the curse makers? Aye, your goodwill toward me will result in your remaining the lord of Penwyth, at least its figurehead, for perhaps longer than you deserve. Aye, I will let you live, let you continue to drink your fine wine and pretend to power over the souls who work and live at Penwyth, but know that I will be the one to rule, and this girl here will be my wife. And King Edward will be pleased."

Lady Merryn de Gay said to the man whose face wasn't unpleasant, whose breath wouldn't fell a horse, "If you do this, sir, you will die. My great-grandfather told my grandfather that the Druid curse came from the sacred stone circle that stands in the plains of southern Britain. I know no more about it."

"Enough! Go and have your ladies make you resemble a female. And have a wedding feast prepared. I want all in readiness by the setting of the sun."

*   *   *

When Father Jeremiah married young Merryn, finely garbed in an old saffron silk gown
that had belonged to her mother, to Sir Arlan
de Frome of Keswick, it was exactly five
minutes before the sun set on another brilliant spring day near the very edge of Edward's England.

The only cheers were from Sir Arlan's
men and those only because they'd heard
that the cellars were filled with beer and rich
Rhineland and Aquitaine wine. They were
also having a fine time making sport with the
Penwyth soldiers.

Penwyth's   master-at-arms,   Crispin,
whose beard was longer and whiter than
Lord Vellan's, knew a great number of fine
curses, but they couldn't kill a man, more's
the pity, and so none of Arlan's men bothered to clout him for his insults. All of Arlan's
men drank and laughed and toasted each
other on the ease by which they'd taken a
very fine keep indeed.

Lady Merryn de Frome sat next to her
bridegroom of two hours at the high table,
her grandfather and grandmother in the middle of the table, one of Sir Arlan's men on either side of them.

They ate from the same trencher. Sir Arlan sopped fine white bread in the thick beef gravy. Because he had been raised with a modicum of manners, he offered her a tasty chunk of beef off the end of his knife.

She took it, chewed and swallowed, all the while looking through him, as if he wasn't even there.

He grabbed her chin in his hand and jerked her about to face him. "I'm your husband. You will show me respect. Look at me."

"I am sorry that you must die," she said and looked him right in the eye.

"By Saint Peter's furrowed brow, you will cease this foolishness about a bloody curse!" He turned away from her and ate all the tender beef on his trencher.

The jests continued, most of them forced ribaldry, because what man in his right mind would want to bed this child? Still, his men wanted to have the form correct.

There were more toasts, one even speculating on the year the new Lady de Frome would produce her first child.

Sir Arlan was laughing at that when he shouted to Lord Vellan, "From this night on I am Sir Arlan de Gay, your heir and grandson-in-law. Aye, I fit your name well, do I not?"

Lord Vellan merely smiled.

There was more cheering, all from Arlan's men. All the Penwyth people were furious and muttering, but softly, since they didn't want their heads cleaved in.

Arlan turned to his bride. "Tell me you have begun your monthly flow."

Merryn looked at the big man who was old enough to be her father, although, truth be told, most men in the Great Hall could have fathered and grandfathered her as well because, she was, after all, barely fourteen years old. "No," she said, "I have not."

"A pity. However, with bed play perhaps it will encourage your woman's body to do its duty. I will draw blood this night. Aye, that should do it."

"Why did you wish to steal another man's holdings?"

Sir Arlan could have struck her, but he chose, instead, to say, laughter rich in his throat, "My father wanted me, his bastard son, to be a priest, bent and celibate, copying texts in musty old chambers, cut off from life. I was to spend my life paying for his sin of fornication that produced me. I could not imagine a more tedious existence. I could have killed him, but I did not. I went to the Holy Land, fought under Lord Edinthorpe, and brought back jewels. But soon they were gone, and there was nothing for me." He shrugged, looked very pleased with himself, and Merryn wondered how much of his tale was true.

"Penwyth is now my home and you are now my wife. There, I have answered your question. You will never again speak to me with disrespect." He paused a moment, looking at her fine-boned face that would surely show beauty someday. "You will not fight me in our bed tonight."

"Oh, no, I won't fight you," Merryn said. "I won't have to."

He didn't understand that, but it didn't matter. He was too happy with himself and his new circumstance to question her further.

Aye, Sir Arlan felt very good. He'd lost no men and he was now the lord of Penwyth, not as large a holding as Wolffeton or St. Erth, to the east, but his sons would wed with their rich daughters and just perhaps, in twenty or so years, Lord Arlan de Gay would be a name to reckon with.

He met Lord Vellan's eyes, rheumy old eyes that made him shiver deep inside himself where, thankfully, no one could see, eyes that had seen many more things than he had—but that was absurd, of course. The old man had never left Cornwall. He was nothing, a relic, content to dine on ancient legends. Sir Arlan picked up his goblet newly filled with deep red wine from Bordeaux, and said to the company gathered in Penwyth's great hall, "To the future. As of here, as of now, I am to be addressed as Lord Arlan de Gay."

"To the future!"

"To Lord Arlan!"

Arlan swallowed, smiled at everyone, then, without warning, he fell forward, his face landing in his trencher.

There was stunned silence, then shouts, howls, men drawing their swords, their knives, racing to where their master slumped with his face hidden in the rich gravy that coated his trencher.

Lord Vellan shouted as he rose, "Sir Arlan is dead. I warned him. All of you heard me tell him of the ancient Druid curse that was carried down and strengthened by the Witches of Byrne. By all the Druids' ancient wisdom and might, the curse has struck him down."

"No," Darrik shouted, so afraid, so furious, he was shaking with it, "You poisoned him, you miserable old man. You poisoned him, damn you, and now I will kill you. I will kill everyone." The man rushed toward Lord Vellan. Suddenly he simply stopped, as if a mighty hand had grabbed him and held him in place. It seemed he couldn't move. He stared, his eyes bulging in terror, crying now since no words would come from his mouth. Tears ran down his cheeks and yet he remained perfectly still, straining, as if pinned in that one spot. Suddenly, his body began shaking and jerking about. His mouth foamed. He hurled himself against a knot of Sir Arlan's men who were standing close, staring at him, too petrified to move.

They all collapsed onto the stone floor.

Darrik was dead.

It seemed that all thirty-one remaining soldiers standing slack-jawed in the great hall instantly realized that they had no leader and that a virulent curse could kill them all at any moment.

Father Jeremiah's voice rose above the wild fear, the cries, the panicked shouts.

"God's will is done. I pray for these lost souls."

Within the hour, thirty-one men rode hard from Penwyth to spread the tale of how Sir Arlan de Frome had been struck down because he had taken Penwyth and wed Lord Vellan's witch granddaughter. There were whispers about how Sir Arlan's man, Darrik, had shouted "Poison" and tried to kill old Lord Vellan. But, in voices lowered to whispers, he'd somehow been held back by an invisible force. He'd jerked and heaved about until finally he'd fallen to the ground, foam frothing from his mouth. And that force that had held him—be it the devil, or the spirits carrying out the curse—had killed him. Not a mark on him, it was said, just the white foam that dried very slowly on his mouth.

2

Present
London
May 3, 1278

King Edward I of England stretched out his long legs, crossed his ankles, and admired the new pointed slippers that adorned his big feet. Perhaps they were a bit too beautifully embroidered for a warrior king, but his sweet Eleanor had fancied they would look splendid on the royal feet. At least she didn't expect him to wear them into battle.

A slice of sun shone down on the royal head from the beautifully worked glass windows installed by his late father, Henry II, making Edward's thick hair glisten an even richer gold—like a freshly minted coin, his mother was wont to tell him many years before. Edward looked about at the expanse of stone and tapestries and lovely windows. He quite liked Windsor, what with all the improvements his father had made.

He looked up to see a large, hard-faced young man walking beside his Robbie. It was Sir Bishop of Lythe, the young warrior who had rescued his dear daughter, Philippa, from one of her own foolish escapades three months before. The king's son-in-law, Dienwald de Fortenberry, earl of St. Erth, obviously hadn't managed yet to control his precious somewhat-royal wife. Edward would certainly give him more counsel about that. At least Dienwald had thanked the young man by knighting him. If Edward had but been there, he doubtless would have thought of it first.

He watched the young man straighten from a low bow, and said, "I called you here, Sir Bishop of Lythe, to give you thanks myself for saving my gentle daughter, my sweet Philippa, from those oily scoundrels.

Is it true that one of them held a knife to her side?"

Sir Bishop nodded.

"He threatened to shove it into her if you didn't throw down your arms?"

Sir Bishop nodded again.

"How did you manage to get the knife from him?"

Bishop paused, then said slowly, "The man wasn't a good fighter, nor was he quick of wit. I managed to distract him long enough to kill him before he could hurt Philippa. No more than that."

"Hmmm." Edward didn't believe it was that simple for an instant. "My daughter was unknown to you, I understand. Yet you still came to her rescue, even though you'd never seen her before."

"She and her men were in my path, sire. I had no choice."

The king laughed and buffeted Sir Bishop of Lythe on his broad shoulder, causing him to stagger a bit.

"You know that Philippa is the wonderful result of my own royal prerogative, do you not?"

Sir Bishop perhaps wasn't certain of this.

"By that," Robert Burnell whispered close

to Sir Bishop's ear, "his majesty means that she is his own personal bastard."

Bishop smiled. "Aye, sire, I know."

"Good, then you will also know that by saving her, you saved a part of the very essence of your king."

"Granted by God, I doubt it not."

The king detected that slap of wit and decided he was amused. "If you are wondering if I plan to give you the hand of one of my own dear daughters who are legitimate and therefore princesses of the realm, unlike Philippa who is only a princess in my heart, disabuse yourself of that notion right now. Nay, Sir Bishop, I intend to reward you far more suitably."

Since the eldest of the king's legitimate daughters was only seven, Sir Bishop was pleased not to be offered such a reward. He pondered the king's words. More suitably? What did that mean? The king fell silent while a servant garbed in crimson and white served him a goblet of wine, after dutifully tasting it, rolling it around in his mouth, and convulsively swallowing it.

In truth, Bishop had believed that being knighted by Lady Philippa's lord husband, Dienwald, was reward aplenty, but his father hadn't raised a blockhead. He wasn't about to question anything the king chose to do. After all, not only wasn't he a second son, he wasn't even a third son. His father had five living sons, and Bishop was the fourth. He'd been given a name to assist him in embracing the Church, the thought of which had always curdled his belly. Like most second or third or fourth sons, he was landless. Unlike his brothers, he was tired of fighting other men's battles, risking his neck for the chance of winning another man's destrier and armor, although, truth be told, he had won enough over the past couple of years to keep him rich enough and his own eleven men content, but still—what did the king have in mind?

A coffer filled with gold would be nice, mayhap some gems from the Holy Land tossed on top. But Bishop doubted this was what the king intended. No king Bishop had ever heard of willingly parted with gold. When the king turned his attention from his wine back to him, Bishop said, as unctuous as a real bishop or any of the king's courtiers, "To be Sir Bishop of Lythe is surely reward enough, your highness." Although, truth be known, his knighthood hadn't brought in a pence more since he'd added the "Sir" to his name, no more respect from other warriors who knew of it either, as far as he could tell. It had, however, bought him some new friends in Philippa and Dienwald de Fortenberry.

That pretty speech was to be expected, the king thought, and didn't mind the bootlicking. Bootlicking kept men's eyes pointed downward, a good thing when power was at stake, which it always was.

Dienwald had told him that Bishop of Lythe was a clever young man, with a bit of ready wit thrown in to please others, and braver than he should be. Aye, a clever lad he appeared to be, Edward thought. Dienwald had also told him that this young man was hungry and honorable, two things that usually didn't sit all that closely together. But in this case, Dienwald had promised him, they did. Dienwald might be feckless and arrogant as a cock, but he usually saw clearly into other men's hearts. As sons-in-law went, he'd set a high standard, if one discounted that he was called the Scourge of Cornwall.

Dienwald had also said that Sir Bishop was a good fighter, wily and devious, proving his worth by protecting Philippa until Dienwald and his men had arrived to wipe up the remaining bandits.

The king shook his head. He'd protected Philippa? He couldn't imagine his sweet, gentle, strapping-strong daughter accepting any protection. He said to his ever-overworked secretary and the Chancellor of England, Robert Burnell, "Robbie, methinks that we finally have found the man to solve the mystery at Penwyth."

Bishop didn't sigh, but it was close. No gold. A pity. *Penwyth? What the devil is Penwyth? What mystery?*

Burnell had been thinking about this, chewing his quill nub until his lips were black, and he finally nodded. "It continues to confound, your majesty. Mayhap, however, more than just a simple man is required to lift the curse."

"Ah," the king said. "You think the curse really derives from ancient Druid priests, Robbie? That the curse has been leavened by the Witches of Byrne? You think all these spirits are still somehow huddled in the castle walls?"

Druid priests? Witches of Byrne?

"The thought must intrude, sire," said Burnell. "There seems to be no other explanation."

"You are a churchman, Robbie, and yet you allow yourself to believe this curse business?"

Robert Burnell said, "I do not know what to believe, sire. It disturbs me that mischief is plaguing Cornwall and that the source of that mischief might be a demon or a spirit somehow unfettered by an ancient curse."

Demons and spirits? This didn't sound good.

The king said, "How many men have been lost to the curse to date?"

"Four, sire. The very first one, Sir Arlan de Frome, died not two hours after he wed Lady Merryn. Evidently he was dead when his face hit the trencher. This occurred four years ago, just a fortnight after the Penwyth heir died in a tourney that you, your majesty, hosted, in April of 1274, I believe it was."

"Aye," the king said. "That was Sir Thomas de Gay. A fine man, ill-timed in his death. By all the saints' endless prattle, I remember that I exhorted the men not to lay each other's heads open, but they didn't listen." The king sighed, and looked toward one of his hounds, a black mastiff who could catch an entire roasted pheasant in his mouth while running at full speed. He said, "In any case, Lord Vellan, a spirited old man with more fire in his gut than strength in his arm, has petitioned me repeatedly for his granddaughter to be made his heir, and the Baroness Merryn de Gay of Penwyth. That is ridiculous, of course."

The king smiled, all bonhomie and good-will, "Aye, I've decided it's to be our young knight here." He looked at Bishop straight on, rubbed his large hands together. "You will wed Lord Vellan's granddaughter, Merryn. As of today, I proclaim that you are the old man's heir. It's an important holding, of credible strategic importance. I trust that you will protect it with your life. It is also not too far distant from St. Erth, close enough so that Dienwald may call upon you if my dearest Philippa entangles herself in more difficulties. I had believed that children would divert her, but the three babes—twin boys, one named after me, and a little girl named after my glorious Eleanor, and the little boys look like me, which is a good thing, I say— all three sit and clap their hands when she tells them her tales of derring-do. The little girl is the image of her mother, bless her."

The king looked down at his slippers, at least a foot long, and wondered if the twin boys would gain his height. Actually, if they only gained their mother's height, that would be sufficient.

"You have told me quite a lot, your majesty."

"Aye, but your brain is clever enough to pick what meat you wish from the bones."

Bishop nodded, but still, he couldn't quite believe what the king had just said. He said, carefully, "You wish to make me heir to Lord Vellan de Gay, your majesty?"

The young man was honestly surprised, overcome, really, and that was nice, as it boded well for his unstinting loyalty to his king. Edward nodded, pleased with his self-serving generosity. "That is exactly what I mean. You will become Lord Bishop de Gay of Penwyth. You have four brothers to carry on your father's name. There is no need of yours. The de Gay line will not die out."

The king wants me to be the girl's fifth damned husband? The king was sending him to his death before he'd even enjoyed a single marriage bed. The king wanted to reduce his bones to dust before Bishop would fully realize that Penwyth was his, all his. He would be Lord Bishop de Gay of Penwyth, the fifth husband, for how long before he died?

Struck down by an ancient Druid curse.

This was not good.

Robert Burnell handed Bishop a piece of parchment. "This is the curse, Sir Bishop. It has to date killed four men who took Penwyth and married Lady Merryn."

"Read it aloud, Sir Bishop," the king said.

Bishop cleared his throat. "It appears to be two separate curses, your majesty."

"Aye, I know it. Read them."

Bishop read,

> *"The enemy will die who comes by sea.*
> *The enemy by land will cease to be.*
> *The enemy will fail who uses the key.*
> *Doubt this not,*
> *This land is blessed for eternity."*

He looked up. "What is this key?"

Burnell said, "No one knows. Lord Vellan said it came down to him in exactly that way."

"Read the rest of it, Sir Bishop."

And Bishop read,

"Maiden's heart pure as fire
Maiden's eyes, green as desire
Maiden's hair, a wicked red
Any who force her will soon be dead."

"Lady Merryn de Gay—she has red hair and green eyes?"

"Evidently so," the king said. "Keep the curse. You may need to give it an occasional read."

Bishop carefully folded the parchment and eased it into the knife sheath on his belt. He was wondering if the king secretly hated his daughter and was thus sending her savior into the maw of almost certain death. A spirit felling him in his tracks, as Robert Burnell had said? Or by poison, at the old man's hand? Or maybe it was the girl herself ridding Penwyth of usurpers and herself of unwanted husbands?

Were the two poems really hundreds of years old?

Bishop didn't know what to say, but this certainly gnawed at his guts. He didn't want the king to believe him a coward, but, on the other hand, he really didn't want to die. He had just barely reached his twenty-fourth year.

Because there was simply no choice, Bishop nodded, bowed. "I thank you, sire, for your generosity and trust. I am honored. I will hold Penwyth until my breath dies in my throat." *And hopefully it will be closer to fifty years than to a week.*

"Nicely said." And, Edward thought, about time, too. He nodded to Burnell, who now handed Bishop the official deed papers, beautifully scripted by Burnell's own hand early in the morning hours before the dawning of this beautiful May day.

Bishop eyed those papers, saw them as a death warrant. Suddenly he smiled. "Perhaps, your majesty, we can have another writ to accompany that one? One that mayhap could save my life?"

The king smiled. "What is this, Bishop? Ah, I see, you are concerned that the curse might strike you down."

"Not an inconceivable notion, sire, given that four men are already dead because of it."

"But there is no need for the curse now," Edward said, sitting forward on his throne. "I have directed Lord Vellan that it is my command that you become his heir. Therefore it is done, the curse is no more. The king commands it."

Robert Burnell said, "It is common knowledge in the west of Cornwall, sire, that the fourth knight to take Penwyth claimed he was there by your command. It made no difference to his fate. He died whilst he was dragging his new bride to the nuptial bed."

"I had not heard that," the king said. He stroked his long fingers over his jaw. "But he lied, and surely the spirits realized that and thus dispatched his soul to hell."

"That is possible," Burnell said and nodded. "Of course, the fourth husband didn't have any papers from you to back up his claim."

Bishop said, "Mayhap I should insist that the spirits read my writ."

There was a snicker from one of the servants.

Robert Burnell frowned.

"Still," the king said, his eyes on Bishop, "I really don't wish you to die, even though that jest you just made didn't amuse me. Robbie, what think you?"

"I think, sir," said Robert Burnell, "that Sir Bishop was striving to calm his own fears through making an unworthy jest. He is not a stupid man. Indeed, I believe he must have a plan."

"Is that true? Have you a plan, Sir Bishop?"

"Aye," Bishop said. "I hope it is a good one, sire, since it is the only one I have."

Three days later, Sir Bishop of Lythe, now officially heir to Lord Vellan de Gay, Baron Penwyth, left London, which didn't smell so very bad in spring, the wind off the Thames sweet in his nostrils. Still, it was a relief to leave the mobs of people, the stench of unwashed bodies and foul waste, the neverending noise. The countryside stretched ahead of them.

He was off to Cornwall with his eleven men, both of the king's two writs, rolled safely inside a sealskin against his chest. Tucked inside the writs was the Penwyth curse.

So she had red hair and green eyes, did she? Hmmm. This should prove to be interesting, if he survived it. He'd never bedded a woman with red hair. He wondered if her woman's hair was as red as the hair on her head. Well, he would see once she was his wife.

But before he could bed her, he had to rid himself of this damnable curse. There were ways to do things. And there were other ways as well. He was pleased that he'd come up with one of the other ways. It just might keep his heart beating.

3

St. Erth, Cornwall

Dienwald de Fortenberry, the very first earl of St. Erth, and the king's damned son-in-law, didn't like the look on young Bishop's face when he rode into the inner bailey, his men following close behind him. He was carrying his helmet under his arm, and his hair, as long and black as an old hound's teeth, was loose down his neck. He didn't look happy. Those bright blue eyes of his were narrowed to slits, darker than Dienwald remembered. What he looked was, oddly, profoundly determined. What was going on here?

Dienwald called out, "Bring yourself and your men into the great hall, Bishop. You have news, and it doesn't particularly please you. Don't tell me—the king, my blessed father-in-law—wishes me to build ships, set sail with every able-bodied man in Cornwall, and attack the damned French?"

Bishop shook his head, smiled, his blue eyes brightening. "No, it isn't that, Dienwald. It isn't all bad, particularly if I manage to survive it, but I would wish your advice."

"Hmmm," Dienwald said, stroking his hairless chin. "A mystery. My fool, Crooky, will weave a tale of it that will survive until our grandchildren." He called out, "Philippa, come here, wench, and welcome the brave knight who saved your hide—and a beautiful hide it is. I added that in a loud voice so you will not be tempted to tell your father that I abuse you." He said to Bishop, "The king would flay me alive if I so much as harmed a curly hair on her head. He has told me that at least a dozen times over the past three and a half years. And I wonder. If I did hurt a hair on her head, how would the king know? She has so much hair, even I wouldn't guess if one or two strands were missing."

Philippa de Fortenberry, a small boy tucked under each arm, walked down the steps to the great hall, waving one of the little ones at him. "Hello, Bishop. Welcome to St. Erth. What is this? You don't look like a man the king has rewarded. Come down, that's right. Give Gorkel the reins, he will see to your destrier and your men. Our neighbor, Graelam de Moreton, has sent us some excellent wine from his father-in-law."

Bishop dismounted his destrier and handed the reins to Gorkel the Hideous, who gave him a very big welcoming smile, a smile so frightful it made gooseflesh rise on his arms. It was said that the sun was loathe to rise in the morning because it would shine on Gorkel's terrifying face. Truth be told, though, this time Gorkel's face didn't seem quite so gruesome as it had when Bishop had first laid eyes on him three months before.

Bishop embraced Dienwald, then walked to Philippa, looked at the little boy she'd waved at him, and said, "Now, are you Nicholas?"

"This one is Nicholas," Philippa, waving

the other little boy, who looked perfectly content. "This is Edward."

Bishop would have liked to embrace Philippa as well. Indeed, he took a step toward her, but Dienwald beetled his brows, and Bishop merely bowed, lightly stroking her hand that was around the belly of the little boy Nicholas. "You go well, I see, my lady," he said, and when she laughed that lovely deep rich laugh of hers, he smiled.

"What happened? You did see the king, didn't you?"

"Aye, I did."

Philippa said, "I heard you ask for Dienwald's advice. Surely you would prefer mine?"

Bishop, no fool, said, "I can use all the advice offered, for it is possible that your father the king has handed me over a beautiful plate of food that could prove quite rotten."

"Aye," Dienwald said, "but you're smiling. I don't believe this gift of the king's gnaws at you overmuch." He ran his fingers through his hair, nice thick hair that his bountiful wife liked to stroke while she was kissing him and nibbling on his ear. "Did you stop at Wolffeton to meet with Lord Graelam?"

"No, the king told me I must make haste," Bishop said. "Also, I couldn't be certain of my welcome."

"He would have welcomed you well enough," Dienwald said. "I suppose I must add that Graelam is a decent warrior. If he says he will do something, consider it done. Most important, he can also lie and cheat and steal quite well, but still he is not as good at it as I am."

"No one can lie and cheat and steal like my husband," Philippa said, and gave him one of the boys. She grinned up at Bishop. "Come and have some wine, and tell us what has happened."

Dienwald said, as he tossed his son into the air—Bishop wasn't certain which son it was—"As for Graelam's wife, Lady Kassia, she is a princess among women." Dienwald brought the little boy back under his arm, sighed and laid his hand on his breast, fluttered his eyes heavenward, then sighed again. "Unlike Philippa here, who would offer you but a single goblet of wine, I daresay Kassia would have given you the keys to her lord husband's cellars."

Philippa punched her husband's arm,

hard. "Speak not too sweetly about the little princess. I am the princess, not she."

"You are my big wench," Dienwald said, gave her a fond smile, and took the other babe. "Where is my little Eleanor? I wish Bishop to look at the most beautiful girl child in all of England."

"He can admire her in due time, husband. Now, Bishop, my lord is mightily pleased that you saved me, even after three years of living with me and watching me waddle about with Eleanor and then our two boys in my belly. He claims that he very nearly did not survive when I was birthing them. He accused me of trying to kill him with guilt since it took so very long. Now, although he doesn't usually do this, he is apparently willing to give you some of his precious stash of wine."

Bishop said, looking around, "Where is your son Edmund, Dienwald?"

"He fosters with Lord Graelam." Dienwald shook his head and snorted. "I saw the lad a fortnight ago. All he could speak about was the mightiness of Lord Graelam's arm, his wisdom in settling disagreements. I tell you, it fair to burned out my gut."

Edmund, Dienwald's son by his first wife,

was now nearly eleven years old. Time passed so very swiftly. Dienwald handed the small boys to Bishop, grabbed a fistful of his wife's curly hair, pulled her face close and kissed her once, twice, big loud smacking kisses. He raised his head, laughed, and said, "It is time to fill our bellies, wench, see to it."

Philippa laughed as she called to the servants to fetch food and drink. Bishop carried in the St. Erth twins, who settled nicely on his forearms.

When only bones remained on the trestle tables, Philippa, her riotous head of hair confined beneath a lovely silver snood, said, "The time has come, Bishop. What has happened?"

"I am the new Baron Penwyth. The king has also given me Merryn de Gay to wed."

Dienwald, who'd been sipping from his goblet, choked and spewed out wine. "By all the saints' leftover bones, that's not good, Bishop. Well, it is, but it's scary, what with the damned curse."

Philippa leaned forward and slapped her husband on the back, the force of it nearly driving him into his trencher. "She's been widowed four times, Bishop. My father wants you to be the fifth sacrifice? Something is very wrong here."

Bishop settled back in his chair, his own goblet of sweet red wine in one hand, and told them about the meeting with the king.

"So my blessed father-in-law has made you Penwyth's heir. You will wed Merryn. Don't frown, Bishop. She doesn't have rabbit's teeth, rest easy. Hmmm. I like it, but not that you could die to gain it, and then, of course, it would be no gain at all."

"No gain! No gain!
Sweet Bishop must wed,
But what will he have?
No gain! No gain! Just pain.
Lots and lots of very bad pain."

Philippa stared at Crooky the Fool, who was standing before them, his head thrown back, grinning like the fool he was.

Dienwald said, "What was that, Crooky?"

"It rhymed, that's what it did. I did well, did I not, master?"

Dienwald scratched behind his ear, smiled, and said, "Crooky, about the pain part. Come here and let me assist you to better understand it.'

"Oh, aye, you'll cave in my poor ribs. I'm gone." Crooky fell into the rushes and scooped them over himself until only his nose was showing.

"He must needs break into song when the spirits strike," Philippa said. "Usually it is much worse. Now, I cannot imagine that you would willingly lay your head on the block. What are you planning, Bishop?"

Bishop said. "Before I tell you my plan, have you any idea why some long-ago Druid priests decided to weave a protective curse on a place that didn't come to exist until centuries later?"

Philippa sat forward, her chin resting on her hands. "It is said that the Celtic Druid priests saw clearly into the future. I suppose that the priests could have divined a Druid descendant building a stronghold near to the edge of the sea, and that is why the priests created the curse, to keep Penwyth safe."

Dienwald waved that away. "I have heard that too. But I am not certain that I believe it. Now, there are other important things to consider. Your future wife has a nice chin, and beautiful hair. Not curly and wild like my wench's here, but red as a sunset over the Pendeen Hills."

"Aye, and eyes as green as desire."

"Where did that come from?" Philippa said.

Bishop handed her the parchment. Philippa read aloud:

"The enemy will die who comes by sea.
The enemy by land will cease to be.
The enemy will fail who uses the key.
Doubt this not,
This land is blessed for eternity.

Maiden's heart, pure as fire
Maiden's eyes, green as desire
Maiden's hair, a wicked red
Any who force her will soon be dead."

Crooky bounded up from the rushes. "What a fine curse! What an excellent rendering! By all the saints' black toenails, I will write a curse as fine as that one, I swear it by every inch of my height!"

Dienwald said, nodding, "That's quite some curse. It sounds like it's directed at Merryn. Since I haven't seen her for several years, I don't know if she has a bosom to be remarked upon. Well, no matter, she cannot compare to my bountiful Philippa."

"I don't know about her bosom either," Bishop said. As for the red hair and green eyes, he didn't doubt for a moment that she had both. "Attend me, Dienwald. If the Druid priests did speak a curse to protect a descendant, mayhap it adds weight, but still, I cannot believe it. This Merryn, a descendant of ancient Druids?"

Dienwald said, "Four men have died because of the curse. You cannot discount it. Nor can you ignore the fact that Merryn is perfectly described in the curse, if indeed she does have green eyes."

"I don't discount it, you may be certain of that. But I ask myself: is it really a curse, something otherworldly and deadly that has come down from the ancient Druids, or is it something we can understand? I think it must be poison. The old man—Lord Vellan— is killing off these men, either he or his granddaughter."

"That means," Philippa said, "that Merryn knew enough to poison her first husband when she was but fourteen years old. That's reaching too far, Bishop."

"Then it is Lord Vellan," Bishop said. "He had this curse all polished up and ready to read to the first husband upon his arrival."

"Aye, he was prepared," Philippa said.

"Mayhap," Dienwald said. "Lord Vellan is known for being a crafty old buzzard."

Bishop said, "I think it's more likely that there was a vague sort of curse that came down from the Druids. Then it got woven into the beliefs of the Witches of Byrne. Mayhap it is the witches who turned it into a specific deadly curse. Doesn't that make more sense? At least there are still some witches about, aren't there?"

"Aye," Philippa said. "I've heard that the Witches of Byrne still cleave to their caves near the Boswednack forest. They don't like to be seen."

"I don't know, Bishop," Dienwald said. "Your idea is possible. I should like to know how each of the four men died."

"That's a splendid idea, Dienwald. Surely their manner of death would prove either a curse or poison," Philippa said.

Bishop said, rubbing his hands through his hair, "By Saint Egbert's shinbones, I don't know how each died. But I must find the answer. I tell you, Dienwald, I would be slapping myself on the back for my good fortune if it were not for the bloody curse." Another sigh, then he said, "Robert Burnell told me Penwyth is a neat holding, nothing grand like Wolffeton or St. Erth, but it has strategic importance."

"Aye," Dienwald said, "that is true. Hmmm. This teases my brain, Bishop. The king has given you the witch and Penwyth. Edward must have great faith in you."

"So now she's a witch?" Bishop said, and felt the very nice lamb he just chewed fall in a knot to the bottom of his belly. "A witch? By all the saints' swollen bellies, before, she had a chin and good teeth and beautiful red hair. And now you can call her a witch?"

"My husband is amusing himself," Philippa said. "Merryn isn't a witch. At least I don't think she is. She's no longer a child. She was first wed when she was only fourteen; at least that is the legend that has grown up about it. The fact is, I've never seen her, and my lord here has seen her but once, two years ago, so you must give all his fine descriptions their proper weight."

Dienwald said, "Be quiet, wench. I feel things, deduce all sorts of brilliant conclusions from the barest of facts. Now, I can see from your face, Bishop, that you have no intention of riding up to Penwyth's walls and announcing yourself as the fifth hus-

band. I have always believed you clever—
at least I've believed it since you saved my
Philippa. Come, tell us what you will do."

And Bishop sat forward and said, "All
right, I'll tell you."

An hour later, after Bishop had once again
admired the small twin boys Philippa had
birthed and lightly touched his fingertips to
little Eleanor's chin, he slept well in a narrow
bed with a single window that gave onto the
beautiful, still spring night and the rolling
Cornish hills.

Before he left the following morning to ride
the twenty-five miles to Penwyth, he thanked
his host and told him, "I am not too young
to be wed, but I am far too young to die trying."

Dienwald said, "Don't whine, Bishop. I
was first wed when I had but eighteen years
on this sweet earth. Since Edmund was the
result, now I am glad of it. But you're right.
If a man must die, he deserves at least a
decent wedding night."

He yelled to his fool, Crooky, who was lying in the rushes, chewing on a bit of
cheese. "Well, dimwit, sing a moving song
for Sir Bishop of Lythe, who is now also

Baron Penwyth. Aye, sing to the man who will battle ancient priests and curses."

Crooky quickly swallowed the cheese, pulled himself up to his full height, which brought him to Bishop's armpit, and bellowed to the rafters,

> *"The pretty knight goes a-wooing.*
> *He hopes he won't be fried.*
> *Be she a witch? Be she a blight?*
> *He hopes he'll know afore he's died."*

"That was miserable," Dienwald said and kicked his fool in the ribs, sending him on a well-practiced roll through the sweet-smelling rushes. "A man isn't fried, you codsbreath—well, if not fried, it's true that a man can be boiled. I saw that happen once. It fair to curdled my guts. Philippa, what say you? Is frying acceptable?"

Philippa said, "It wasn't all that good an effort, my lord. Shall I kick him as well?"

"Nay," Dienwald said. "Nay, I hoved in his ribs and he did his roll, and did it well."

"I'd rather be kicked by an almost-royal princess," Crooky said, and gave a deep bow to Philippa. "The master has hard toes."

"The last time she kicked you," Dienwald

said, "she nearly knocked your ribs out your back."

"Sir Bishop," Crooky said, bowing low, "I wish you Godspeed and I will strive to adjust my rhymes more pleasingly when you are next here. *If* you are next here. I wonder, can a knight be baked?"

Bishop wanted to kick the fool himself.

4

Penwyth Castle, Cornwall

The closer Bishop drew to Penwyth, the drier it became, which was odd, because from all he'd been told, from all he himself had seen, there should be as much rain in Cornwall as anywhere else in England, and there was more rain in the rest of England than most folk could bear.

It was as if a pall were hanging over the land, as if the Penwyth curse had burrowed into the earth itself. The ground wasn't just dry, it was baked. Every rock, every bush, every tree had a thick layer of dust covering it.

Not good, he thought. A keep had to have farming, gardens, and orchards in order to survive, particularly out here at the very rump of England's shores.

Something of a wild, harsh place at the best of times, the far west of Cornwall was, at the moment, a miserable hot baked hell. He wondered if King Edward had known this.

They came over a small rise, and there it was—Penwyth. Built during the reign of Richard Coeur de Lion, Penwyth dominated the land, a squat giant's fist with thick outer walls. It brooded, its shadow nearly touching the small town of Penwyth that lay just to the east of the huge castle. It was built on a slope of land that gave a fine vantage in all directions. The gray stone walls looked dry too.

Bishop slowed Fearless as he looked up at Penwyth's walls. His eleven men arranged themselves in formation behind him, their lances held upright in their left hands, their shields in their right hands, alert and ready for a fight. He knew they were scared, which was a good thing, since they needed all their wits about them.

He saw only five soldiers atop the Penwyth ramparts. That made no sense. On the other hand, four other knights had taken Penwyth without an arrow being shot.

Well, he wasn't leading an army. That would be obvious to the meanest brain. Let the five soldiers look down upon them, let them be certain that there were no other possible enemies hiding behind him and his eleven men. Although he didn't know where additional soldiers would hide. There weren't many trees around the castle.

The castle was well fortified, the moat was deep, but it was empty now because of the drought, and the drawbridge was winched up tight. There were four round towers, each a good forty feet tall. He couldn't see any soldiers in those watchtowers. This was passing strange.

He pulled Fearless to a halt at the edge of the moat and yelled, "I am Sir Bishop of Lythe. I have been sent by King Edward. I mean no harm to any of you. Let me and my men enter so you may hear the king's command."

A helmeted head disappeared. Time

passed. A hot, dry wind blew that carried fine dirt to film the skin and find its way into every crevice of a man's body.

His master-at-arms, Dumas, said from behind his right elbow, "I swear, Bishop, that I saw some gray hair flowing from beneath one of those helmets. What is this place?"

"I hope we will find out without any of us dying in the process."

At last an old man appeared on the ramparts and called out, his hands cupping his mouth, "I am Lord Vellan de Gay. You say you are Bishop of Lythe. I have never heard of you. How do I know that you are come from the king?"

"I cannot very well overrun your castle, Lord Vellan," Bishop called out, head thrown back. He'd removed his helmet, and now felt the hot breeze dry the sweat on his face. "I have only eleven men with me. You can see that there are no rocks or trees for other soldiers to hide behind. Surely you can risk allowing me to enter Penwyth. I swear on God's holy brow that I mean no harm. I am merely the king's messenger."

Lord Vellan stood there, his thick gray hair, grown halfway down his back, lifted off his forehead by the hot wind. Bishop wished he could see his face, but he wasn't close enough and there was too much hair whipping about the old man's head, mixing with the long beard.

Lord Vellan said no more. In the next moment, the mighty winches ground harsh and loud, and the heavy wooden drawbridge began its slow descent over the dry moat.

Once down, the portcullis was raised. Bishop nodded to his men and lightly touched his spurs to Fearless's sides. Suddenly his destrier jerked back on the reins, tossed his head, and whinnied loudly.

To Bishop's surprise, there was a loud answering whinny. That was all he needed, to have a mare in season anywhere around Fearless, the most able and willing stallion in the kingdom. He should have had Fearless gelded, but he liked him tough as a soldier's boot and mean as a viper.

He led his men beneath the portcullis, looking up for a moment, to see the thick, sharp iron spear points directly above his head, which, if released, could cleave a man in two. He realized in that moment that this was *his* holding—or would be when Lord Vellan went to his rewards. Aye, it was *his* portcullis, *his* drawbridge, *his* empty moat.

He passed through the outer bailey, then through the open gates into the inner bailey, letting all the sounds fill his head. The smith's hammering sounded like booming thunder. But just below it were dogs barking wildly, children screaming, and adults laughing and yelling. When he and his men rode into the inner bailey, silence fell, the smith's hammering went quiet, even the animals stopped their racket.

Bishop knew what they were seeing. The soon-to-be fifth husband, the soon-to-be dead fifth husband, and they wondered how he would die. No, that wasn't going to happen. He was smiling when at last he pulled Fearless to a halt not half a dozen paces from the deep stone steps leading up to the great hall.

He looked at the old man standing there, a sword hanging almost to the ground, fastened to a wide leather belt that cut him nearly in half. Tucked into that thick belt was the pointed end of his long gray beard.

Here stood more pride than in Bishop's own father, a harsh man who'd had more honor than a man should have.

Bishop said, "Lord Vellan. I am Bishop of

Lythe, here as a representative from our king."

From behind the old man came a girl's voice, not high and fluttery but sharp, filled with suspicion. "A bishop, Grandfather? He expects us to believe that the king sent us a churchman?"

Was this the girl who possibly had no bosom and no rabbit's teeth and a nice chin? And beautiful red hair?

"You have misreckoned my name," he said mildly.

She stepped from behind her grandfather, this girl he was to wed, this girl who would be his damned wife until he shucked off his mortal coil. She wasn't smiling, so he couldn't tell about her teeth. It was a good chin, raised too high at the moment, and stubborn. There was distrust seamed into what was possibly a nice mouth, but distrust, in this case doubtless laden with fear, hid all sorts of things.

"You say your name is the Bishop of Lythe. You are obviously a churchman. Why has the king sent us a churchman? Does the king wish you to exhort Grandfather, to tell him he will go to hell if he continues to insist that I, his granddaughter, a female, and thus of no value at all in the Church's eyes, not be made his heir?"

"If your reasoning is as tortuous as those words you just spoke to me, then mayhap I should despair at your lack of wits," Bishop said, knowing he'd insulted her just to see what she would say.

Actually, she looked eager to shove her grandfather aside and leap on him.

After a moment of dead silence, he said, seeing her fists clench, "No. That isn't why I'm here at all."

Lord Vellan said, even as he took his granddaughter's hand and lightly squeezed it, keeping her in place, "This is my granddaughter, and heir, Lady Merryn de Gay. If you are not a churchman here to inform me as my granddaughter just said, then why do you come to Land's End in the midst of a drought when everything is slowly dying around me?"

"The king sent me to expunge the Penwyth curse, my lord. I am not a man of the Church. I am a man of profound knowledge, a man of science. I am considered by many to be a wizard, gifted in the understanding of otherworldly phenomena.

"I have heard that this curse has smitten

four men to their death. It is doubtless a powerful curse, but I will get rid of it." Bishop smiled; he'd made all his claims without hesitation, looking Lord Vellan straight in the eye.

Lord Vellan blinked, and Bishop thought that was probably good. The old man then pushed his heavy silver hair back from his face and said hardly above a whisper, "A wizard, you say?"

"Aye, I say that."

"I have never before met a man who is said to be a wizard. Well, then, about the curse. It has been good to us, that curse, for the four men who forced my granddaughter to wed them—all were villains, every single one of them. And now you're telling me that the king wants you to rid Penwyth of its curse?"

"Aye, that's it."

"But don't you understand? We want the curse," Merryn said, stepping forward again, chin up, shoulders back, ready to slit his throat if given the opportunity, his men's as well. "The curse has saved us four times." She waved four fingers in his face. "The curse has saved me."

"Madam," Bishop said in a voice as stern

as his father's, "you have buried four husbands. You will bury no more. The king for-
bids it."

"If it is the king's wish, then so be it. We
will not bury another one. Aye, we'll let their
miserable bodies rot in the fields. As for my
four husbands, one of them was so repellent
he didn't have a single tooth in his mouth
and I doubt he was much older than my father, who had all his teeth when he died, at
least all of the important ones. Listen to me,
sir. They were bad, all of them. I am very
glad they are dead."

"Which one didn't have a single tooth in
his mouth?"

"The third one, Flammond de Geoffrey,"
Merryn said. "A mercenary who spoke little
English."

"When he forced her to kiss him, he
gummed her," Lord Vellan said, and shuddered. "It was dreadful to watch. Merryn
clouted his ear. He couldn't kill her since he
had to have an heir from her, and so her
punishment was to be the death of one of
my men. He lifted his sword to run it through
Crispin, held by six of his men, then he suddenly dropped it, stared straight up at the
beams overhead as if someone were there,

and started screaming and screaming. Then he vomited up mounds of white foam."

"Aye," Merryn said. "It just kept pouring out of his mouth as he screamed and choked. Then he finally fell to the floor, gagging and ripping at his own throat."

It was a nice performance, Bishop thought. They did it well. Anyone listening would be petrified to his toes. He wondered if it was true. He said, "Your third husband has nothing to do with me, Lady Merryn. Now, I doubt any of the husbands particularly wished to wed you either, but a man does what he must to gain what he wishes to have."

He could have sworn he heard her curse him behind her teeth. It would be a major task to educate her on the manners befitting a widowed lady. He went right ahead, ignoring her. "Now, again, you have misunderstood me, apurpose this time. I will speak it plainly so the meanest brain can understand: *There will be no more deaths at Penwyth. It is the king's command.*"

She said something under her breath, but not under enough. "By God's divine angels, this is idiocy, brought to us by an idiot."

"I am not an idiot." Bishop knew it was

time to get all of them in line. A dose of fear should do it. He spoke loudly so that all in the inner bailey could hear him. "Heed me, madam. I am a wizard. I have my own powers. And if my powers chance to fail me, why then I am also a warrior, able to split a man's head open with my sword."

The girl shouted, "You, Sir Bishop, wizard and warrior, just how would you split open the head of the spirit of a Druid priest?"

"I should use my invisible sword," he said and slashed his hand through the air. One of the old men-at-arms jumped back. "You see, he felt the sting as my invisible sword sliced through the air."

She laughed. Bishop sheathed his invisible sword, smiling a bit himself. There was talk among the people in the inner bailey. He heard a woman say, "I felt the hiss of the blade, I did."

"I smelled the heat of his sword," another man said, and crossed himself.

Good, Bishop thought, *that pleasing threat of the supernatural should bring even this loudmouthed girl in line.*

A little boy said, "Father, is he the pope?"

"He is a sinner," Merryn said. "Ah, but just

look at how I'm quaking from the threat of his invisible sword."

The sneer on her face was full-bodied, inviting a clout, but he contented himself with the high ground. "You will see. Now, are you and Lord Vellan agreed? No more deaths at Penwyth?"

"We have not the magic to prevent death, Sir Bishop," she said, the sneer still well in place. "Think you that we are witches here?"

A witch, he thought. *Aye, she could easily pass for a witch, what with that mouth of hers.* He said, "I will speak even more plainly. There will be no more strange deaths at Penwyth, be they a husband of two hours or a tradesman who has cheated you."

"Must we include a man who calls himself a bishop and expects us to treat him with unwarranted respect?"

He drew a deep breath and said, "If you kill me, you will have the king on your necks, doubt me not." He paused a moment. He was content that Lord Vellan and the little witch understood him. At least Dienwald was right about her hair. Red as a sunset. Actually, red as sin, a wicked red, just as the curse said. He couldn't tell the color of her eyes just yet.

He said, "I am thirsty, as are my men. We have ridden from St. Erth."

"That is but twenty-five miles away," she said. "If you barely had the endurance to cross that paltry distance, then as a wizard why did you not simply wave your hand above your head and present yourself to us in a puff of smoke?"

He ignored her. It was that or leap off his horse and strangle her on the spot. It was a pleasing idea. Bishop sighed. "Will you allow us to enter the great hall, Lord Vellan? I have the king's writ for you so you can see that I am only stating his wishes and his commands."

"Oh, aye, come in, come in," Lord Vellan said. "Merryn, speak to the servants, have food and drink brought for the false church-man here and his men."

"I am not a false churchman," Bishop said. "Bishop is my name, given to me by my father. One should not mock a man's father or the name the father heaped upon his son's head. He had hoped that I would seek out the Church ranks, but that was not to be. Now I have a 'Sir' in front of my name so that no one need be confused." He paused a moment, looked directly at Merryn, and said, "Unless one happens to be a block-head."

"Sir Bishop," Merryn said, seemingly savoring each sound as she looked him up and down. "That sounds ridiculous."

"No wonder you are a widow four times over, madam. Your viper's tongue would make any man eager to totter to his grave."

"Not you, apparently, sir," she said.

He gave her a fat smile. "Ah, but I am not here to wed with you, my lady." He crossed himself, and heard her hiss.

He was still grinning when she turned on her heel and walked up the remaining stairs, through the wide-open wooden door and into the great hall. Ah, now that he was paying attention, he realized that he admired the worn depth of those stone steps, each of them just wide enough for a single man, each too narrow to fight well, so the man above always had the advantage. Aye, it was a splendid dozen stone steps. He wondered how many men had trod them over the past hundred years?

He prayed he would be setting his own feet on those stairs many times before he became dust and bone. From the low, nervous voices behind him, he didn't think his men believed he would grow as old as Lord Vellan.

5

Penwyth's great hall was a huge rectangle with a high, beamed ceiling, going up a good forty feet, smoke-blackened from years of roaring fires in the immense fireplace that stood in the center of the east wall. It was a strange thing, but Bishop immediately felt as if he'd come home.

Home?

It was true. It felt comforting. He felt as though it was his great hall already. He breathed in the lingering smell of old smoke, the smell of the wolfhounds, six of them, all at attention in a straight line behind Lord Vellan. He also smelled the air, stale and dry. It made his mouth dry, parched his throat. Lord Vellan was right. The drought was devastating Penwyth.

"We are fortunate," Lord Vellan was saying to him as he eased himself down onto his magnificent chair, its arms beautifully carved with two lions' heads, their mouths open on silent roars, "that we have a very deep well. There is no shortage of water for all our people and animals. The land, however—if it doesn't soon rain, our crops will die and I shall fear for all our lives."

"How long has there been a drought?"

"Off and on since the first man came to wed Merryn and fell over dead, his face in his trencher. Maybe it began before. I'm not certain."

"Mayhap if you rid us of the curse it will rain again," Merryn said, and brightened. "It would at least be one good thing to come out of it."

Not the only good thing, he thought, and decided he would fit quite nicely in Lord Vellan's grand chair.

Lord Vellan said, "Come, you and your men may sit at the trestle table. Bring it close so I do not have to yell at you."

The men's boots crunched through crackling rushes. Bishop helped his men pull the table closer to Lord Vellan. He remained standing, waving his men to sit on the long wooden benches.

Suddenly, it came clear and sure in his mind, just as it had always come to him since he was a small boy. He breathed in deeply, through his nose and his mouth, just to make sure. Bishop smiled. "I have good news for you, my lord."

Merryn said, "What is your good news? You will depart after you have survived drinking our wine?"

"No, it is far better news than my leaving."

She said, "I can't imagine what could be better than that."

Bishop was still smiling. "In that case I will leave you to wonder, though it will tax your few wits."

He saw that she couldn't think of anything worthy to say back to him. He could see every feeling on her face. He imagined she was a bad liar. That face of hers, it was an uncommonly interesting face, not really beautiful but fine-boned, vivid, strong, the mouth full. And her eyes, incredible eyes, were just as the curse had said—as green as desire. He felt a bolt of lust looking at her eyes. Not a bad thing, since he was going to wed her, but it was a surprise. To be suddenly as hard as the stones in the mammoth fireplace, it wasn't a common occurrence.

But it was true. He'd gotten hard just looking at her eyes. He realized he'd like to see that red hair of hers brushed out of the tight braids to hang loose and free about her face and shoulders. Wicked as sin? He'd surely find out. He smiled even bigger. If he didn't die, why, then, things were looking up.

"Ha!" said Merryn, and knew it wasn't worth anything. No way around it, he'd bested her. She said on a sigh, "All right, Sir Bishop, I am listening. What is better than another dead husband?"

Bishop merely shook his head. "Perhaps when you have learned some manners, perhaps when you can bring yourself to entreat me in a sweet, submissive voice, I will tell you."

"We will all grow old if we wait for a show of submissiveness from my granddaughter," Lord Vellan said.

"You are already old, Grandfather."

"I am beyond old, Merryn. Now, I entreat you, Sir Bishop. What is your good news?"

Bishop stared at Merryn.

"Very well, what is this ridiculous news?"

"It is going to rain."

Lord Vellan was shaking his head, back and forth. "Rain? You make that prediction? No man can predict such a thing."

"You will see," Bishop said.

Merryn said something under her breath that he couldn't make out, then she said aloud, "Sit down, Sir Bishop." Once he was seated, she rose to pour some wine for him into a lovely heavy pewter goblet. "You actually claim to predict that it will rain? Do you have a closer knowledge of the Witches of Byrne or the Druid priests, Sir Bishop? Are you in truth a wizard? It was not just a lame jest?"

"I have told you that is said of me." *The virtues of lying cleanly and fluently,* Bishop thought, remembering the lessons of his two elder brothers, two of the best liars in England. "As for the rain, the fact is that I can smell the rain coming in the air, I have always smelled it, even as a child." Bishop tapped the side of his nose. "And it has never left me. It will probably rain tomorrow, or the next day at the latest."

She snorted.

"How do you do it, Sir Bishop?" asked

Lord Vellan. "From whence did this gift come?"

Bishop said, "Perhaps from my grandmother. When I was a small boy, I heard my mother speak about my grandmother being able to do inexplicable things." He shrugged. "I suppose you're right, that it is a gift of sorts, this foreknowledge of the rain." He saw the naked hope on Lord Vellan's face, the stark disbelief on Merryn's face. Of course they didn't believe him. Why would they? He'd just walked into their lives, claimed he was a wizard, and now he was predicting rain for this rain-starved land. At least he wasn't lying about that. Predicting the rain—he'd first done it when he was but three years old.

Bishop listened to the servants and soldiers speaking behind him, and he raised his goblet. He eyed Lord Vellan as the girl poured him wine from the same carafe. Still, he was afraid to taste the wine, hated that he was afraid, but knew it was that simple, and that the damned witch saw the fear on his face.

She laughed, grabbed his goblet, and took a healthy swig. She wiped her mouth with her hand and set the goblet back down in front of him. "Since you have not forced your way in here and forced me to wed you, you are quite safe from the ancient curse." She paused a moment, then frowned, a studied frown meant to enrage him. "At least for the moment. Who knows with ancient curses? Maybe confusion arises after centuries of moldering." And the witch actually laughed.

Lord Vellan raised his own goblet. "If it rains, I will be in your debt, Sir Bishop. All of Penwyth will be in your debt." He gave a quick look toward his granddaughter. Was that a threat toward that red-haired witch in his old eyes?

Bishop was pleased, thinking it only right that all his future people be in debt to him. It was a very good feeling. He called out, "Bless God and all his armies of angels," and wondered where that salutation had come from as he tipped back the goblet and drank deep. He was expecting something vile, but the wine was excellent. He even licked a drop off the rim of the goblet. If it was poisoned, he certainly couldn't tell. In any case, it was now too late for both of them, since his future wife had been his taster. He drank the rest of the wine, looking her right in the face as he drank it down. He had no choice, for she was staring back at him—a sneer and a dare in her eyes.

He heard his men speaking quietly behind him, knew they were watching him drink, believing him a fool. He couldn't blame them. He'd gone into battle with more confidence than he'd drunk a single goblet of wine, served him by a witch who was watching him with a heavy sneer, a witch who should have had tangled black hair and a black tooth or two, but instead had neat braids wound around her head in a sort of plaited crown. That hair—it was as red as a drunkard's nose, mayhap as red as an Irish sunset, mayhap a wicked red. As for her teeth, they were straight and very white. Very well, he supposed that she could have something pleasant about her, he just wasn't aware of it yet.

He allowed her to pour more wine into his goblet, knowing that she was enjoying every moment of it. Then he raised the goblet toward his men, toasting them, "Drink up, lads. It is a tasty grape."

"They don't have wine, Sir Bishop. They have ale, made here in our own alehouse. Nay, sirs," she said to his men now, who looked ill at ease, all of them sitting on the edge of the wooden benches, ready to bolt— all except Dumas, who looked ready to strangle her if need be. She said to him, "The ale is the best in all of Cornwall. It is my mother's recipe."

Dumas cleared his throat. "My lady, if you would be so kind, we would all prefer sweet water from your castle well."

She laughed, the witch actually laughed at his stout, brave men, after she had nearly scared them out of their tunics. What gall.

"What is your name, sir?"

"I am Dumas, my lady."

"Have you long known the churchman here?"

"Aye, my lady, since he was an unripe lad of seventeen summers."

Merryn looked back at Bishop. "I see he has outgrown his unripeness." Actually, since she wasn't blind, there was absolutely nothing at all unripe about him. He was well made, looked to be as strong as Prince, her grandfather's most vicious wolfhound, his muscles stark and hard. His hair was thick, richly black, his eyes dark, dark blue, and that damned face of his was finely hewn, his cheekbones all sharp, and his mouth—no, she wouldn't look at his mouth because his mouth made her feel some very strange sorts of things. He was magnificent, truth be told, and he probably knew it. He'd probably had maids swooning all over him since he'd reached an age to have that mouth kissing and those muscles flexing. Even his teeth were straight and white. Surely there had to be something ugly about him, but she didn't see anything. She would have to look more closely.

Merryn forced herself to look away from him. She sipped at her wine, waiting for her grandfather to read the king's writ.

Lord Vellan didn't say anything. Evidently, she thought as she turned toward him, he wasn't through studying this man who claimed it would rain, this man who claimed he was a man of science, a man who understood things that mortals couldn't begin to comprehend.

A man who was a wizard.

A wizard.

Surely there was no such thing anymore than there were still witches roaming the caves hereabouts. The Witches of Byrne were so few now that no one ever saw them.

Lord Vellan sliced off a hunk of cheese

from a huge wheel that one of the servants held in front of him on a big wooden platter, then slipped his knife back into the sheath at his belt. He frowned as he chewed, and Bishop wondered why he ate it if he disliked it. He cleared his throat, and at last he said, "Sir Bishop, give me the writ."

Bishop pulled the rolled parchment from his tunic and handed it to the old man. His veined, gnarly hands trembled a bit as he unrolled it, but unlike his hands, Lord Vellan's hair was thick and healthy, albeit gray as a thick morning fog. Bishop couldn't get over how the tip of that long, long beard of his, tucked beneath his belt. How old was he? Surely he was somewhat older than the dirt in the inner bailey.

Bishop said suddenly, "I was only a boy at the time, but I met your son, Sir Thomas de Gay. He was a fine man. I was very sorry to hear that he had died in the king's Windsor tourney four years ago."

Merryn went utterly still. She didn't say a word, just waited. He'd met her father? She felt a jerk of pain. She could no longer picture her father's face.

Lord Vellan said, "My son should have remained at home. But men revel in violence, they seek it out to test themselves, only there was no need for him to do so. He was not as lucky as his father. He should have stayed at home, but he didn't and was done in." He handed Merryn the fine parchment.

Bishop's mouth dropped open. "Why do you give it to her? She is a girl. She has no idea what mean those marks on the paper. She hasn't—"

He shut up when wine splashed against his face. He couldn't believe it. He was a visitor, a guest—*a wizard*—and the lady of the keep had thrown her wine at him. And all he'd said—

She was frightened, embarrassed, and scared. He saw all of it clearly on her face. He could read her more easily than he'd ever read a parchment. She said, "I acted without proper thought. I accept it as a fault. If you are really a wizard, then will you strike me down?"

He slowly wiped the wine off his face with his sleeve. He looked at her as if she were naught of anything, and he was pleased when she stiffened up and said, "I read better than you do," but in truth, she really couldn't. She still had to sound out many words when she saw them, but she wasn't about to let him know that. She backed away from him and studied the parchment. Thanks be to all the precious martyrs' shinbones, she could make out most of it. She raised her head and smiled sweetly at him. It was a nice smile, he thought, albeit as false as a minstrel's tales. "Forgive me for throwing my wine at you, Sir Bishop. It was rude and I most sincerely and humbly apologize for it. I thank you for not striking me down."

"Your apology is about as sincere as your desire for another husband, my lady. You make it just because you're afraid that I will indeed strike you down. I am tempted, so you will mind your tongue and swallow your rudeness."

"Of course I don't want you to strike me down. I am not stupid, nor am I rude. For the most part."

Bishop heard his men, to the man, sigh with relief. He knew they were praying that he wouldn't take offense, that he wouldn't rise up and throw the female into the rushes, and then fall over dead from the curse. After all, they might be included.

He smiled at her, not at all a nice smile.

"Do tell me what you think of the writ, my lady. Do you agree with the king's bidding?"

"It is my grandfather's opinion that is important here," she said, and he hated it that she'd so easily slipped out of the mild humiliation he'd planned for her. A woman reading, it was ridiculous. Why, he had only learned to read because Lord Lisenthorpe had a brother who was a monk and revered such things. He hadn't liked learning it, but now he appreciated actually being able to read a bill of sale or a contract, or a keep's records. It was true that a man who couldn't read could be easily cheated.

"Aye," he said, unwilling to give it up just yet, "but it appears that Lord Vellan gives you great latitude. He must think your brain holds less air than most ladies? The king said that your grandfather has petitioned many times for you to be made his heir, Baroness Penwyth. Mayhap if you'd told the king you could read, he might have granted it." Then he gave her an evil smile. "Although I doubt it. A woman who can read is something akin to a duck who can sing."

He thought she would burst with rage, and he felt the sweet warmth of it all the way to his belly. He also thought it a good thing that she didn't have any wine close at hand.

But she didn't burst. She stood there as still as a warrior's pennant on a windless day. She showed control, and that was important, particularly since he would be her husband. After a moment, she said, "It is something the king should do. He should trust my grandfather's judgment."

"Don't be foolish," Bishop said, unable to help himself. "The king would sooner give a sheep into the tender keeping of a wolf than allow a holding of strategic importance deeded into a woman's hands. It is nonsense." He realized, of course, that he was gravely insulting Lord Vellan along with his witch of a granddaughter, and he hastened to add, "I doubt not your good intentions, my lord, but Penwyth must be held by a strong man, a warrior with experience."

"You are not old enough to have much experience."

"I have more experience than my years could expect. Now, I remarked that many of your men-at-arms—at the least the five who are standing against the wall over there— are nearing advanced years. And that is why, is it not, that you had to give over your castle to the four marauders?"

Surprisingly, Lord Vellan laughed. "You will meet my men soon, Sir Bishop. Right now they are guarding me and Merryn, all their attention focused on you. They aren't nearing advanced years, they have long since gained their advanced years. They cannot fight like the wily young rats they used to be, but they can still think and give me good counsel. They are still healthy, and fit enough."

One of the old men coughed into his hand. Without a word, a servant took him a goblet of ale.

"And what did your men think when at four different times in the past four years, landless knights have come to lay claim to Penwyth?"

Lord Vellan said, "They thought it absurd to fight. They thought it efficient to let the curse deal all the blows for them. And so it happened as we all prayed it would. All of them, dead by the curse, and all of us still here."

Bishop said slowly, "So you allowed all the invaders into the keep? You offered no resistance at all?"

"No, I did not. I opened the gates, welcomed them, warned them. None of them went to his death without due warning. I read each of them the curse to be certain they understood. I entreated them to leave and take their men with them. When they refused, I provided them fine hospitality. I wanted none of our people hurt as many are in the rage of battle. I wanted no siege." Lord Vellan shrugged. "It is unfortunate, but none of them believed me."

Merryn said, "I believe my fourth bridegroom—a Sir Basil of Ware, did believe my grandfather, but you see he had fifty men at his back, and he'd promised them riches and a home, and thus he could not back down. I could see that he had heard stories and that he was afraid." She sighed. "He told us that the king had sent him. It was a lie, and the curse knew it. He didn't seem too greedy a man, but it didn't matter. The curse said he would die and so he did."

Lord Vellan said, "He refused to eat at his own wedding feast, claimed he wasn't hungry, but it was obvious to all that he was afraid of poison. He claimed he simply wanted to take his new bride to the marriage bed."

"What happened?" Bishop couldn't help himself, he sat forward, nearly knocking over his goblet.

"He took my hand," Merryn said, "and forced me to rise with him. He kissed me in front of all the company. He told me to drink his wine. I drank it. Then he lifted the goblet and drank himself.

"He kissed me again and again. Then he drank more wine. He was laughing and laughing when suddenly he fell, dragging me down with him. He whimpered as blood spurted from his mouth and nose. It took him a long time to die. All believe it was because he lied about being sent by the king.

"His men were terrified. They were gone before I could even drink a toast to Sir Basil's untimely death."

"None of your four husbands ever bedded you, Lady Merryn?"

"That, Sir Bishop, is something I share only with God at my evening prayers."

Lord Vellan said, "The king writes that you are to relieve Penwyth of its curse, that you are a man versed in dark and ancient lore, that you have powers many do not comprehend, and that if anyone can succeed in cleansing Penwyth, it is you. This is what the king commands."

"Aye, it is."

"If you do succeed, then you will leave me open to the next man who wishes to steal Penwyth. It is a bad thing, Sir Bishop."

"The king, wisely, does not wish to have long-dead curses plaguing his lands, killing his people. This is what the king wishes. I am his emissary. I hope that the purveyors of this curse, be they spirits or mortals, realize that if I am killed, the king will simply take Penwyth and you will all be dispossessed, likely slain."

"It is a terrible thing," Merryn said. "The king punishes us. It makes no sense. My grandfather's grandfather was given these lands by King Henry II in 1174. You would give us to the next greedy landless knight who comes along."

He shrugged, said nothing at all. He watched her face turn nearly as red as her hair. *Let her explode with rage. Let sweat trickle down her face.* He looked at Lord Vellan. The old man had no expression whatsoever on his seamed face. Then, quite suddenly, he smiled, a ferocious smile that was filled with enmity and guile.

Bishop knew in that instant that he had to tread very carefully around the old man. If the king had asked him at that moment, he would have sworn the old man had poisoned all four husbands, that no curse was at work here at Penwyth. But he could do no more. He'd already done the best he could to protect himself.

6

Merryn raised her face to the sky. "Did I feel a raindrop on my nose?" She wiggled her nose, batted at it, and said, "Oh, my, no, no rain. I do believe it was just more blowing dust. So where is this rain you predicted, Sir Bishop?"

Bishop turned at the sound of her voice. He was standing atop the ramparts, near one of the four circular towers, looking out over his future lands. He was congratulating himself on still being alive. He leaned back against the thick stone wall. A guard stood some twenty feet away from him, his gray hair blowing in the hot wind. Another old man. Did Penwyth breed old warriors or perhaps old warriors from other places congregated here for their final years? He didn't mind them at all. Once Penwyth was his, he would find out.

He crossed his arms over his chest. He saw that Merryn's sneer was back in full force, and said with as much control as we could muster, "I do not believe the rain will come today. Perhaps by tomorrow evening. How long has it been dry here?"

The sneer fell away as she said, "Nearly six months without rain. People hereabouts believe it has something to do with the curse."

"Ah, I see. They believe the curse to be both a blessing and a blight."

"That's right."

"So you believe that witches control the weather, with ancient Druid priests chanting at their backs, adding their power?"

"No, I would not say that, but it is what some people believe."

"The drought started four years ago when the first husband came?"

"It's hard to remember. I think the weather began to change about that time. This last dry period started with husband number four, Sir Basil of Ware. There hasn't been a drop of rain since."

"It sounds like Sir Basil cursed you."

She nodded. "Oh no, he was merely a man. It's difficult to accept that the Druid priests are behind it, because truly I want to believe that God controls all things, including men's fortunes."

She was standing beside him now, looking toward Land's End and the sea. There wasn't a cloud in the sky. The sun was high and hot, the wind harsh and gritty against her face. "Truth is, I don't really know what to believe anymore."

"I told you that it will rain, which means that when it does, the people will believe that the ancient sprits have got their grit and strength back."

She shrugged, then said without turning, "You are the first comely young man to arrive at Penwyth."

"What?"

"I was only fourteen years old when Sir Arlan came to wed me and steal Penwyth. After that, no man who came here was young, comely, or up to any good. Once, about three years ago, there was a merchant whom we allowed inside because he had goods to trade and sell. What he had, really, was a wagon covering ten men, and they were out to take Penwyth. It wasn't the curse that time, it was our own men who slew them." She shook her head again. "We lost Rupert, one of Grandfather's oldest friends. Grandfather decided after that to allow the curse to work its will."

"I can see that. But about this comeliness, why do you say that about me?"

"You are excellent to look at. Surely you must know that. Are you blind?"

"No, I am not blind. Are there no young men hereabouts?"

She paused a moment, pushed hair out of her eyes. "So you want comparisons, do you? Well, no young men to speak of, at least none I could consider marrying." She paused, then frowned. "I came to tell you that my grandfather is ready to talk about how long you will be staying at Penwyth."

"I will remain here until everything is resolved."

"Then you will leave?"

"Why are you so anxious that I leave?"

She said nothing to that. As for him, he didn't say anything either, because he was looking into those green eyes of hers, the color of a spring leaf freshly rained upon, and he was as hard as the castle stone he was leaning against.

He said, "Do you fear that I will lift the curse and then another husband will ride in and force you to wed yet again?"

"Given that it's happened four times, only an idiot wouldn't be concerned."

"What do you mean exactly that I look excellent?"

"What? Oh, you wish me to fill your gullet with compliments, do you? Very well. You have the most beautiful eyes I've ever seen in my life. The blue is so dark as to be nearly black."

Beautiful eyes? A man with beautiful eyes? Hmmm. "You force me to be honest here," Bishop said, looking down at her. "My eyes are nothing out of the ordinary. It is your eyes that make me want to—well, never mind that."

"Make you want to what?"

"I have forgotten, and you would do well to forget it too. You know, Merryn, I really am quite competent as well as excellent-looking. I will lift the curse, then we will see. You could consider trusting me."

"Trust a man who just rode into Penwyth

hours ago, flinging his orders about? I don't think that's possible. Not after the four husbands who did the same thing. It occurs to me that you are here to lift the curse and then take me, just like all the others, only you're smarter."

She was smart herself. He said, stroking his fingertips over his chin, "Do I have other excellent parts?"

"Your feet."

He grinned. "What would you know about my feet?"

"Your feet are big and that's good because you're a big man. I think all of your parts work well together."

"So my parts are in harmony."

"Exactly so. Do you want to know more about your excellent parts?"

He very nearly nodded, but he had to keep his focus here, and that meant he had to avoid looking into her eyes. So she thought his eyes were beautiful, did she? He said, "How odd it would be to marry a girl who had already been wedded to four other men."

"I will tell you what is odd. To be wedded to four different men and have each of them drop dead before your eyes."

"Mayhap God will give you a man who will outlive you."

"That's a nice thought, but I will not hold my breath waiting."

He wanted to tell her that it wasn't going to be all that long a wait, but he didn't. Instead, he turned to look east, toward a field where he saw six large stones in a rough circle. He pointed. "The stones set upright— I have seen many of them in Cornwall, and also in the western part of France."

"I do not know about the ones in France. The ones yon are called Menya Alber, and have stood there for as long as any can remember. There is also a place called Lanyon Quoit that is perhaps a burial chamber, but so old it probably existed before men walked on the earth. And if that is so, then how can it be a burial chamber? There is also the Nine Maidens Stone Circle, not far from Penwyth. It is said that the maidens were girls who danced on the Sabbath and turned to stone."

"I can feel the age of them," he said. "I can smell their age in the air. It makes my skin itch to think about it."

She blinked, said, "Mine, too. How odd that we are the same in this."

"Let me add that I also admire your feet, perhaps more than you admire mine."

She couldn't help herself. She looked down at the toes of her dusty old slippers sticking out from beneath her equally old gown. "My feet? You cannot even see my feet. Are you trying to drive me mad with jests?"

Without a word, he came down on his haunches and lifted her gown until he could see the narrow cords that bound the slippers to her feet. He untied the knot, eased one slipper off her foot. "Ah," he said, and raised her bare foot to set it on his thigh. "Would you just look at that foot? I thank the saints it is reasonably clean."

She wanted to snatch her foot away, but she didn't do anything, just watched him look at her foot. Then he was running the pad of his thumb over each of her toes. Her toes quivered and curled. Then his hand cupped around her foot, stroking the arch. He said, "I was wondering if your feet would be too big. What a blessing that they are not." He looked up at her and smiled. "What do you think about the curse?"

Her breath whooshed out of her. Still, she left her foot where it was. She felt his hard thigh beneath her sole, the soft wool of his trousers, and the warmth of his big hand now closing about her ankle to steady her. This was all very odd. His fingers were now molding themselves around her heel. She said, "My feet aren't too big. My grandmother has always told me my feet were just like hers and therefore perfect." He was making her foot feel warm. It was absurd. She said not another word until he replaced her slipper and tied the cord together again. Slowly, he rose.

She looked at the wine stains on his dusty gray tunic and said, "You will sleep in the steward's chamber. I will send a servant to fetch your tunic. It must be washed. I do not want it to be ruined, at least by my hand. I know no more about the curse than you do. It is odd to see so many young men."

A black eyebrow went up.

"You and your men. You are all young."

"Dumas, my master-at-arms, is nearly forty, a grand old age."

"You call nearly forty a grand old age? Our master-at-arms, Crispin, has reached his sixty-eighth year. As for you, you have yet to reach your twenty-fifth year, despite all that experience I see in your eyes."

"To gain sixty-eight years and still talk and walk and make sense and lift one's arm— that's an amazing thing."

"Aye, it is. I don't want you to die."

Bishop thought that sentiment boded well. "Why not?"

It was as if she'd just realized what she'd said. She closed down like a clam.

"Is it because you admire my excellent parts so much?"

"That could be a small measure of it," she said, and looked down at the foot he'd stroked.

He grinned. "I have been here for nearly four hours. I am still breathing." He pressed his palm to his stained tunic. "My heart still beats." He took her hand and flattened her palm against his chest.

"Aye, it beats. Very strongly. I believe it is beating faster than it was just a moment ago. Why is that?"

He quickly moved her hand. "My heart beats just as it should," he said. "I think I may be safe, particularly since my death would mean yours and your grandfather's as well. The writers of the curse couldn't have intended that."

"No, they couldn't."

"I will discover the truth, Merryn. I must. You know I cannot leave. If I did, my task unfinished, the king would knock my head into a stone wall."

She smiled at that, and showed him a deep dimple on her left cheek. It was the first glowing smile she'd given him. "You fear the king more than ancient curses?"

"Oh, aye, I do. Do you believe the curse was fashioned especially for you, that some Druids hundreds of years ago said, 'This is for Merryn de Gay and none other'? "

"Do you believe my hair is as red as fire? A wicked red?"

He looked at her wild red hair, blowing fiercely around her head in the dry wind. He nodded. "Aye, at least as red as fire, and beyond wicked."

He reached up, touched his fingertips to her hair. Slowly, never looking away from her, he wrapped some strands around his finger, over and over, until he was tugging her toward him.

She shook her head and he released her hair. She said, "And are my eyes as green as desire?"

"No, your eyes are as green as lust."

"Oh." She blinked at that. If he wasn't mistaken, and he knew he wasn't because he was, after all, a man, she blushed.

He said, "What do you know about this key? 'The enemy will fail who uses the key'?"

"An odd line, but I know nothing at all about any key. No one does, not even my grandfather."

"So the curse is for any and all females with red hair and green eyes who just happen to live at Penwyth?"

She said nothing.

"All right, tell me this. Is there a mare in season within the walls?"

"Why, yes, my mare, Lockley. There isn't a stallion about to cover her."

"My Fearless will cover her, willingly. He whinnied when he heard her; he caught her scent."

"I will think about this. I want to know his bloodlines, Sir Bishop. I want to inspect him, see that he is worthy of Lockley."

"I will swear upon Saint Cuthbert's scabbed knees that Fearless's withers are the finest in the land."

"You jest. I don't know anyone who jests like you do."

"Do you consider it one of my many excellent parts?"

"I have known you for a very short time, only the length of a well-attended banquet. This is all very odd."

"You may inspect Fearless. If it will gain him the mare, then he will doubtless allow it. You must explain his reward to him simply, no difficult words. As a wizard, I have merely to think my words to him and he understands."

"You claim you can predict rain. Just maybe your damned destrier can understand what a person says as well. I don't believe a man can be a wizard. Wizards are old and bearded, and they have strange mad lights in their eyes."

"Even a wizard must begin young."

"I still don't believe it. You are a man, just a man, albeit a clever one."

"So you believe me clever?"

"No. I didn't mean to say that."

"You will see. Now, the curse. The Celtic Druids had no written language."

"The curse has come down from father to son or daughter from each succeeding generation. It was Lord Vellan's grandfather who finally had a scribe record it. There's nothing more to it than that."

She was lying and he knew it. He felt frustration boil in his belly. What was going on here? He said, "It is said that the Druids put their prisoners in wooden cages so they could burn them at night for warmth and sacrifice. Can you begin to imagine the smell of that?"

"When my third husband vomited up white foam, I remember that the stench was beyond anything."

He did not want to imagine that. He said, "Very well. Now, the Witches of Byrne—a small cult of women who paint their bodies with white lead, color their hair black as a rotted tooth, and rub their teeth with the red berries of the brickle plant to show their ferocity and their desire for raw flesh—even the Witches of Byrne are difficult to find now, since they despise men. It is difficult to continue if there is no man to plant his seed in a woman's belly."

She said, "My grandmother told me that the Witches of Byrne don't despise men. They merely don't trust them. They observe the horror that men bring, know that those same men would destroy them if they could. Surely you don't deny that?"

"Your grandmother?"

"Aye, Lady Madelyn. You will meet her soon."

"She is as old as Lord Vellan?"

"Aye, and like my grandfather's, her wits are as sharp as the point of Crispin's sword."

"You spoke of the harshness of men. I imagine that women, like men, would bring horrors if they had the chance. The truth is that men themselves have few choices." He shrugged. "I live the best I can. I wouldn't kill a witch unless she threatened my life. Isn't that fair? And just?"

She brushed away his words with a sweep of her hand. "You have few choices? You are a knight. You ride to Penwyth from the king. I have never ridden anywhere at the behest of the king. You take it as your right to give orders to females. You have men to do your bidding. You can do exactly as you please. You took off my slipper and played with my foot. What you claim is nonsense."

He said, "There is death all around us, Merryn, an inevitable end to all of us, men and women alike. We all want to survive, and that means knowing how to think, how to act, how to defend ourselves. A man is honorable or he is not. I believe a woman too is honorable or she is not. But honor is nothing if your very survival is at stake. It is true what I said: I live the best I can. I do not kill unless I have to. Look at you, Merryn. Your survival depends upon a curse."

"It's a difficult thing, all these dead husbands, living in the shadow of this curse."

"I know the words to the curse. Indeed, I very nearly have it memorized. Tell me what you know, Merryn."

She studied her thumbnail, then slowly shook her head. "I don't know anything."

He smiled down at her, but not too far down, for she was tall, mayhap as tall as Philippa de Fortenberry. "Robert Burnell, the king's secretary and the Chancellor of England, is a very learned man. Before I left the king, he gave me all the parchments he had collected on the Celtic Druids and the Witches of Byrne. Reading of them made the lice jump out of my hair."

"Another jest." She looked at his thick black hair blowing off his neck in the hot, dry wind. "I always wanted black hair, thick just like yours, with the sun gleaming through it."

"You think my hair is excellent?"

"Aye, it is, I admit it. You say you're a man of otherworldly knowledge, Sir Bishop, a man who understands curses and magic and dark ways—in short, a wizard."

"I am. It is my habit to open myself to those of the otherworld, to those in other times, to let their knowledge seep deep into me so that I may understand what they are, and why they still keep themselves close to this earth." By the time he finished speaking, he'd lowered his voice almost to a whisper. He nearly had himself believing what he was saying.

He watched her rub her arms. A little fright, that was good. What was she keeping from him? He said, "Aye, and now I must gather more information to reach the beings that put this curse into motion."

There was a sudden gust of hot wind. It whipped her hair loose from its plaits and back from her face. He saw that she had small ears, nicely shaped. She hadn't been beautiful to him just four hours before, but it seemed that he might have been mistaken. He reached out his hand yet again to touch her hair, but this time he didn't. He dropped his hand back to his side. At least, he thought, his children wouldn't be ugly, and that would surely be a relief to their future spouses. The dimple in her left cheek was long gone. She was still too afraid to smile.

"Tell me of the husbands."

She couldn't keep the remembered horror out of her eyes as she said slowly, "I watched them all die. The first one, Sir Arlan, was seated next to me, since he was my bridegroom, and we shared a trencher. I watched him eat. He fed me from his knife. I was a child, and yet I never doubted that he would be my husband until I died."

"So you didn't believe the curse."

"I will tell you, when my grandfather stood there and quoted the curse in a loud, clear voice, I believed every word. It would have sent me on my way." She paused a moment, and he knew she was seeing the scene from four years before. "Did I believe it? No, I did not.

"Then, it was so sudden that I couldn't quite grasp what was happening. Sir Arlan jerked, shuddered and quaked, then fell forward, his face in the beef chunks and gravy in the trencher. One of his men, a very brave and foolish man, rose up and yelled that my grandfather had poisoned his master. He, too, died. All the other men fled Penwyth within the hour."

"That sounds like poison, not some bloody curse."

She was silent a moment, then nodded. "Aye, I thought that it must be poison, but you see, he and I ate from the same trencher. He speared pieces of beef on his knife and slid them into my mouth. I drank from his goblet. How could it be poison?"

He looked down at her. "It could be poison, if you were the poisoner and clever about it."

"I was a young girl. I did not kill him. It would not have occurred to me to kill him."

What was she keeping from him? Bishop said, "Then, I believe, there was Sir Gifford de Lancey, the second husband. Tell me about him."

"Do you know all my husbands' names?"

"Certainly," he said. "A wizard makes it a point to steep himself in knowledge. Tell me more about him."

"He didn't believe the curse, and neither did his men. After he wedded me, he began to fondle me and kiss me and smack his lips when he saw what he'd gained with no effort at all. He called all our men old cowards, my

grandfather a useless relic, said my grandmother was the mother of all ugly witches.
He wanted to strip me naked before he wedded me, but my grandfather managed to talk
him out of it. By this time, Sir Gifford was
laughing at the curse, said my first husband
had been a fool, and then he killed two of
our people just because he wanted to show
Grandfather what he would do if thwarted."

"What happened?"

"All of a sudden, with no warning, blood
spurted from his nose and mouth. He became a fountain of blood." She shuddered,
then turned on her heel and walked to the
wide wooden ladder that led down into the
inner bailey. She looked back up at him.
"There is a lot of blood inside a person's
body. He lasted longer than anyone wanted
him to, and in truth, it wasn't long at all.
There are still bloodstains on the stones."

Then she turned, and he watched her
stride like a young man, her gown swaying
around her ankles, a gown that was too
short. Four husbands. The second one had
died three years ago and it still distressed
her. It would distress him as well, watching
a man's blood pour from his nose and
mouth. Could a poison do that?

What was she keeping from him?

7

Bishop was shown to the steward's small chamber by an ancient serving woman who had no teeth in her mouth and never stopped smiling at him. She left him alone, standing in the middle of the small room. It smelled of ink and parchment, and the air was heavy and stale, as if the single narrow window had been closed for a very long time. He pulled away the goatskin that covered it, and sunlight poured into the room. He saw dust hanging in the air from the spears of bright sunlight. He looked at the shelf of parchments, each one tightly rolled and stuck into one of the little circular slots that filled an entire wall. There was a small trunk at the end of a narrow cot, and one blanket.

Bishop pulled out a parchment at random and unrolled it. It was an accounting from three years before—the crops, the sales, the births and deaths and marriages of Penwyth. He looked at several other parchments. Nothing to make him believe the steward was cheating Lord Vellan. Mayhap he'd keep the fellow.

He heard the sound of a very old throat clearing behind him. His right hand on his sword, his left hand quickly pulling the knife from inside his tunic, he whirled about, half expecting to see some mad spirit hovering near him, or an ancient warrior, sword trembling in a knotted, veined hand, ready to strike him down. But it wasn't a spirit or a warrior in the steward's chamber with him. It was a very old woman who looked so frail she was nearly transparent. He prayed she never stood on the ramparts. The wind would blow her away. She stood there, watching him, saying nothing at all, and he felt a frisson of fear. He hadn't heard her come in. One moment he was alone, and the next she was here. Mayhap she was a spirit, mayhap she was a Witch of Byrne.

Bishop shook his head. He calmed himself. She was an old woman, nothing more. She was also wearing a beautiful gown, so she wasn't a servant, then. He said, "Madam? May I be of assistance to you?"

Old, so very old she was, but she still stood tall, her frail shoulders pulled back. She had a knot of white hair high on her head, held with half a dozen blue ribbons that floated about her face. He could see her pink scalp through the ribbons and the strands of hair. Once, he thought, once, a very long time ago, she'd been beautiful. He could still see traces of it in her faded blue eyes, wide, beautifully shaped, and in the sharp slant of her cheekbones. She continued to stand there, just staring at him, saying nothing at all, just looking, and then, suddenly, she began humming, and that made gooseflesh rise on his arms. "Who are you, madam?"

She took three steps toward him, paused and blinked. She extended a hand whose fingers were long and naught but flesh and bone. He carefully raised that delicate old hand and lightly kissed her wrist. The skin looked so thin he wondered if eventually it would just fade away and then the fragile old bones would just crumble since there would be nothing more to hold them in place. But her hand wasn't light. She wore heavy gold rings, some of them set with stones he'd never seen before, weighing down three of her fingers. Aye, the bones would crumble and the rings would clatter to the floor. He caught a sudden image in his mind of those rings rolling across the floor, stopped by a man's boot. He shook his head, clearing his mind of that strange image.

She said in a faint, wispy voice, "I am Lady Madelyn de Gay. You are in the steward's chamber."

"You are Lord Vellan's wife?"

She gave a scratchy old laugh, high and thin, and lightly slapped his shoulder. "I could not be his daughter, now could I? I am three years older than that doddering old man, and yet I don't dodder. Watch me."

Bishop watched her walk away from him, the heavy fabric of her gown trailing the floor, then take a turn around the small room, then turn back to face him. She smiled at him, showing a full mouth of very white teeth. Come to think of it, Lord Vellan had most all of his teeth as well. That was unusual.

"No, madam," he said. "You don't appear to dodder at all."

"You are a very handsome boy, well knit, with manners and grace. Merryn told me that you were too excellent for your own good. She said you were riper than a man should be. I am not certain I understand that, but mayhap she is right. Still, I wonder why you are standing here in the steward's chamber."

"Your husband granted me this chamber during my stay here."

"The steward, Ranlief, is old—not as old as I or Lord Vellan, but his brain slows and his hands tremble. I cannot imagine his ancient bones resting well on the floor of the great hall."

"Why don't you give him Merryn's chamber?"

"My sweet dear little granddaughter. There are too many men who would seek to ravish her were she to sleep in the great hall."

"I have seen few men here of an age to ravish anything, madam."

"Aye, you're right. That is an amusement

that even I haven't considered for a very long time, mayhap in the last century. But I am a woman, not an eternally randy man. Even Lord Vellan is randy, though his man's lust must remain in his brain, since there is no other part of him to make use of it.

"Nay, I must protect my little Merryn. Old or young, all of them want her." She sighed, perhaps waiting for him to relinquish the steward's chamber, which he had no intention of doing. She said, "My Vellan looked like you. Aye, he was all proud muscle and sinew, a formidable warrior, an even more formidable lover. He had beautiful dark hair, flowing about his head to his shoulders. Ah, what a ferocious laugh he had." She frowned, her pale blue eyes fading for a moment. "At least I think he did. It was so long ago, mayhap even before the last century. Are you here to be Merryn's fifth husband?"

"I'm alive, so why would you think that?"

Her bony fingers pleated and smoothed the skirt of her gown. It was lovely, that gown, all pale blue, just like her faded old eyes, just like the ribbons in her hair. The style wasn't one he had ever seen. Mayhap, he thought, it was from the last century. She said, "Aye, now that's a good question. By

Saint Francis's white brow, you are still alive, now, aren't you? Odd that the curse didn't strike you down." She peered at him, up and down. "At least not yet. I think you are also too beautiful to be a husband. Vellan was beautiful as well. I do remember clearly that my mother wanted him for me. She did nothing but praise him to my father, tell him that Vellan would dance with me in the moonlight and make me shriek with delight."

"Did you, madam?"

"Oh, aye, I danced in the moonlight, but usually alone."

He smiled at her.

"Aye, I shrieked, too, and I was never alone, thank the merciful heavens, when I did that." She paused, then said on a frown, "I haven't shrieked in more years than I can count. I will ask Vellan what this is all about—not that he will tell me anything. He lies, fluently and cleanly, you see. So if you are not here to be Merryn's fifth husband, then what is your purpose? Did Ranlief die and no one told me of it?"

"No, the steward still breathes. I am here at the king's behest to rid Penwyth of its curse."

"The king? The king sent you?" She laughed. The old lady threw back her ancient head and laughed and laughed. It scared him down to his toes, that laugh. It was all thin and sharp and, truth be told, there was something veiled and secretive buried in that laugh, something beyond what was real and expected.

Bishop didn't like this at all. He was becoming as fanciful as a young girl. He wondered if she would swoon she laughed so long and hard—that, or just fall into a heap of bones on the floor at his feet. He held himself perfectly still, waiting to see if she would survive that mad laughter.

She did. She smoothed her skirt, pulled down her sleeves, clenched and unclenched her fingers. "If you have forgotten, my name is Lady Madelyn de Gay and I was once a great beauty. I remember my sweet mother told me I was a princess, the most beautiful girl in all of Cornwall." She frowned, a far-distant cast to her eye, seeing something he couldn't begin to imagine. "If I was a princess, then why wasn't I married to the king? Why aren't I living in London, in beautiful Windsor Castle, not here hidden away on witches' land?"

"Witches' land, madam?"

"Oh, aye, the Witches of Byrne. They first began on the small rolling hills hereabouts, dancing on the barrows, chanting into the hearts of storms. Then they moved to caves closer to the sea. They love to eat fish, you know."

"No, I did not know. Madam, never in my life have I tried so diligently to understand, but what you say makes no sense to me."

"You are a man," she said. "Rarely do any of you look beyond the flesh to the grit and sinew that lie beneath."

"Mayhap that is true of all people," Bishop said. "Sometimes life is too pressing in its demands to look beyond what you are able to see. The curse, madam. Why did you laugh when I told you I was here to remove the curse?"

"Oh, you are so young, so innocent of evil. But there is evil, there will always be evil, whether it breeds and festers inside men or is an old evil that hovers just above the earth, swooping down to bedevil poor mortals, but always there, just waiting, waiting."

"I might be innocent of all evil, madam, but I would know it if I saw it. Do you believe the curse to be evil?"

Suddenly, in a flash, something changed. She was no longer ancient, with the light of madness in her pale eyes. She was hard as steel and alert, standing tall, right in front of him. She said low, her voice harsh and deeper than it should be, "You know nothing. You know less than nothing. You will not do well here at Penwyth, not if it is your wish to rid us of the curse."

"Why won't I do well?"

"The curse will never die. It protects us, that curse. I have heard the witches talk about life after forever is finished and done with. Is there evil in life after forever?" The old woman shook her head. A delicate wooden pin fell to the stone floor. "It is enough to muck up a mortal's brains."

She paused, then just as suddenly she seemed to fade, to shrink back from him, to become the old woman she was. He fancied he could see that old heart beating beneath her shrunken chest. She said, "What is your name?"

"I am known as Bishop of Lythe. Sir Bishop now, knighted by Lord Dienwald de Fortenberry of St. Erth."

She nodded. "Ah, the Scourge of Cornwall. Another fine boy is Dienwald. His is a spirit as wild as a witch's curse rising to the black heavens. His is a brain that is fresh and perverse. He looks at things differently, does Dienwald, so I have been told. I have heard many stories about him. Is it true he is wedded to the king's daughter?"

Bishop said, "Aye, for three years now. He knighted me because I saved her life."

"If I was a princess, then why wasn't I wedded to Dienwald?"

"He would not yet have been born, madam." The old woman appeared to chew this over for a while, then floated away from him to stand looking out the narrow window.

"That was a jest that pleased me. Ah, just look. The land is dying. Isn't that curious?"

"It will cease to die once it rains."

"There won't be any rain. Until my granddaughter is proclaimed the heir, there will be no rain."

"There will be. Sometime tomorrow."

She turned to look at him again. "I heard the servants whispering that you're a wizard, that you understand ancient laws, that you hear old spirits at play, that you can speak to the old spirits. No good can come of that. Aye, and there's your name—Bishop—a fine name. You will not remove the curse, you will not. You must leave Penwyth before it is too late. How do you know it will rain?"

"You just said it. I am a wizard, madam. I know things. It will rain."

"Then tell me, sir, how many children did I birth?"

Suddenly he simply knew. "You birthed five children, madam, but only one sur-vived—Sir Thomas de Gay, a fine man I once met."

It was difficult to tell if her eyes looked startled, but he believed they did. She said at last, "Your answer is correct. All those dead babes. It seems that more babes die than survive in this bitter world."

"I am sorry, madam. Now, would you tell me about this curse?"

She yawned in his face. Her breath wasn't sweet, nor was it foul. It was simply old and faded, nearly sheer, like an ancient whisper. "I don't think so. I am vastly tired." She waved her hand, then let it fall to her side, as if it had a will of its own, as if the rings were so heavy she couldn't keep the hand up.

She said, "I have met you and I have given you warning. Mayhap you are a wiz-ard. You knew about my children, and that surprised me. You said it will rain. But you are not as strong as the curse. Leave now, Sir Bishop of Lythe. Rain, it is a wondrous thing. I long to see curtains of rain, to feel it against my skin. Rain tastes good on a tongue. All this is very curious."

She turned slowly and walked toward the door of the small chamber. He watched her gown pick up more dust from the stone floor. She paused at the door, looked over her shoulder at him, cocked her head, then whispered in that parchment-thin voice,

"The enemy will die who comes by sea.
The enemy by land will cease to be.
The enemy will fail who uses the key.
Doubt this not,
This land is blessed for eternity.

"Maiden's heart pure as fire
Maiden's eyes, green as desire
Maiden's hair, a wicked red
Any who force her will soon be dead."

When she finished, she smiled at him. "The Penwyth curse is a good curse. It is strong. It has meat and gristle and bone. It will last a very long time. Aye, something you don't know, my beautiful boy. My mother was a Witch of Byrne. She knew of the curse when I wedded with Lord Vellan, told me it would protect my home even after I was long dead. Then she whispered that she didn't know if I would ever die."

"Did your mother the Witch of Byrne die?"

"My father slew her," she said, "and buried her heart away from her body." She gave him a vague smile and left the steward's chamber.

Bishop stared at the closed door, stared at it for a very long time. He felt cold.

He wondered if Merryn was a witch, like her great-grandmother.

He was still alive in the early evening when the servants brought in bread and cheese and ale to feed the forty people, only twenty of them soldiers to guard the keep, and six wolfhounds that sat on their haunches in a straight line, jowls quivering.

Bishop saw a very old serving woman carry a heavy wooden platter to Lord Vellan. It was piled high with stark white bones that had been boiled clean.

Lord Vellan picked up the biggest bone and tossed it to the first wolfhound in the line. He caught it in midair. The other dogs didn't move. One by one, each caught his own bone and fell to.

Only then did the rest of the company begin their meal.

"The hounds are well trained," Bishop said to Lord Vellan.

Lord Vellan looked over his shoulder, saw that the first wolfhound was back on his haunches, and threw him another big bone.

"Aye, those that aren't stay in the bailey."

"I met your lady wife, sir. She came upon me in the steward's chamber."

Lord Vellan threw more bones, then smiled at Bishop. "Poor Ranlief. My steward hasn't stopped his complaining. He has three blankets, what more could he want? Ah, my wife. Twisted you up, did she, lad?"

"I confess that a lot of what she said I did not comprehend."

A serving maid, this one sprightly—not a day over fifty—handed Bishop a fat loaf of white bread and carefully placed a platter of cheeses in front of him. He heard a soft rustling, turned to see Merryn ease into the chair beside him. The chair beside Lord Vellan was empty. Bishop supposed it was for Lady de Gay. Why wasn't she here?

"You're still alive," Lord Vellan said. "All of my men are surprised. My wife said you drank a magic potion to ward off the curse."

"No, I have not drunk any today," Bishop said. He gave Merryn a hunk of his bread, paused only an instant before he broke off another hunk and ate it himself. He didn't taste any poison, but that didn't mean much. If the four husbands had tasted poison, surely they would have yelled it out before falling dead. The truth was that the bread was delicious. He ate another hunk. The miller here at Penwyth ground the flour well—there was very little grit.

Merryn nodded and looked over the platter, finally picking up a piece of yellow cheese that he could smell from two feet away.

She grinned at him. "It tastes much better than it smells. It's made from Beelzebub's milk."

"It is said that Satan roves the land. I did not know that he also gave milk."

More wit, she thought, and smiled. "No, not Satan. Her name is Beelzebub. She is one of our goats. She makes the best cheese of all of them."

"It does have a powerful smell."

"Aye, it does, but your breath will remain as sweet-smelling as the roses that bloom in my garden. Here, try it."

He did, and was surprised that the cheese was mellow and sweet. He ate more of it, chewed more bread. The miller would grind his flour and Beelzebub the goat would make cheese for him. He devoutly prayed that the cheese wasn't poisoned. Made from a goat named Beelzebub, who knew?

He looked down the trestle table at Dumas, who was deep in conversation with one of the old warriors. The old man was nearly bald, but his dirty gray beard was stuck into his belt, the tip of it showing below his waist, just like Lord Vellan's. He hoped Dumas had discovered something useful, because he himself hadn't.

"You're not dead," Merryn said.

"No. I'm not married to you, either."

"You think I'm disappointed?"

He looked at her for a long moment, then said, after he'd swallowed more of the wonderful bread, "I don't know what you are. I know only that you are not telling me things that are important."

Not a sound from her mouth.

Bishop waited until Lord Vellan had

thrown all the white bones to the wolfhounds and drunk a full flagon of wine, then he said, "My lord, as I said, I met your wife, and aye, she twisted my brain. She told me that her mother was a Witch of Byrne."

There was sudden silence in the great hall.

8

Lord Vellan continued to chew on a hunk of Beelzebub's cheese. "She said that, did she?"

"She told me that her mother knew all about the curse that promised Penwyth would always be protected."

Lord Vellan shook his head, making his thick white hair swing into his face. "Ah, my ancient Madelyn," he said. "She tells me every day that she wishes to bury me. I wonder if she will. Ah, but her mother—Meridian was her name—now there was a one. She was a witch, no doubt in anyone's brain. One of the Witches of Byrne? I don't know.

I never saw her paint herself white or color her teeth red. Indeed, she hated fish.

"The woman plagued me. Whenever I displeased her, she would send a curse to land on my head. I swear to you, Bishop, once my armpits itched until I nearly went mad with it. You see, I had only lightly buffeted my wife's shoulder, and Madelyn snuck away and told her mother. The itching, it was fairly bad, but not to be compared to the sores that appeared on the soles of my feet. Big sores, open, with pus flowing from them. I thought I would die. I begged her to heal me, swore to her that I would never again harm a hair on her beautiful daughter's head."

"You mean you struck your wife again? After you'd already endured the itching?"

"No, I did not." Lord Vellan snapped his fingers, and the third wolfhound in the line came forward, tail wagging, to curve his huge body against Lord Vellan's leg. "Madelyn was angry with me and told her mother I had struck her again. I'm not a codsbrain—naturally I didn't ever strike her again. As for Meridian, she cursed her husband once too often. He wasn't stupid, he knew if she became really angry, he'd be dead. So he killed her in her sleep, stuck a knife in her gullet, took her heart and buried it fifty feet from her body. A cautious man, was Sir William." Lord Vellan chewed thoughtfully on his cheese. "Now Madelyn roams about the castle, pours lime in the jakes, sleeps on the ramparts when the weather is warm, stitches small shirts for Beelzebub so that her cheese will remain sweet, and prays every morning to the ancient ones to bring rain. She told me you would bring rain. She says she felt it."

Bishop was a straightforward man. He disliked artifice and guile. He watched people, observed what they did. He also observed various phenomena—he loved violent storms as much as he admired rainbows—and tried to understand what it was he was observing. When he listened to another person, be it the king himself, he knew and understood the words that were spoken, knew exactly what to think, knew what to do. But here? At Penwyth? He almost shuddered. He drank some ale, which was really quite good. He said, "I can't bring the rain. I have not that gift. I merely forecast it."

"How?" Merryn asked.

Bishop frowned a moment, then shook his

head. "I don't know. It's just there, a sense of it inside me. It's part of me, I guess you would say."

"Both one and the same," said Lord Vellan. "Both a mystery to man. Call it what you will."

Merryn said, "Did my grandmother scare you to the roots of your hair?"

"She confused me more than scared me," he said, knowing he wasn't telling the exact truth. "She did not make a great deal of sense."

"You just don't know how to listen to her properly. She tells me her brain is seasoned from so many years dealing with this earth. A seasoned brain, she tells me, is a brain that can comprehend the meaning of a leaf that lies atop a rock."

Bishop rolled his eyes. "I am tired of this." He turned to Lord Vellan. "My lord, I wish to hear what you think about the Penwyth curse. If there is really no curse, then mayhap you will tell me that it is poison, that you have saved Penwyth and your granddaughter by poisoning the men who have forced their way in here. It is one or the other, my lord. It is time you told me which it is."

The great hall fell quiet for the second

time. More old faces than he could count, all seamed from years in the sun, were alert, their eyes fastened on the lord's table.

Lord Vellan cleared his throat, drank more ale, then said in a voice that carried to the blackened beams overhead, "I did not poison any of the four husbands. Even though I struck my wife once, I more than paid for it. I am guilty of nothing else."

Lady de Gay called out as she floated across the vast stone floor toward them, "I will tell you, Sir Bishop, all about the curse. It came from the spirit of an ancient Druid priest, B'Eall was his name. He was bloated with the blood of many sacrifices. He had held scores of dripping hearts in his hands, caressed them, squeezed them, the blood flowing through his fingers, until there was no more blood in them. B'Eall said he knew when he stood on this land, looking over the rocks and the hills and beyond to the sea, that it was his duty to proclaim this land sacred. He buried many bloodless hearts in this earth to make it so. And so it happened."

Lord Vellan shrugged. "Who knows?"

"It is deep and complex, this curse," Merryn said, and sneered at him. "Beyond a mortal man's brain."

Lady Madelyn's tale was meant to paralyze a man with fright. It was enough. It was too much. He realized they were playing with him. No one could be as artfully mad, as artfully perverse, as these people. It was all a ruse to frighten him, to make him ride as fast as he could away from Penwyth.

Bishop rose slowly from his chair. He looked from the old woman, gowned so beautifully this evening in a long-ago style, to her husband, to their granddaughter, with her pretty feet and small ears. He wiped Beelzebub's cheese off his knife and eased it back into its sheath strapped to his forearm, inside his tunic sleeve.

He looked yet again from Lord Vellan to Lady de Gay and said, "My craw is full to overflowing with all your crazed words meant to terrify a man. They do not terrify me. They enrage me. I have had enough of it."

No one said a word. No one's attention faltered, except for two of the wolfhounds, who began to snore. "Listen, all of you. I have told you all that I am a wizard. I have told you all that it will rain, that the drought will cease. I have told Lady de Gay that she birthed five children. I have told you that I understand otherworldly spirits and their ways, that I can hear ancient voices and understand them. I will not tolerate any more of these mad, mad puzzles, your ill-disguised threats cloaked in mystical trappings." He looked at Merryn. "I will not tolerate your secrets and your lies." He paused, then spoke louder, reaching every ear in the great hall. "I will now give you my own curse."

The two snoring wolfhounds stirred, then looked up at him. Bishop stood tall. He raised both arms above his head, his palms out, stretched to the beamed ceiling. He closed his eyes. His voice boomed out deep, thunderous as a prophet foretelling doom on the heads of the people. "I pronounce that this spot of earth upon which I stand will flow with endless rain until all my inquiries are answered clearly and truthfully."

"Endless rain would be a pleasant thing, Sir Bishop," Merryn said, not a whit moved, not even mildly alarmed. "It is not our fault that you are too dimwitted to understand words spoken to you."

"And those words not spoken to me? Am I too dimwitted to understand them as well?"

She crossed her legs and kicked her foot up and down. There was that damned sneer on her mouth again. He was so mad he wanted to spit, to hurl her into the moat once it was full again.

Then he looked around the great hall. The servants and the soldiers were all of them frozen in place, their faces showing their fear. That pleased him. He looked at Lord and Lady de Gay. They were calmly chewing on bread and cheese, acting as if they hadn't heard him. But the wolfhounds, all six of them, were alert now, all eyes on him, standing tall like soldiers ready for battle. Or waiting for more white bones.

"We have answered you as clearly as we can," Lord Vellan said, and just maybe he looked a bit apprehensive, the old fraud. Good.

It hit him then that he'd just up and announced a flood. He'd done himself in with a curse—he who knew nothing of curses or their origins, he who had no power at all. A flood. He couldn't believe his own stupidity.

But maybe his curse had come from somewhere deep within him. After all, he'd

known about Lady de Gay's five children.
He was a blockhead.

It had been happenstance, it meant nothing at all. He was a fool and a blockhead.
He could but hope that it would rain at least
two days. Were two days of hard rain
enough to fulfill the curse?

There was no hope for it. He had to do
something dramatic, something so shocking
that it would shake them to their very core.
He was smiling as he turned to Merryn,
grabbed her arm, and jerked her to her feet.
Her mouth opened to yell at him, but he
slammed down his palm, and she couldn't
even squeak. "No. You will be quiet." He
tightened his grip, knowing he was hurting
her but not caring at the moment.

He leaned down until his mouth was an
inch from hers and said, his voice just as
loud, just as carrying, "You will come with
me, Merryn de Gay. You will remain on one
of the parched hillocks until the rain comes.
You will feel the rain strike your flesh, fill
your mouth, blind your eyes. I will keep you
away from Penwyth until you tell me the
truth of the curse."

She kicked him in the shin.

His blood throbbed wildly with rage,

coursing through him like madness itself, ready to overflow into violence. He jerked her off her feet and threw her over his shoulder. He saw Lord Vellan's master-at-arms, Crispin, raise his sword. "No, Crispin, be seated. None of you will interfere. I am here to remove the Penwyth curse, and that is what I will do. I will tolerate no more lies and evasions, no more attempts to drive me to madness."

She was struggling, trying to rear up, pounding his back with her fists. Bishop smiled as he slammed his palm against her bottom.

She yelled, reared up again, and tried to bite him. He loosed his hold on her and she fell, head down, toward the stone floor. She screamed. He tightened his hold, looked over his shoulder and said, "You will be quiet and hold still or I will drop you and your head will crack open like a ripe melon."

She was still as a stone.

Good. It was an excellent threat, although not a particularly believable one. Bishop slowly pulled her back up. Her gown came up and his mouth was not more than two inches from a very white thigh. He smelled her flesh and he was instantly hard. Damnation. He was a man. There were just some things he could not control. But it didn't matter. He was set on his course now. He would bring peace back to Penwyth. He would learn the truth, and he would kiss that leg of hers as soon as he got her out of the great hall.

It was Dumas who stopped him before he reached the stables. "Bishop," he said, knowing she could hear him, "you must have supplies and protection from the rains when they come. You need protection as well. The men and I will come with you."

"I thank you, Dumas," Bishop said. "But I want you and our men to remain here. Bring supplies to the stable and my tent."

She reared up again, yelling, "You fool, let me go. This is madness. I don't want to drown in a rain that will never come because you don't know what you're talking about."

He slapped her bottom again. "No, the madness is right here at Penwyth. What I do is the only sane course open to me. I am taking one witch from Penwyth. Or perhaps I will not, if you but tell me the truth."

"There is no truth! There is only the damned curse. It is what it is. There is no more. My grandfather knows more than anyone. If he doesn't choose to tell you everything, it is his affair. Now let me down."

"Then he will have to find us and tell me before I will consider bringing you out of the rain. I hope you like rain, Merryn, for I do plan to tie you down and let you drown in it."

Not another word out of her mouth. This was better, he thought, and smiled. When he rode out on Fearless a short time later, the sound of her mare's whinny following them, Merryn on her belly across his legs, and supplies and his tent lashed down behind him, he realized that if he did tie her down in the rain, he could kill her. Lying under an endless torrent of rain would likely send her to her just rewards.

Just what those just rewards were, he didn't know.

"My belly is cramping."

"Shut your mouth. We have left Penwyth. If you can, look back. The ramparts are lined with old faces, including your grandfather's. The servants are likely alone in the great hall, eating all of Beelzebub's cheese, possibly wondering how you will look with rain choking you."

"You can't mean to drown me. Ha, do you hear me? Ha! There will be no rain. It's a drought, you fool. It hasn't rained in months. I will not drown, I will die of dry air in my throat."

"Now wouldn't that be a sight."

"So you admit that there's nothing to your prediction?"

"You will see, as will everyone else."

"Where are you taking me?"

"Be quiet."

"But I—"

He smacked his palm against her bottom. She yelled, then didn't say another word.

He began whistling. It covered the sound of her harsh breathing. He looked up at the beautiful night, the stars filling the sky, the moon a narrow scythe, yet giving off plenty of light. It was warm, the air soft on the flesh. Was there really rain waiting somewhere in all that vastness? He knew there was, knew the rain would be here soon. Before, this gift hadn't been of any great importance to anyone. But it was now. Mayhap he really was a wizard and this was a bit of proof.

Bishop thought about the Penwyth drought. He doubted that keeping the curse potent had overtaxed the Witches of Byrne or the shadows of the ancient Druid priests. It was simply nature herself that had brought the harsh, dry winds that baked the earth around Penwyth.

She was gagging.

He didn't hesitate, pulled her quickly up to sit in front of him.

"That was wise," she said after a good dozen deep breaths. "I would have puked on your boots."

"I wonder what I would have done?"

"Would you beat me again?"

"I didn't beat you. Don't exaggerate your plight."

"Where are you taking me?"

It was in that moment that he realized he had no idea where to take her. Because he didn't know, he simply said, "Be quiet."

Fearless, without hesitation, headed southwest. He was going to Land's End. So be it. It wasn't long before Bishop pulled him in at the cliff edge. The calm sea stretched out in front of them, smooth and black beneath the sickle moon as far as the eye could see. The jagged black rocks stood like armless giants on the narrow beach, reaching far into the water itself. He could hear the slap of the sea against the rocks, feel the spume from the waves as they crested, only to fan out onto the night-black sand.

"This is the most beautiful spot on the earth," Merryn said. "Look yon, you can see the nests of a thousand rooks tucked into the crevices of the cliff."

"You have never been anywhere else. Of course it is beautiful to you."

She twisted about and looked straight at him. "Have you ever seen anything more beautiful?"

"It is too dry, too barren a landscape," he said.

"That will change when this vaunted rain of yours begins to fall, won't it?" she said, with credible sarcasm. "Do you intend that we stay here? Will you tie me down to the ground and let the crows peck my flesh?"

"When it rains, I doubt any bird will want to come out of a dry nest to attack you, not even the rooks." He dismounted, then clasped her beneath her arms and lifted her down. "Don't run or I will be angry." He untied the big bundle of supplies from behind Fearless's saddle and tossed it on the ground. "There is a tent. Set it up."

She kicked a pebble and did nothing.

"Of course I doubt that you are capable of doing anything useful at all. You're but a girl, a lord's daughter who's never done anything in her life save count her ribbons. Mayhap when the time comes, you will have the ability to birth and suckle a child. One can but hope."

She kicked the bundle, then went down on her knees and began unwrapping the supplies. Bread, cheese, and three goat-skins filled with ale. It looked like Dumas had cleared off the trestle table at Penwyth. She pulled out the tent. It seemed to be well made, but she didn't know how to set it up. She examined the narrow poles, the flaps, and sighed. She laid her palms on her thighs and looked up at him. He was brushing Fearless's back.

When he saw her annoyance clearly in the dim night light, he laughed. "Brush my horse."

She did it well, speaking to Fearless, kissing his nose, telling him how her beautiful mare would make him dance to her music, making the brute whinny in return and butt his head against her shoulder.

When the tent was set on flat ground, Bishop rose and walked to the cliff edge where she stood, her back to him, her skirt blowing about her legs in the night sea breeze. He thought she was saying something.

She was probably chanting a curse.

He said, "We have no need of a fire. It is late. This has been a day like none other and I am weary. Come here."

Slowly, she turned to face him. He would have sworn that there was a circle of light around her head. He felt his heart lurch in his chest. He shook his head, furious with himself. He'd come to this ridiculous place that would eventually be his and then it would not be ridiculous, and now he was thinking he saw a witch behind every rock.

"Come here."

"I wish to enjoy the lovely night."

"I don't care what you wish." He raised a rope in his hand.

"What will you do? Beat me with that rope?"

He said for the third time, "Come here."

Merryn realized in that moment that things had changed irrevocably since she'd awakened this morning. He was here and she knew to her soul that he wasn't going to leave. Would he die? Would the curse fell him? "I cannot tell you anything more about the curse."

"Come here."

Slowly, she walked to him.

"Hold out your hand."

She did. He tied the rope around her wrist. "Now, we're going to sleep."

She looked at him helplessly, swallowed, and said, "Please, I must have a moment before we go into the tent."

"A moment to do what? Chant more curses down on my head?"

She shook her head. "Please, just a moment. I must relieve myself."

"Very well. If you attempt to escape me, I will tie you to Fearless and let the two of you sleep close tonight."

There was one bush, some ten feet away. He waved toward it. "Go."

He was standing in the same spot when she returned a few minutes later. Slowly, she raised her arm.

He tied the rope around her wrist. "Come," he said, and pointed to the tent.

The tent was barely large enough for the two of them. He'd spread a blanket on the ground, stacked the supplies at the back to use as pillows. He'd tethered Fearless close by.

Once she was lying on her side, her back

to him, he stretched out on his back beside her. With the other end of the rope tied to his wrist, he realized neither of them could move. "Turn toward me." When she didn't move, he said, "I won't rape you. I'm tired. It has been a very long and strange day. I wish to sleep. Do as I tell you."

She sat up, pulling the rope tight between them. "You shouldn't have brought me here. It isn't right. I am a lady."

"That remains to be seen. Come here."

Merryn didn't want to lie down beside him, touch him, rest her cheek on his shoulder, even though he still wore his tunic. He was a stranger, a young stranger, a young stranger with power and excellent parts. She was afraid of him and yet she wasn't. It was a conundrum. "What if it starts raining?"

"The tent is sturdy, solid. However, if it rains hard, we will get a bit wet."

"I know of a small hut just down the way, toward Sennen. We could shelter there."

"No. I'm tired. I don't want to take another step tonight." He jerked on the rope.

She rolled over toward him and very slowly, afraid of touching him, she eased down beside him. She was stiff as the wind that was picking up outside the tent. A hard, dry wind, one that didn't carry the scent of water. At least not yet. He pressed her face against his shoulder. When he realized she didn't know what to do with her hand, he merely picked it up and laid it on his chest.

"Go to sleep," he said. "You are safe from me, unless you start your chanting again."

"I wasn't chanting. I was singing. What will you do if I start chanting?"

"Tether you to my horse's saddle and let you walk behind us."

She didn't know him well enough to judge if he would really do something like that. Better not to risk it. "I won't chant."

"Good." He said nothing more. She lay there, thinking she'd never before in her life lain this close to a man. He was big, too big. His heartbeat was steady beneath her palm. She realized that every breath carried his scent. He smelled nice. No, it was more than that. He didn't smell old. That was it. Merryn closed her eyes. Why had he brought her here? Was he really going to stake her out in the rain?

If it rained.

9

Bishop was a light sleeper, something that had saved his life at least three times. He would awake, instantly alert at the sound of Fearless nickering from a distance of twenty feet. He would awake at the sound of twigs breaking beneath someone's foot beyond the next hillock. He would awake if someone was breathing ten feet from him.

But this time he hadn't awakened, hadn't even stirred, when sometime during the night Merryn had climbed on top of him. He lay there, amazed that this could have happened. She was sprawled, arms and legs spread, just like a blanket, her head pressed under his chin, and every female part of her nicely placed against him, very *closely* against him.

He forced himself to lie still, get his wits together. He could hear the wind off the sea coming over the cliffs, a light wind, but constant, as it usually was from the sea. He could smell the salt water, but he couldn't scent any rain in the air.

Not yet. It was too soon for the rain.

As he lay there, he was aware of everything about her, not just the soft body that fit so nicely against his. He could feel her deep, easy breath against his neck, feel her fingertips curled around his shoulder.

How in the name of Saint Malcolm's hoary palms had she gotten on top of him without him even stirring?

He heard Fearless blowing outside the tent. He pictured his stallion, head to the cliff, the light wind in his face as he bobbed his head up and down, doing a dance with the wind.

She was on top of him, her belly was against him, and he was harder than the ground beneath his back. She was too close, too close. Surely she would wake up soon, surely she would feel him hard against her belly. Surely she would open an eye and be shocked to her toes, toes that he'd caressed. He felt one of her feet lying across the top of one of his.

By Saint Anthony's wristbone, he could reach his hands down and ease them up her gown, feel those legs of hers. He knew they were long, he'd seen her walk, seen the wind flatten her skirts against those legs of hers, but he wanted to feel them, stroke her flesh. He wanted to hold her foot again, lightly touch her small ears.

Please, God, let her awaken soon.

Oh, aye, she'd leap up and yell like a blooded witch, and all the ancient Druid spirits who still roamed the land would jump upon him and stuff him in a wooden cage.

He didn't care. Even as his hands came over her back to hold her tight against him, he said, "Merryn."

"Hmmmm."

"Merryn, wake up." He let his hands move down, nearly to her bottom. "If you don't, I will simply take you right now and then it will be done."

He lifted his hands off her. He shouldn't touch her. That was madness, what with that curse hanging about, but it didn't seem to matter because he did anyway. He was kneading her hips, wondering if he could just flip her over and take her. Yes, just come inside her, and it would be done. If he got her pregnant, would the curse still strike him down? Would the curse even know that he'd taken her? "Merryn, open your eyes. It's morning. If you don't, you'll be under me in another breath."

He'd expected her to jerk up, a scream ready to explode out of her mouth. But no. Slowly, so very slowly, she arched up, inch by inch, until she was above him, not six inches from his mouth. She was staring down at him even as his hands were kneading her, his fingertips going inward, his sex hard against her.

She said, surprise in her voice, "By all that is holy, that feels far too good not to be a grievous sin."

That wasn't what he'd expected. By Saint Gregory's calluses, who and what was this young girl who'd already buried four husbands? Who was keeping secrets from him?

His hands kept moving, pulling her now tightly against his sex, so hard now he wanted to groan like a wounded man at the nearly painful pleasure. He continued to look up at her. "Of course it feels good. It's supposed to feel good."

"Is it a sin, do you think?" And then she eased down a bit, her breasts nearly touching his chest.

"Listen to me. You should be yelling at me, trying to jerk away from me and run."

"Aye," she said, her mouth even lower now, not more than three inches from his.

"When did you climb on top of me?"

She hadn't realized she had. "Oh, my." If she had turned any redder, she could have competed with a St. Ives sunset. But he also saw the excitement in her eyes. No, more than excitement—immense curiosity.

He said, "If you wanted me, why didn't you just wake me up? A man can sport at a moment's notice." He pushed up against her belly, and at the same time his fingers were pressing in.

"I don't know what happened," she said, still not moving, her breath sharp, jerky now. "Mayhap you tugged on the rope and pulled me on top of you."

"Nay, I'm not such a fool." But evidently he was. He began pulling her gown up, knew what he was doing, knew he was a fool.

She stared down at him, just couldn't look away. "If you keep doing what you're doing, the curse might strike you dead."

"Possibly, but why would you care? I might not tie you down in the rain when it comes if you tell me everything I know you're keeping from me."

She didn't say a word, but her breathing was rough now. If he wasn't mistaken, and he knew he wasn't, she was more than interested.

"You deserve to be punished," he said, sounding bored and indifferent, even as his fingers cramped and itched to touch her bare leg. "When it pleases you to remove yourself, it would relieve me."

She said, looking down at him—no, she was still looking at his mouth, "You feel very different from me."

He moved, just couldn't help himself. He was harder than he'd been but a moment before, so hard he wanted to take her, fast, by the saints, very, very fast. He moved again. Then he just couldn't bear it. He wrapped his arms around her back and quickly rolled her off him and came down over her.

She didn't yell or curse him, she just lay

there, her hands on his shoulders, and said, "I've seen naked men before. They didn't look like you feel like you look."

He laughed at that. He kept his weight on his elbows. Her hair was tangled around her head, her lips were slightly parted. This was more difficult than having her on top of him. It would be so easy to pull up that damned gown of hers and come into her, hard and deep. Oh, God, yes, very deep and deeper yet until he touched her womb. He nearly groaned with the thought of that. He said, to distract himself, "Did you touch these naked men? Did you, a lady, touch these naked men here?" And he pushed against her, just to make sure, he supposed, that she was clear on what he'd said. He was killing himself.

"Nay, I meant that I looked at them and they didn't look at all like you feel against me."

"A man is a man," he said, and felt himself puff up like a gamecock at her words. He grew even harder. Was she trying to seduce him?

"Well, mayhap that is true, but I did look and they weren't at all like you."

Then he realized the truth of the matter

and felt himself deflate. "They were all old men."

"Well, of course. There are nothing but old men at Penwyth."

"I'm moving off you now."

He didn't want to move off her, he truly didn't. But he forced himself to move just a bit to the side. She didn't move until he said, "Damn you, Merryn, you are sorely trying me. Get away from me."

She tried to slither out from under him, moving back and forth, as if she was afraid that he would force her if she moved the wrong way. He could have told her there wasn't ever a wrong way for a man.

When he was on his side next to her, she quickly sat up. But she didn't stop looking. Oh, no, she looked at him and by Saint Peter's toenails, he swelled even more.

He immediately sat up and began to untie the rope.

"What are you going to do this morning?"

He hadn't thought about that. He hadn't thought beyond his rage of the night before, his desire to punish all of them for making him feel like a fool, to punish her for keeping secrets from him and being the one who'd pushed him over the edge. He kept working on the knot, which had somehow tightened during the night.

"Do you really believe it will rain today?"

"Aye. Sometime today it will."

"If it rains, then you don't really intend to tie me out in it, do you?"

At last he heard some worry in her voice. She should be worried; it was a believable threat.

Her head was down, her red hair tangled.

"If you will finally tell me the truth, if you dump out all your secrets, tell me everything you're keeping from me, I will reconsider my plan."

She raised her head then and stared at him straight in the face. "There aren't any secrets. You have whiskers."

As a distraction, it was very good. "I am a man. It is morning. Of course I have whiskers. You have suffered through four husbands. Naturally you know exactly what has happened. You know everything."

To his surprise, she raised her hand and lightly touched her fingertips to his cheek, feeling the coarse hair. She touched his chin, his other cheek. "It's a curse. That's all I know. I can't explain any of it. You are very different from me."

"Merryn, there are young men about Penwyth. I saw at least a dozen. Everyone in that damned castle can explain exactly what is going on."

"Aye, but the young men are peasants and they aren't supposed to have me look at them with any interest beyond the tasks they are to accomplish." She paused a moment, still fretting with the rope about her wrist. "I never saw one of them naked. They didn't bathe often, and if they did, it wasn't in the barracks, where I did once or twice see a naked man-at-arms."

He laughed, just couldn't stop himself. Suddenly, without thought, he leaned forward and kissed her mouth. She fell as silent as the rope she now held in her hands. He saw that her wrist was chafed. His wasn't.

She touched her fingertips to her lips, then looked at him. "No one has ever kissed me before."

"Your second husband kissed you until blood came out of his mouth."

She actually shuddered. "Aye, Sir Gifford de Lancey. It was horrible. I don't want to remember that."

"He's dead. Sufficient punishment."

She nodded slowly. "Aye, I suppose it was."

"Did he touch you?"

Her hand touched her breasts, but she didn't say anything.

He fell back laughing again. "In the normal course of things, still being a virgin after four husbands would be impossible to believe."

She went up to her knees, looked around the small space. "I must relieve myself."

"Aye, I have to as well."

It was a beautiful morning, not as warm as it had been the day before. It was at that instant that he smelled the change in the air. It was always so. This shift in the very feel of the air itself. The sun was low on the horizon. It was still early. The sea was calm. He watched her walk to the one bush. He turned and relieved himself, thinking for the first time in his life that it was a much easier task for a man.

He saw to Fearless, who was bored and ready to butt Bishop's shoulder with his great head. He rubbed him down, moved him to another place, this one closer to the cliff edge so he could see all the birds at play below.

When she came out from behind the

bush, she sniffed the air as he had and smiled. "I'm quite hungry. Let me see what Dumas packed for us."

He could but stare at her. Was this just a simple pleasant outing for her? She didn't appear to be afraid of him at all. This wasn't good.

He said, his voice all hard and rough, "Go through the supplies. Then after we eat, I will tell you what I've decided to do with you."

That made her wary again, made her afraid, which she should be. He was getting used to the idea that he would marry her. Since he'd been told by every man he'd known that it was a wife's duty and obligation before God to obey her husband, give him children that survived, and never disagree with him, he realized that she could pose something of a challenge. After all, she wanted to be the heir to Penwyth as much as he did.

Then, suddenly, he clearly saw a small boy in his mind's eye, a boy whose hair was as black as his. Ah, but the boy's eyes, they were green as the Boskednan swamp grass, not dark blue like his. This was nonsense. He wasn't a damned seer. He wasn't a wizard, either. He knew no secrets, no ancient truths that floated through the eras to come into the modern day, evidently still fully potent. No, he couldn't conjure up a meal for himself, much less curse a man and make him keel over dead.

So where had that boy child come from? Likely from sleeping on the hard ground, a female sprawled on top of him. The result was painted images in his brain.

He knew only about rain, nothing more. He didn't know much about females, either, just that to have a willing body beneath him made him feel very good for a number of hours after. Every man he'd ever known was just the same.

She said, "My grandmother whispered to me how you, with no hesitation at all, told her that she'd birthed five children. How did you know that?"

He took the piece of Beelzebub's cheese she handed him and chewed on it, gaining himself some time. He shrugged, swallowed the cheese, and said, "I have told you. I am a wizard. I know things."

"Or mayhap the king mentioned it to you."

"How would the king know such a thing? Why would he care?"

That was true enough. She gave him a loaf of bread that she unwrapped from a cheese cloth, watched him break it apart in his big hands. She said, "My grandmother was frightened."

"Good. She should be. However frightened she was, she still wouldn't tell me anything of any use at all. She is a very strange lady, Merryn. Did she raise you?"

"Aye, she did raise me, I suppose you could say. More often than not, though, I simply did what I wished until our steward, Ranlief—"

"At least the steward got to sleep in his own chamber last night."

"Aye, I'm sure he appreciated that. He says his bones pain him during the night. My grandfather had a special mattress made for him. It's filled with feathers from chickens and geese. Ranlief was the one who taught me how to read a bit and to write. You said my grandmother was strange. I have always found her fascinating. She prides herself on her strangeness, her contrariness. It drives my grandfather quite mad, always has, and she knows it full well. But you know, I believe that he hit her only that one time, never again, not even after Meridian died."

"What about your mother?"

"My own mother died shortly after she'd birthed her third son. All the boy babes died. Only I survived. My father, Sir Thomas, wasn't often at Penwyth after my mother died. He didn't seem to care anymore."

"Your great-grandmother—Meridian. That is a very strange name. I'm very sorry about the boy babes, but to survive to manhood is difficult."

"Aye, it is. I heard talk that I should have died, not the boys, but I didn't."

"Where did Meridian live?"

"In a castle near Tintagel. She knew things, just like you know things, and they happened. I'm not lying to you. Did the curse really come from her? Or through her? I don't know. You see, I am telling you everything I know." Then she fell silent, chewed on the bread he handed her, and he wondered if she were chewing over her lies as well, her secrets, damn her eyes. "I think if my great-grandfather did kill her it was because he was simply too frightened of her to let her live."

The wind died. From one moment to the next, the wind simply stopped. The air seemed to thin, to flatten. It was a very strange thing, but Bishop felt it happen, deep inside him. He didn't move, just let this strangeness seep into him.

Merryn said, "What is wrong, Bishop? Why do you look so strange?"

Suddenly Fearless whinnied.

Bishop jumped to his feet and looked around, but there was nothing—no one was anywhere near them. He'd picked this spot because he could immediately see anyone coming.

Nothing. Just the morning haze that stretched as far as he could see. He saw the west tower of Penwyth in the distance. Were men staring toward Land's End, trying to see them? He didn't know, couldn't know.

"Nothing is wrong." He finished the bread, drank down a goodly amount of the ale, and said, "I have decided what I'm going to do with you."

10

He didn't say another word to her, just gave her a hand and settled her in front of him on Fearless's back. They rode northward along the coastline. He made sure they were always on or very near Penwyth land. He wanted to see the span of his property. The situation, he saw, was very bad. Planted fields were on the very edge of survival, and, Bishop realized, most of the people were as well. He prayed that his rain gift wouldn't fail him this time, because it was clear to him that Penwyth was dying.

"It doesn't look very good," Merryn said.

"No, it does not."

"You haven't done anything with me yet," she said after another long silence between them.

"I am looking for the perfect spot to stake you out for the rains that are coming soon."

But he didn't seem to find the perfect spot. He stopped, and they ate the rest of Dumas's supplies. He saw that she was looking very pleased with herself. In that instant he knew that he had to do something or she would have her foot on his neck. She would believe him naught but an empty bladder. He couldn't allow that.

"Here," he said, seeing that they were still on Penwyth land. "This small hillock. This is where you can drown in the rain that's coming. Actually, since it's a hill, you won't drown because all the water will flow off you, but you'll still get pounded."

She didn't believe him. "I wish to go back to Penwyth now. Everyone will be very worried about me."

"Why would they worry? They know I am punishing you. Do they believe I will kill you? Hmmm." He grabbed her wrists and tied the rope around them. She fought him. She was strong, and she tugged and jerked and yelled at him, but he just tightened the knot until he was satisfied. He dragged her to a sturdy bush atop the hillock, locked his foot behind her knees and knocked her over backward, then came down over her. "Hold still. I told you what I was going to do."

"No. I won't let you." She managed to bring her bound wrists up and clout him in the jaw, catching him off guard. He fell back, and she scrambled to her feet. "You will not tie me down like some animal." She ran. He could see her chewing on the rope, trying to loosen it as she ran.

He was nearly on her, careful of his own balance because they were running down the hill and there were rocks and brambles everywhere. He could hear her furious breathing. She was looking over her shoulder at him when her foot struck a rock. She yelled as she went flying forward, her bound hands out to break her fall. She landed on her hands and knees and rolled over and over, until at last she came to a sprawled stop at the base of the hillock.

"Damn you, Merryn." He nearly fell himself, but managed to keep his balance until he could get to her. He went down on his knees beside her. She was unconscious. He sat back on his heels and closed his eyes.

The day wasn't going very well.

He lightly touched his fingers to her head and felt the growing lump behind her left ear. Thank God her hair was thick. He hoped it had protected her a bit.

He turned her over on her back, felt her arms, her legs, and could find nothing broken. But her insides, that was the question. Bad things could happen if the insides were jarred and pounded. He paled. He raised his face to the heavens and cursed.

"A bishop shouldn't say such things."

"I am not *a* bishop. I am *the* bishop. And that is *Sir* Bishop to you."

She heard the relief in his voice. She was both angry and afraid of him, and yet she wished she could smile at his wit, but the truth was, she wanted to hit her head with another rock so she could ease away into that lovely oblivion.

It wasn't to be. She closed her eyes. She'd never felt such pain before—pounding pain, ferocious pain, nearly blinding her. She felt him untying the rope, rubbing her wrists. Then his palm was on her brow and he was leaning close. She felt his warm breath on her skin.

"There is nothing I can do to help you."

She knew that. She also heard the worry in his voice. "I can't move."

"No, don't even try. Just lie still."

He was gone. She heard Fearless whinny, heard Bishop speaking low to his stallion. Then there were two blankets covering her. He lifted her and placed a folded blanket beneath her head.

She didn't make a sound, but it was hard, very hard.

She felt his fingertips on her cheeks and knew he was wiping away her tears.

Then, with no warning at all, the heavens opened up and the rain poured down.

Bishop looked up through the incredible sheets of rain and cursed again. The precious rain, bringing life to the parched earth. Why couldn't it have held off just a little while longer?

"You don't have to tie me down," she said, then turned her face away. "I will drown anyway because I can't move and the ground is flat here."

He huddled over her, trying to keep the worst of it off her, but it wasn't possible. Fearless whinnied. He was miserable.

Bishop crouched lower over her, his nose not an inch from hers. He didn't know what to do. The skies had darkened a bit, he'd realized that in some part of his brain, but with his future wife lying nearly unconscious at his feet, he hadn't really paid attention.

He cursed again and touched his nose to hers. "Listen to me, Merryn. I cannot take the risk of moving you, so I'm going to set up the tent. It will keep us a little dry."

"Why didn't you think of that sooner?"

"Mayhap I was thinking that you might have the gall to die on me."

"If I am to die, please let me die dry."

He set the tent up right beside her. Thank God the ground was more level than not, since she'd rolled all the way down that hillock before she'd struck her head.

Slowly, knowing she was awake, knowing that the pain was ripping through her head, he eased into the tent and slowly, his hands beneath her arms, he pulled her inside. The blankets were wet, but he couldn't help that. She couldn't very well lie on the bare ground. Once he had her inside, once he knew for sure that the tent would keep the worst of the rain off them, he lay on his side next to her, close, to give her his body heat. Her red hair was wet, plastered to her head. He saw a bruise rising on her cheek.

"Breathe very slowly and lightly," he said. "Come on, Merryn, you can do it." He knew this was the right thing because once, when he'd been lying on the ground, trying not to moan with the immense pain in his shoulder from a bandit's axe, Dumas had said over and over, right in his ear, "Breathe, Bishop, but keep it calm and easy. Don't suck it in, no, just light and easy. That's right. I'll take care of this."

And so it was that Bishop repeated the same things to Merryn. He touched his fingertips to her forehead and began to massage her; then her scalp, drawing closer and closer to the lump over her temple. Slowly she began to ease.

The rain was battering the tent, and he knew the canvas was sodden by now. Would it withstand the force of the storm? He didn't know. He'd never before been in a rainstorm this heavy.

He felt her take his hand, squeeze his fingers when the pain was bad. To distract her, he began to talk. "I fought in Normandy with the Duke de Crecy, a villain of a man, more cruel and ruthless than the legendary Richard Coeur de Lion. He had not a care for his own hide. He was happiest, I think, when he was slicing his mighty sword, cleaving men in two, kicking the two halves apart. That last battle earned me a goodly amount of wealth, and so I came home to Cornwall. That was when I chanced upon Philippa de Beauchamp surrounded by a group of bandits."

She was quiet, too quiet, no longer squeezing his fingers.

Bishop laid his palm on her forehead. Cool, no fever—at least not yet.

"Who is Philippa?"

"Good, you're awake. Just keep breathing and listen to me. Philippa is the king's illegitimate daughter, married to Dienwald de Fortenberry, earl of St. Erth. You will not believe this, but she was riding with half a dozen men and found herself in the middle of a trap. The leader had grabbed her and was holding a knife against her ribs. I managed to free her and kill the leader. Then Dienwald arrived. It all ended well, and then I was—"

The day suddenly became night, black as the sand on the Land's End beach. A flash of lightning cut through the blackness. She cried out.

He gathered her against him, knowing

that if the rain came down any harder, the tent would collapse.

Another huge slash of lightning burned his eyes with its fierce brightness.

Thunder rolled overhead, making the earth tremble.

Then suddenly thunder crashed right over the tent, so close, so very close, and Bishop heard a rock explode just feet away. He pulled Merryn more tightly against him, protecting her head as best he could.

"It will be all right," he said, and said it again, as much for himself as for her. The minutes passed, the rain pounded down, and he knew that the tent would soon collapse on top of him.

A slash of lightning lit up the inside of the tent, bright as the noonday sun. The thunder struck, and the earth shook, but the light didn't fade.

It made no sense.

Still the light didn't fade. It grew even brighter.

And brighter yet.

He stared up at the dome of the tent, at the sturdy pole that kept it up, and it seemed to him that the light was now hovering right above his head. In the deepest part of him, he could feel the darkness trying to come closer, to consume the light, but the light held it at bay.

There was another earsplitting clap of thunder, then yet another.

Then it was utterly quiet. Too quiet, as if the air itself had been swallowed, sucked into something deep and black, something he couldn't see, but he could feel it.

Then just as suddenly the light was gone, swallowed by the blackness, only now the blackness was heavy and thick. He felt light-headed with the weight of it.

There was another explosion, but this one wasn't the sound of a rock blasted apart by thunder outside the tent.

This explosion was inside his head.

He fell over her.

11

Sometime Else

He awoke slowly to a still and heavy darkness, a darkness that blanketed him, that held him snug within it. He didn't want to open his eyes, he really didn't, but finally, slowly, he did, and saw that the darkness was more pervasive than he'd imagined. Nothing but darkness, all around him, and surely that was beyond odd. He felt the weight of it all the way to his soul—solid, heavy. It was hard to breathe. He knew, somehow, that if he didn't move, he would soon have that darkness inside him. But he didn't move just yet; he sucked in what air he could.

Something was very strange here.

He rolled over. He'd been lying outside, asleep and alone, and there were no stars overhead, nothing but this thick blackness. He heard a man's voice, close and coming closer. By all the gods, an enemy was nearby—it had to be Mawdoor. Somehow Mawdoor had brought him here and surrounded him with this darkness. But how?

Had he been unconscious, not sleeping? How was that possible? He drew a deep breath. If it was Mawdoor lurking close by, then so be it. Both knew there would someday be a reckoning between them. Would it be now? He called out, his own voice scratchy as a rusted blade—and that startled him—"Who goes there?"

A man was suddenly standing over him, looking down at him, speaking. He nearly pitched over, he was so startled. By all the ancient gods, it wasn't Mawdoor, it was rheumy old Callas in his dirty robe, his scraggly gray beard hanging in tangles to his sunken groin. Wretched-looking old relic.

Not Mawdoor, thank the gods. He felt appallingly weak, as if his wits were scattered like the stars behind that black, black sky.

Then he remembered, but it was a memory that didn't make any sense. He remembered that he'd finally found Brecia's sacred oak forest, had known to his marrow that it was hers. He'd felt it, let the knowledge seep into him, and he'd been more pleased than ever before in his life. He also knew he would search that dark forest until he dropped dead from exhaustion or she somehow managed to smite him down. Aye, he would search until he found her, the damned witch.

And now here was Callas, one of her ancient priests, outside the forest, standing over him. This was interesting indeed.

Why was he lying here on the ground? Had he been somehow caught in a dream, its images woven around him, freezing his brain? It was odd, these residual feelings snaking through him. He felt himself, knew that it was indeed himself, and yet—and yet, there also seemed to be the shadow of another, close by, nay, even deep inside him—but no, it was gone. No, no, he was only himself, none other. That sort of thinking was madness. All of it was enough to make a man's head pound off his neck.

Callas laughed, deep and thick with pleasure, waving his gnarly old stick around.

He cocked his eyebrow at the old sot, came up to a sitting position and wrapped his arms around his knees.

"Are you comfortable now, prince? Sitting there on the ground, so alone I can hear your heart beat. So what say you, you damnable black wizard who claims to know everything? I saw you lying on your back, helpless as a wingless sparrow. Did some being greater than you dash you down? Was it Mawdoor? You know that Mawdoor lives near. Did he bring you here?"

The prince watched Callas laugh again, louder this time, meanness and triumph heavy and hard in that ancient laugh of his.

Slowly, he unclasped his hands and got to his feet. He shook himself, frowned. No one had bound him, no, nothing like that. He'd simply been lying on the ground on his back. And now he was awake, Callas standing over him. He'd been vulnerable. If Callas weren't such a gutless coward, he just might have been dead.

Or perhaps he'd fallen asleep and this

was a dream spun out of another wizard's spells and heaped upon his head. Maybe it was one of Mawdoor's dreams. The prince still felt the echo of another's presence. But no matter. Mawdoor wasn't here, old Callas was.

Callas hadn't carved out his heart, and now the prince wouldn't allow him to.

"What is this, prince? You won't claim to strike me down? You're as silent as that stone beside your left foot."

The prince leaned back against a spear of stone, one of a small circle of stones that soared some eight feet into the air and had probably stood here since just after time started up. He looked insolent and languid, and said, his voice calm and deep as the night darkness surrounding them, "Why would I strike you down, old man? You are nothing to me. You are barely a speck of dirt on the bottom of my foot, a runny blister on the butt of an ass."

Callas drew himself up as straight as he could. "I do not like the sound of either of those things. Listen, prince. I am Brecia's first counsel. You knew of me through your mother's heart before you were born, you knew me since the moment that small boy wove his first spell. But look at you now. Standing against one of the Divas so you won't fall over—ah, you cannot harm me, aye, one of the ghosts just felt it to me. Aye, you're helpless, just leaning against that damned heathen stone, all alone, your power sucked dead as a hollow reed."

"Have you been drinking too much earth wine, you old buzzard? You think I'm helpless? I could turn you into a red-tongued toadstool like this—" The prince snapped his fingers, and Callas jumped a foot off the ground and yelled.

"Be quiet, Callas."

The old man was panting. The prince started to tell him that he preferred him the way he was—old and gnarly—when suddenly he felt something strange hovering just at the edge of his vision. If he turned his head quickly, he knew he would see something, someone. He turned. There was nothing, of course. He nodded. He understood now. That strange something was a leftover dream from the last full moon, when he'd meted out punishment to the wretched mortal cowards who'd sought to kill a witch they'd found, unconscious from her own potion. The prince shook his head, let it go.

He had a witch of his own to find. She'd escaped him, but he'd hunted her down, exactly how he wasn't certain at this moment, but it didn't matter. He would worry about all of it later. He knew in his wizard's bones that Brecia was somewhere in that sacred oak forest, knew she had to be—it was, after all, her forest.

He continued to ignore Callas. The ancient collection of beard and bones wasn't panting anymore, nor did he seem at all anxious to open his black-lined mouth.

It occurred to him suddenly that of course Callas was afraid of him. He had every reason to be. The prince was one of the greatest wizards of all time. The old man was an idiot, but he wasn't stupid.

The prince walked to Callas, towered over him, then stepped closer, nearly to his nose so he could intimidate him even more. Aye, let the old man's teeth chatter, although he had so few left there wouldn't be much sound to it.

The prince lightly touched his fingers to Callas's mouth, skimming the flesh, the beard tickling his fingers. "Did you bring other priests with you, Callas? Are they awaiting your signal to attack me? It doesn't matter if there are ten, nay, even a hundred ancient graybeards, even a hundred of your ghosts. I will cut off their heads, weave their dirty beards into leads for my dogs. Or I will turn them into black rocks to be pounded by the waves for all time. What do you think, Callas?"

"I think that something is wrong, prince. Just look at you. You pretend to arrogance, yet there is something strange going on here, something I don't understand. Do you?

"No, prince, don't threaten me. I mean you no harm. Aye, just look at you—you look more dangerous than your father looked when he blew the tide into that pitiful town called Londinium that lies toward the east."

"My father is rarely capricious. A mob was stoning an old man, someone accused of witchcraft. He stopped it."

"Why didn't your father simply smite them all?"

The prince shrugged. "He was trying to keep his temper, and he began blowing out to calm himself. Instead, his breath became a mighty gale, washing the water over all the land."

"Aye, and that old man he saved drowned like the rest of the mob. Like your father, you would rather slice a man into two parts with your sword than simply lock your fingers together and turn him into acrid blue smoke or a tarantula."

The prince stroked his chin. "Hmmm, I haven't thought of spiders in a long time. Now, you are here alone, are you not, Callas?"

"As you see, prince, as you see."

"Why?"

Callas cocked his old head at that question, he frowned, he pulled on his beard, but in the end he just shook his head. "I don't remember. This is all very strange. Don't you believe it's stranger than a ghost who wishes to copulate with a mortal?"

"Aye, everything is passing strange." So neither of them knew how he'd gotten here.

The prince said, "I will not kill you. That is not why I am here. This is Brecia's oak forest, isn't it?"

"No, it is not. You must leave, prince."

The prince raised a dark eyebrow at him. "Leave? I don't think so. I will tell you the truth, Callas. I have looked and looked but could never see where Brecia was. She is good at concealment, I admit it. But now I am here, how I don't exactly know, but this is the very edge of her oak forest. I feel it to the very core of my being. Now I finally realize why you are here, Callas. You are here to guide me into her fortress. The gods sent you here, just as they sent me. It is time, and Brecia knows it."

His heart began to pound. Soon he would see Brecia. It had been too long since that first time they'd stood beneath a sarsen stone lintel at the vast sacred stone circle.

"You weave a silly tale. Why would Brecia want to see you, prince? You're a black wizard. You want to own her, control her."

"Only that?"

"Listen to me, you black prince of Balanth. Brecia is the soul of the body. If she is taken, coerced, controlled, then she will die, then we all die."

"You think that is true, Callas? That this is what I want?"

The old priest snarled like a cornered wolf. "That's what she thinks. She came to realize that you lied to her, that you were not to be trusted. She found out that after you saw her at the sacred stone circle, after you told her you wanted her above all others, you disappeared and you took that witch from across the sea as your wife."

The prince shrugged. "I did not lie, not really. The fact is, I had no choice but to wed Lillian. I did not even know of it until my parents and the council told me. It was my duty." He paused a moment, felt a quivering of regret in the silent air. "Lillian died birthing my child."

"How is such a thing possible?"

"She was flying at the time. I told her not to, that it was too close to her time, but she must always do the opposite of what I counseled her to do. At least the representatives of the Spanish Karelia agreed to keep to our treaty, since her death was a natural thing and not my fault."

"Did you tell them what you told me? That she disobeyed you?"

"No, I did not."

Callas shook his head. "They would have kept the treaty anyway. They knew what your family could do—you would commit random acts of wizardry that would explode their innards."

The prince smiled. "Mayhap. But the Spanish Karelia are a powerful lot, not easy to discount. The treaty serves all, keeps all passions at a simmer. Now, enough talk, old man. I wish to see Brecia. I will walk with you or I will kill you and go by myself. You may decide."

Suddenly the prince had that sensation again—someone, something, just to his side, perhaps a bit behind him, just beyond what he could touch and hear and see. He turned quickly, but there was nothing, no one there. Had something happened whilst he was asleep? He controlled the strange feelings, furious with himself for allowing them to overwhelm him for even a moment.

"I will take you, prince, but I don't wish to. We will see what Brecia decides to do with you."

The prince's eyebrow shot up. *"What she will do with me?* Come now, Callas. You're here to take me to her. Or did you intend to try to kill me whilst I slept?"

The old man shook his head back and forth. No, Callas was more likely to wave his priest's stick at some poor ass and turn him into a roach or a dung beetle. He looked like all his brethren, thin, hollow-chested, wrapped in a dirty white wool robe tied with a frayed rope that was as old as he was. His sandals were held to his bony feet with thin strips of leather. For as long as the prince could remember, Callas had worn these same clothes, or ones just as dirty. He wondered if when a priest departed the mortal plane, he left his robe for a younger priest. Mayhap this robe was as old as the forest itself.

He said, "You look like those damned hermits who spin out their lives in caves beneath desert cliffs in the Bulgar."

"What is this Bulgar?" Callas said, staring at him. "I know of no place called Bulgar."

"You are so provincial, Callas. The Bulgar is a hard, brutal land from whence come many of the greatest wizards of the world."

"There are hermits in this place? In caves? Why have I never heard of this?"

The prince laughed. "You cannot travel like I can. Forget the Bulgar. Enough. I wish to go now into the forest. I wish to see Brecia."

"She will kill you, prince."

"Let the witch try," the prince said, rubbing his hands together. He felt a burst of pleasure at the thought of actually seeing her face when she beheld him, seeing her seething rage that would surely bubble and boil. He said, "Just smell you, Callas. You are filthier than usual." The prince stepped forward.

Callas raised his hand. In it he held his priest stick, his *kesha*, at least two feet long, its length signifying to all who knew of such things that he was one of the most learned of the priest seers, having spent more than seventy years of his life in study. It was carved deeply with the symbols of life. Its tip glowed black.

The prince waved at the *kesha*. "Where did you get that thing?"

"My dead mentor," Callas said. "An ancient priest who became a ghost four or five years ago. It's mine now, and it will remain mine until I give it to a student upon my own passing, and only the gods know when that will be."

"In fifty years? A hundred?"

Callas just smiled. "You know the worth, the power of the *kesha*."

The prince nodded. The black tip of the *kesha* had always seemed to the prince to be like a small candle that simply never went out. It illuminated the darkest night, lighted the deepest passages through the oak forest. He'd heard stories of the *kesha* all his life, knew it had come down from the ancient beings who had built the vast stone circle at the very dawn of time. Now, in the present, wizards used these mighty stones—fifty-six of them standing in a rough circle like huge, silent sentinels—to go beyond to another place where sights and sounds intermingled and light became lighter still, and all was whole and safe, and there were answers there, perhaps answers to questions no one yet knew to ask. If the prince closed his eyes, he could see the circle of stones, hear the wind blowing through them, hear the low, rhythmic chants of the priests, placating ancient beings they didn't really understand but knew to be potent.

"What is this game you play with me, prince? You know the power of the *kesha,* you know that if it touches you, your heart will shrivel in your chest and you will gasp for breath and then you will fall bloodless to the ground."

The prince threw back his head and laughed. "You touch me with that and I will send you to live on an ice floe in the northern seas." The prince crossed his arms over his chest and looked intimidating. He remembered that he had a knife fastened to his wrist, hidden by his long woolen sleeve. The wool was soft against his skin.

Callas didn't move either himself or his

kesha. He said, "You are wearing new woolens. They are far too white. You stand out like a streak of lightning in a black sky."

The prince shrugged. "The wool is soft and clean, something you should consider."

"You don't look quite right," Callas said. "There is something that is different about you, prince—"

In a flash, the prince pulled the knife out of his sleeve, a move so practiced it was merely a blur.

Callas jerked back. He swallowed hard, his eyes on the slender knife.

The prince said, "You've always been afraid of me, and that is very wise of you. I can see you more clearly now. The night darkness has thinned a bit." He paused, then shook his head. "It is a strange time we live in." The thick blackness was receding. Now directly overhead was a sickle of moon. The inverted black cup of the gods was full of stars, shining so fiercely that the prince could see the small scar from a long ago cut on his right ankle.

Callas said, "Aye, you're right about that."

"At least the darkness isn't what it was. Now, Callas—"

"I am now the highest priest, prince."

The prince snorted through his laugh. "I hope this means you know the right direction. Let us go, Callas. Take me to Brecia." Just saying her name made him hard. It was an excellent feeling, this instant, overwhelming lust he felt just saying her name. Soon he would have her. At last.

Callas stroked his long, dirty beard, plaiting it in his fingers, then smoothing out the plaits. A long-standing habit, the prince knew. "Brecia won't have you, even though she wants you. She said if you come near here again she would kill you."

The prince gave him an evil grin, filled with white teeth and infinite malice. "I tremble with fear at that threat. Now, let us go, or I will slit your ancient throat. Then I just might turn you into blue smoke and send you back to puff out of one of Brecia's witch's pots."

Callas extended his *kesha* closer, but the prince just laughed and shoved it away with his hand. "Old man, don't even try any of your dismal magic with me." He smiled, sheathed the knife, and pulled out his narrow, beautifully worked wand, not much longer than his forearm. "Or," he said, grinning now as his fingers caressed the length of the wand, "I will make you itch."

The prince flicked his wand, nothing more, just flicked it in Callas's direction. The old man leapt back, then yelled. "No, don't, prince, no! Damn you, prince, no!"

The prince watched for a moment while Callas tried to scratch all the places on his body that were itching so badly he was nearly dancing with it.

"Make it stop. Please, make it stop!"

"Will you take me to Brecia?"

Callas yelled, "Aye, I will take you to her. Let her destroy you with her magic. She is strong now and—yaagh, make it stop!"

The prince flicked his wand once again, still smiling. Callas shook himself down, scratched violently at his left knee, then paused, blinked, and looked immensely relieved. "I wish I could do that. Will you teach me? It really is a stupid curse, but it is very effective."

"I will consider teaching you if you take me to Brecia."

Callas turned his long *kesha* in his hands, watching the tip glow. "A dark wizard such as you should not come into the forest. Your darkness destroys the holiness of our sacred oak groves."

"Leave go, Callas. I promise I will destroy nothing. Take me to Brecia. I am sure the witch will see me." So close, he was now so close to her. He laughed. "Perhaps I will cast a spell on her. Not itching, no. I will make her desire me above all men. I will make her want to strip me down to my hide and caress me. Aye, I would like to have that witch in my power. Do you think she would like that?"

The prince thought Callas would fall over in a faint. "Brecia would not do that, even under a spell. She is inviolate. You should not make sport with us, prince."

"All right," the prince said agreeably. "Since I am a wizard, I can snap my fingers—" And he snapped his fingers right in Callas's face. The old man yelped and jumped back. The prince laughed. "Aye, I can snap my fingers and we will be there, at your most sacred shrine, right in front of Brecia." If only he really could do that, he thought, glad Callas didn't realize he couldn't. "Is that what you wish me to do? Only the gods know what shifts and changes that would bring."

Callas groaned, then swallowed it as if realizing that a priest should not show weakness, particularly to the dark prince. "No, no. You will not do your evil magic on me. No, stay away from me. Follow me. It is not far, only as far as Brecia deems it to be."

That sounded ridiculous to the prince, but he would be the first to admit that Brecia was cunning, mayhap just that clever. He fell into step closely behind Callas, who was walking as nimbly as a mountain goat. The floor of the forest was soft with rotted leaves and pulpy vegetation beneath his boots. It was still darker than not, and he stumbled several times.

He wanted Brecia, and he fully intended to have her this time. No more treaties to dictate his mate. He was free to follow his own way. He began whistling in the darkness, and Callas looked ready to spit with fear.

The prince smiled.

12

Present

Bishop lay still, waves of pain crashing through his head, the stark image in his brain of a filthy old man and a young man—no, the young man was more than that, aye, the young man was a prince, by all the saints, he was magic, he was a wizard, he had a damned wand and he could use it. It was impossible, but there they were, alive in his brain, their faces as clear as if they were standing right in front of him. But even in the next instant, they were fading into the mist that covered that thick, ancient oak forest.

For an instant he swore he heard the young prince's laughter, and he thought, *He is going to get Brecia.*

Then there was nothing. Just nothing.

Bishop didn't move, perhaps afraid to move. A dream, he thought. He'd dreamed— a vivid, very strange dream, nothing more than that, no matter the rich, detailed colors, the strange speech they'd spoken, which he'd understood.

He drew a deep breath, shook his head. The images were gone.

But there was one thing he was very sure of in that moment.

There was no oak forest near where he and Merryn had lain in that tent beneath the drowning sky.

"Wake up, Bishop. Come on, wake up."

"I don't want to."

"Good, you're alive. In the single day I've known you, I've learned a lot about you. Now I'm seeing that you're also selfish. Just listen to you—*I don't want to*—" She'd mimicked him quite well, actually. "Well, I don't care what you want. Get up before the tent collapses."

He opened his eyes to see Merryn not an

inch from his nose, her warm breath fanning his face. His brain righted itself. What was this? She was the one who had gone head-first down the hillock. He said, frowning, "Are you all right? You fell and hit your head. I remember that."

"I'm better than you are. I opened my eyes and I saw you hunkered over me. You jerked your head up at this loud clap of thunder, and a flash of lightning streaked your face white. Then you just fell on top of me."

"A loud clap of thunder," he said.

"Aye, something must have happened. There aren't any lumps on your head that I can tell. My lump is good-sized, but you don't see me flat on my back, do you? You're a warrior, aren't you?"

"It's raining."

"It's more than raining. It's making up for the months when there was nothing at all except blowing dust. I don't know how much longer the tent can stay up. You have to get yourself together, Bishop."

He looked past her, saw the blur of rain battering down on the tent. Surprisingly, it was holding. But for how long?

"You were right about the rain. It is incredible. You are a wizard, aren't you?"

"Aye, I am a wizard," he said without thought, without any consideration at all. Now wasn't that odd? He felt suddenly filled with energy, the pain gone, and he wanted to draw his sword and leap out of the damned tent and kill bandits. No luck there. No self-respecting bandit would be out in this deluge.

"We can't stay here. How do you feel?"

"I healed myself," he said, just to see what she would say, just to see how she would react to that.

She reared back, alarm in her eyes. "You are jesting again, aren't you, Bishop?"

"Of course," he said. "We will stay here until the rain stops or the tent collapses in on us. Come down beside me and we can warm each other."

She hesitated only a moment before easing down beside him. They were both damp, and that wasn't good, but she realized soon enough that the heat from his body would warm her quite well. Even in the dead of winter he would warm her. She said, "When I woke up I realized that I didn't know how much time had passed. But it's dark. It wasn't dark when I fell down the hillock. It was full into the day, wasn't it?"

"Aye, it was, but then the sky darkened, don't you remember?" He was remembering that huge flash of white light that stayed and stayed until suddenly—there was just nothing. The dream, there had been the dream. Gone now, all of it.

"Aye, just before the rain came down it darkened, but look now, Bishop. It's night. Did you do something?"

"By all the saints' knee-bent prayers, what do you think I am? A god to change day into night at my whim?"

She was silent. He felt her fingertips wandering over his chest. "Could you?"

He wanted to laugh. The cost of coincidence. He'd been right about the damnable rain and now he'd moved beyond that simple task—now he could change the march of the sun. "Very well. I am a god, not just a wizard."

She giggled. "You are jesting with me again. My head hurts a bit, but it isn't bad." She paused a moment, then said, "Were you really going to tie me down? Let me lie there in the rain?"

"Yes."

She didn't say anything more, just settled

her cheek against his shoulder. Soon both of them slept.

And when they awoke it was still raining and the tent still hadn't collapsed. They could see dirty light outside. How long had they slept? Had it really been night? How long had that bloody dream lasted?

He knew suddenly, knew with absolute certainty, that if he left Penwyth land, there wouldn't be any more rain. The rain was for this land only. But how could that be?

Five hours later, Bishop, with Merryn in front of him atop Fearless's back, rode beneath a now sunny sky to St. Erth Castle. The torrential rain had turned to billowing dark clouds that hid the sun, and then the clouds turned white and the sun was bright.

All this happened the moment they left Penwyth land.

He shouted to the porter at St. Erth's gate, waved at Gorkel the Hideous, and Eldwin, the master-at-arms, and shouted out greetings.

The last thing he wanted was an arrow through his gullet because someone believed him an enemy.

When he rode Fearless into the inner bailey of St. Erth, he was nearly deafened by all the noise.

It was warming, that noise, because it was normal. It didn't hide any mysterious dreams, or any—what? He couldn't remember. The children shrieked, animals grunted, butted each other and any humans close enough. Chickens squawked as they pecked at the children's bare toes, sending them running and yelling. Above it all was the armorer's hammer, striking iron, making it ring and echo throughout the bailey.

The main thing was, the noise was all young.

Bishop breathed in the scents of baking bread, horse dung, human sweat, and fresh rosemary. He saw Philippa holding a basket in her hand, and in that basket was a pile of rosemary she'd just picked.

"Bishop. Welcome. Who's this? Goodness, neither of you looks very good. What happened?"

Merryn could just imagine how they looked. Their clothes weren't yet dry, but she knew her gown was wrinkled and torn, her hair whipped into tangles around her head.

She looked at Bishop, saw that he was smiling.

"It is good to be back to something I know and understand," he said, "something that is utterly normal. Merryn, that bent little man is Crooky the Fool and the other is Gorkel the Hideous, well named indeed, a man endowed with the ugliest face in Christendom. And that is Eldwin, Dienwald's master-at-arms, out of breath from running down the wooden stairs from the ramparts."

Bishop looked down at Dienwald and Philippa. "This is the maid of Penwyth who's been married four times. Merryn de Gay, this is Lord Dienwald de Fortenberry, earl of St. Erth. And this is Philippa, his wife and helpmeet, the king's sweet daughter."

Merryn had never before visited St. Erth. She'd heard stories about the Scourge of St. Erth, but he didn't look at all wicked. And Philippa, the king's bastard daughter, was beautiful, all that thick, curly hair, plaited through with pale yellow ribbons.

Dienwald laughed and clasped Merryn beneath her arms to lift her off Fearless's back. "You're just a bit damp, both of you. Why? Look at the sun overhead. You were sporting with her, weren't you, Bishop, and you both fell into a river or perhaps a small pond somewhere?"

"Ah, Dienwald, no sporting around with her." Bishop laughed, dismounted, and handed Fearless's reins to Gorkel, who gave him a blinding smile. "Actually, it is raining hard on Penwyth land."

"But not here?" Dienwald arched an eyebrow. "How is that possible, Bishop?"

Bishop could do nothing but shrug. "It is a bit unusual, I suppose. I cannot explain it."

"Bishop made it rain," Merryn said.

That brought instant and complete silence.

"No," he said, all calm and indifferent, "I didn't. She jests."

Dienwald gave him an odd look, then stepped aside as his wife said, "We can have explanations later. Come in, come in. First, dry clothes for both of you. Ah, it is a very good thing that we have more than enough sheep now to weave wool for clothes. Merryn, you're about my height, so my gowns should fit you well enough."

"Ha," Dienwald said. "You're a giant, a maypole. This is but a little bit of a girl and—"

Philippa stuffed a bit of rosemary into her

husband's mouth. He spat it out, laughed, and said, "Come along, Bishop. Gorkel will take good care of Fearless. Indeed, he is the only one to take care of the brute, since he's the only one Fearless won't try to bite."

"Aye, Fearless is afraid that Gorkel will bite him."

Not long thereafter, Merryn walked beside Philippa de Fortenberry, countess of St. Erth, up the deeply worn stone steps into the great hall.

There was so much noise, everyone talking at once, everyone moving here and there, going about their tasks, half their attention on Bishop and Merryn. And the laughter and the sounds of children playing, shouting, arguing.

"At Penwyth," she said to Philippa, "there isn't this noise."

Philippa raised an eyebrow at that. "Every keep I've visited shatters the eardrums, even the inner bailey at Windsor."

"It's all old men at Penwyth," Merryn said. "They don't usually speak loudly. Thank you for the clothes."

"These lovely clothes were given to me by Kassia de Moreton some years ago. They fit you well enough. What do you mean there are only old men at Penwyth?"

They'd reached the great hall. "Oh, no," Philippa said and rolled her eyes.

Crooky the Fool had hopped on top of one of the trestle tables. He sang at the top of his lungs:

> *"Here's the king's Bishop*
> *Not here to play at chess.*
> *There's a maid he's got to wed,*
> *Then he'll haul her off to bed.*
> *All the while he'll pray*
> *That the curse won't strike him dead.*
> *All hail Bishop the 5th—husband."*

Merryn looked up at Philippa. "That rhymed, Philippa—at least some of it did— but it wasn't true what he said. What is wrong with him? Bishop didn't come to Penwyth to marry me. He came just to remove the Penwyth curse."

Dienwald roared, leapt over to the trestle table and cuffed the fool so hard he flew off into the rushes and rolled and rolled until he lay on his back and grinned up at his master.

"Master, heed me, I will do better. Until the

evening arrives on night feet, I will practice until I can find rhymes that will rhyme even with themselves, mayhap even a few choice words to rhyme with 'husband.' Another line? Aye, I'll even add another line. What think you, noble master?"

"Enough, you brainless sot," Dienwald said. "Bishop isn't to wed her."

"But he is, I heard all of you—" Crooky's eyes rolled back in his head and he clasped his own hands around his throat and started squeezing. "Oh, dear, oh, begorra, and oh, my mother too, I will be smote down because my brain has grown warts and died."

"Aye, it has," Dienwald said. "Keep your mouth shut." He looked over at Bishop, who hadn't moved an inch. He still held the goblet of fine St. Erth ale in his hand. He was staring at Merryn. He was wondering if Crooky the Fool had just signed his death warrant.

Merryn cleared her throat. "Why, Fool, do you call him Bishop the 5th? Why do you think he came to Penwyth to marry me? Tell me."

"No," Bishop yelled at the top of his lungs. "I would cut off my toes before I would marry you. The fool here mistakes his bishops.

Bishops litter the land. It is another one of them he cackles about, not me."

"Aye, thass true enough, mistress," Crooky said and stopped strangling himself, then rolled in a ball until he came to a stop at Merryn's feet. He came gracefully upright, which was only to Merryn's shoulder. He fingered the sleeve of her lovely pale-green gown. "I remember when the beautiful princess Kassia, so dainty and gracious she is, brought this gown. The mistress here gnashed and ground her teeth and yelled that she'd throw it to the wolfhounds, ah, but she didn't, she—"

Dienwald came toward Crooky and the fool quickly rolled beneath one of the trestle tables.

"He's a fool," Dienwald said. "Actually, since he's my fool, he's all right. Come, Merryn, and have some of the wench's delicious bread and ale. Aye, the gown, given to her by the beautiful little Kassia, so incredibly soft and gentle, looks much better on you than it did on my wench here. I say, wench, did you ever wear this lovely gown? Or was it too small for your bountiful charms?"

Philippa cuffed her husband's shoulder. He laughed and laughed, then threw back his head and shouted, "Where are my babes?"

Margot came scurrying forward. She had a little boy under each arm, and a little girl was plastered to her gown, her fingers in her mouth.

Dienwald looked sideways at Merryn and said, "Come look at my babes, Bishop. They have grown in these few days since you last saw them. Is that not true?"

"They will be giants, Dienwald," Bishop said.

"Aye, and if ever you wed"—Dienwald shot a look at Merryn—"which I know will not happen for many years yet, particularly since you are not here to wed Merryn of Penwyth—why, then, these are the babes you will want to have. Toss me Edward, Margot."

And Margot, not strong enough, thankfully, to throw the little boy to his father, instead handed him over, cooing over him even as Dienwald brought him close.

"Aye, look at Edward, Bishop. You too, Merryn. Look at this perfect babe who looks just like his brother, Nicholas. Ah, wench, is this Edward I'm holding?"

"Aye, my lord, that is Edward."

Nicholas began yelling. Eleanor took her fingers out of her mouth and began yelling in harmony.

"When you have children, Merryn de Gay, which won't be for many years yet—you have to wed, and that won't happen until many more suns have sunk low in the sky, and it doesn't involve Bishop—you will wish to have babes like my little ones here. My precious Eleanor is the loudest, isn't she? Just like her mother."

Dienwald now held all three of his babes.

Philippa was laughing so hard she was holding her sides. She was also looking out of the corner of her eye at Merryn, wondering if she was thinking about Crooky's ill-chosen words.

She wasn't. She was looking about the great hall, taking in all the talking, laughing people—scores of people—most of them young with few wrinkles to share amongst them. And the children, so many of them, crawling or walking or skipping. It was amazing. She'd never seen such a thing in her life. And Philippa's three babes. They were still in their father's arms, laughing, yelling, bouncing up and down.

Bishop took her hand and sat her on the

end of the trestle table bench. He gave her a piece of bread and a hunk of cheese. "It probably isn't as good as Beelzebub's, but it is tasty."

"Thank you," Merryn said and ate, never taking her eyes off the activity in the great hall of St. Erth.

When she'd eaten, she rose from her seat, placed her hands on her hips, and said, "Thank you, my lord and lady of St. Erth. I should have realized that this man, Bishop of Lythe—"

"It's Sir Bishop. I knighted him myself."

"—was a base liar. So that was your plan, *Sir* Bishop, to pretend to be at Penwyth only to root out the curse. All along you were there to marry the heiress." She raised her arm and pointed her finger directly at him.

"You believe what the fool sang?" Philippa said, an eyebrow arched upward. "It is his job to make up fantastic tales."

Merryn said, her foot tapping now, "He spoke the truth, even though the rhymes weren't very good."

The great hall fell silent as the grave. Even the children, even Dienwald's babes, were quiet, staring at Merryn and her outstretched arm.

"—she's going to strike him down."

"—she's going to kill him through the end of her finger."

Bishop heard the frightened whispers from just behind him. He slowly stood, stared at that pointing finger of hers, and walked toward her. He grabbed her arm and pulled it back to her side.

She was heaving, her breathing was so hard and fast. "Let me go, you bastard."

"Oh, no. Listen to me, Merryn. This curse—I don't know what it means yet, but I will discover what it is all about and I will get rid of it. And yes, then I will marry you."

"Bastard!"

She yelled so loudly that his eardrums nearly heaved into his brain.

She drew back her arm and let loose, striking him hard in the jaw. Bishop reeled back and grabbed the edge of the table. For a moment he was so angry that he saw red creeping into his vision, felt his attention narrowing until it was solely on her. *She had struck him. She had actually struck him.* He looked at her, knowing that if he touched her in anger, he could kill her. He didn't want her dead, curse her eyes.

He threw back his head. "Listen, all of

you. I have taken the maid from Penwyth far away from the seat of the curse. I will wed her right now, within the next hour, by Father Cramdle, who will ignore any screeching, any vile curses from my bride's mouth."

"You cannot make me wed you, Bishop." She ran at him, came onto her tiptoes, and shouted right in his face, "I won't have you, you miserable liar. You are worse than all the husbands. At least they were honest in their greed."

Bishop grabbed her, jerked her about so that her back was pressed against him, and held her arms firmly at her sides. He leaned down, whispered in her ear, "The king has given you to me. That is enough."

She said with no hesitation, with complete conviction, "Don't you understand, you half-wit? As long as there is the curse, you will die if you wed me."

Damnation, he did believe her.

Bishop said against her face, "Very well. I won't force you to marry me."

"Good. Let me go or I'll kick you until you yowl."

"You do that and I'll bare your bottom and thrash you. Right here, in front of everyone."

He was silent for a moment, a thoughtful silence she didn't trust.

"Let me go, you bastard."

"Oh, no. Do you know, Merryn, I think I'll do something else with you."

He loosened his hold enough so that she could turn to face him. She wanted to hit him, he could see it on her face, that open face of hers. But she held herself back. "A lot has happened since you came to Penwyth, Bishop. Tell me you understand now. If you marry me, you will die. It's that simple. I won't allow that to happen. I won't marry you."

He gave her a long look and said, "I understand. As I said, I'm thinking about something else now."

13

Bishop pulled Merryn away from the center of the great hall into a corner where there were three servants staring at them from the shadows and two small dogs chewing on an ancient leather strap. He waved them away, then whispered in her ear, "Aye, I understand, all right, but heed me, Merryn. The king has given you to me. There is no lie in that, no greed, no dishonesty, just my wish to remain alive until I get rid of that damned curse."

She punched him in the stomach. His breath whooshed out even as one of the nearby servants gasped in horror. Merryn said right in his face, all the while shaking her fist under his nose, "You're just a man, damn you, just like all the rest of them. Does the king hate you, then, that he sends you to your death?"

"No," he said once he could breathe again. "He merely wants it done to his satisfaction, and that is you safely wedded to me and the curse a past memory."

"Listen to me, Bishop. If you wed me, you will die."

He stared down at the top of her head. She was strong. His belly still hurt. That bloody curse—by all the saints' crooked teeth, Bishop hated what he couldn't see, what he couldn't examine, what he couldn't understand. *Sometimes*, he thought suddenly, *sometimes he couldn't bear a wizard's knowledge, a wizard's gifts, a wizard's obligations.*

He blinked, shook his head. He felt a moment of dizziness, and his vision grew dim. He managed to hold himself still until he was steady again.

Where had that bizarre thought come from? It had to be the curse creeping toward him, eager to topple him into his grave. Would foam ooze from his mouth? Would all his blood spurt out of his nose? He said, "I am tired of your evasions, your secrets, Merryn. I want the truth—the curse comes through you somehow, doesn't it? And you manipulate it in some way, don't you?"

The great hall was as silent as stone. How had anyone heard him here in this shadowed corner with two damned dogs gnawing and growling over a leather strap near his left foot? But they had, and everyone had gone silent, leaning toward him. Suddenly one of Dienwald's twins started crying. Bishop heard Philippa say quietly, "It's all right, sweeting, come to Mama. If Bishop can't fix this, why, then, your father will tend to it."

Merryn said, "It's true I have red hair and green eyes, it's also true that there always has been a girl with red hair and green eyes for as far back as anyone can remember. But the curse—it was fashioned hundreds of years ago. How could it have anything to do with me, Merryn de Gay?"

"Then why are four men dead?"

She shook her head. "I'm not a curse bearer, nor am I a poisoner. I haven't the skill or knowledge of such things."

Bishop slowly turned her to face him. He

held her shoulders, leaned down, and said in her face, "When will you stop your damned lies?"

He managed to grab her wrist the instant before her fist would have slammed hard into his stomach. He drew her up against him, but it was she who said against his mouth, "I'm not lying to you. I have no secrets."

But he could see that she did, and it enraged him. The pulse pounded in his throat, "Very well, Merryn. I believe that even if I married you here—away from Penwyth—I would still die."

"You will return me to Penwyth?"

"No." He smiled down at her, not at all a pleasant smile. "I told you, I have other plans for you."

She looked up at him, studying his expression, trying to judge what was in his mind. "A lot has happened since you came to Penwyth, Bishop."

"Aye, you are right about that. It's now been just two full days since I yelled up to the old men on Penwyth's ramparts to let me enter. By all the saints' sour breaths, just two damnable days." His eyes darkened, now nearly as dark as the shadows that surrounded them. "If you wished to marry me, if you weren't coerced, then I wouldn't be struck down."

She said, so close now that her warm breath fanned his face, "Listen to me, Bishop. I believe that even if I stood on the Penwyth ramparts and yelled for all to hear that I wished to take you as my husband, you would still die."

"How do you know the curse would fell me if you agreed to wed me?"

"I don't know, but I'm not about to take the chance."

"What is this? You don't want me dead?"

She looked at him for a very long time, until one of the dogs slapped her foot with the leather strap. She raised her hand to touch him, then dropped it to her side again as she said, "No, I don't want you dead."

He smiled then. "Ah, you're protecting me."

She shrugged.

He knew everyone in the great hall was still listening, but he didn't pause. He said, "All right. I won't marry you."

Crooky jumped atop a trestle table, poked out his chest, scratched his armpit, and sang out:

"The maid has won.
But she won't be glad.
She'll die a virgin
Alone and sad."

The fool's song actually rhymed, and rhymed well, Merryn thought, but those rhyming words weren't true. They weren't. Something would happen, something would change, something had to change. She wouldn't die alone. She thought of all the old men at Penwyth she'd known all her life, as had her father before her. Had they ever been as young as she was now? They would die, they had to sometime, since they couldn't last forever, and then there would be no one to grow old with her. Oh, God, would she die alone? Alone and sad? Those weren't comforting words Crooky had sung.

"No," Bishop said, loud enough so that all heard him, "she won't die a virgin."

"I was worried about dying alone," she said. "I hadn't yet considered the virgin part."

His anger, boiling but two minutes before, was now at a simmer. He didn't want to smile, but it was difficult to keep his mouth straight.

Crooky pointed at Gorkel the Hideous,

who was chewing on a sprig of rosemary, and yelled, "Old Agnes told Gorkel that the rosemary would make his breath so fine all the young maids would follow him about, demanding kisses. Tell us, monster, what think you of all this Penwyth witchery? Come, let your words flow from your sweet mouth."

Gorkel made a face as he swallowed the last of the rosemary, but most couldn't tell because he was so very ugly. "I say the maid shouldn't prick t'young soon-to-be lord of Penwyth, thass what I say."

"But what does that have to do with witchery, monster?"

"There is no witchery," Gorkel said, standing not a foot from Crooky, his head thrown back so even the wolfhounds came to attention. "A maid should dedicate herself to making her husband's rod hard and strong, jess like our own sweet mistress does for t'master."

Philippa waved her fist at Gorkel, and he laughed, a deep belly laugh that was a terrifying sound.

Crooky held his nose and fell backward off the trestle table to roll in the rushes. He lay there on his back and said, "My dearest mistress, give the monster a sweet kiss, for his breath is so pleasing it knocked me flat on my arse."

Merryn couldn't help it. She laughed, as did every person in the great hall.

Bishop, however, was suddenly aware that there was something wrong. But what? *Someone or something was close, he felt it, saw the shadow of it, felt the air change, felt the prickle on the back of his neck.* He whirled about. There was nothing save one of Dienwald's wolfhounds scraping his nails on the stone floor.

By all the saints' flapping tongues, what was wrong with him?

He waited until Philippa, a small boy under each arm, stretched on her tiptoes, let the little boys pat Gorkel's face and tug on his hair. Gorkel leaned down and Philippa kissed his forehead. "It's a sweet breath you have, Gorkel," she said, and his face split into a huge ugly grin.

"Hear ye, Crooky, the rosemary wrought wondrous magic. T'mistress said so."

Crooky yelled out, "All you fair maids, come and kiss the monster."

Not one of the fair maids moved. Old Agnes cackled through her two remaining teeth. "I'll come kiss you, Gorkel."

Gorkel gave a whistle of fear and took a quick step back, covering his mouth with his hands.

Bishop said, "Philippa, if you would please give Merryn some more clothing. We are leaving within the hour."

"Oh, aye," Dienwald said. "I'll give you some as well, Bishop. And some supplies. Eldwin! See to it."

Merryn raised her eyes to his face. "You're taking me home?"

Bishop shook his head.

"Where are we going?"

He just shook his head. "I will tell you just one thing, Merryn," he said, loud enough for all to hear, "you will not die a virgin."

"I suppose that is good to know," Merryn said as the great hall filled with laughter, cheers, shouted advice on how to relieve the maid of her maidenhead.

"I trust," Dienwald said to Bishop, "that you know what you're doing."

Bishop was staring after Merryn, who was carrying the two little boys while Philippa carried Eleanor. "I hope so, Dienwald, I surely do."

"Where do you plan to go?"

"Two days' travel—to the northeast."

"You sound like you know exactly where you're going."

"Oddly enough, I do."

"I have a friend, Roland de Tourney, who lives that way. If you have need of any assistance, stop at Chitterley. He'll help you."

"Thank you." Bishop plowed his fingers through his hair. "Nothing is as I expected it to be. And now I'm off and I know where I'm going, but none of it makes any sense." Then the words just leapt out of his mouth. "Dienwald, do you believe me capable of magic?"

Dienwald didn't laugh. He looked out over his great hall. He saw Margot scrubbing one of the trestle tables. Gorkel was picking small sprigs of rosemary out of the rushes on the floor, whistling through the space between his large front teeth, then popping the sprigs into his mouth.

Dienwald didn't like such bald talk that smacked of things unknown and powers that could easily plow down a mortal man. He sighed as he laid his hand on Bishop's shoulder. "Aye," he said. "I believe that, but I don't like it."

Bishop closed his eyes a moment, shadowy images racing through his brain through a haze of red. *Why red?* He said, "Why do you believe it?"

"When you saved Philippa," Dienwald said slowly, still looking out over the great hall, "she told me there was simply no way you could have known that the leader of those bandits was holding a dagger against her side. No way at all. Yet, somehow, you did know."

Bishop had forgotten that. It was true that sometimes he simply knew things, saw them in his mind's eye, but that wasn't unusual. That was just a warrior's training based on what he knew of other men and how they fought.

He said, "Mayhap it wasn't really like that, mayhap it was something as simple as realizing that I had to go very carefully, that if I didn't slit the man's throat quickly he'd have warning, and then he would—" Bishop shrugged.

"You knew something bad would happen, is that it, Bishop?"

"Aye."

Dienwald turned to face him. "This has happened to you before, hasn't it? You have this sense, this awareness, when something isn't right?"

"There's nothing mysterious about it. You know that in battle you simply know what to do. Don't assign such mystical knowledge to me. My wizard role for Penwyth—that's all it was, as you well know, a role, so I could intimidate and frighten off anyone who would try to kill me. I'm nothing more than a man, just a man, just like all other men."

"Aye, sometimes that's true," Dienwald said slowly, then gave him a long look. He grabbed Bishop's forearm, shook him. "Listen to me. This damnable curse. There are forces at work here, forces neither you nor I can begin to understand. I will be honest with you. I had firmly believed a poisoner was at work at Penwyth, probably Lord Vellan, the villainous old sod, and that's why I thought your wizard role was a good one. As for Lord Vellan, by God, you wouldn't believe the things he's done over the years. Well, not that I've seen any—I was too young. Ah, but the stories that still float about. Lord Vellan is and was ruthless, without mercy. It is said that the only one who could ever control him was his mother-in-law. I don't understand that, but there it is. Did the old man poison the four husbands? I don't know.

"Listen, Bishop, whatever you are planning to do with the girl, you must not trust her."

"No," Bishop said slowly, "you are right. It isn't poison. It is quite something else, and that something else is somehow pushing me to go. And do what? I don't know, but I must go and I must have her with me. No, I don't trust Merryn. I'm not that great a fool. There are not more than three females I would ever trust."

"I am afraid to ask you their names."

"Good, just know that Philippa is one of them. She is full-hearted, Dienwald. A joy."

"Aye, full-hearted." He grinned, a laugh rumbled deep in his chest. "Aye, that's my wench."

An hour later, fed, clean, and garbed in their hosts' clothes, Bishop and Merryn rode out on Fearless.

The sun was lowering in the afternoon sky, the air was cooler now, but just as sweet.

Merryn said, "I've decided that Fearless is an excellent horse. I will let him mate with Lockley."

"He will doubtless be pleased."

"Where are we going, Bishop?"

He said nothing, merely looked between Fearless's ears. He started whistling.

"It is already late. Why did you not wish to remain at St. Erth for the night?"

He whistled louder.

She slumped back against him. The silence stretched long between them. She heard birds in the yew bushes as they rode past, some taking flight, fanning black across the blue sky. She saw a single huge stone sitting in the middle of a field. "How long will it take us to get where we're going?"

"Two days, mayhap more, since we're sharing Fearless."

"What are you going to do with me?"

"Turn around and face me."

She did.

He said, eyeing her from not more than two inches away, "I'm glad you combed your hair. You looked like a witch."

"Is that a good thing or a bad thing, I wonder?" She turned again, facing the rutted road in front of them. She began whistling.

Bishop laughed. "No," he said, leaning close to her ear, "you won't die a virgin."

"Is that what you're going to do with me? Force me?"

"Oh, no, I would never force a woman." He began whistling again, loudly.

Bishop called a halt just as the sun was setting behind them. He hadn't stopped sooner simply because Dienwald had given them enough food to last a week. He didn't have to hunt their dinner.

It was a hidden spot, in the shadow of a small maple forest, safe enough. He set a fire going while she laid out the food.

"I hope it doesn't rain," she said, looking skyward.

"If it does, we know the tent won't collapse," he said. He sniffed the air, smiled even as the certain knowledge filled him. "No rain."

"Do you think it's still raining at Penwyth?"

He thought about it a moment, then turned his head and looked back—why, he didn't know. He felt just a very slight quiver in the air. And he knew, just knew. "The rain stopped." And then he knew even more.

"You said it wouldn't stop. You said it would be a flood. You said you'd tie me down and let me drown in it."

He grinned as he gnawed on a rib of beef. "I thought that had a nice frightening sound to it."

"You made that up?"

"I did. Did I tell you I think it's very nice that you don't want me dead like the other four?"

She broke off a piece of bread and shrugged. "I don't want you dead. I'm probably a fool. Will it rain again?"

"Aye, it will. The drought is over."

"How can you know that?"

He shrugged, frowned into the fire. "I just do."

"I wonder why," she said, sat cross-legged, handed him another broiled rib of beef. "Do you think it's because you came?"

He said without thinking, "No, I don't think so. There is activity in the far reaches of—" He stopped dead in his tracks. Those strange words had just flowed from his mouth without his brain's permission.

She was sitting forward, all her attention on him, not on the fresh peas from Philippa's garden that she was chewing. "Far reaches of what?"

He stared into the small fire he'd built, listening to his own voice and wondering at the words that came so easily out of his mouth. "There are ripples leavening the air. Mayhap they portend ancient conflicts, violent quarrels, in the oak groves. There is confusion, strife." He stopped talking, his eyes closed.

"Bishop, what's the matter? What oak groves? What sort of ancient conflicts? What quarrels? What are you seeing?"

"I'm not seeing anything," he said, and he looked both baffled and angry. "I don't like this, I really don't." He knew deep down that things were changing, churning up mysteries, dredging out long-buried secrets, like muck from a swamp, secrets that weren't even necessarily his. He rose, dusted off his trousers. "I am going to rub down Fearless," and he left her to stare after him.

She sat there and wondered what he had meant about her not dying a virgin. Her life was suddenly out of control, but oddly, she wasn't at all afraid. Did he really know she wouldn't be cursed with virginity until she died?

14

When she was settled against him, her warm breath on his neck, Bishop said, "It's a balmy night. A night that makes a man think of things other than sharpening his sword or splitting an enemy's head open."

She wondered what those things were, but she said, "I've never seen heads split open, since my grandfather and all his soldiers were already old when I was a little girl. I'll never forget he told me that since his strength was failing, he would learn other ways to survive. He is always weaving his plots, arguing with all the other graybeards. They have a fine time of it. When my father died with no male heir, they all knew that there would be trouble. As long as there were covetous men, they said, there would be endless trouble. But they weren't worried because there was the curse."

"Aye—that bespeaks a great deal of luck."

He waited for her to say more, but she didn't. What was she keeping from him? Her fingers touched his neck, trailed down to his shoulder, paused, then continued, over and over, her touch light, smooth.

Was he, he wondered, nothing more than a big dog for her to pet and use for warmth?

Didn't she realize he was a man? More than that, didn't she realize that he was a young man and a young man could easily be harder than the tent pole in the flick of an eyelid? Evidently not.

He reached up and took her hand and brought it down to his belly. He smoothed her palm open. His muscles tensed. He felt awareness streak through her and grinned into the darkness. If he'd been a dog before, he wasn't one now.

Her fingers moved, just a bit.

"Lower," he said.

"What do you mean, 'lower'?"

"Move your fingers lower."

"You mean like this?" He gritted his teeth and held his breath as those fingers of hers slowly stretched downward. She actually squeaked when she touched him. As for Bishop, he shuddered like a palsied man. He wanted her fingers on his naked flesh.

"Yes, like that." Oh, God, not really, not just like that. He wanted more. He nearly rose straight off the ground when her fingers traced over him, so light was her touch. He couldn't help himself. He grabbed her hand and laid it on him, held it there.

"Bishop? Are you all right?"

By all the saints' gnawed knuckles, no, he wasn't all right. He was nearly ready to spill his seed on his clothes, and that would be humiliating. He could barely breathe, and she now wanted him to speak as well? He felt her fingers curve around him, his own hand holding hers there. All he could think about was her fingers. "What did you say?"

"You sound like you're in pain. Should I move my hand?"

He groaned behind his teeth. "I'm all right," he said, and almost bit his own tongue straight through.

"You are very different from me. At least you are by the feel of you."

"I know," he said, and nearly exploded when her fingers tightened.

"Just what do you do with all this?"

He laughed, just couldn't help himself. It brought him a moment of sanity. He said, "I would come inside you with all this."

He felt her legs move against his, knew her knees were locked together. Oh, yes, she knew what he meant. Only if she'd been raised in a convent was there a chance she wouldn't understand what a man did to a woman.

"My grandmother occasionally bathed male guests when she was younger. She once told me that men were just men, some gnarlier than others, and when they were naked in the bathing tub, you just hummed, perhaps whistled, and stroked them down with the sponge. She said the trick was never to dwell on it."

He laughed. He'd never been an important enough guest in someone's keep to warrant the lady scrubbing him in his bath. "Would you scrub my back, Merryn?"

"I don't know," she said slowly, and stroked him again. "It would have to mean that we were married and you didn't die from the curse. That, or you would visit my keep once the king makes me the baroness of Penwyth and I would do just as my grandmother told me to do."

"You would whistle?"

"I don't know," she said again, and he could just see her frowning even though it was dark in the shadowed canopy of the maple trees. "Perhaps you are worth more than just a whistle. Mayhap a rhymed song like Crooky sings."

Her hand left him and he wanted to weep. She moved restlessly against him. He didn't know if she realized she was petting him, like a dog again, his belly up to his chest, his shoulders to his neck. He felt her shake her head against his shoulder, heard her sigh. "I don't want you to die."

Something moved deep inside him at her words, something that scared him witless. No, he wouldn't think about it. "If I take your virginity, I won't die."

That got her attention. She reared up and stared at him. "My virginity?"

"Aye, we could just get that part over with. I wouldn't be your husband yet. Am I safe from the curse?"

"Oh, yes," she said, then shook and shuddered at what had come out of her mouth.

He laughed. Why not? He was lying here, she was plastered against his side, and his sex was harder than the pebble that had worked its way into his boot. Why not? Suddenly, he felt something else tugging at him, tugging him away from her and her virginity. But wasn't a virginity a wondrous sort of thing that a man shouldn't ever be tugged away from? But now, somehow, he was. He didn't understand it. *Something was just there, nearly touching his face, or mayhap that something was inside him, and his brain went inward, toward it.*

He heard his own voice say, "No, I won't take your virginity. Go to sleep, Merryn, go to sleep." Maybe he'd spoken those words for himself, because in just moments he fell into a sleep deeper than a sword thrust into a man's belly.

Sometime Else

The prince followed Callas into the oak forest. On and on they walked, at least a mile into that deep, dark tangle of trees that swallowed the sound of their footfalls and hunkered over them, the leaves twitching and blowing, from no wind that he could feel. There were no shadows in this forest, no room for them. There were just scores upon scores of oak trees, like sentinels in place since the dawn of time, huddled so closely together that all vegetation falling to the earth soon became fetid and quickly rotted into nothingness.

Finally, after it seemed that eons had passed, they came to a large clearing. The prince saw that in the middle of the clearing was a rise. It wasn't a natural rise, but one that looked as if men had piled mud and stones and straw there, high and higher yet, wanting this prominence, wanting it to dominate.

Or magic had made the prominence. Aye, magic was more likely. Why waste energy piling up muck when you could just roll your eyes and snap your fingers? He looked up to see the moon, still a thin sickle, but light was pouring off it, making the clearing nearly as bright as day. The heaven was filled with stars, so bright that they made the leaves on the oak trees shimmer and glow. A very interesting effect the witch had wrought.

"Callas."

The old man turned. For an instant the prince saw a spasm of fear cross his face. It pleased him. Puking ancient priest, so knowledgeable about things that interested the prince not a whit. Fear became the old varmint. He wondered idly just how old the old relic really was.

"What is it you wish, prince?"

The fear was gone. Was there smugness in the old man's voice now? Did he believe him cowed at the unnatural brightness pouring onto this clearing? The prince said, waving his hand, "What is this place?"

Callas cocked his head to one side, his filthy hair tangling down over his shoulder and arm. "You are blind, aren't you, prince? I did wonder, you know, and now I am certain that your powers don't extend into our magical forest." He laughed. "You are in our stronghold now, prince. Even though you see no one, many are watching, wondering why you are here, ready to kill you if you so much as whisper a violent thought."

The prince laughed, felt a hank of hair fall into his face, and pushed it back into the club at the back of his neck. He said very softly, "Let any of your kind come to me,

Callas. Let us see how much harm they can do me. I will tell you true, I see nothing at all but this naked prominence your people built. Why did you build this place?"

Callas raised his *kesha*. The tip glowed madly, pulsing with power. He pointed it directly at the large mound of earth.

"What are you doing?"

Callas said nothing, merely continued to point the *kesha*. What was the old relic up to? The prince grabbed Callas's arm, careful not to touch his priest's stick. The old man was so startled, he would have fallen if Bishop hadn't held him up. Bishop shook him. Suddenly, Callas seemed boneless, not real, a figure stuffed with feathers. Had he killed him so easily?

"You black-blooded bastard, leave him alone."

It was Brecia. His heart nearly burst in his chest.

At last.

He was smiling so widely a ghost could have flown into his mouth when suddenly a wooden fortress appeared atop the prominence. Narrow wooden poles, at least eight feet high, were lashed together with ropes. The tops of the poles were whittled to sharp points. And behind that wall stood a wooden tower, at least forty feet high, mayhap higher.

A damned tower, a big one. Worthy of a witch, a very important witch. Where was Brecia?

The prince didn't like this. He was used to controlling everything around him. He'd seen the man-made or witch-made prominence, nothing more. And now there was a large fortress atop it. He felt a jolt of raw fear all the way to his feet, something very rare for him.

Why hadn't he seen the fortress? Was Callas right? Did he lose power here in her oak forest?

Where was that damned witch who'd called him a bastard? *His* damned witch.

He dropped Callas's arm, watched the old man stagger. Suddenly there were a dozen, nay, two dozen faces, maybe more, close, all staring at him from the trees lining the clearing. He heard her yell again, "Don't you dare kill him!"

The prince couldn't stand this. Where had her voice come from? He whirled about, but the fortress looked inviolate. It could be an illusion conjured from a witch's brain that wasn't really there, that didn't really exist. But it was here.

He drew a deep breath. This was nonsense. He was a wizard; nothing before had ever been closed to him. What was this?

The prince threw back his head and yelled, "Brecia! You damned witch, come here this instant or I will crush this foul old man." Then he smiled. "Nay, I won't do that. I will create a pond just for him, nice and deep and clean, and force him to bathe himself and his filthy clothes. Show yourself, or it is done."

Nothing.

The prince pulled his wizard's wand from his sleeve and pointed it at Callas.

"Don't you dare humiliate him, you wretched excuse for a wizard."

He smiled even as he watched Callas scamper away, more agile than an ancient old priest should be. The gates to the fortress were slowly swinging outward. The prince settled his wizard's wand back into his sleeve, felt it warm against his flesh, part of him really, and he walked forward through the wide gates.

They seemed to be wider now that he was

walking through them than they'd appeared but moments before.

He heard voices, knew the ghosts that hid behind the trees were wondering what to do. He called over his shoulder, "Callas, reassure your people. Tell them that my business is with the witch. I won't kill them if they leave me alone."

He was inside the fortress. He heard the huge wooden gates close behind him. A dozen small campfires were dotted around inside the compound, a huge area, surely much larger than the fortress he'd seen when he'd stood outside that gate. She was doing this, he knew, and somewhere deep inside him he appreciated her efforts to provide him such a charming and confounding illusion. It showed skill, and he admired that. Aye, she would suit him quite nicely.

He looked more closely at the fires and saw at least fifty ghosts, all of them hovering just a few inches off the ground, so pale they were nearly transparent, but he could see their feet dangling, and their feet had more substance. Their feet were bare. They made absolutely no sound at all, just hovered, the air humming around them. They were there, yet he couldn't feel their presence, and that was odd, but he could see their damned bare feet, long, narrow feet with the toes too long.

Was Brecia somehow shielding the very feel of them from him? No, he was too powerful for her to do that. He knew they were ghosts, but he simply couldn't sense them. But why? Mayhap they weren't really ghosts, but shadows from another realm. Unreal beings Brecia had called up to frighten him? Simply props like those the mummers used in their plays? He shook his head. What they were didn't matter. She could have conjured up mad dogs flapping around him, snarling, and he wouldn't have been bothered. But all in all, the ghosts with their long, naked toes were a nice touch.

He had never before been to Brecia's sacred place. He let himself settle into it, and soon he could feel the power pulse around him, though the feel of it wasn't familiar to him. It was like a lover's lips, light, nipping, flowing over his flesh, coming close to him, but never touching, a lover he'd never yet had. He would swear that that power dipped quite near him, almost alighted on his shoulder, on the back of his hand, then flowed softly away. A power he didn't recognize, that was something new to him. What would happen if it did touch him? If it went into his mouth, his eyes, his nostrils, and he breathed it in? He felt his wizard's wand grow warmer against his forearm.

He realized then that the lazy orange threads of fire from all those small campfires seemed to connect, entwining, dancing through each other, then soaring higher and higher. They warmed the entire space inside the fortress.

He smiled. He pulled out his wizard's wand and flicked it at one of the small fires. It blasted upward, threads of orange scattering, sending sparks leaping up at least fifty feet. The ghosts soared, seeming to dissolve into each other, all heads craning upward to watch the sparks burst high over their heads. He would swear that their feet became even clearer. Well, he'd announced himself, given Brecia warning. He smiled. He wanted very much to see the witch.

He slipped the wand back into his sleeve and walked forward to the tower.

Bedamned, the fortress was bigger now than it had been just a minute before. He would say that it was now more than forty feet high.

He threw back his head and yelled, "Brecia! Where are you?"

"I am in here, prince," she said, and he wondered for a moment how her voice could be so clear when she was inside the tower. Clever witch. He saw random small windows, all cut in geometric shapes—triangles, circles, squares—and each shape seemed to glow in the night darkness.

Clever magic from the clever witch, he thought, but nothing more than that. Nothing compared to what he could do. He wouldn't let himself forget that.

The prince pushed open the door to the tower and walked in. The floor was bound wooden planks, smooth, stretching endlessly. He smelled lavender, and other fragrances he didn't recognize, saw that their leaves were scattered over the wooden floor. A huge fire burning in the middle of the large chamber went all the way to the roof, escaping through a wide hole in the top. The air was faintly blue with the smoke.

Then he saw her.

Brecia.

Three years since he'd first seen her, at the ancient sacred gathering place where representatives from all known tribes had traveled to the flat plains in Britain to speak within the great sarsen circle of stones and look at the rising sun balance for a few precious moments atop the great sloping stone. All knew it was the moment of the summer solstice.

She'd been so beautiful then that just to look at her made his tongue dry in his mouth. She was even more beautiful now, standing on that immense dais, looking down at him, her arms crossed over her breasts. Her effect on him was even more dramatic now after three long years. He swallowed. The damnable witch, she'd escaped him, nearly cursed him into oblivion, but at last he'd won.

He'd managed to find her—only the thing was, he still had no idea how he'd come so close to her sacred forest or why he'd been lying there alone on the ground with that old man Callas standing over him. He remembered Callas had been with her at the great stone circle, standing beneath one of the huge lintels, staring at him, and he'd seen fear and hatred in the old man's rheumy eyes.

Like Callas and all those damnable ghosts outside, she was wearing a white wool robe.

Hers, however, was so white, it shone like pure light. He could have read ancient parchments in the light cast from her gown. No dirty rope around her waist, rather a thin golden chain that pulled the gown snug, made a graceful knot, then hung down nearly to her knees.

No one else seemed to be in the chamber.

Were there indoor ghosts? He walked closer.

She had the same incredible hair, longer now, perhaps. So very red, a pure red, pure as a flame fed by magic. It hung down her back, nearly touching her hips, and because his vision was excellent even without magic, he could see her mysterious green eyes, and knew they hid her secrets and skills more dangerous than a curse ripe with vengeance. Her skin was pale, smooth. She smiled at him, showing very white teeth. That smile—it was a smile of triumph, a smile that told him she'd bested him and was savoring the knowledge at this very moment. He wanted to take out his wizard's wand and force her to her knees in front of him. Perhaps before that, he would make her fall to her knees and crawl to him, kiss his feet. Aye, he liked that image. Then she could pull off that white wool gown and show herself to him, and then he would—

"So, prince, why in the name of all the evil demons that surely created you did you come here? How did you find me?"

15

His heart pounded hard and fast. He hadn't felt like this in the three years since he'd first seen her, since she'd gotten away from him, the damnable witch, furious because she'd heard of his upcoming marriage to Lillian. He'd tried to hold her, tried to explain, but she'd managed to escape. He'd yowled with fury, tried desperately to forget her, but couldn't. He said easily, drinking her in, "Callas brought me."

"He would never allow you anywhere near to me, particularly here in my own grove."

His wizard's wand lay calm and smooth against his forearm. He could feel it faintly pulsing, making his flesh warmer now than it had been just a moment before. He knew he had to go carefully, knew in his gut that he couldn't let her suffocate his magic, not again. He couldn't allow her once again to reduce him to a mortal man's lust, a mortal man with no brain at all, no sense of himself and who and what he was, reducing him to just his pounding, hard sex, wanting beyond reason to be inside her.

The prince said, "Callas did bring me. Sufficient proof, even for a witch, since I am standing in front of you."

"You must have threatened to kill him to make him bring you here."

"No. I made him itch."

She stared at him. He knew she wanted to laugh, but she managed to hold it in. Slowly, she stepped off the dais and began her lazy walk toward him. The white wool swung at her ankles, as if there was a slight breeze teasing the fabric, showing golden sandals. But the air was stone still. Where were all her priests, all her servants? Where were those bloodless lurking ghosts with their naked feet?

She stopped a good six feet away from him. She seemed taller to him now than she did three years before, taller and more stiffly proud, arrogant in her own power. He would change that soon enough. Or maybe she was afraid of him now that he'd found her, had actually come into her sacred grove, proved that her power wasn't inviolate.

Ah, just to look at her. He watched as she slowly raised her left arm, the white sleeve, full and billowing. Smooth as magic, which it was, in her hand was suddenly her witch's wand. It was more like his wand than like the *keshas* carried by Callas and all the other Karelian priests throughout the world. It was elegant, finely carved, just like his, no more than ten inches long, gleaming with gems so old they seemed to carry the finger marks of the gods who had flung them to earth at the beginning of time.

Where were her other priests? Why was she seeing him alone?

"You are here, prince. What do you want?"

He looked at her face to see some sign of what she was thinking. He said nothing, just kept studying her. As always, a shield was firmly in place in front of her mind. He couldn't penetrate it, and that infuriated him.

She came closer. She pointed her witch's wand directly at him.

He said, "Don't point your ridiculous stick at me, woman."

"A stick? You arrogant, black-brained bastard."

"I am not a bastard. I was born as the result of a hallowed joining. As for you, what can you claim as your antecedents?"

"I had no beginning and will have no end."

He laughed. "That is nonsense and you well know it. You come from good wizard stock, only it is different from mine. Your sacred grove, all these oak trees that rustle in the night breeze, this fortress that you've spun from fancies in your mind, none of it means anything to me. No more than those ridiculous ghosts hovering outside by those puling campfires, their feet dangling in the air above the ground."

"Ghosts? Why do you think they're ghosts?"

"Don't mock me, woman. They have no substance, no presence."

"Ah, so you mean you cannot sense them."

He hated it, but he had to nod.

"Aye, they are ghosts. It's hard for anyone

from outside the oak forest to sense them. Callas will become a ghost sometime in the future. Ghosts all live and breathe and worship and ply their crafts. Eventually they grow so old that they begin to fade—the last part to fade is their feet. They finally fade into the very roots of the oak trees, becoming one with the oak. It is an ancient, revered ceremony."

"I have heard that the ghosts exist in all times."

"Yes. They are my people, past, present, future. They are my closest followers."

"All your followers are ancient? Nearly faded away, all of them?"

"No. Many of my people dwell in the forest. The old ones—the ghosts—feel uncomfortable in the forest. They feel threatened, they are always cold. They like to remain close to me, and thus all the fires with the magic flames. They are so very old in their power, their strength beyond what either of us can imagine. As for my people who live in the forest, they will remain hidden until I tell them it is safe."

"It sounds like all your followers are as insubstantial as this fortress you've conjured up."

"Don't mock what you don't understand, prince. That is stupidity that even a wizard can't afford."

"They worship you, Brecia?"

"Of course they worship me. I give them food and water and shelter. I provide them harmony and order and balance so they can become all they wish to be, with no impediments."

"Is this fortress real or is it just a special treat for my eyes only?"

"It is real enough to those who see it."

Since he had said something like that many times, he let her get away with it. "When will Callas begin to fade?"

"In perhaps a hundred years or so. I'm not really sure. So many of them overlap in age, it is difficult to know individual ages."

"And who will the old priests and all the hiding ghosts worship when you are dead?"

"You're right, of course, I will have an end, I will die. They will worship my heir."

"Who is your heir?"

"I am very young, prince. I have no need as yet for an heir."

"Good solid witch blood for your heir?"

She inclined her head gracefully, sending thick red hair over her shoulder. By all the ancient powers that poured through his blood, he wanted to touch that hair of hers, wrap it around his hand, over and over, and keep wrapping until she was not more than an inch from him, and then he would wrap again until she was against him, then he would put her under him. He blinked away the image.

"Yes, as you say, good solid witch blood."

"You need a powerful wizard to bring forth a decent heir, a wizard to strengthen your sputtering blood."

"I have yet to meet a wizard who could meld his powers with mine in a way that would blend properly. Wizards are too unbending, too contemptuous of anything that isn't of their making, of their beliefs.

"Perhaps I will travel to Spain. I understand the Karelia there have fashioned incredible sacred places, all hidden from mortal eyes. Aye, there I might find a Spanish wizard who would complement my own powers, who wouldn't seek to control me, make me a slave."

"I have been told that the Spanish Karelia capture men and stuff them into wooden cages. At night they burn them for warmth."

"I had not heard that. It is something I

would not accept." She shuddered as she said, "The smell. It would be offensive."

"It makes me think they are weak and cruel. Who needs to burn a mortal in a cage when all you have to do is cast what warmth you need with your wand?" He slipped it out fast, flicked it upward, and the faint blue smoke became a narrow funnel. He watched her look at the smoke, now swirling upward in a tight circle to the hole in the ceiling.

"Now your eyes won't burn, will they?"

"They didn't in any case. A clever trick, prince, but then you—" She raised her own wand from where she'd held it against her skirt, and smiled at him. He waited, doing nothing, watched her lips move. Suddenly he was in a wooden cage, suspended by a long iron chain from the roof of the fortress. The cage swung back and forth.

The prince said nothing at all. He was cramped, his left leg felt ready to break. He gave a soft whistle, lightly flicked his fingertips over the wooden bars. The cage disappeared, and he was once again standing at his ease in front of her.

He smiled at her, pointed his wand at her, nothing more than that. Suddenly she wasn't standing in front of him, she was lying on her back on a bluestone altar, her white woolen skirts fanned around her, hanging over the sides of the altar.

"Bluestone," she said, slowly sitting up. "You stole the bluestone from the sacred circle of stones in Britain."

"Aye, it's a mighty stone, beautiful and thick. A fitting resting place for a witch."

Quick as a swallow, Brecia raised her wand. In that same instant, the prince tilted his head back, his throat working over strange words. Suddenly her wand was in his left hand. He smiled, waved his own wand toward her, and there were ropes tying her down, quite thin beautiful leather straps that even a wizard couldn't break. She was at his mercy now, and still he smiled.

He held the two wands up in front of her, hers so beautiful and graceful, his hard and deep, solid power with little ornamentation. "See these, Brecia? If I cross the two wands, then it is very possible that the world would end. What think you?" He slowly brought the witch's wand and the wizard's wand close, until only a breath separated them.

She tried to jerk free of the ropes, but

couldn't. She raised her head, stared fixedly at the two wands so close to each other. "Don't, you fool. You have no idea what would happen."

Since he had no idea what would happen either, he pulled the wands apart and held one loosely in each hand. "Have you any power without your wand?"

"Of course."

"Then free yourself, Brecia."

She was speaking, some sort of chant, he imagined, and closed his eyes to see the words in his mind, and to counteract them.

She was sending him to hell. No, wait, not exactly to hell. She was with him, there, deep in an oak forest, and he was tied to an ancient oak that shuddered around him, branches trembling as if in a high wind—but there were no high winds deep in an oak forest.

He walked to the altar, stared down into those green eyes, and felt the force of her and himself, tied to that damned oak tree. He stood over her, and lightly, very lightly, he touched his finger to the tip of her nose. It broke her concentration. She looked up at him, and he knew she would slay him if she had the chance. She would send him to the

Spanish Karelia to roast in a cage during one of those cold nights. He touched the tip of her nose yet again, smiled.

"Listen to me, Brecia. Shall I make you itch like I did Callas?"

"Black bastard."

"I have told you I am not a bastard. Is my magic black? You say that only because you like to imagine yourself some sort of angel, decked out in pure white."

"You are a fool. Release me."

"No, not yet. A fool, am I? I learned my lesson with you three years ago, after you managed to escape. You refused to understand that the marriage was one I had to make. There was no choice.

"When I awoke from that fathomless sleep that was steeped in dark dreams with phantoms chaining me to boulders at the edge of the sea, I also awoke with the knowledge of how to control you. I have your wand now, too. You can't bring me down, Brecia. I have all the power."

Her lips weren't moving, but he knew, simply knew, that she was fashioning another curse, one designed specifically for him.

He lifted his wizard's wand high, lightly

skimmed it over her, from her bare toes to the top of her head.

The white robe didn't disappear. She wasn't naked. Now what was this? He didn't use his wand again, merely thought her naked, dwelt on it with precise concentration. Her damned robe stayed just where it was. So she wasn't cursing him. Instead, she was fashioning chants to keep her clothes on.

He leaned over her. "You will yield to me, Brecia. You can struggle all you like against those ropes, but they can hold you—until forever and beyond."

She was suddenly silent, staring up at him, and then she cursed him in vivid words that called upon every power from Satan himself to the first Druids who'd lived in caves and dyed their hair green, to the crude, barbaric Karelia from the south, who filed their teeth to points to better rip the meat from the bones of their sacrifices.

"Don't think your curses do any more than make me laugh," he said, and still he was laughing even as he leaned down and kissed her. But it wasn't her mouth he felt, it was something raw and slick. He lurched back and saw not Brecia lying there naked, but a dozen ropes all looped and tangled together, like twisted snakes, and there was wet blood on them, dripping onto the dirt floor.

Brecia was gone.

In the next instant, the bluestone altar was gone. There was naught but a white gown lying on the ground.

The prince was so surprised that he was held quiet. He *had* taken her gown, but she'd managed to give him an illusion that she was still clothed. How had she done that? He threw back his head and bellowed the only promise he knew she wouldn't ignore. "If you don't come back, I will leave and take your wand with me."

She was standing in front of him again, the white robe that had been lying on the ground suddenly on her, neatly belted by the gold chain at her waist. But her feet were bare, her golden sandals probably left in oblivion.

She was his now, and he knew it. He hoped she knew it as well. "Now," he said, "if you are so powerful even without your wand, then you will cast a grand spell that will provide your multitude of ghosts, all the old priests, and all your followers with enough food, water, and shelter to last them a thousand years."

"Why would I do that, prince?"

"Because I'm taking you with me. To-gether we will produce a son to master any wizard now living or ever to come on this blessed earth."

"I will have nothing to do with you. You lied to me. You wed another. I could kill you if I really tried."

"The marriage—it is over. I am free and now here for you. Now, you say you want nothing to do with me simply because I am more powerful than you. You say that be-cause you fear me, since you know I can overcome you. Aye, Brecia, you will come with me. You will mate with me."

She was silent, but he knew she was sort-ing through his words, even seeing herself breeding a fine heir, one for each of them. A wizard and a witch.

He said, his voice more gentle, drawing her in, that voice, "I remember when I first saw you in the sarsen circle, just behind the altar stone. You held both your hands flat against it. You were whispering something to it. A wish? A curse? Then you turned and you saw me."

"Aye, I turned and there you were. You looked dark and powerful and infinitely wicked. I believed I could come to trust you, but I was wrong. All you want is to best me, to conquer me, to possess me."

He looked at her thoughtfully. "All that? I remember thinking then that you recognized me as your mate, just as I recognized you as mine. Now there is nothing to prevent our joining."

She laughed at that. "Oh, no, I wasn't recognizing you as anything, prince. Actually, I was looking at you and thinking about my great-grandmother, whose hair was so red that some claimed flames leapt out of it."

He waved away her words. "That is enough. It is time for us to mate. You know you can trust me."

She shrugged, studied his face, looked into his eyes. Was she trying to look into his mind as well? She couldn't—he was closed to her. Then she snapped her fingers right in front of his nose, huffed a little breath.

And she was gone. Simply gone.

She hadn't managed to rescue her wand. It still lay flat on his palm, stone cold, the gems flat and opaque, as if stripped of all light, all power, all meaning.

The prince stood there, miserable to his feet. Why was nothing ever easy?

16

Present

"Bishop, wake up." She shook his shoulder. "What are you dreaming about? You're laughing, nearly choking on your laughter. Come, wake up and tell me what you're see- ing in your dream. Are you dreaming of me and how clever I am? Is my wit making you laugh?"

He was standing inside a huge tower, some sort of stone altar in front of him. He saw no one, heard no one. He wanted to howl, he wanted to kill her—Brecia—it was Brecia, with her glorious red hair. He really wanted to take her throat between his hands, and at the same time he wanted her beneath him, her legs spread wide. Then, quite suddenly, he was laughing and shaking his head at her cleverness.

He awoke to Merryn's hands shaking him, lightly slapping his face, and he was still laughing, but it wasn't a funny sort of laughter, he knew that. He was laughing because there was simply nothing else to do.

He shook his head, not laughing now. "I begin to believe that nothing in this beleaguered life is ever easy for mortals." He paused a moment, frowned. "Nay, maybe even for those who are not mortal, those not from our time."

"What," she said slowly, "isn't easy for mortals? What do you mean about those who are not mortals? Come, Bishop, why were you laughing your head off? What is this about those not from our time?"

"I don't know," he said slowly. What had happened? What was going on here? He shook his head, sat up too quickly, and hit his head against the tent pole. No laughter in him now. No, he felt niggling fear from the sharp stirring in his blood, from the still-faint images in his brain, but it was all retreating now, slowly, very slowly, until the echoes of his laughter, the echoes of that stone altar faded away. Brecia faded away.

Bishop wanted to leave Cornwall right now. He wanted to go to the far islands to the north where the Vikings had settled. He wanted to hunker down in a stone hut with a warm fire. He wanted no mysteries, nothing he couldn't grasp with his hands, with his mind. He wanted to look at the icy sea water crashing against those islands, feel the water cascade over his bare feet—for an instant, he saw bare feet, scores of them, faint, somehow hovering above the ground. No. He shook the thought away. Damnation, he wanted to actually feel the cold water on his feet. Aye, he wanted what was real, what was solid.

"You look very strange. What did you dream?"

"I don't know, but it really wasn't funny at all," he said.

"Well, that's good, isn't it?"

Wit at this hour. He shook his head at her and crawled out of the tent. The early-morning air was sharp on his face. He raised his face skyward, looking at the sun, still low in the heavens because it was just past dawn. As he stood there he wondered why he was riding to Tintagel. It came into his mind and he knew, simply knew, that he was going there. But what was there? He shook his head and breathed in deeply. Whatever it was, he knew without a single doubt that it would become clear to him.

He turned to see Merryn on her knees making a fire. He stood there, making no sound, just watching her, the way her hands moved on the twigs, twisting them exactly the way she wanted them, leaning down to blow the small spark into life. She sat back, her palms on her thighs, and nodded, satisfied, as the nest of fire spread to the larger sticks and sent out warmth. Her gown was wrinkled, her hair falling out of its braids, long red tendrils touching her cheek, curling at her neck. Suddenly, she looked up at him and smiled, a sweet smile that was only for him, a smile that reached her eyes. He saw awareness of him as a man, awareness of what they'd done the previous night, how she'd touched him and held him. And she'd liked it, a lot, he'd known that. And he realized that she liked reflecting the memory of it now. He couldn't think of a thing to say other than *Would you like me to pull up your gown and put my mouth on you?*

She said, that smile fading now, "Bishop, I'm worried about you. Can you remember anything about your dream?"

He joined her at the fire, coming down on his haunches, taking the hunk of cheese she handed him. He chewed, tore off some of the bread Philippa had wrapped in thick white woolen cloth, and in that instant he saw a gown that was as white as that woolen cloth—Brecia's gown. Then it was gone.

"When I first awoke," he said, looking into the flame, "I saw myself, only I wasn't really me, and I was laughing because I simply couldn't believe what had happened."

"What do you mean?"

"Think of yourself standing in the middle of a great hall, filled with people. Suddenly your clothes disappear. Everyone stops talking and stares at you." He shrugged. "Would you laugh, because there was simply nothing else to do?"

She looked at him blankly.

He grinned. "Ah, mayhap a man would do that, not a woman. Women have many more interesting parts to cover than men."

"I think your parts are far more interesting than mine. I'm just me, but you're—"

"What?"

She sighed and chewed on a piece of cheese. "Your parts are undoubtedly more interesting than poor dear Crispin's when I saw him naked. But I did feel you. That part felt very interesting."

For a long moment he couldn't speak. He hurt. "You got me off track," he said at last, staring into the fire, not at her, because if he did he just might take her down and rid her of her virginity.

She said, "You mean about being naked in a hall full of people and laughing?"

"What would you do, Merryn? Would you yell a nice full-bodied curse, even though it wouldn't help?"

She was laughing and nodding. "No. Nor would I run away because that would make me look even more foolish."

"That's right. That's what the end of that dream was like. There was simply nothing else to do but laugh." He chewed on the bread. She handed him a flagon of Dienwald's ale. It was tart and fresh and it warmed his innards, settled him back firmly inside himself, which was a grand relief.

She realized he wasn't going to say any more about the dream. It was probably faded now, nearly gone. She was looking at his hands, strong and tanned, and she could see his hands stroking her arms, maybe even the length of her legs, maybe even scratching her scalp. Who knew what men did with their hands? She thought of his mouth going where his hands went. *Oh my, oh my.* She swallowed and cleared her throat. "Where are we going, Bishop?"

He swept his hand to the north, saying nothing.

"Do you know what is there?"

"No, but I know I have to go there and I have to take you there with me. I also know that we must go now, without delay." He paused a moment. "It has something to do with the curse."

She shook her head, looking at the fire spark.

"What is it, Merryn?"

She was silent.

"There are a lot of things I don't understand, you know that. Do you think you could trust me, Merryn?" He waited, watching her intently.

Merryn stirred a stick in the embers, sending more sparks into the air. Finally, just at the point when he was ready to curse the air blue, she said, "Yes, I trust you."

His breath nearly whooshed out. Relief poured through him, relief and something else. Gratitude, perhaps, that she was willing to go into the unknown with him.

"But you don't trust me, do you?"

He was looking at her mouth as she said the words. He wanted her mouth on him. *Stop it, just stop it.* He looked at her eyes and hated the pain he saw there. He said simply, "I would trust you if you would just tell me what you're keeping from me."

She more than trusted him. In two short days, she'd come to admire him—his humor, his rage, his smile. She'd come to look at him as she'd never before looked at any male, and she wanted to touch him just about all the time. Hmmm. This was more than trust, and so she said without hesitation, "I think my grandmother poisoned Sir Arlan de Frome, my first husband. I didn't tell anyone, particularly you, because I don't want you to punish her, to hang her for murdering that man, because that is what the king would expect you to do."

Not the curse? No, he refused to believe

it. It went against everything he felt. "Tell me why you think this."

"I heard her laughing with my grandfather the next morning, saying she didn't want to give Sir Arlan's trencher to the pigs, they just might keel over dead."

"That's all you heard?"

"Aye. It was enough."

"And the other husbands?"

"I don't know. All their symptoms were different. She wasn't ever near them. Some died sooner than others. My grandmother learned all about plants, their uses and how to mix them, from her mother, Meridian. She knew all about different plants that could kill."

"But you have no proof that she poisoned Sir Arlan?"

Merryn shook her head. He reached out his hand and lightly touched his fingertips to her nose, smoothed her brows, touched her mouth. "Thank you, Merryn. Aye, I trust you."

"Were you dreaming about a woman, Bishop?"

"Yes," he said without thinking. He frowned. "Perhaps, but not entirely. It is strange, Merryn."

"Something very odd is happening to you, isn't it?"

There, she'd said it aloud.

He said, "Aye, but I'm not yet certain what it all means."

"You will tell me when you are." She wanted to leap to her feet and do a little dance, maybe even sing a little rhyme. *He trusted her.* And he needed her to be with him. But why did he need her with him? "The curse," she said, "it always came back to that. All this strangeness, this quest of yours. Maybe my grandmother didn't poison Sir Arlan."

"Stop worrying about it. We'll find out the truth."

She nodded. She had no idea now what to believe. One thing she was very certain of—she wasn't at all afraid, not of him at any rate. She knew Bishop would protect her if attacked, knew to the soles of her leather shoes, finely stitched by the weaver Crake, who was so old his hands shook as he sewed.

"Merryn, did your grandmother and grand-father write the Penwyth curse?"

"Not that I know of." She paused a moment. "There were whispers, of course. And

I wondered because the second part of the curse spoke so specifically to me—red hair, green eyes. But I truly don't know."

He nodded, gave her his hand and pulled her to her feet. He wanted to kiss her, wanted to bring her hard against him, but he knew he wouldn't. It wasn't the time. He was being pushed and prodded to ride ever northeast. And so they rode throughout the morning, staying close to the beach. The sea was beautiful, the water glistening beneath a bright sun as far out as she could see, and the sea air settled on her skin. As the afternoon lengthened, fog billowed from the water over the land and over them as well. Bishop pulled Fearless back from the cliffs because of the thick fog.

The sun was lowering behind them when Bishop said, "If there is a curse and we don't get rid of it, then you will die alone and sad, just as Crooky said. No man could risk wedding you."

"I know. But there is a solution, Bishop. You must ask the king to make me Grandfather's heir. I can protect the western end of England from all possible invaders. Truly, my father and grandfather taught me strategy, taught me to use a bow and arrow, to throw a knife. It's true that I do not wield a sword well—they are too heavy for me. But I have guile, Bishop. I have incredible guile. If the French wish to invade, why, I'll drive them into the sea."

"I'm strong, Merryn, and I can wield a sword, and yet I have eleven soldiers always with me."

"Except for now."

"Yes, that's true, and I am taking a risk, not just with my own life but also with yours. So who will be your soldiers, Merryn? Who will fight for you to protect Penwyth? Surely not all those old men?"

She was silent.

"A man-at-arms must be able to draw back a bow and aim it as he holds it steady; he must be able to fight on horseback; he must be able to see the enemy creeping up on him and fight him with his bare hands if necessary. He must wield an axe, and as you know, they are heavy, those axes. All those old men must die one day, Merryn, and then what will you have?"

"They have never died for as long as I've been alive."

"You are only eighteen."

"None died during my father's lifetime, either."

Silence fell between them and time passed.

He said, "Let us say that you do stave off any enemies of Penwyth and England. Who will come after you, Merryn, when you die? What will happen to Penwyth then?"

She remained silent. He heard her whisper, *"Must I laugh because there's nothing else to do?"*

17

Something was pushing him ever forward, and the shortest way to the northeast was along the coast. Just as something was pushing him away from taking her virginity.

They skirted villages, several small keeps of no particular significance. Bishop was wondering where were all the thieves and bandits and assorted other people who would whistle even as they killed him, when Merryn saw dust rising in the distance and pointed. "A band of horses," he said. He couldn't afford to fight now, couldn't afford to be killed, because Merryn would be helpless. He slowed Fearless and rode him a bit inland into a small copse of larches. Bishop dismounted and stood by Fearless's head, holding his nostrils to keep him from whinnying. They waited silently until the dust cloud disappeared to the south.

Then they rode, stopping but once so Fearless could rest. They were drawing close, Bishop felt it in his bones.

"Will you know once we get there?"

He smiled over her head. "I'll know."

"How will you know?"

"I'll know." *That was exactly what the prince would have said.* Bishop nearly fell off his horse. What was going on here? He was suddenly afraid that he would know exactly where he was when he got to where he was going.

He tightened his hold around Merryn.

The skies darkened toward evening of that second day. Bishop said, "There is a cave close to the sea, just ahead."

"How do you know of this cave?"

"I just do," he said. "And I have no idea how I know. I also know that it will rain soon. We will be protected in the cave."

"Just a while ago you really didn't know where we were going, did you?"

He shook his head. "Did your grandmother have red hair?"

"You've seen my grandmother. Her hair,
even when I was a child, was stark white,
never a bit of red, but truly, I really don't
know."

"And your mother's mother? Was her hair
red?"

"My mother's mother. I never knew her,
but I remember hearing my grandfather talking about Constance, my grandmother, and
how she'd just gone away, probably spirited
away by the devil himself. Then he looked
at me sideways, as if he were wondering if
I'd be spirited away too. I didn't understand."

"And your mother? Did she have red
hair?"

"My mother had hair blacker than a sinner's heart. My father loved to tell her that,
and then he'd push her against the wall and
kiss her." She was silent a moment, then
twisted about to look at him. "I just remembered. My mother told me when I was very
little that I had the look of my grandmother,
that she had hair that was like flame it was
so red."

He couldn't believe this, didn't want to believe this. No, it was simply the same choice

of words, nothing more. He said, all indifferent, "Did it seem that fire came from her hair?"

"That's a strange thought, but you know, I remember my mother said my grandmother liked to leave her hair loose, particularly when the wind was strong because it looked like fire whipping about her head. I don't remember anything else, Bishop. My mother died when I was only six years old. There is so much I never heard her say because she died."

"I'm sorry."

"My hair isn't all that red."

"It's quite red enough." *As red as Brecia's hair, rich, rich red.*

He looked into Merryn's smiling face, at the incredible hair framing that face, and thought, *She's herself, not some phantom, just herself, and that is very fine indeed.*

Bishop directed Fearless down to the beach just below Tintagel Head, an immense promontory that belonged to the Duchy of Cornwall. The going was treacherous. The rocks were sharp black spikes and spires, poking up like thick fingers or lying like fists on the dirty sand. The water was dark with seaweed and driftwood. Seabirds were loud above them. He pulled Fearless to a halt in the dying light. "See, yon is a Celtic monastery."

Merryn looked at the ruin standing jagged and fierce atop the promontory. "It is very old," she said. "It looks haunted and sad."

"The monastery is not so very old," he said, then wondered how that could be so.

"You've been here before, haven't you, Bishop?"

"Aye, I've been here," he said, but she didn't believe him. He dismounted and lifted Merryn down from Fearless's back.

"Is this a magic place?"

He laughed. "Certainly not. It's just a place that is somehow important, for a reason I have yet to learn."

Fearless didn't balk when Bishop led him into the cave through a tall, narrow opening overhung with the tangled branches of a bowed old oak tree. "We won't go very far in," he said over his shoulder.

Fearless whinnied. Bishop stroked his neck. "Here," he said, "we will stay here." Bishop handed Merryn some of the supplies.

To her surprise, once inside the cave, she saw that there was wood stacked against the wall. To her even greater surprise, Bishop seemed to accept it with no question at all.

When night fell but moments later, the fire was their only light. The walls of the cavern weren't damp. They were actually warm, as Merryn discovered when she happened to lean one of the tent poles against a wall. Warm to the touch. How very odd.

"Do you know, Bishop, everything about this cave is odd. Just feel the warm walls. It is almost as if the cave is somehow welcoming us. But that's impossible, isn't it?"

She was right.

He just shook his head, and stretched out his arms. He felt the smooth sand beneath his palms, no hidden pebbles or sticks, and the air was clear and sweet. Fearless, once inside, immediately settled down to eat from the bag of oats from St. Erth's stables. Every once in a while, he looked around him into the part of the cave that extended beyond their campfire, into the deep shadows, alert, as if someone was calling to him, and he shook his great head and blew.

Once Merryn had settled beside Bishop, both sitting atop the flattened tent, she said, "Can you tell me why we're here yet?"

"Did I tell you that your hair is redder now than it was this morning?"

She touched her fingers to her hair. "No, you didn't. That isn't possible, Bishop."

He said nothing, merely lay back against the cave wall, folded his arms behind his head, and stared at the cave ceiling. "It's true." Even in the dim light he saw flames dancing around her head. *I'm going mad, there's nothing else for me to do.*

The fire was burning down, but the warmth didn't diminish at all. The air was still, calm, warm. Bishop looked at the opposite cave wall, at the faint shadows cast there by the fire. As he watched, one of the shadows suddenly seemed to spread, darken, and grow larger. Merryn didn't notice. She was drawing Penwyth Castle in the fine sand with a stick. She didn't seem to notice anything at all. But Fearless did. He was nodding at that shadow.

Bishop couldn't look away from it. The shadow was shifting, darkening here, lightening there, until it became a man. *A man,* he thought. It was a man, nothing else. Then it shifted again, twisting back on itself, and was only a shadow again, falling into strange forms like clouds in a summer sky.

But it was more than a simple shadow. He said nothing to Merryn. He didn't want her to be frightened.

He realized in that moment that he recognized the man buried in the shadow. Bishop felt his heart begin to pound, loud, deep beats, but he wasn't afraid. He waited quietly for the shadow to come to him. It moved. When it finally covered him, and he felt the sweet, dry air inside the cave fill his body, his fingertips began to tingle.

He heard Merryn's voice as if from a great distance. She was calling to him, but he couldn't quite grasp what it was or who she was. Slowly, he rose and stood in the middle of the cave, the shadow twisting around him, wrapping him tightly, and he said, "My wand. Where is my wand?"

And it was suddenly there, in his hand, and he was staring down at it. It wasn't more than a foot long, beautifully worked, but still stark, elegant, and it fit into his hand as if it were part of him. It pulsed with light and power; he could feel that power fill him, become one with him, and he smiled into the fire, which was burning fiercely once again, much larger now than when he and Merryn had built it an hour before.

He turned and walked toward the back of

the cave. The air was redolent with the smell of incense, a heady odor that filled him just as the huge shadow had. No, not incense, but the smell of a thick oak forest. Where was it coming from?

He didn't know. He didn't really care, he just kept walking. The cave seemed to go on forever, yet he knew it didn't. He knew also exactly where he was going. He was striding through the cave, the roof now high above his head, the passage widening with each step he took. And his wand—surely just a finely wrought stick of some sort, but he knew it wasn't—he held loosely in his right hand. It felt natural there.

He called back to Merryn, "Stay where you are. I'm all right."

He heard her say something, but it was faint and distant.

Suddenly there was a low noise that was sharp and steady, a buzzing like a hive of bees flying toward him, louder and louder until he clapped his hands over his ears. The buzzing stopped.

He lowered his hands, realized that he didn't have his wand. No, he had to have his wand. Where was it? He looked down at the floor of the cave, searching, but he didn't see it. Rather, he saw a small circular set of stones some three feet high that surrounded a hole. Flagstones, just like the sarsen stones at the huge meeting place on the plains of southern Britain. He knew what sarsen stones were, knew the feel of them. He knelt beside the circle of stones and looked down into the hole. He could see nothing at all, just blackness. He had no idea how deep the hole was. He leaned down, reaching, but felt only air. He cupped his mouth and called downward, "Where are you? Come to me now."

Nothing, just blackness.

He called out again, this time louder. "I await you. Come to me now."

A light flickered far down in the blackness, just a small pulse of light, flickering wildly, like a candle flame in a wind. It grew stronger and stronger. He didn't move, just watched the light come upward, and when it nearly reached him, he drew back as if stung by a bee from that buzzing hive he'd heard just moments ago. No, it wasn't a bee, not a brief prick but a full-bodied hit, something else—

A hand slapped him.

He reeled back, but not far enough.

A hand slapped him again. Hard.

18

Present
Penwyth Castle

Lord Vellan, chest-deep in his bathing tub, said to Crispin, "What do you mean there's another band of men outside the walls? Another brainless ass is here to claim Merryn? But the king himself sent Sir Bishop of Lythe."

"It seems this man doesn't know about that, my lord. He's got at least twenty men, and he's demanding to come in. He's demanding to wed Merryn."

"He can't do that," said Lady Madelyn.

She stroked the soapy sponge down her husband's back, thinking his bones were too thin and meager now. She could feel the bones through the sponge. On the other hand, it was no surprise, for she'd felt his bones through the sponge for more years now than she could remember.

Lord Vellan ran his fingers through his wet, grizzled white hair, his magnificent hair still so thick, his pride. "By all the arrows that pierce Saint Sebastian, it is madness, their leader is mad. Aye, I will come."

Ten minutes later, Lord Vellan climbed the ladder behind Crispin, ready to catch him, for Crispin's balance wasn't all that good anymore. Both men were panting by the time they reached the top of the ramparts. Lord Vellan looked down at the bald-headed man who'd just pulled off his war helmet. The man looked up. Lord Vellan knew when a man was determined, and this one was. He was young, and like all young men Vellan had known, he believed himself invincible. Vellan said to Crispin, "This isn't good." He yelled down, "Who are you and what do you want?"

The man smiled, showing very white teeth, a full mouth of them, something Vel-

Ian hadn't seen in his own mouth or any of his men's mouths for many a long year. "Old man, I have come to claim Penwyth. I have come to wed the heiress."

"If you take my castle, you will die."

The man threw back his head and laughed loudly. The men behind him looked uncertain, then slowly each man began to laugh. It was a pathetic effort. Lord Vellan could see that they weren't nearly as convinced of their master's invincibility as he was himself. The man waved his hand, covered with black gauntlets that went up nearly to his elbows. His tunic was black, as was the rest of his garb. What affectation was this?

The man shouted, "Just look, it is as I was told. All those ancient old sods wearing chain mail, helmets covering their gray heads, none of them strong enough to fight off a frail woman. Aye, Lord Vellan, I have heard of the four husbands, how all of them died right after wedding your precious granddaughter."

"Aye, all of them did. Are you mad that you want to be the fifth one?"

"I won't die. You have a strange poison, all realize that now, despite the wild tales carried around by these husbands' former soldiers. Aye, I've heard some of their tales. They speak of witches flying over their heads, flinging black smoke into their eyes, and strange white-garbed priests grabbing throats and choking the husbands to death. I've even heard that the devil himself strode in to stomp the husbands beneath his cloven hooves. Aye, there are all sorts of stories, but they would frighten only boys, not men.

"Aye, I know it is poison, for it could be nothing else. This curse of yours, it offends a warrior's brain. I won't touch the food you give me for my wedding feast. Bring your granddaughter. I would see her."

"The fourth husband didn't eat," Lord Vellan said. "And he died as well. Just fell over dead."

"That is a lie I refuse to believe."

"She is to wed Sir Bishop of Lythe, sent by King Edward himself."

He was silent, but just for a moment. "I have not heard of this, and thus it is a lie as well. Let me and my men in, old man, before we scale the walls and smite all the old warriors down. Think you they could do anything more than heave great curses at us?"

Likely not, Lord Vellan thought. He said, "Who are you? Where do you come from?"

"I am Fioral of Grandere Glen, here to claim my inheritance."

"I have never heard of you. What is Grandere Glen?"

"It lies near the mouth of the great Loch Ness, in Scotland. I am a second son and thus must make my own way. Let us in, old man, or I will kill everyone in this keep."

Lord Vellan knew there was no hope for it. He shouted down to Fioral of Grandere Glen, "Listen, Sir Bishop of Lythe took my granddaughter to"—*oh, God, where did Bishop take Merryn*?—"Aye, Sir Bishop took her to the earl of St. Erth. Since she is not here, you cannot wed her."

Fioral cursed. The old man was lying, he had to be lying. Who the devil was this Bishop of Lythe? Here by the king's command? Was he in league with Dienwald de Fortenberry, the king's precious son-in-law? Aye, a rogue he was said to be, but the king merely waved away his misdeeds. If Sir Bishop of Lythe had taken her to St. Erth, then he would not be able to get to her.

Ah, but when Sir Bishop came back to Penwyth with her, and of course he would return, then Fioral would simply kill him and wed her himself.

He would be the sixth husband. The number six had always been lucky for him. He smiled. No doubt the priest in residence here at Penwyth had memorized the marriage ceremony by now. He smiled at his own wit. Aye, this felt right to him. He spoke to the men behind him. One by one, slowly, they nodded.

Dolan, his master-at-arms, came close and said, out of the hearing of the rest of the men, "Fioral, we could lie in wait between here and St. Erth, kill this Bishop of Lythe, and bring the granddaughter back here."

Fioral thought about that, then shook his head. "Nay, we must be in the position of power. I will be here, sitting in Lord Vellan's chair, alive and laughing when this Sir Bishop returns with her. Then he is a dead man. And I? Why, then I'll soon be the fifth husband."

"Or the sixth, more likely," said Dolan. "If this vaunted curse hasn't laid Sir Bishop in his grave."

"Or the sixth," Fioral said, "if he wedded her elsewhere and has not been struck down." He eased his helmet off his head again because it chafed the back of his head. "I think the old man is telling the truth. Were I this Bishop of Lythe, I would take her to St. Erth."

"If he did," Dolan said, "it means that he believed the curse and took her away from here so he wouldn't be butchered when he wed her."

"The fool. It is poison, plain and simple poison. No ancient Druid spirits are lurking hereabouts, no Witches of Byrne are crouched down in the scrubby trees."

Dolan sincerely prayed his master was right.

Fioral called up to Lord Vellan, "We are coming into Penwyth. Lower the drawbridge or I will kill every man, woman, and child within. I will spare none. If you allow us to enter, then all of you are safe."

"But not the animals," Dolan said. "We need to eat while we wait for this Bishop of Lythe."

"I wonder, does the wretched Penwyth curse travel around with the heiress?"

Dolan shook his head. "That is hard to accept."

Fioral chewed that over, then paused a moment.

He laughed as he watched the mighty drawbridge being winched slowly down over the moat, which, he saw, had only three feet or so of water in it. The water didn't look stagnant, green with rotted vegetation. It seemed fresh.

He'd heard about a drought plaguing Penwyth, and perhaps the plants and trees and crops he'd seen were a bit dry, but the air was fresh and there was water in the moat. No drought, just another wild tale, like that wretched Druid and witch curse. He thought he would perhaps kill one of the old warriors, just to show Lord Vellan that he was serious, that he was here to stay, that this was now his keep, and these were his animals and his old graybeard warriors, whose brains, he hoped, were not frozen back in time with the desperately foul King John.

He was smiling even as he spurred his destrier forward, hooves clattering on the thick wooden drawbridge. Mayhap he'd kill old Lord Vellan. Then everyone would know that any poison would bring death to all of them.

The Tintagel Cave

Bishop grabbed for the hand that had struck him. He caught only dead air.

This slap to his cheek caught him off balance and sent him onto his back on the floor of the cave. He sat there, angry and utterly confused.

He crawled back, leaned over the black hole, stretched his arm down its full length. That damned hand it couldn't be all that far down. The hole couldn't be deep at all. "Damn you, come out of that hole."

He heard laughter, he knew it was laughter. It was growing fainter, as if whoever had struck him was climbing back down into the hole. That meant there must be a ladder of sorts.

Bishop leaned over the edge of the circular stones, and felt around for a ladder or a rope, something. He paused, listened. He could hear nothing now, could feel nothing, not even any movement in the air.

Then, suddenly, he heard soft breathing right beside his left ear. He jerked around, but no one was there, nothing was there—but then he knew, just knew. He looked down in the blackness. He didn't want to, but he did. He even leaned down into it.

When two very strong hands grabbed his shoulders and pulled him into the hole, he wasn't surprised, but he was terrified. Then he was free, no hands on him, and he was falling and falling.

And he made no sound at all.

Sometime Else

The prince awoke slowly, stretched. In that instant he knew he wasn't alone. *Someone else was drifting over him, through him, settling in, but he was still himself. He felt the other's hunger, his aches from sleeping on the floor of the oak forest.*

The prince of Balanth shook away all the nonsense and took stock. He knew he was still in her oak forest, and he was alone. Yet again, he was alone.

He threw back his head and yelled, "Brecia! Come here, you damnable witch. Show yourself."

There was a slight shifting of the air, making it shimmer, and she was suddenly standing there, right in front of him, her arms crossed over her breasts. She looked furious.

"Brecia," he said, and stuck out his hand to take hers.

She looked at that hand, brown, strong, the blunt nails. "Your hand, prince? Why, were I stupid enough to touch your hand, you might just turn me into a toad. Where is your wand?"

"You, a toad? You would make a dangerous toad. You would gather all the toads together, overthrow the local toad government, and make yourself their queen toad. My wand? That is a good question. I don't know where my wand is. It seemed to leave me, not long ago. Isn't that odd? I don't remember. I don't know why I'm here, sleeping in your forest, either. Something strange has happened that I don't understand. Did you put a spell on me, Brecia?"

When she didn't take his hand, he finally drew it back.

She said slowly, "There is something different about you, prince. Mayhap the gods came to you, ordered you to curb your arrogance, your violence?"

He seemed, to her eyes, to take this seriously. "Why, no, I don't think so. Do you believe I am too arrogant? Too violent?"

Something was strange here, he was right about that. She nodded slowly. "Aye, sometimes I have seen you so."

"Why was I sleeping, Brecia? In your oak forest, away from your fortress?"

"It was night. It was good that you slept."

He looked around. "But here? Alone in your forest? Nothing at all to protect me?"

"Why would you need anything to protect you? Aye, I see. It's because your wand is gone."

"I don't think so," the prince said. "I was in your fortress. I'd tied you down, but then, even without your wand, you disappeared. Where did you go, Brecia?"

"I didn't go far, just off to your left, if you would know the truth. I wanted my wand back. I heard you laughing." Why, she wondered, had she told him the truth? She never had before. He was too dangerous, this wizard prince was too powerful, this prince she'd wanted so desperately three years before. She said, "I think you simply decided to leave my fortress, to leave my oak forest, but you tired and decided to sleep here."

He frowned.

"And why not? You are so arrogant, so above all mortals and immortals alike, you wouldn't believe any wild animal would dare come near you. As for your enemies, why, they are as nothing to you. You could whistle at them and they would sink into swamp mud."

He gave her a quizzical smile. "You believe I am that good?"

"Don't toy with me, prince. I am not one of your women, eager to fall at your feet, praising your skills."

"I can see you at my feet," he said. "I can see my hands sifting through your hair whilst you are there before me." He could also see her coming up on her knees, see her hands touching him, see himself in her mouth, and he nearly expired on the spot. By all the ancient gods who ate men's flesh, he would spill his seed right here in front of her if he didn't get himself under control. He focused on her, on that exquisite face of hers, and realized he didn't want to look away. He'd wanted her for so very long, perhaps even forever. Such wild red hair she had, long down her back, braided in the front with white ribbons. Hair red enough to burst into flames. He smiled at that, and said, "Would you like to?"

"Like to what?"

"Fall at my feet and praise my skills? Perhaps you could also vow eternal devotion to me? Mayhap do other things as well?"

"I am your equal, prince. I do whatever I wish to do. But you refuse to accept that, don't you? I must be your slave, bow deep to you. Let you put your foot on my neck."

"My equal? Well, you did get away from me, Brecia. You were lying there on the altar I created for you. Such a beautiful slab of stone. You looked remarkably beautiful lying on it. I would have liked to whisk away your clothes and have you stretched out there on the bluestone and I would come over you—"

Brecia's eyes nearly crossed. "You arrogant son of a witch's cursed alliance! Think you I would ever willingly mate with you?"

"Oh, yes," he said. "Oh, yes. You know that we are meant to mate, Brecia. Why do you fight me? I don't wish to make you my slave. Actually, I believe I should prefer your foot on my neck. You have lovely feet, Brecia, not like the ghosts, whose toes are far too long."

He was not acting the way he should. He

was different. She was tempted to blink at this idiocy from a powerful wizard's mouth, but she didn't. She held firm. He was probably playing a game with her. Since she didn't have her wand, it could lead to bad things. On the other hand, he didn't have his wand, either. Were they equal in power? She didn't know. She said, "I don't like you, prince. I wish you to leave my forest. I don't know how you managed to find me, but it doesn't matter. Leave. I don't wish to see you again."

He laughed, held out his hand to her. "You will never bore me. Never. Come, Brecia, it is just the two of us. A man and a woman. Forget our skills, our magic, our sense of what is of this world and what is not. Come with me."

He was different, she thought yet again, staring at him, staring at that hand of his, and she didn't know what to do. She'd believed he was the most beautiful man in all the earth until she'd realized what he really was, what he really wanted, and that had been to take her and to take a wife as well. He was a wizard who wanted a son by her—and not just another wizard, but the most powerful wizard the world had ever seen. He would destroy her and her sacred grove and all her people in his quest to mate with her, if he deemed it necessary.

But then again, he seemed different. It knocked her off balance. When she'd come across him sleeping as soundly as if he'd still been in his mother's womb, she'd stared down at him, not really wanting to look away, but then he'd awakened. She'd expected him to try to enchain her immediately, to overwhelm her. But he hadn't. She still didn't move. "Where do you want me to come with you?"

He looked thoughtful at that. "I suppose I must retrieve my wand first, yours as well, then we will go to my fortress atop the Balanth promontory."

"I have never been there before. I hear it is frightening, so tall that if a mortal falls, he dies."

"No, it is merely my home. It's true that the fortress stretches not only to the heavens, but also to the shadows deep in the earth beneath the promontory, but it is for protection. You would be safe there forever, with me. I haven't yet had a mortal fall into the lower reaches." He paused a moment, frowned. "I cannot remember if a mortal has ever even seen Balanth. It was not designed for a mortal's eyes."

"No."

"Neither is your fortress. I didn't see it until you unveiled it to me."

She waved that away. "How came you to be here?"

He frowned a moment, scratched his head. Ah, she loved that black, black hair of his, thick and long. The bastard. "I suppose I must have been searching for you. As you know, when you disappeared, I was nearly beyond anger." He raised his hand. "Nay, listen to me. You know I didn't roast any of your ancient ghosts over their campfires. I didn't send them hurtling into an uncertain pocket of space to gasp out their breaths and wiggle their naked toes."

"No," she said slowly, frowning. "You did not even try to do that. I saw you turn away from the bluestone and yell, yell very loudly, your voice so strong that the blue smoke dissolved and re-formed like clouds in a mortal sky over your head. And then you walked out of my fortress. My people and I watched you go, watched your anger simmer in the very air, turning it red as a human heart."

"You believe that I merely became tired and lay down here, built no fire to warm me, and fell asleep?"

"It would seem so. But your wand is gone, prince. No wizard is safe when his wand is gone."

19

She seemed disturbed that his wand was gone. And why was that? He said easily, "Your wand is gone as well, Brecia. Surely you can feel by now that I don't have it."

She withdrew into deep silence, and he knew she was worried, about both their wands. It meant an enemy. It meant Mawdoor. Finally she said, "I know you don't have it, damn you to demon's hell. You slept while Mawdoor took both our wands. That bespeaks a fine mind and a keen awareness."

He looked thoughtful, then shrugged. "At first I thought you had somehow gotten it back from me yourself. But I see that you haven't. Is that why you searched for me, Brecia? You wanted your wand back?"

She turned her head a bit, and red hair curtained her cheek as she nodded. "Perhaps that was part of it. I must have my wand back, as you must have yours. Do you know where they are?"

He didn't say anything.

"Without his wand, a wizard is in very big trouble."

"As is a witch," he said, but he didn't seem all that concerned.

"A witch has more tools, I've discovered, than a wizard."

He said without hesitation, "That is nonsense, Brecia."

She said nothing to that, surely that was another strangeness. He would swear she was looking at him differently, as if he were somehow not himself, but another, and that damned other found more favor with her.

She shook her head at him, not understanding why he was acting so differently, why he hadn't tried to tie her to a tree and force her to mate with him, why he hadn't told her she would do exactly what he wanted—she knew he didn't need his wand to do that, did he? She'd been a fool to come to him and look down at him whilst he slept. A fool to believe he somehow still had her wand, when she'd known, all the way to the soles of her sandals, that he didn't have his own.

She said, "Mawdoor has our wands."

He nodded. "Ah, so you have dealings with that wizard."

"He lives close by. It's impossible not to have dealings with him. And there's more."

"What? What more?"

She shook her fist toward an oak tree, and the prince would swear that the tree shuddered. "Say it or you'll choke," he said.

"He wants to wed me."

The prince threw back his head and laughed loud and deep. He sobered quickly, gave her an insolent grin. "I don't think that will happen."

She shook her head again, this time at herself. Her hair danced like flames around her head. He wanted very badly to rub his face in her hair.

He said, shrugging, "My wand will return to me, if it is able. It would take a very strong wizard to keep it from me. And you believe it is Mawdoor?" He spit and laughed. His arrogance—it shimmered off him. He recognized no limits, no beings more powerful than himself, no weaknesses within himself. And most saw him as he saw himself. Strong and invincible. She had always admired that even as she hated him for his specific arrogance, his inborn conceit, for all that was unbending in him—directed at her. Once, he'd repelled her more than he attracted her. But now—because she wasn't a fool—she recognized that he was the more powerful and she always had to go carefully around him.

She said slowly, "It seems to me that your wand is not with you because Mawdoor came upon you here in the forest and took it. And took mine as well."

"Aye. I wonder why he didn't try to kill me? He's always wanted to."

"You were sleeping. Isn't there a long-unwritten code that two opposing wizards must face each other?"

"Aye, the code has existed almost since the beginning of time, its purpose to ensure that the winner of any fight wins only through his skills and nothing else."

"Would Mawdoor stand by that code?"

The prince shrugged. "I don't think he

would. Mawdoor has always gone his own way, and that means that he didn't kill me because he wants something else, wants something more from me. A battle on his land? The chance to kill me and have you admire him, accept him?" At her silence, he said, "He knows that you and I will mate; therefore he must rid himself of me."

"And he mustn't make me too angry in the process," she said.

The prince nodded. He saw Mawdoor's dark, fierce face clearly in his mind, even though it had been at least a year since he'd seen him. At the stone circle—that was where he'd last seen Mawdoor. He was not a nice wizard. He was vicious and vile, stronger than he should be because of his damned demon blood, and the most lustful wizard in many a long year. The prince said to Brecia, "You will never wed Mawdoor."

"No," she said and looked down at her sandals, straightened the golden chain around her waist. "Of course I will not wed him. Neither of you has anything to say about that. Prince, I know that you can do magic without your wand, but can you truly protect yourself without it?"

He frowned at that. "I don't know. It has never been a question until now."

The words came out of her mouth, startling her more than him. "I can teach you magic to protect yourself, magic that doesn't require a wand."

He could but stare at her. "You don't want to see me kicked off the edge of the earth? You don't want to see me crushed beneath a mountain of black stone that will hold me in darkness forever and beyond? What is this, Brecia? Why would you want to teach me magic? Why would you want to help me?"

Because this is the first time you have ever needed me, that's why. But she said nothing. She turned away from him, and he watched her long fingers stroke the white wool gown.

He said, "You could stroke me like that."

"What?"

"Your fingers. You're stroking your gown."

To his surprise and delight, she looked like a maid caught up in a man's words, not a witch who with just a wink and a tap of her fingertips could send him to his knees, eating dirt.

Could she do that to him since he didn't have his wand? He didn't know.

She said, "Forget my fingers, prince. You are not acting the way—"

"I'm me, Brecia, none other. Come, what's wrong with you?"

"You should be furious, screaming curses to any god who will listen to you, blasting incantations all over my sacred grove, exerting every sort of power you possess to locate your wand. Why are you talking about my fingers stroking you, when your very existence is at stake?"

"I suppose because I don't think it is," he said. "Is that odd of me? Perhaps. Would you really show me magic, Brecia?"

"You don't trust me, do you, prince? You believe my offer of help is somehow a trick."

He gave her a look of great hunger, nothing else, no threat, no struggle between them, just hunger. "I have wanted you since the first moment I beheld you at the sacred meeting place. I have admired you since that first moment. I will trust you to my dying breath."

"Stop this, do you hear me? Just stop this. You are not behaving like yourself, like you always act when you are around me, and I won't have it."

He looked at her face, at the faint line of freckles over her nose, and wondered for the hundredth time if her hair would feel warm against his skin. "Did you come looking for me, Brecia?"

"I just wanted to make certain you were out of my forest. Aye, and I hoped you had my wand, but you didn't. You were simply sleeping."

"Did you see either of our wands disappear from my hands?"

She shook her head. "At first I thought Callas had managed somehow to steal my wand back. But he hasn't the strength. He fears you more than hates you, and he believes you will destroy all that I am, that I might forget what I owe to my heritage, to my people, to my sacred oak grove."

The prince said thoughtfully as he brushed leaves from his legs, "Maybe I should have killed the little sot."

She laughed. That was the prince she knew and understood, the prince she'd like to kick off the Balanth promontory to sink into the depths of the sea below.

He realized that he'd heard her laugh only

once before, at the sacred meeting place. She'd hummed with pleasure and laughter until he'd had to wed Lillian and Brecia had just disappeared.

"Callas is my man. If the need ever arises, why, then I will deal with him in my own way."

"Brecia, I don't need my wand. I can move a mountain without my wand. Perhaps, though, I would need my wand if I wished to move the earth."

"Yes, but—"

"But even with my wand, I cannot change a woman's mind." Then he smiled and waved his left hand in a wide fan in front of her. A wind came up and blew her hair into her face. He waved his left hand in the opposite direction, and the wind stopped.

"Aye, that is a clever trick, prince, but the wind isn't a mortal enemy or another wizard. The wind comes when you command it to come because it has no will of its own. But because the wizard who holds your wand— Mawdoor—is very likely now more powerful than you, you need my help."

"How very odd it is," he said, stroking his jaw. "You seem to like me better now that you see me as weak."

"You, weak? Ah, prince, you make sport with me. It's just that—"

He took a step toward her. "What, Brecia?"

She smiled, raised both her hands, and trickled her fingers downward. In an instant he was naked.

He didn't move, just stood there, hands at his sides, smiling at her. He made no move to leap upon her. And surely that was odd. He said, "That is clever, Brecia. Do you like what you see?"

She studied him, and he knew it, and he also knew that he pleased her. If she continued, even he—a very powerful wizard with or without his wand—would become harder than a sarsen stone.

She trickled her fingers upward, and his clothes were back in place.

"Perhaps you are at my mercy now, prince. Do I have more skills without needing my wand than you, a powerful wizard?"

"Oh, no," he said. "Oh, no." He smiled at her, touched his thumbs together even as he spread his fingers wide, and raised his chin perhaps an inch. Suddenly, her hands and feet were bound. She toppled over onto the ground.

"You can't fan your damned fingers now, Brecia."

"I had thought you more reasonable," she said. "A mistake, I see now." She wanted to ram his head into one of her oak trees. He held her easily, and he knew it. She'd been a fool to feel any lessening fear or honest misgivings of him. "What will you do now, prince? Force me? Make me bow to you, kiss your feet?"

He cursed, clenched his fingers into fists, lowered his chin, and she was free. She rose, brushed off the white woolen skirt, and knew more surprise than she'd felt in a very long time.

"So," she said, her voice as flat as the sacred ale he'd had to drink at the meeting place, "you have no need of me at all. It is merely a competition with you, prince. A matter of proving that you are more powerful than I. It is nothing else at all."

He laughed at that. "Whisk away my clothes again, Brecia, and you will see how there is a lot more to it than that."

"You are a man withal you're a wizard," she said in that same flat voice. "A man's body changes with a thought, a glimpse of a woman's ear or the sound of her voice.

Show him a naked woman and he becomes crazed."

"I would not be crazed with you."

"Perhaps not," she said. "But you would demand that I give you everything."

He didn't say anything, just smiled at her, and felt his blood thrum heavy in his veins, bright and fast, his wizard's blood.

He said, "If you were with me, we would have a better chance of finding our wands. What do you think, Brecia?"

She said slowly, "You mean something like a partnership? We would work together?"

"Yes."

It seemed at that moment that the forest became as still as Brecia. There wasn't a single oak branch rustling, no sound at all from any bird or insect. If her ghosts were hidden amongst the trees, they were more silent than the air itself.

He felt deadened with it. "Now you don't trust me, Brecia?"

"I know that if I trusted you, you would try to bind me to you, or, mayhap you would even use me to barter for your wand."

The earth shook beneath his feet, and both of them felt it. His rage was that great.

"Damn you, you obstinate, blind witch, I would die before I let anyone harm you!"

His words hung in the air, hard and heavy between them, the air undulating as if unseen fingers were sweeping through it.

She stared at him for a very long time before she said, "There is much between us, prince." He knew she could see the shimmering air, knew she was using her own breath to warm it, sending her soft breath to him, to stroke his face, to calm him. "I will believe you until you become again as you once were."

"Whatever that was," he said, blowing that warm air back into her face.

"Mawdoor is dangerous," she said, and it was true. His fortress was too near her oak grove for her peace of mind. Her people, even the ghosts so old they could see into the future as easily as they could the past, spoke very quietly when Mawdoor was the subject. All feared him.

"Mawdoor has never tried to harm either me or my people. He's never come into my forest as far as I know." She paused a moment, and he saw a flash of fear on her face. "I remember late one night, several years ago, Mawdoor—just to remind me of his power, I suppose—sent a powerful bolt of lightning down to strike not a foot away from my fortress. A huge plume of smoke rose high above the forest, and I knew he'd sent it."

"Not much of a warning," the prince said. "What did you do?"

"I? I did nothing. I have heard stories of his power, of the devastation he brings when he is displeased."

He frowned at that. "He knows where you live, where your fortress stands."

"Oh, yes."

"Somehow he must have divined that I was there also."

"And he was surprised," Brecia said slowly. "And then enraged. You're right, he must be planning something quite spectacular since he didn't kill you right here."

"He could not divine that I was with you. Even I could not divine that. Perhaps one of your ghosts is his spy."

The ground shook.

He smiled. "Well done, Brecia. Do you really wish to help me fetch our wands?"

The ground stilled. He heard a bird flying overhead, actually heard it, and the march of an insect near his foot.

"Aye," she said, "I'll help you. There is something else you must know, prince."

"I don't think I'm going to like this, am I?"

She merely shrugged. "Mawdoor sent one of his advocates into the forest to see me. Three months ago, at the time of the full moon."

He waited.

"It was his offer of marriage. But it was much, much more. It was also a threat if I refused him."

"What did you do to his advocate?"

"I did nothing, merely told him that I had vowed celibacy until the third millennium."

"What did he say to that?"

"The advocate suggested I rethink the millennium."

"Did you turn him into a snail and step on him?"

"I wanted to mix him into my blue smoke and have him meander out the top of my fortress, but I feared Mawdoor's retribution. I sent him on his way with blessings and kind words. I am not a fool, prince."

"No," he said, "you are not. And no, you will never wed Mawdoor."

"You know this for a fact?"

"Oh, yes. You will be mine."

20

Mawdoor's fortress was stark black and forbidding. It was the kind of forbidding that made a man's toenails fall off, as grim as a Druid priest's altar ready for sacrifice. It was an immense circular black wooden tower standing on a hillock that he himself had created, a thick black spear aimed some fifty feet toward the heavens. A ten-foot wooden wall—a perfect triangle—surrounded the tower, with other towers at each of the three corners. The wood was blacker now than when it first appeared, because, it was said, every time a mortal saw it and fear sank deep into his heart, the wood became blacker. No one knew how much darker the darkest black could get.

This was true. Local tribes avoided the fortress; indeed, they walked carefully, eyes on their feet, when they were within a mile of Mawdoor's lands.

Mawdoor had named his fortress and all its lands Penwyth, a name that had come to him in a dream, he'd said to his acolytes, a name that meant nothing really, but it sang softly in his brain. His dream was of a not-so-different future with his fortress still here, just changed a bit, perhaps not so very black. It pleased him.

The prince had never been inside Mawdoor's fortress. The only reason he'd come this far west was because he'd wanted Brecia. He looked up at the fierce black fortress and knew he didn't want to go inside it now either. He'd heard for years that Mawdoor had become quite mad and shut himself away in his black tower for long periods of time. Then he would emerge, looking fit and enraged and ready to string mortals' entrails from one end of this huge island to another. It was a pity, because the madness hadn't interfered with his powers. Nor his brain. He was very proud of his brain, an instrument that could see the fastest birds flying in the sky, could tell him what sorts of birds they were and whether or not he wanted them for his dinner.

His brain gave him great beliefs. He was convinced that the gods themselves had sent the great bluestones at the sacred meeting circle in the British plains from the ancient land just north of the Erin sea. He also believed that the gods had hidden a treasure in one of those bluestones, a fabulous prize for a wizard who was clever enough to figure it out.

The prince agreed that there was madness in Mawdoor. There were always rumors about wizard treasure, theories exchanged behind cupped hands, but no one really believed them. Besides, what sort of treasure could be hidden in a bluestone?

He said to Brecia, "Mawdoor cursed me in my cradle. My father told me that, told me he hated that I'd been born because he feared I would be more powerful than he. My father said Mawdoor was only seven years old at the time. I hope he has skills and imagination above the ordinary. I am ready to be impressed by wizardry."

Brecia chewed on that a moment, then

said, "I've been thinking. Maybe he couldn't hurt you because you were in my forest. I have always put a stop to any violence in my forest, if possible."

"You're saying that you protect your forest?"

"Aye, that's what I'm saying. I don't know if it's enough to stop a wizard as powerful as Mawdoor. Perhaps it is."

The prince said nothing, but he didn't believe it for a minute. No, Mawdoor wanted him to come to his home.

He paused, watching Brecia pull her hood over her head, hiding her hair.

The prince pulled his soft woolen cap down over his head, pulled it tight. All he needed was a gust of wind to knock it off. The fitted cap was blacker than Mawdoor's fortress, as black as a moonless midnight, and softer than a mink's fur. The cap would hold him invisible, but for no longer than one hour, because he didn't have his wand to steady the spell for a full twenty-four hours. An hour had to be enough. He knew no one could see him, not even Brecia.

"We must hurry," Brecia said, eyeing where she knew he was because she could hear him breathing. "I wish I could do that, flick my fingers, or curl over my toes, or stick my elbow at an odd angle, and conjure up a cap like that. If I could, my cap would be white, the purest white imaginable."

He smiled at that, and said, "I saw you disappear, and you didn't have your wand."

"Aye, but I couldn't go far at all. I was no more than two feet away from you, prince. I would fall flat on my face in view of anyone looking if I moved any distance at all away from my wand."

"You have just told me one of your secrets, Brecia."

She had indeed, and she wondered at herself. Why had she said anything at all to this wizard who threatened all that she was and all that she could become in the mists of the future? "Mayhap I'm just speaking aloud because I believe I'm alone."

"Mayhap," he said, and laughed, pointing, even though she couldn't see him. "I can see the cook chopping up something green on his table. Maybe Mawdoor is eating plants now. I wonder what that would do to his disposition?"

She laughed, and it warmed him.

The prince looked up at the black fortress, felt his blood pound thick and hard. He wanted Mawdoor, wanted his neck between his hands. To take another wizard's wand, that was a very bad thing. He said, "We must go in. We must get this done. Time runs short."

Brecia walked up the impossibly steep stone steps that led to the fortress gate, a huge structure that was banded with iron, the prince invisible at her side.

A querulous old voice yelled down, "What do ye wish, woman?"

"I wish to see Lord Mawdoor."

"Why?"

"If I wished to speak to an old graybeard with fewer teeth than my ancient cat, I would. I am a witch. Open the gate, now, or I will turn you into a lily pad."

"Ha! There bain't no lily pads hereabouts, no place for them to sit."

"Then you will be a lily pad sitting on a rock," Brecia said.

She saw that he still wasn't sure. She nearly smiled when he said, "A woman or a witch who has no respect for her elders isn't worthy of anything. I think I'll leave you until you rot clean into the dirt and roll back down the hill. What do you think of that?"

"Mayhap I would roll onto a rock and land

on you, an old withered lily pad, baked from the sun and brittle with age and no water. What are you called, old man?"

"I am called Debbin, I guard the gates on Tuesdays, and I am not an old man. I am in my prime."

"Prime of what?"

The old man shook his fist at her, he opened his mouth and yelled out several full-blooded curses, all aimed at her head, only to have Brecia nod pleasantly at him. When he opened his mouth again, he discovered that his tongue was so fat he couldn't begin to stuff it back in. Debbin wanted to spit it out, no, he wanted to gag. He stood there, looking at the cloaked woman, and wanted to howl, but he couldn't do that either—his tongue was just too big.

"If you would like your tongue to fit again into your mouth, then let me in."

His cheeks bulged, and his face was red as a sunset off the western coast.

She said, "Or, if you like the size of your new tongue, and still refuse me entrance, then I will send you to the underworld, where they fry old men like you over huge, smoking fires. Demons are fond of human tongue, I've heard."

The old man cursed and choked on that big tongue of his, but the old gate swung open. She smiled at him and splayed her fingers in front of him. His tongue fit once again in his mouth.

"That was well done," the prince said in her ear. "A creative use of a body part." She felt his mouth suddenly touch her earlobe, lick, then bite gently. She squeaked.

"What is wrong, witch?"

She shook her head at old Debbin, who was pressing his palm over his mouth, and walked through the open gate. She stopped cold, heard the prince draw in his breath beside her, and heard the old man cursing under his breath. He was probably wishing her in the depths of Mawdoor's dungeons, but he was afraid to curse more loudly, and of course Brecia knew it.

She cleared her throat and gave him a little wave.

The prince said in her ear, "If you are through performing your little tricks, we must get inside."

She snorted.

"Or are you trying to impress me so that I will judge you to be worthy as my mate?"

"I wonder how you would look howling around a fat tongue, prince."

"Don't even think of trying that on me, Brecia. However, it was well done of you."

They walked into a vast courtyard. There were no horses, no animals, no children, just old men and old women, shuffling with shoulders bowed, eyes to the ground, saying nothing at all.

"This is all very strange," the prince said, and she heard the rustling of his clothes. "There is no magic in any of these people. There is only despair."

"You're right," she said. "I don't feel anything coming from them. They are quite mortal. But they are all old. Why?"

He said nothing. She felt his hand under her elbow, leading her toward the immense black tower door.

"They cannot die because their misery keeps them alive. I remember my father telling me that he should have killed Mawdoor's mother before she mated with a demon and birthed a black stain on all wizards. I wish that he had managed to rid the world of her, but he didn't." She could practically hear him frowning.

Brecia said, "Why not?"

"I believe Mawdoor's mother talked him out of it, swore to him that her son would be pure of mind and heart."

"And your father believed her."

He nodded.

He realized that Brecia had stopped and was staring upward. She said, "I had believed my own tower to be the state of a witch's art. But this?"

He laughed. "I can feel that he has spent many, many years constructing this fortress. It is designed to terrify both mortals and other wizards. He doesn't feel your presence yet, Brecia, nor can he know I'm here with you."

"How can you feel that, prince? How can you know what he knows? Mawdoor might be staring down on us right this minute, rubbing his hands together, deciding how to kill both of us."

The prince said, "Brecia, if Mawdoor knew you were here, he would have this tower studded with gems to dazzle your witch's eyes. He would fill this dank, barren courtyard with budding fruit trees and lovely blossoms to inflame your simple witch's heart. He wants you, doesn't he?"

She didn't say anything, just kept walking

toward the huge black door at the bottom of the tower.

The prince said, "If he guessed I was with you, he would have that door open onto a viper pit."

"But you know such things fade quickly."

"Aye, in the normal course of things, but with Mawdoor? I don't know. There are tales, of course, about black deeds and blacker sacrifices."

The huge black door flew inward before Brecia could open it.

Mawdoor stood there, staring down at her. He was tall, too tall for a man or a wizard, but that simple spell would fade as well. She craned her neck and said, "Hello, my lord."

"Brecia, is it you? It is about time you have come to Penwyth. I have been waiting for you."

"I have come to fetch my wand."

"So, it is true, you cannot work your magic without your wand." In a move so fast it blurred, he pulled her wand out of his sleeve. He gave her a slight bow and handed it to her. "I was holding it safe for you. How did you know I had it?"

"It seemed to me that it was something you would do, Mawdoor."

"Ah, something clever, something you wouldn't immediately realize. Is that what you mean?"

"That is," she said, "more or less exactly what I mean."

Mawdoor looked around the vast courtyard. "Where is that damned prince?"

"I don't know. I left him in my forest sleeping away the spell I placed on him."

"You truly guessed that it was I who had taken your wand?"

"Aye, there could be none other," she said. "May I come in, my lord?"

He stood back, watched her enter, and stiffened suddenly. "There is something else here, something that came in with you, Brecia. What is it? What are you hiding?"

21

Brecia whirled about. In a voice no louder than a whisper, she said, "Did the wretched prince of Balanth somehow manage to slip in with me? But how?"

"Oh, no, but—" Mawdoor took two steps back. He stilled, closed his eyes a moment. She could feel him searching in the air around her, poking, prodding, and she held herself very still. She couldn't hear the prince breathing, wondered if he'd managed to shield himself in yet another layer of invisibility. Without his wand? If so, that was impressive indeed.

When Mawdoor opened his eyes, the air

was still and flat again, sweet-smelling from the lavender he'd sprinkled on the stone floor, probably in the last few moments. He smiled. "No. I must have simply picked up the trace of him on you. Take off your cloak, Brecia. Let me see you."

She was a witch, she had her wand, but she wasn't a fool. A witch who wasn't a fool was always cautious. There was a darkness in him that bespoke thoughts and dreams that were powerful and crude. Heinous dreams he reveled in, and dominated every act in them. She knew he was not many years older than the prince, but still he looked much older, maybe because of black thoughts, blacker deeds that had to take a toll, even on a wizard. But still he was a man in his prime, fit, not so tall now as he'd first appeared but strong, thick with muscle. His eyes were bright green, perhaps another affectation, she didn't know, but they just didn't look natural.

Slowly she slipped her cloak off her shoulders, shook back the hood, and handed it to him. She watched as he brought it to his face and rubbed it against his cheek. "It smells like you," he said. "Make the cloak disappear, Brecia."

She lifted her wand, her lips moved, and the cloak was gone.

"Is it in limbo or did you destroy it?"

"It is in limbo. It is a lovely cloak, woven long ago by a ghost with great talent and flair. Why would I want to destroy it?"

He shrugged. "Because the prince touched it, perhaps. But it wouldn't matter, would it? You would just fashion another for yourself."

"I was not taught to do that. The cloak belonged to my mother and her mother before her. When I touch it, I touch them. I would be distraught if something were to happen to it."

"If the prince saw it, knew it was precious to you, he would shred it like wheat in a miller's wheel."

She cocked her head to one side in question.

"Come, Brecia, all know that the prince saw you at the sacred meeting place, in the shadow of a mighty trilithon, and he wanted you. Not to wed and cherish you like I would, but to force you to bow to his will, to render you helpless, to make you his slave."

"I have not heard this, Mawdoor."

He shrugged. "Oh, the prince wanted you

all right, but it doesn't matter now since you are here, in my fortress, my honored guest. Now, I have returned your wand to you. You owe me a great deal for that, do you not?"

"You did not tell me how you got my wand. Did you take it from the prince?"

"Aye. One of my acolytes found him on the edge of your oak forest, sleeping like one of the heavenly angels, which he isn't. He was afraid the prince would awaken and smite him. He then decided that if he didn't try to take both wands, I would smite him."

"I can see that would give him courage."

"Aye, it did. Unfortunately, it also killed him before I could contain the prince's wand in a special place."

Mawdoor walked away from her to a small golden chest that sat atop a rich malachite table. He flicked his fingers and black leather gloves covered his hands. He took a key from his hand, slid it into a small, strangely wrought lock, and watched the lid of the chest fling itself open.

She saw pulsing light within the small chest.

Mawdoor stuck his hand inside, and she saw him grimace. But he set his teeth and pulled out the prince's wand. The wand was straining to get away from him, but Mawdoor was expecting that. He was using a great deal of force to keep control of it and to keep it from touching his flesh as well. What would happen if the prince's wand did touch his naked hand?

He said over his shoulder, "Do you think the prince will come here, Brecia?"

The prince stood very still. He could have reached out his hand and touched Mawdoor's left shoulder. He could feel his wand trying to escape Mawdoor's hand to get to him, but Mawdoor's hold was too strong. The prince concentrated on the wand, spoke ancient words to it, stroked it with his mind, called it again and again. His wand began to vibrate, sending pulses of warmth into the silent air.

"It is strong, this damned wand," Mawdoor said. "Stronger now than it was when it first came to me. But my grandmother's chest held it, and so can I."

Brecia said, shrugging her shoulders, "I don't care if he comes here if I am already gone. Why do you think that I would? I came here only to fetch my own wand. Where is the prince? I don't know." Her voice dropped, and she leaned toward him. "The prince is dangerous, Mawdoor. I have witnessed his magic. He is the strongest wizard I have ever seen. It is said that his sire and his mother were more powerful than any in Britain, and thus their seed formed a being even stronger than they."

"Nonsense," said Mawdoor, "all nonsense. It is a tale he himself has spread about the land. I laugh at his claim. I spit upon the idea that he could be the strongest wizard in this land." He turned and spat onto the bare stone floor. "I am the strongest wizard of all time. I will prove it to you. I can even control the prince's wand." His green eyes were even greener now, the thick hair on his head now blacker than the blackest night. He smiled and nodded at his spit on the stone floor. A blood-red carpet suddenly appeared. She didn't know if the carpet was real or not. He pointed the prince's wand at her, again careful not to touch its tip to his bare skin. He was smiling. "Ah, Brecia, you came to me, just as I wished you to. I wish you to remain here, with me. Aye, you will stay here at Penwyth and wed me."

Brecia was tempted to turn his head into a mushroom, but she wasn't certain she could do it. By all the gods, time was growing short, too short. Any moment now the prince would be visible and Mawdoor could scatter pieces of him throughout the earth, using his own wand against him. Was that possible? Why couldn't Mawdoor feel the prince's presence?

"No, Mawdoor," she said finally. "I will not remain here and wed you." *Now—she had to do it now.* Brecia felt the prince's breath on her cheek. She whipped up her arm, wand in hand, and mind-trapped the prince's wand even as it rose in Mawdoor's hand.

It was in his left hand. Oh, no, oh, no. How did it get in his left hand? There was nothing she could do. She was frozen to the spot.

Suddenly the prince was so close to her that it seemed he was covering her with himself.

He laughed and rubbed his fingertips together and watched his wand heave and jerk against Mawdoor's hand. "Just a bit more," he said. "Come to me, you can do it."

Mawdoor yelled, "Why can I not sense you, you evil spawn of a witch's seed? I know you are here. You're trying to get your wand, but I won't let you."

The prince laughed again, and for a instant he let himself be heard and seen. He stood there in front of Mawdoor, glittering in gold cloth, a gold crown on his head, and he laughed even as he drew in his breath sharply, then blew it out. His wand rose straight up, pulling Mawdoor's arm with it, up, up, at least twenty feet into the air. Mawdoor hung on. He shouted words unknown to either of them. The wand stopped rising. It held him there, twenty feet off the floor, swinging back and forth like a clock pendulum.

"Let it go, Mawdoor, or you will remain there for the rest of time."

"No," Mawdoor yelled, swinging over their heads, a gentle arc, back and forth. "No, damn you, you wretched creature."

Brecia realized then that Mawdoor couldn't get to his own wand; it would be his downfall.

The prince laughed again, raised his arms, and clapped his hands over his head. The wand simply disappeared from Mawdoor's left hand. Mawdoor hung there, cursing, and the prince blew him a kiss. A cage came around him, wooden bars, blacker than the black of his hair.

"Only a mad fool takes another wizard's wand, Mawdoor," the prince said. In the next instant, the prince, his wand now safely in his own hand, flicked it, and both he and Brecia were gone.

Mawdoor whacked his left hand at the bars. The cage fell apart, spilling him out. He got to his feet, still breathing hard, wondering how the prince could have gotten the wand away from him, not that it mattered where he'd sent the prince and Brecia. Still, he'd held it in his left hand, fought with it but managed to hold it firm. His left hand had put a powerful drugging hold on the wand, kept it safe from Brecia, but not from the prince.

But losing the wand was only a moment of humiliation; hanging in the air, then being slammed into a damned cage, that was only another moment of humiliation. Even as he'd hated it, he smiled.

He rubbed his hands together, smiling in triumph. He threw back his head and shouted, "You believe me stupid, prince? You are trapped, you abominable creature. I have both of you, and you will stay here until I call you forth."

He saw his splendid prison. His magnificent brain had plotted out every last detail. Now that he was able, he pulled out his wand, closed his eyes, and chanted a prayer of thanksgiving to his antecedents.

22

The prince said, his voice disbelieving, "We can't get out. I will kick myself for my conceit, for believing that Mawdoor would be crude and violent in his plans to kill me. But look what he has managed, Brecia. We're trapped." He then cursed loud and long, remarkable curses really, come from all over the land, and from all over time, enriched by wizard curses from faraway Bulgar and Byzantium. He stopped, got hold of himself. "Look, Brecia, the bastard has created a lock on the very air that flows over his fortress. I wanted to be impressed, and I surely am."

She nodded. "You were too arrogant," she said, and looked at the nothingness that held them. She couldn't see a trace of the trap, couldn't feel it either.

"I am not arrogant," he said. "I was over-confident and I confessed it."

"Ha. You showed yourself all garbed in gold with a crown. You wanted to enrage him, and look what it has brought us, and—"

"He would have done this had I appeared to him in rags."

"—then you put him in a black wooden cage."

"He would have done this even if I'd set him on a golden throne."

"Humph."

The prince wanted to throw back his head and howl his anger, his fear, but he knew he couldn't. She was watching him. He had to stay in control, had to figure a way out of this. "Very well. You're right, I was arrogant. I wanted to flatten him with my power. I should have known it was too easy. I should have known he had some complexity in him."

She said, "Good. You finally admit it. That gold crown, though, it was really quite mag-nificent. Do you know, prince, your arrogance is something so deep inside you that you cannot control it."

"I can control anything, dammit. Maybe I was arrogant on purpose."

"Whatever the reason, it doesn't matter. We are in this together."

"Stop arguing with me. It does no good. We will get out of here."

Brecia knew no one could see them because now that he had his wand, the prince could keep both of them invisible from everyone, Mawdoor included. Unless the prince got distracted—in which case they would suddenly appear and everyone would be able to see them.

"Prince, we are invisible."

"Yes."

"But I can't see any of the old mortals. I don't see anyone at all. Oh, God, the heat. It's getting hot! What's happening?"

Then she knew what was happening to him. She grabbed his hands, cupped them in both of hers. They were suddenly visible. No matter. She had to stop this.

The prince's golden cloak was glistening strangely—no, now she saw the shadow of glowing flames billowing behind the rich golden cloth. The cloak was shimmering in the still air, and it was giving up great blasts of heat. The golden crown was gone, as was his wizard cap. If he still wore it, it would probably be burning on his head.

"Stop!" she yelled right in his face. "You must be calm, prince. You are turning this space into a fire." She dropped his hands and slapped him, hard. Once, then again, and a third time. "Get hold of your rage! Listen to me. You must quiet down or we will die. We can figure this out."

He quivered where he stood. He gulped in great quantities of air. He forced himself to step back from the edge. The heat grew less. His cloak hung loose again, cool to the touch. The air calmed, cooled.

"I'm sorry," he said. "I'm very sorry I lost control like that."

"I probably would have lost control if you hadn't," she said, and lightly touched her fingertips to his sleeve. "We must find a way out of this bubble."

They moved about their invisible prison, probing for weaknesses, plying their wands, but they could find nothing. The prince spoke incantations, old ones from before the early fires, chants so old they made her skin skitter with cold. Nothing happened. He fell silent. He looked at her.

It was her turn. She spoke every old incantation she knew, searched out ancient spells and balms, but nothing worked. The air didn't move. They were still trapped.

Brecia watched his golden cloak fade into nothingness, and he was again garbed as he had been, in a tunic and leggings, clothes any mortal would wear.

She waited, but he fell silent again, and she knew he was not happy with his thoughts.

She said, "I want to try something." She raised her wand, spoke softly, and there it was, her beautiful green cloak, inside the space with them. "I did it. I called the cloak, but I wasn't sure it could come through the bubble."

He said slowly, testing yet again the space that seemed clear as the open air but wasn't, "Your cloak is filled with ancient magic, woven in through the millennia." He ruminated on that a moment, then said, "There is something to this, Brecia. That was well done. A weakness, there is a weakness in this prison, and we must find a way to use it before Mawdoor burns us to ashes."

"He doesn't want to burn me to ashes, just you. He wants to wed me."

"That seems to please you."

She just shook her head at him, ignoring him, something he wasn't at all used to. She was evidently thinking about something more important than his words to her. Before he could tell her what he thought they should do, she said, "His eyes, he'd done something to his eyes. That green—it was like an emerald with the life leached out of it."

"Aye," the prince said. "That is something I have never tried. My father told me that if you changed your eyes, all that you saw changed as well. Thus what you saw was either an illusion or it was real. You wouldn't know which and that would lead you to make mistakes."

"Do you think that is the reason he couldn't sense you? He'd changed his eyes and they didn't see what they should have seen?"

"It makes sense. Do you want to live in that black tower?"

She actually shuddered. "I would never

stop fighting to get out of that black fortress of his."

He snorted at that. "Good. You have some sense, at least enough for a witch. Don't forget, though, that you're here with me, and you know what that could mean."

"Aye, ashes to ashes, both of us."

"That didn't amuse me at all. Now, the cloak you brought in here to you. I want you to try to send it back out."

Brecia drew in a deep breath. She cleared her mind as she'd been taught by her mother, her mother's mother, and all the ghosts who had lived with all of them.

Then it became clear to her. They were inside a small hole of space, a bubble, although it wasn't round. Rather, it stretched upward to curve over the highest point of Mawdoor's black fortress. Now that she saw their prison, she began her search. Time passed. She found nothing.

"I can see our prison," she said.

"Send your cloak through. Watch where it goes."

She raised her wand, closed her eyes just a moment, and her cloak was gone.

He said, "Now call it back."

She did. Her cloak fell into her hands. "But

it just seemed to appear. I can't find a weakness, a seam, nothing. It seems impenetrable."

The prince sniffed the airless air. "It makes no sense. I have decided what we must do, Brecia. There is no choice. Mawdoor could destroy us at his whim. We must risk it." He drew a deep breath. "You will touch the tip of your wand to mine."

She whirled around, appalled. "Oh, no, we cannot do that. I have heard it could destroy the earth, it could bind me to you forever."

"There are certainly worse things than being bound to me."

"Of course there are worse things, you fool. That is just the beginning of the things it could do to us. I have also heard it could make us mortal. No, we cannot take the chance."

"All old witch's tales. Wizards never take any of that nonsense seriously. End of the world? That is absurd, Brecia. Make us mortal? Beyond absurd."

"What about binding me to you?"

"Ah, now that doesn't seem at all absurd. Enough, Brecia. I don't know how much time we have left to us. I know to my very core that it would give us the power to break through this ridiculous bubble."

She thought about it, hard.

"You're carrying on like a witch looped in her own curses."

"Stop with your infernal insults against witches. Without a witch you wouldn't exist, you miserable fool who got us trapped in this wretched invisible bubble."

"I think it is more of a dome. Look at the shape. Listen to me. If you were alone, he would force you to mate with him. At least since I am here, you have a chance to escape him. We won't know what happens when wands touch until we do it."

"No, not yet. There has to be another way."

He was silent. He let the idea slide away. She was right, it was a huge risk. There had to be another way. But the curved dome over their heads seemed impenetrable. He touched his palm to it and kept it there as he rose, tracing its outline until it curved high over his head and began to curve downward again.

A perfect dome, seamless. He stayed at the highest point of the dome, and touched his fingertips to it again. He felt it pulse, but it wasn't warm. He pressed his palm hard against it and felt it turn icy cold. Nothing there, he thought, there was really nothing at all there. Now he could see the gray-beards far below going about their tasks. But they hadn't seen them before. What had happened? Couldn't Mawdoor hold the illusion together?

He called out. They didn't hear him. What had he expected, anyway?

If he and Brecia couldn't get out of this miserable fortress, then it made sense that the old people couldn't get in, either. They probably didn't even realize they were here.

He came back down to stand in front of Brecia. "Let me ask you a question. Why are there no young people here? No animals?"

"You said he sucked the hope out of people."

"I was guessing. What do you think?"

"Perhaps Mawdoor fears them."

"Why?"

She shrugged as she fingered her beautiful cloak. "The young are vibrant. They believe themselves invincible, and that is indeed what saves them many times from catastrophe. Mayhap the young keep Mawdoor from using his full powers because in some way they drain him. I am not at all certain about that, prince; don't think that I am."

He thought about it. "I wonder if I can make some changes down there at Penwyth."

"Prince," she said, seeing that he'd retreated deep inside his head, where the most ancient curses and chants and incantations resided—wizard's curses, ancient gods' curses—all wanting to burst into this world and wreak havoc. "Prince, listen to me," she said, drawing him back to her. "I have an idea. Focus your mind and your wand on this one spot. I will do the same. Let us just see what we can do with our combined powers."

The prince looked at her, frowned, then forced calm to flow over him, through him. "Maybe," he said. "Maybe." He didn't hold out much hope, but who knew? He looked at the exact spot, stroked his fingers over his wand, speaking to it in its own tongue with his mind, and then he pointed it directly at the same spot to which Brecia's wand pointed.

Nothing happened. Brecia wanted to yell with the failure, but then, suddenly, the air itself began to tremble. Her wand shook in her hand. It took both hands to hold it steady. It grew cold, becoming colder still with each passing second. It was if they'd somehow managed to open the doors to the ice world that was far to the north. "Keep your thoughts right here," she said. "Keep pointing, right there, that's it."

Wind whistled, tangling their hair about their heads. The bubble began to tremble with the power that blasted against it. The invisible point at which their wands pointed began to breathe. They could hear it, like a giant breathing fast, then faster still, then suddenly there was utter silence. It was if they were held suspended.

Next came incredible grinding sounds, as if an underground mountain were being shoved up through the earth by a giant's magic fist.

They heard a loud crack, then flames shot up around them, hot flames, coming close, closer still. The prince yelled, "Hold steady, Brecia. Hold steady."

But her wand was on fire, so hot she could see her fingers turning black. "By the sacred ancient mother of the oaks," she whispered, but she held on because she had no choice; she held on despite the awful pain, the smell of her own flesh burning. His hands weren't burning. She saw that his eyes were steady on the point of power, and she redoubled her concentration despite the pain. Why weren't his fingers burning like hers were?

It wouldn't be long now. She knew the pain was going to kill her, burn her to ashes. No, no, she had to concentrate, she had to send all her power to the tip of her wand, hold steady—hold steady.

Suddenly the bubble burst outward, flinging flames high into the sky overhead, as far as the eye could see. There was the sound of crashing glass, and it was everywhere. Shards flew up around the flames, merging together to encase the flames, and flame funnels flew so high into the air, they met the clouds. The prince and Brecia waited, not moving. No broken glass fell back down into the courtyard. Nothing at all fell back down. The flames seemed to snake through the clouds. Brecia could have sworn she heard a hissing sound, like water poured on a fire. The funnels disappeared.

The prince saw that Brecia was lying on the ground, unconscious. And her hands—

by all the gods—her hands were still burning. He didn't think, just touched the tip of his wand to hers, now lying on the ground beside her.

From one instant to the next, they were no longer in that wretched courtyard, they were lying on their backs on a deserted beach, as if flung there by an invisible slingshot. How far away their wands had sent them, he didn't know. At the moment it didn't seem all that important.

They were free.

Brecia's beautiful green cloak was lying on the warm sand next to her, smoldering, the wondrous fine-woven material blackened, tattered, as if torn into strips by an animal's claws. It was ruined.

She awoke to see her cloak burning. Incredibly, it was her cloak that got her attention, not her burning hands. She began scooping up sand and throwing it on the cloak to bury the flames. "Oh, no, oh, no."

He couldn't stop her. He looked at her cloak, wished it whole, but nothing happened. He wished it whole with all his being, directing it through his wand. Nothing happened. The cloak continued to smolder sullenly.

He didn't understand; whatever was burning the cloak was beyond him. He said, "Brecia, leave go. By all the gods, look at your hands."

She looked down at her outstretched hands, saw her blackened fingers, felt her skin peeling and bubbling, felt pain so deep, so foul and vicious, that she didn't think she could bear it.

"Don't snivel. I'm not going to let you die, you careless witch. I'm not going to let your hands burn off. Close your eyes and hold still, dammit."

He took her hands in both of his, saw that the fingers were raw, bent, so badly burned that they were curved like claws. He leaned down, kissed each of her fingers, touching his tongue to her burned flesh. He kissed each one again, his tongue cool on her flesh. And yet again.

The pain was gone. Her fingers were white again, whole. She was crying silently from the awful pain, tears running down her cheeks and dripping off her chin. He touched his fingertips to her eyes, and the tears fell onto his hands. He turned his hands over, cupped them, and let her tears flow. When his hands were filled with her tears, he looked at her smoldering cloak and whispered two ancient words that he'd never spoken before. *"Blashen norna."*

He opened his hands and let the drops of water fall onto the cloak. Nothing happened. He said nothing more, merely looked at the cloak lying there on the ground, burning sluggishly. Then he smiled, lifted her right hand and touched it to the cloak.

The cloak became brilliantly clean and fresh again. There was no sign of fire, no smell of burnt fabric. It was exactly as it once had been. She sucked in her breath, and he felt her joy, her bewilderment, and he smiled at her even as the cloak came around her shoulders. He made a cup again with his right hand, flicked his fingers, and the hood came over her head.

"You saved me. How did you do it?"

She heard his unspoken words in her mind: *My father is a great wizard. I am a greater wizard, and you and I will birth a wizard who will be known throughout the ages, for all time, forever and beyond.*

She stared down at her hands, flexed her fingers, felt the smoothness of her flesh, felt the blood flowing easily. It was as if she'd never been burned. Her cloak was soft and warm around her shoulders.

"We're sitting on a beach." She tasted the salty air, inhaled it deeply.

The prince came to his feet and stretched. She wondered if he was testing all his parts, making certain that he'd not left anything of himself at Mawdoor's fortress.

"I touched our wands together once more. This is where they sent us. I'm very pleased you're all right, Brecia."

She had no choice, and it didn't seem at all difficult to say. "I thank you, prince."

"I believe it is time we left Penwyth—aye, we're still close to the fortress, I recognize this beach at the western end of Penwyth— before Mawdoor finds us and thinks of another challenge."

He took her hand and pulled her quickly up and against him. She felt her cloak spreading out, as if under a spell, enclosing him against her, making them one, and then they were gone from the beach, gone from Penwyth. Only an instant passed, she knew it, felt it, but still it seemed a very long time before her feet were on solid ground and she knew herself to be home.

He'd actually brought her home, despite

being close to Penwyth and Mawdoor. She breathed in the very being of her oak forest, felt it comfort her, enclose her.

They were still pressed together inside her cloak. She said against his throat, "We're home," she said.

"Yes," he said, and she felt his mouth against her temple. "I brought you home."

23

They stood at the edge of the dark, ancient oak forest and felt the brilliant noonday sun, full and hot overhead, beating down on their faces. "It doesn't seem that any time has passed," she said.

"Time has passed," he said. "It is another day."

He started to say something else, but stopped when they saw seven travelers, four men and three women, some walking, some riding mules, coming toward them.

Mortals.

An older man walked at the head of the small group, a gnarly stick in his hand. He saw them, stopped, leaned on his big stick, and said, "We saw you coming from the dark forest. There's danger in there, you know. Are you all right?"

The prince, Brecia realized, was garbed just like the mortals, as was she. She hadn't noticed that he'd whisked away her white robe. She looked down at the long green woolen gown, at the soft leather slippers on her feet. She fingered the delicate gold chain at her waist. He hadn't done away with that.

"Oh, aye," the prince said to the man, nodding to the rest of the travelers. "There is nothing in that forest save very old trees that block out the sunlight, nothing menacing."

The man said, "My name is Branneck, and these are my people. We are traveling to the plain to see the sacred stone circle."

"You are a religious group, sir?" Brecia asked, aware that the women riding the mules were all studying her. Why? She fingered the gold chain at her waist. The women's eyes followed her fingers. They wanted her gold belt. Why couldn't the prince have put a leather belt around her waist?

"Aye," Branneck said. "We come from

Caledonia, to pour the Loch Ness monster's tears on the stones."

There was no end to human foolishness, the prince thought. He smiled at them and said, "My wife and I are returning home. We spent a week deep in the oak forest. It is said a woman will conceive a child if she is taken standing up, her back against one of the ancient oak trees."

"Ah," Branneck said, staring now at Brecia, at her golden belt. "That is an interesting notion. Think you that you are now with child?"

Brecia closed the distance to the prince's side. She took his arm and leaned into him, smiling up at him. "Mayhap I could be with child if only my husband could have brought himself to a proper size to accomplish it."

The seven men and women stared at her. The men blinked, looked toward the prince to see if he would cuff this disrespectful woman, but the prince threw back his head and laughed.

Branneck said, his fingers tightening around his walking stick, "It seems that you are alone."

"One wants to be alone when one is bent on impregnating one's wife," the prince said.

Then he withdrew a golden disk from beneath his tunic, a beautiful creation fashioned during the time of the Romans, and set it just so that it gleamed beneath the brilliant sun. Brecia wondered if he'd gone mad. The men were eyeing that gold disk just as the women were eyeing her golden chain.

Branneck smiled, all complacent and confident, nodded to the men, and raised his stick. He ran at the prince and brought the stick down to crack open his head. The other men were on the prince in the next moment. Brecia eyed the women, who were smiling, watching the four men against one.

Brecia called out, "Attacking a single man amuses you?"

"Shut yer mouth," one of the women said. "Else we'll let the men plow you until it is certain you do conceive."

Brecia turned to watch the prince. He'd blocked Branneck's stick with his arm and shoved the man back onto the ground. The other three men had closed in on him, and were ready to kill and rob him. His life meant nothing to them, save a few coins in their pockets.

"Brecia," the prince said, "would you like to deal with these kind fellows or shall I?"

"It will be my pleasure to watch you," she said. She expected the prince to blink them into oblivion or dash them into a pile of small black stones, each one's arms and legs inseparable from the other's, but he didn't do either. He watched them as would a mortal man, bent forward, hands extended, and he said, "Come here, my brave fellows. Let me how you how a real man treats scum like you."

She realized then that he had made himself a vulnerable mortal man. He'd blanked out his wizard skills. Did he believe himself so beyond mortals? He had run mad. She felt a sharp hit of fear. Why was he doing this? She nearly yelled at him, then stopped herself. No, he was strong, well made. He could protect himself, just as a mortal man would.

One of the men yelled in rage as he rushed forward, motioning the other two to come at the prince from the side. The man Branneck, whom he'd knocked on the ground, was on his feet again, moving around behind the prince.

One of the men ran forward swinging his stick at the prince's head. The prince laughed, grabbed the man's stick and swung it in a full circle, striking the other three men in their bellies. There were cries and curses, and a moan from a fellow who now had a broken rib.

The women were getting worried. One of them yelled, "Branneck, bring him down, stab him in the back! I want the woman's golden belt. Do it!"

Brecia walked to the woman, grabbed her arm, and pulled her off the mule's back. The woman shrieked as she fell to the ground at Brecia's feet. The woman cursed even as she flew at her, her fingers curved like talons, her fingernails aimed at Brecia's eyes and face.

Before Brecia could react, the prince picked up one of the moaning men and threw him at the woman. They went down together.

The men looked at Branneck, nodded. Each of them drew a knife, long and sharp, and it was obvious they knew how to use them, had used them often. The prince merely laughed again and said, "What will you do with those, lads? Do you want to feel them dig into your ribs? Then come here, and let me assist you to your mortal sinners' hell."

Branneck hung back, not rushing forward in rage with the other three men. The prince clouted each of them, a fist to the side of the head, a fist to the belly, a knee to the groin of the unluckiest. He had turned to smile at Brecia, preening, very pleased with himself, when Branneck, silent as a cat streaking through the oak forest beneath a full moon, crept up behind him. Brecia didn't think, she just shouted, "Behind you!"

The prince turned, but he was too late. Branneck's knife stabbed him in the chest. Branneck jerked the blade out and stood back, panting. "Now you can die, you devil."

Brecia couldn't believe it, she just couldn't. Because the prince was enjoying himself playing at mortal games, she'd let him have his way. But it had gone wrong, terribly wrong. Now it was too late, too late. The women were coming at her, the men rising, coming with them.

". . . teach the bitch a lesson."

". . . plow her belly."

". . . aye, give her the blade too."

Branneck said, "I want that gold chain she's wearing."

The prince was lying on his back, his eyes closed.

"You miserable fools!" Brecia slipped her wand out of her sleeve, screamed words she'd scarce ever spoken in her life, and pointed at each of them. They were all suddenly on the ground, hands and feet tied. As for Branneck, she sent him straight up into the air. "You will stay there for all to see," she said. "Forever."

She heard him screaming even as she knelt over the prince, covered both of them with her cloak, closed her eyes over the awful fear, and whisked them back into the oak forest.

"Don't you dare die, damn you," she said over and over. He was quiet, too quiet, and now he lay on her bed inside her fortress, his blood flowing over his tunic, staining it deep red, the blood of a man mortally wounded.

Callas was at her side in an instant. "Move, mistress. He might try to kill you."

"Go away, Callas. He isn't my enemy. By the gods, what do I do?"

The prince opened his eyes and looked up at her. "Brecia," he said. "I didn't make a very good mortal, did I?"

"You were a splendid mortal," she said,

"but there were four of them and they were bent on killing you. Hush now."

But he wasn't a mortal, and that was the point. She nodded herself back into her long white woolen gown.

"Tell me what to do."

"There is nothing," he said. "I was a fool. I'm very sorry. I don't want to leave you. I wanted to impregnate you."

"You're saying you can't fix yourself? What sort of wizard are you, prince? Damn you, do something! Tell me what to do!"

His eyes closed, and that ironic smile fell from his mouth. She knew in that moment that he was dying. He was dying as a mortal man would die because as a mortal man he'd been stabbed in his heart.

"NO!"

She stretched out her full length over him. She felt his blood seeping into her gown. She felt his heartbeat, slow, faint.

She closed her eyes and stretched herself so that her arms covered his arms, her legs covered his legs, her heart pressed against his heart.

She closed her mouth over his mouth, breathed in his breath. "You will not die," she said into his mouth. "Do you hear me, you pathetic wizard? Where is your magic? Damn you to beyond—shuck off the mortal's skin and heal yourself!"

She felt his pain, pulsing up now, coming through her gown, coming from the deepest part of his heart where the blade had entered and torn. She began to shake with the pain as it grew and grew, pouring itself into her, digging into her very being, hard, stabbing deep. Her eyes rolled back in her head as she felt the knife blade sinking into her, felt her own blood explode around the blade, felt the icy cold of the blade's tip vibrating, the death bringer. Then she felt the blood— his blood, her blood—begin to seep out of her chest.

She held on, closed her eyes and kept the pain deep and close, not making a sound. She whispered against his mouth, "Prince, you will not die. Give me your pain, all of it."

"No, Brecia," he said, and she heard the death sound in his throat. "I was a fool, I wanted to prance about like a mortal man, and now I will die, but I will not allow you to die with me. No, Brecia." With incredible strength, he threw her off him. She landed at least six feet away, rolling onto the floor. The soul-deep pain was suddenly gone.

He lurched up onto his elbow, looked at her. "I didn't mean this to happen," he said, and fell back. "I wanted to amuse you, fight those ridiculous men, make you laugh."

"You will not die, damn you!" She shouted his name, surrounding it with every curse she knew, screamed it to the roof of her fortress, as she leapt back up and threw herself on top of him again. His chest against her chest, her arms against his arms, her legs against his legs, his bleeding heart now bleeding into her heart.

She held him down with her strongest spell, pressing her forehead against his. The pain grew and grew. She didn't know such pain could exist. It was beyond the pain of her burning hands, beyond anything she could have imagined. She heard Callas screaming at her, telling her to leave the miserable wizard to the fates.

She felt the prince trying to throw her off again, but he was weakening. Her spell was holding, and she was too strong for him. She realized that she could easily die as well.

It didn't matter.

She pressed harder and moaned her pain against his forehead. She felt his breath whisper against her flesh. "Get off me, Brecia, it's no good. It is my fate." He knew in his wizard's soul that no one could change fate.

Brecia didn't waste time worrying about fate. She prayed to her mother, to her mother's mother, to all the long line of witches who had come before her, who had nurtured and taught her, and she cried, her tears falling on his closed eyes.

The pain was breaking her. It was beyond a mortal's pain, beyond a witch's pain. It was a shared pain, a final pain, and it would break her.

She didn't know how, but she managed to hold on. She felt the last of her own blood flowing into his now, and then, suddenly, she felt empty, a husk that meant nothing anymore. She was above that husk, looking down and wondering what was wrong.

Then she sighed softly and laid her cheek against his cheek. She was falling, but he was with her. It seemed they were falling into a deep hole and it was black and warm in that hole. She wondered vaguely if they would ever stop falling and what would happen if they did.

24

Present

Bishop walked back to the front of the cave to see Merryn warming her hands over the small fire she'd made. He stood there watching her for a moment and thought how much like Brecia she looked.

No, no, she wasn't Brecia. Brecia was from long ago.

Bishop wondered how long he had been away. And he had been away, he knew that now, knew it to the soles of his boots.

"Merryn?" He started. His voice sounded

rusty, as if he hadn't spoken for a very long time.

She looked up, smiled just a bit. "Did you find anything in the back of the cave? What you were looking for, whatever that was?"

He shook his head. "How long was I gone?"

"Just a few minutes. You came back because you were hungry or because there was nothing for you to find?"

Only a few minutes? Longer, much longer. No, he didn't know. "I suppose there is some truth in both things," he said, and no longer knew what he was talking about. He rubbed his cheek where the hand had struck him.

"I have some bread that is stale, but I was going to put it on a stick over the fire. What do you think?"

"I should like that," he said, and realized he was starving. He also realized that his chest hurt, as if someone had punched him with his fist. He rubbed his hand over his chest, and the ache receded.

He watched her slice the remaining bread into thick slices and fix it to a stick. She began waving it close to the flames. She said, without looking up, "What have you been doing?"

"Nothing much," he said, and sat cross-legged beside her. "It is dark in the back of the cave. There's nothing there."

"You weren't gone long enough to see everything, surely."

"No," he said, taking a toasted slice of bread off the stick she was pointing at him. "Just a few minutes."

"Fearless whinnied while you were gone. I looked outside but didn't see anyone."

"I will look again after I've eaten this delicious bread. This was a very good idea, Merryn." He wasn't about to tell her that he'd been pulled into a black hole by someone who'd laughed and then slapped him. And then—As he chewed on the toast, he closed his eyes, and there was Brecia, lying on top of him, trying to save him, killing herself in the process, and he felt what the prince had felt, anger at himself for his foolishness, his failure, his anguish that he would die and never have Brecia.

But it all happened in his head. He had no death wound. He'd been gone but a few minutes. A dream—it had been some sort of dream that they'd wanted him to relive.

Why? So that he would know they were real, that he would accept them? Why?

The curse. It always came back to the curse.

He calmed himself. They would show him what must be done. He ate more of the delicious toast. Whatever was, whatever had been—it was fading quickly from his mind, from his memory.

Merryn said as she pulled a burned bit off her own toasted bread, "You said you had to come here, that it has something to do with the curse. I don't understand that. You said you didn't find anything. What will you do now?"

He kept chewing on his toast, looking directly into Merryn's small fire. He said, "This is the origin of the curse." He frowned. "Or this is where the curse has to end. I don't know yet." He had no intention of telling Merryn that someone had slapped him hard and laughed when he'd leaned over that black hole, and pulled him into a long ago death scene.

She said, "But you don't know what you're supposed to find here? What you're supposed to do here?"

He shook his head. "I feel like a blind

man." But he was no longer scared. The dreams that weren't dreams—they'd made him a part of them, made him feel them.

He shook his head and ate the final piece of bread.

"What are you going to do now, Bishop?"

He looked at Merryn's hair, the red dulled in the dim cave light. It was braided tightly around her head, not long and flowing down her back with white ribbons. "I don't know," he said. "I just know that we must be here. All of it happened so long ago."

"What happened so long ago?"

He hadn't realized he'd spoken aloud. "Many things," he said, "were long ago." He watched her apportion the remaining strips of salted herring. His pile, he saw, was three times larger than hers. She was humming softly under her breath. A lock of red hair had come out of the tight braid and was curling lazily around her breast. Without warning, he felt a bolt of lust that nearly stopped his breath in his chest. Overwhelming lust, such lust as he'd never felt in his life, not like this, like thunder striking him, pounding into him, prodding him, sending him into madness. It was too much, this lust. He had to have her. He had to have her now. He saw the prince, he saw Brecia. "Now. I want you now."

She dropped her small pile of herring into the fire, stared at him, and saw something that scared her to her toes. "Oh, no!" she said. "Look what you've made me do, Bishop. Stop what you're thinking and help me." She was leaning over the fire, trying to pull the separate strips out of the flickering flames and ashes, but it was no good.

"Take mine, I don't care, but first, I have to have you, Merryn. Now."

"What's wrong with you? You eat toasted bread and suddenly you're overcome with lust? How could you want me? You wanted me before and then you pulled away. Admit it, you don't really want me, you just want what I would bring you. What is different this time?"

How could he not want her? Oh, God, he wanted to come inside her and she wanted him to admit something? He liked the toasted bread. Hadn't he already told her that? He shook his head, but nothing was there except roaring lust and he simply couldn't control it, not now. He reached for her. To his surprise, she handed him a strip of the dried herring. He ate it, reached for her again, only to have her stick another strip into his mouth.

He said around the fish he was chewing, "I want to see you naked. I want your legs open wide. I want your hands on me, right now."

"You're not afraid that the curse will smite you?"

The curse? What utter nonsense. "Come here, Merryn. Take off that gown and come here."

Slowly, she came up onto her knees, then stood, hands on hips, looking down at him. "No," she said. "Go away, Bishop. Don't talk like this. I've never heard you talk like this. Your face is shadowed, but I can see that your eyes look strange. No, stay where you are. Go away!"

"I cannot do both." He saw her eyes nearly cross as he spoke those words, not bad words, with a bit of wit in them. He was the same, dammit. It was just the lust for her that was driving him over the edge. He heard the quick hitch in her breath before she turned on her heel and ran out of the cave.

"Merryn! Damn you, woman, come back here. It's dark, there are wild animals and—"

Of course she couldn't hear him. What was wrong with him? He was harder than the wall of the cave he'd been leaning against. He was pounding with need—no, he should be honest about it, he was drowning in his own lust, and it was pushing him and he knew he had to have her, knew that soon she would be his wife and so it wouldn't matter if he impregnated her. Wouldn't matter, wouldn't—God would surely forgive him.

He yelled her name over and over as he chased after her. He saw her running toward Fearless, who was looking at her, shaking his great head. No, she wouldn't steal his horse, would she?

He grabbed her leg just as she managed to swing up onto Fearless's broad back.

He jerked her hard and she fell against him. He held her close. Oh, God, it wasn't the first time he'd held her, felt her breasts against him, but now it was more. He wanted those breasts of hers naked, he wanted her flesh against his mouth. He wanted her long legs pressed against his, and he could feel every bit of her. He was breathing so hard he almost couldn't speak.

She was hitting him, his chest, his shoulders, and now she smacked her fist on his jaw. She didn't have any leverage, so it didn't hurt much. Not like those two slaps from the black hole. Actually, he didn't notice. Just the feel of her, her breath coming in gasps, fanning his face, and it was simply too much.

He finally realized that she was afraid of him. He'd shocked her, frightened her with his talk. He had to do something, he couldn't just throw her to the ground and take her. He grabbed her shoulders, shook her until her head fell back. He wanted to kiss that mouth of hers, but he yelled, "What is the matter with you? You will be my wife. There is nothing wrong with lying with me. It matters not that a priest hasn't yet blessed us. It will happen, Merryn. Stop fighting me. Don't be afraid. You're a strong girl, you shouldn't be afraid of anything. I just want to take you, surely you want that too, don't you? Can't you see how bad it is?"

"How bad what is?" she shouted in his face and slammed her fists against his chest.

Her words made no sense at all. He'd said his piece, and now it was time for him to take her. "Tell me you're not afraid anymore. Tell me you want me."

He was hard against her belly. He knew she could feel him clearly, the shape of him, the size of him, and he knew it scared her. It didn't matter, nothing mattered except getting between her legs. Now.

"Tell me."

She pressed her palms against the sides of his head, harder, until she got his attention, at least a bit of his attention. "Listen to me. You will be my husband for as long as I live, if the curse doesn't strike you down. Ah, that stupid, evil curse."

He kissed her. Merryn felt something really quite nice settling low in her belly. She cradled his face between her hands and kissed him back. The feelings were bolting through her belly again, spreading through her insides up into her breasts, and surely that was strange. And now she was having trouble breathing. Just because she felt his sex against her, shoving against her? Now his hands were on her hips and he was cupping her, raising her and pushing himself against her, and he didn't stop. And his kisses, she never wanted him to stop kissing her. His tongue pressed against her lips and she parted them. Her brain nearly stopped when his tongue touched hers.

She yelled, then slammed her mouth back against his for more. By all of Saint Jude's finger bones, it was too much, and yet not enough, not nearly enough. She didn't know what was happening, but she didn't want it to stop. In the small part of her brain that was still thinking, she realized she knew what men and women did to each other, and she'd always thought it was ridiculous, horribly embarrassing, surely an abomination to the woman. That part of him was harder than it had been just the moment before, and it was pushing against her, and she felt his length. He closed his arms around her and pulled her close, pressed her so tightly against him she was almost part of him. She wanted to get closer. It was overwhelming, this need to push and shove herself against him. And touch him. She wanted to touch him, even that part of him that was molding against her. She felt the pounding of his heart and it seemed to connect to her own heart and now she was panting and breathing hard, wanting, wanting.

"This is a wonderful thing," she said just before his mouth closed over hers again and he not only swallowed her words but took what they were deep inside him. She came up onto her toes, trying to get closer to him, yanking at his hair to bring his mouth down.

"Forget the curse," she said, and yelled again.

Bishop was pounding with lust. Dear God, her mouth, her breasts, all of her. It was too late. Nothing else mattered. He would have her, right now. He jerked her feet off the ground and carried her back into the cave, her arms around his neck, his mouth on hers. He stumbled over a rock and nearly went down. Since he was swimming in lust, it wouldn't have mattered. She was squirming against him. He couldn't stop kissing her, nor, it seemed, could she stop kissing him. She was his and now he would have her. She would be his wife.

He realized just before he came down over her, in some sane corner of his brain, that despite four husbands, she was innocent, she was a virgin, but even though he knew it, recognized what that meant, it simply made no difference. He had to have her, right now, not an instant from now. She didn't yell—this time she moaned.

He pressed her down upon her back and

jerked her gown up. He saw a stretch of white legs, shoved her shift out of the way and saw the red curls that covered her woman's mound. Oh, God. He nearly swallowed his tongue.

"You're mine," he said, freed himself of his trousers and came over her.

"Bishop?"

Her voice was a thread of a sound. He heard uncertainty in her voice. He forced his eyes away from her belly and looked into her eyes. "I don't want you to be afraid. I'll try to slow down, but I think it's too late, Merryn. I'm sorry." He bent her legs, spread them wide. He was hard and ready and he wanted his sex shoving inside her.

He sucked in his breath when suddenly she hit his elbows with the sides of her hands and he collapsed on top of her. He was too stunned to move. Then she grabbed his head, fisting her hands in his hair, and brought him down to her. She kissed any part of him she could reach—his ear, his jaw, the tip of his nose, his chin. "I'm not afraid now. Do you hear me?" He felt her naked against him, felt her heat or maybe it was his or both of theirs, and he wanted to explode, it was that close. No, he had to get

inside of her first, then he could die. He had
to—

"You're not afraid?"

"No," she whispered in his ear.

"Naked," he said into her mouth. "You're
naked and I want to come inside you, Merryn. Now. I must."

He tried to rear up again between her legs
so he could come into her, but she came up
with him, her arms wound around his neck,
holding as tightly as she could. He couldn't
free himself. She was kissing him again, all
over his face.

When his tongue was in her mouth, he
was saying, "Your hair is as red as the hair
on your head. I can feel you against me, and
it's making me—I've got to touch you, taste
you—"

She was whimpering, not understanding,
but she knew what she wanted—his tongue
in her mouth, his warm breath fanning her
hot flesh. And his heat—she wanted all that
wondrous heat on her, covering her, inside
her. His hands, they seemed to be everywhere and what parts of her they touched
made her frantic. She wasn't about to let him
go. She couldn't get enough of his mouth,

of his breath warming her to the soles of her leather slippers, one falling off her foot.

He was panting into her mouth. "I've got to come inside you now, I've got to. Don't you understand, Merryn? Now. I've got to or I'll spill my seed."

She felt him shoving frantically against her, but he couldn't come inside her unless she let him go. She wasn't about to do that, there was too much pleasure having him just where he was. His tongue, by all the gods' astounding miracles, his tongue, wet, probing, was the biggest miracle of all, and she didn't want it to stop.

"Kiss me, Bishop. Don't stop kissing me. That's what I want. Don't stop."

"I want to kiss your damned belly." He was shuddering, nipping at her bottom lip. "I want your breasts, I want—"

"All right, but if I don't like it will you kiss my mouth again?"

"You will like it, I swear." She let him go. He came up on his hands and knees over her, panting, looking down at her face, seeing how wild she was feeling, knowing she wanted him, but—

His hands pulled her thighs apart, and he was staring at her, and he couldn't help himself, it was just too late. He couldn't take the time to kiss her belly, to rub his cheek against her red hair. "Merryn," he said, "try to like this, all right?"

He clutched her legs, pulling her up, and yelled as he went into her, hard and fast. He heard her scream, felt her fists hitting his chest, his shoulders, but nothing mattered. He tore through her maidenhead, felt the wonder of it even as he pressed against her womb. Oh, God, her womb. He drew back, went into her again and again. He heard her shouting his name, trying to shove at him, but he didn't care. He felt himself explode, fly apart, felt himself scattered and free, and he was held there in her, part of her, as he found his release. He would have accepted death in that moment, because that was what it felt like. He'd been freed, released, and now he was floating, and he couldn't breathe because his heart was pounding out of his chest. His strength was gone. He fell on top of her, his head beside hers. And he felt a wonderful peace come over him. He felt immensely tired.

He didn't think she'd liked it. Damn.

Next time—next time he would make sure she yelled until she was hoarse.

In the next moment he was asleep.

25

Sometime Else

His brain began to clear. The pain was nothing now, just a heaviness in his chest, as if someone had punched him there with his fist, but Brecia—she was sprawled on top of him, not moving.

He felt a shock of fear so great he nearly yelled. No, she had to be all right. The fear scored his gut, his heart began to pound. He lifted his arms and wrapped them around her, squeezed her. She didn't move.

"Brecia."

He began stroking her back, up and

down, and he wondered how she'd managed to save him. It had been a mortal wound, delivered by a mortal into the chest of a wizard who had foolishly made himself mortal, and it had nearly killed him. Because he'd been arrogant, because he'd wanted to show Brecia how strong he was, how powerful, how the number of his enemies wouldn't matter. Mortal or wizard, it wouldn't matter. But it had. By all the powers that watched over stupid wizards, he should be dead, but he wasn't, and all because of a witch.

Brecia had saved him.

She didn't move. No, she couldn't have given her life for his. He wouldn't accept it. He held her tight against him and slowly turned until they were on their sides, their faces close. He eased his hand between them and pressed it against her breast. "Damn you, you brave witch, let your heart beat. Do you hear me, Brecia? I am tired of this. Let your heart beat!" He began pressing the heel of his palm against her heart, rhythmically, then stroking her and kissing her still mouth. "Open your eyes. You're supposed to want to survive, to fight to survive, you know that? To do something so stupid, it beleaguers a wizard's brain. Brecia, open your witch's eyes or I'll thrash you."

He felt her heart pound against his hand, and smiled. "All I had to do was threaten you and you obeyed me."

Her eyes opened. She was nearly cross-eyed, she was lying so close to him. "Get your hand off my breast, you dim-witted wizard."

"Why? Dim-witted, am I? Well, you have a point there. No, my hand stays here. You feel very good to me. Just a moment." He eased his hand inside her gown. His fingers touched her breast.

They also touched wetness.

He frowned, then shoved her onto her back and came over her. "What is wrong here? Why are you wet?" He jerked open the wool gown and saw that there was blood streaking over her white breasts, over her heart. Oh, God, she'd taken his wound into her. He'd known that, but seeing the blood, his blood and hers, mixed together on her white flesh, knowing the pain she must have endured, knowing she could have died and had been willing to, to save him, he couldn't bear it.

"You healed me." He pressed his palm against her breast. Her blood was drying even as his fingers pressed down hard. "Is there pain, Brecia?"

"Not so much now. Just a slight ache."

He pulled away from her and sat up. The blood had dried on her chest. As he looked at her, the blood began to fade, then it was gone and her flesh was white and pure again.

He said, "I'm alive. My blood is pulsing through me. I'm strong again, invulnerable. Never will I make myself mortal again."

"That was a smart thing you just said, prince."

He managed a smile. "I have never before heard of a witch saving a wizard."

"I haven't either." Her fingers closed around his wrist. "How do you feel, truly?"

"I am strong again. I am myself. Why?"

She sighed, dropped her fingers from his wrist. "I have always believed that a man or a wizard should die when he harms another, but not when he is arrogant, because he believes all the way to his big feet that he can overcome all odds. No, that is not such a bad thing. And your arrogance, prince, it is such a deep part of you. It pleases me."

He liked hearing that. "What did you do to those assassins?"

"I tangled them all together, arms around legs and legs around necks, all crisscrossed and wound through and about. As for that man, Branneck, I left him in the air, unable to fall to the ground, and he was howling. I don't know how long the spell will last. Perhaps if they free themselves, they'll be able to pull him down."

"They were from Mawdoor."

"Oh, yes," she said. "I believe he was testing for weakness. He didn't care about any of them. He probably believed you would simply kill them, but the way in which you did it, aye, he would have learned more about you, and perhaps he would have seen a weakness."

He started to say that he didn't have any weaknesses, and instead he sighed. "He found it."

"Aye, this time he did."

"If Mawdoor was watching what happened, then he saw that I was also a fool to challenge them as a mortal. Mayhap he believes me dead. It is very possible, you know. A wizard cannot follow you in here, can he? With his mind?"

Slowly she shook her head. "You came into my forest at great risk. I believe the sacred oaks flatten a wizard's powers, I suppose you could say, since they are my oaks, since they are filled with my own power. I am very well protected."

"Then I was smart to have Callas lead me to you."

"Aye, you were." She smiled at him, lightly touched her fingertips to his chest. "We both survived."

"Aye, through no skill of mine. I wanted to make you laugh, Brecia, to make you admire me. I wanted you to see how I could reduce those miserable sots to wallowing pigs, but I failed. Damn you, you saved my life."

"Touch me again," she said. "My breast."

If there was a wizard's heaven, he knew he was there. He couldn't believe what she'd just said. He looked down. Her breast was white, all the blood gone. He kissed her, took her nipple into his mouth. Ah, so warm, her warmth filled him. He raised his face, breathed in her flesh. She brought him back down to her. He said against her warm flesh, "No one has kissed you, Brecia?"

He'd said something, she knew that, but

what it was couldn't matter as the wild feelings crashed through her. She felt as though she could fly—she could even carry him whilst she flew. She wanted to shout, wanted him to kiss her until she was unconscious.

What was happening to her?

She'd never felt anything like this in her life.

Whatever they were, these feelings were pounding and digging at her, bringing near pain in her belly and her breasts, aching, making her want to gasp and laugh, and yell, all at the same time. And here he was, at his ease, stroking her so gently it could have been the wings of a hummingbird, not a wizard's fingers. What was wrong with him? Didn't he feel anything that she was feeling? Was he a block of oak?

She reared up and pushed him over onto his back. "Prince," she said, and began ripping off his clothes. He lay there, unblinking, wondering what was happening to her. Whatever it was, he wasn't about to do anything that would stop her from this incredible madness. Lust was turning his innards molten. Did a witch feel such lust? Evidently so.

In an instant she was naked, straddling

him, and he felt her belly pressing against his sex. She was rubbing her hands down his chest to his belly, and then she was moving down on him, sliding between his legs, and he knew this was going to be a close thing all around.

"Brecia, slow down. You must slow down. I am not like you, I—"

"No," she said, and closed her mouth around him. He rose six inches off her bed, her on top of him, and stayed there. He sucked the blue smoke close and breathed it in. It tasted like an aphrodisiac. He laid his hands on her.

He hadn't imagined anything like this. Then he didn't have any more time to imagine anything. She was clutching him between her hands now, and he was so hard he could have thrust through time itself. And then she was straddling him again and she was bringing him into her, slowly, and then she cried out and shoved down on him, taking him all the way to her womb.

The pain was something she hadn't known about. It was sharp, deep, and she screamed, but it wasn't just pain that sent her scream through the oak forest, it was mad joy and possession—her act of possession, of him, a wizard of her choice, a wizard whose blood she now shared. She was apart from him, driven by powers that had overwhelmed her.

He'd never before seen such lust, such incredible strength and intensity in either a woman or a witch. She wanted him and she was taking him.

The witch was taking him. The instant he thought it, he moaned deep in his throat. He grabbed her, brought her down to kiss her. She was frantic, kisses not enough, she was moving on him, and moaning, her witch's eyes wild and vague. She was pressing down on him, but he felt the power of his own lust lifting him even more until he could feel the sweep of sweet air on his naked back and buttocks. And he said, "Brecia, I will give you all that I can." He eased his fingers between their bodies, and found her. He stroked her, felt the softness of her, the frenzied desire, the explosion of her power, all mixed together and he wanted to weep that she was his and would remain his forever.

His fingers pressed, stroked, and pushed her closer to something she knew was there but didn't yet understand. The heel of his hand was pressing against her, his fingers dancing on her flesh, and his sex, probing deep inside her. She saw it all in her mind, felt every breath he took all the way to her soul. She stiffened over him, threw her head back and yelled to the heavens themselves. He watched her in that instant before he took his own release. By all the gods, it was fine. He held her close, knowing they were together in the madness, and then they both flew upward into the blue smoke, out of the fortress, and took wing into the skies above them.

When Brecia came to herself, she didn't know where they were—she just knew they weren't lying above her bed. She was on top of him, he was still inside her, and she was content.

He was kissing her ear, licking, nibbling at her earlobe. He said, his voice deep, almost an echo, "What you and I do, Brecia, it is only tricks and games. But this"—he squeezed her hard—"this is the magic, the madness."

"Where are we?"

He said after a moment, surprise in his voice, "I don't know." But then he did know, and he was pleased with himself, with his instincts.

"It doesn't matter. We can breathe and talk and it's warm. I can feel the warmth on my flesh."

She was still on top of him, lying flat now just as she had when she'd pressed her heart against his, taking the wound, the pain, the blood, into her. She leaned down and kissed his mouth.

"You could have died, you stupid witch."

Since she was kissing him, his words slurred into her mouth, and she bit his tongue. She said to him as she nipped his nose, his chin, "I see. So you would have let me die if I'd been the one hurt? You'd have done nothing?"

"I know spells, I know potions. I would have done something that would have saved you."

"That is a good thing to know."

He wrapped his arms around her, pulling her very tight against him. They were naked and he felt his seed on her belly and her legs. "You conceived my son," he said, and squeezed her again. A wizard's squeeze this time, and she yelped.

"Don't break my ribs, you fool."

"I, a fool? I was not the one who attacked you, Brecia. Actually, I would have gotten around to it, but I was still lying there, wondering if I would live or die and wanting to beat you for what you'd done. Hmmm. I have never known a woman to attack a man before."

"I don't know what came over me," she said, but there was pride in her voice and wickedness, and he smiled as he kissed her throat.

"Whatever came over you can come again and again." He lifted her so he could kiss her breasts. He breathed in deeply, licked her soft flesh, and pulled her tightly to him again. "Attack me, Brecia, whenever it pleases you to do so."

"All right," she said, and he felt her smile against his cheek. "There is only one thing that concerns me, prince. It would appear that you don't know much about dealing with mortal men. Just look what happened—one of them managed to stick a knife in your black heart. It just doesn't seem possible."

He said slowly, "It didn't seem possible to me either, until I realized that they weren't men, though they were mortals, vicious ones."

"What do you mean they weren't men?"

"I realized that Mawdoor gave them a bit of power by enhancing their skills beyond the ordinary, adding to their strength. He hoped it would be enough to kill me."

"Thank the ghosts that the power he gave them wasn't enough. Do you really believe you impregnated me, prince?"

She was on her elbows above him, and she was looking at his mouth. He smiled at her, touched his fingertips to her chin, the tip of her nose. "Aye, my child is in your womb. I will not be such a fool again. If there is to be a next time, *I* will be the one protecting *you,* Brecia."

She felt a sudden chill, or maybe it was a ruffle of wind through her hair, drying her sweat and his as well. "I don't like this," she said, sniffing the air. "I want to know where we are."

He didn't answer her. She stared down at him, realized he was still inside her, hard again. She could feel herself stretching around him. His breath was warm in her face, and he wanted her.

"We're in a cave," he said finally, yawned, and was even harder than just the moment before. "We're in my cave."

"Your cave? You have a cave? How could that be possible? Which cave is your cave? There are no caves in my oak forest."

"No, there are no caves in your forest. I suppose this is where I always felt safe when I was young. The cave isn't very deep, so there was never any fear of monsters or enemies hiding to come upon me and slay me. Aye," he said, "I somehow brought you here to my cave."

"It's warm, the air is warm. It smells sweet, like newly grown grass."

"Aye, all of that. I just brought you a breath of breeze. Did you feel it?"

"It dried our sweat. And you even brought blankets for us to lie on."

"Aye, I did. In your bed, if you will remember, once you began having your way with me, I never touched it. You brought me off your bed, Brecia, with your lust."

"Now that I think of it, I did think it was very easy to put my arms around your back," she said, and nipped his chin.

He was a wizard. He found no surprise in what he'd done without even focusing his mind on it. Truth be told, she hadn't thought of anything either. She'd known something was happening when her body had flown upward into the heavens, but she hadn't thought, hadn't begun to realize that even in his own lust his will had preempted hers. His will was the stronger.

She was suddenly afraid. He was the more powerful. To admit that to herself would be to admit to a lesser position. She hated that, and it frightened her. And now this. Had she really conceived, after just one joining? No, it wasn't possible, was it? When she returned to her oak forest, she would consult the old ghost who was blind but could see into the heart of an oak tree, into a streak of flame, into a witch's womb.

He was moving again inside her, hard, smooth, deep. "Brecia," he said into her mouth as he drew her down, "come with me again. We may end up this time back in your fortress. I will set my mind to it if you wish."

And it was his will that would take them back, not hers. She kissed him and forgot to worry, forgot to be afraid. Lust roared through her, making her ears ring. "Oh, yes," she whispered against his temple. "Oh, yes."

Present

Bishop awoke and wanted her again, so powerfully that his brain couldn't even focus on the specific words that possibly could convince her to let him have her, again.

He merely rolled on top of her, spread her legs, and came into her.

Her eyes snapped open. He was big and he was inside her body. She wasn't afraid; she wasn't even overly concerned. She knew to the soles of her bare feet that it would be different now. It was already beginning. He was part of her—such an incredible thing—a man inside your body. He was deep inside her, then pulling back, only to come in again.

She kissed his shoulder. He came up on his elbows.

"Merryn? I swear you will like this."

"I know," she said. "I think I'm already beginning to."

He kissed her, and each time he lifted his mouth off hers, he told her in great detail what he wanted to do to her. And as he spoke, his fingers slid over her belly to find her. She stared up at him. The wildness came over her so quickly, she didn't think, just screamed and screamed again.

She heard him over her, his breathing hard, fast, and then he wrapped his arms around her and rolled onto his back, bringing her over him, and he was still deep inside her, and she didn't want to scream now, just wanted to mayhap whisper how she felt, let it flow through her, and know that if she had to move she would die on the spot.

She lay on top of him, felt his hands moving down her back, onto her hips, and he was kneading her flesh, squeezing, pressing her down on him, and he said, "What do you think, Merryn? Did you enjoy me?"

"Oh, yes," she said. "Oh, yes." She sounded absurdly pleased with herself.

"Now, we must solve that damned curse so we can marry, because you have conceived my son."

That gave her back a modicum of strength, and she sat up on him. "Surely that isn't possible. How would you know such a thing? Surely men don't even think about that when they begin roaring and pounding."

"I just know. If you wish to speak about roaring and pounding, then think about the yells that came out of your mouth. You nearly deafened me with your pleasure."

He had a point there. She said, "You think you are that potent, my lord?"

He pulled her back down, kissed her mouth until she was mewling, little sounds that drove him to madness, and she was moving on him, and he knew she wanted him, again, and he was hard inside her, and once more it began.

"Surely all this can't be what is done." She was panting the words and he was drowning in lust, drowning in this seeming endless need for her.

"Oh, yes, this is just right. Trust me. Scream for me again, Merryn."

And she did. On the other hand, he yelled like a drunk warrior attacked by bandits. Merryn imagined just before she felt into an exhausted sleep, that after all this, she should be pregnant with at least three strapping sons.

She heard a laugh as she sank into sleep. Not a man's laugh, a woman's. Was it her? Her mouth wasn't moving, was it? But then the laugh was gone, and the air was still. She breathed in his scent, tasted the sweat of his shoulder, and smiled. She fell asleep with his heart pounding solid and steady against hers.

26

Bishop leaned over the black hole, waiting to be slapped again, waiting to hear that laugh again.

Nothing. There was no movement in the air, no sense that something else was near, something that he should understand, should be able to see, or sense, or at least feel.

He had a torch with him. He raised it high over the hole. He saw only blackness. He held it down in the hole. Nothing but darkness—no ladder, nothing.

He was ready to believe he was mad, when suddenly the torch went out with a

bang, as if someone had slammed it between two hands. Bishop was standing in
the pitch black. He took a step back and
stumbled over something. He landed on the
sand floor of the cave.

Then, just as suddenly, the torch flamed
up again, even though it was lying there in
the sand. It was burning as brightly as it had
been before those invisible hands had
slammed together. Invisible hands? He'd
surely been tossed into a witch's pot of madness. Aye, he'd been gaining in madness
since he first saw Penwyth. Slowly he eased
himself up, picked up the torch, and looked
at what he'd tripped over.

He saw a stick half buried in the sand. A
stick? Why hadn't he seen it before? Had he
knocked it free of the sand when he'd
tripped on it? It made sense, yet it didn't, not
at all. Fear nibbling around the edges of his
consciousness, Bishop studied the stick before he planted the torch in the sand, feeling
it sink down a good six inches—and surely
that was strange, for there was nothing beneath the sand save rock, was there? But it
didn't matter. He reached for the stick, gently shoved away the rest of the sand, and
lifted it.

His hand burned, suddenly, fiercely, as if he'd stuck it into a flame. He dropped the stick, rubbed his fingers, and just as suddenly the pain was gone. Without thinking, without pause, he reached out his right hand for it and lifted it. It was warm, that damned stick was warm against the skin of his hand. There was no burning, nothing but steady, pulsing warmth. It seemed that the stick was settling in, that it was made for his hand and no other's, and it fit his hand perfectly. It was perhaps a foot long, no longer. It felt like nothing he'd ever touched in his life. By all the saints' muttered prayers, he thought, he could tell it was old by the very feel of it. No, it wasn't just old—"old" was a word that didn't apply to it. No, it was beyond old, it was something from before anything a man could understand. He knew it, deep inside.

Nor was it just a simple stick, torn from a tree limb. He held it close to the torch. No, it was finely carved, indentations all around it where there had been stones, perhaps. Precious stones? He didn't know. He wasn't at all certain that it was wood. But it wasn't metal, he knew that. But then, what was it?

"Bishop?"

He looked up to see her standing not three feet away, watching him.

"Look, Merryn, I found it."

"What did you find?"

"My torch went out and I stumbled over it. It looks like a stick, but it's not. See, there were possibly precious stones worked into it." He reached toward her with it. "Tell me what you feel when you touch it."

Merryn reached out her hand.

"That's it, your right hand."

"Why?" she said as she took the stick.

"I don't know. I first picked it up with my left hand and it burned me. How does it feel to you?"

"Warm. The wood feels almost soft."

"Aye," he said. "That's it."

She sat down beside him, the stick still in her right hand. She touched it with the fingers of her left hand, and her fingers felt scalded, like she'd just dipped them in boiling water.

"Be careful. For whatever reason, it won't accept your left hand."

"I wonder what it is," she said, holding it so gently, as if it were something very precious, something very fragile.

"It's the reason I came here," he said, and in that instant he knew it was true.

"There's something strange at work here, isn't there, Bishop? Something we don't understand."

"Yes, and it has something to do with the damned curse. We will figure it out. It's why we're here."

Merryn stared at the stick, turning it in her right hand, feeling the warmth of it against her palm. It was so strange, so very strange. Then she said, "Once when I was a little girl, my grandfather showed me a drawing in a very old parchment. I'll never forget the drawing, it was so vivid, the inks so bright. It was so real, as if someone had pressed it there, an exact image of real life."

His heart began to pound slow, deep strokes. He sat forward, not touching the stick, but watching her turn it slowly on her palm, caress it. "Tell me," he said. "Tell me about the drawing."

"There were three old men, all with long gray beards, smooth, like they'd just been combed, coming nearly to their waists. All of them wore long white robes with lovely worked-leather belts, studded with gems. One of the old men held a stick like this, and the stick looked very new. It was shining and shooting off sparks, as if from a fire. He was pointing the stick outward as if at the person looking at the drawing. My grandfather leaned over my shoulder and said in his rolling, deep voice, "These are wizards, young Merryn, from long ago. The one in the middle, he is holding his wand."

"Was he holding the wand in his right hand?"

She closed her eyes, tried to remember that wonderful drawing. "Yes," she said after several moments. "He was."

"This is very interesting," Bishop said. "You think this is a wizard's wand? It's like the one in the drawing?"

"I don't know, Bishop, but you came here because something pushed you to come here. You found this stick. It must have something to do with the curse."

He said, still looking at that wand in her palm, "It wasn't on the ground when I came in here before. I am very certain of that."

She felt fear prickle her skin. "How can you be certain?"

"I just am. Now, the question is what to do with this—this wand."

She rolled it back and forth in her right

hand, and let the warmth of it sink into the sleeve of her gown, touch the skin of her forearm, warm it, and she felt good. Deep down, it made her feel very good.

He said, never looking away from the wand, "I know that Penwyth has stood where it stands now."

She looked at him, her head cocked to one side. "Not longer than a hundred years."

"Oh, no, Penwyth was there long before then. Aye, it was there, all right—not the castle, not the moat, something else—but it was there and it had that name."

"How do you know this?"

He started to say, *I was there,* then he realized how mad that sounded. But he saw it now. By all that was holy, he saw Mawdoor—saw himself as well, only he was the prince and Brecia was with him. He saw all of it very clearly. He looked at the wand in Merryn's right hand, and he saw it all even more clearly. He saw the flecks of gold in Brecia's eyes.

Bishop blinked, shook his head to clear it. He'd touched that wand, and now everything was as clear as if it had all occurred but moments ago. Was it the prince's wand? Brecia's wand? A witch's wand, not a wizard's?

"So very long ago," he said. "It all happened so very long ago."

"How do you know this, Bishop? Are you a wizard?"

"No, I'm not a wizard," he said and knew down to his bones that he wasn't, only—"but the past is coming through to me. Don't be afraid, Merryn. I'm not, at least not any-more."

She swallowed. "I'm not afraid."

He looked at her, that red hair of hers braided in a tight circle around her head, the green eyes, alert and dreamy at the same time. He looked at that wand in her right hand and felt a lurching in his heart.

She looked like Brecia, that witch who'd lived in a time far distant, the witch who'd mated with the prince. And just who was the prince?

He realized in that instant that he was glad she wasn't Brecia. Brecia was a very long time ago. Merryn was here, with him, right now. His seed was in her belly. He shuddered with the knowledge of it.

Bishop carefully took the wand from her in his right hand, and rose. He had to learn more.

He stood there, in the shadows, holding

that wand, the torch flame wreathing his face in darkness and a glowing red light, and he wasn't himself in that moment. She knew it, but she wasn't frightened. She sat staring up at him, wondering what was happening.

She watched him raise the stick high above his head. But surely the cave ceiling hadn't been that much higher than Bishop's head was. Surely. But now it seemed to go up and up, no ceiling at all in sight. And Bishop, he seemed somehow larger, shadows and light and the flame from the torch making him look like a demon called from the bowels of hell.

She said, her voice as thin as the grains of sand that fell through her fingers, "Bishop, come back."

The moment ended.

Bishop looked white. Slowly, he came down onto his knees. He gently laid the stick on a small stone ledge that protruded a few inches from the cave wall. That ledge had been there all along—it had to have been—she knew that, but now she saw that it was there because it held the wand. She reached out her hand to touch it, drew it back.

"I must think about this," Bishop said. He

raised his head and looked at Merryn, and she saw the blast of hunger in his eyes, eyes focused completely on her. It was the same lust she'd seen in him the night before, the utter loss of control. She picked up her skirts and ran.

Sometime Else

Brecia was brooding, worrying the golden chain at her waist as she brooded. She said, "Mawdoor sent those men. The women were with them because Mawdoor knew they would lull you, just in case."

"Aye, he did." The prince took another bite of a partridge leg, roasted to perfection over one of the ghost fires. He knew that her people were throughout the oak forest, close if they were needed. It was the ghosts who stayed in the courtyard, near their fires, and watched. She handed him a wooden bowl of soup, filled with carrots and cabbage and garden cress.

"Will you eat until the next full moon comes?"

He swallowed and smiled up at her. "You

exhausted me, Brecia. I am only a wizard. I must rebuild my strength."

She threw a plum at him, which he caught and brought to his mouth. "Ah, the smell. Sweet plums."

"We must beat him, prince. We cannot let him continue to terrorize the countryside. He might succeed in destroying you, maybe even in taking me."

"I am thinking about this, Brecia."

"No, you are not. You are thinking about me being naked. I know because just look at how you're licking that wretched plum."

He took a final lick, the final bite, and tossed the plum pip to her. "You should eat something as well," he said.

She took some sloe berries out of a beautiful old glass bowl that was filled with red and green shadows and popped them in her mouth as she paced back and forth in front of him. She stopped suddenly, in midstep.

"I know what to do," she said, and she drew in a big breath. "I know what we will do."

He suddenly heard a soft sibilant sound coming from outside. It was different levels of voices, and they were humming, in harmony. It was a gentle sound, and it pulsed through him.

"My ghosts," she said, her head cocked to the side, her incredible red hair falling halfway to the ground. "They are pleased. Isn't that strange? I believed they wanted me to remain as I was, but I was wrong. They are pleased with you, pleased with what has happened."

"Are they also pleased that my son grows within you?"

"Aye," she said, "they are."

He smiled, nodded. "Now will you tell me what you think we should do about Mawdoor?"

She ate some more sloe berries, then said, "We will leave at first light."

"Should I take off my clothes?"

"Why would you do that?"

"If you already know what we're to do to Mawdoor, then I don't have to think about it. I can have you again."

She whirled about, fisted her hands, then opened them with her fingers splayed in front of her face. She grinned at him through them.

He was naked.

She began to laugh when he realized that

he was sitting in the midst of huge platters of food—deer, squirrel, hedgehog, hare—wearing only his knife sheathed on his forearm.

"Replenish yourself first, prince. I can now judge how the meat improves you," she said, and laughed when he settled his perfect naked self cross-legged on the floor in the middle of all those platters of meat. He spent a few moments making his selection, then picked up a small bit of hedgehog. He never looked away from her face as he ate it. She looked at his strong, beautiful body and stepped toward him, such a powerful urge it was, and she didn't deny it. He gave her a slow smile—blinked once, then twice at her—and she too was naked. He made room for her between the woodcock and the quail.

"I'm a demanding wizard," he said. "You need to keep your strength up as well." He fed her, caressed her just as she was caressing him between bites, and the air was pungent with the smell of the blue smoke and the roasted meat rising above their heads.

And outside in the courtyard, the smell of sweet woodsmoke filling the air, the ghosts

sat by their small fires and sang their blessing, their sweet harmony rising and dipping,
floating through the branches of the oak
trees, and into a night that was warm and
soft, and all knew that no enemies were in
the oak forest that night.

27

Sometime Else

Mawdoor hadn't laughed so hard since the time fifteen years before when his vicious grandmother had granted him two wishes because he'd cut out the heart of one of her enemies. He would never forget the look on the old witch's face when his second wish was to have her walk into the sacred oak forest blindfolded, and stay there.

Aye, the look on her face had made him feel very clever indeed. He'd waited, his own cleverness pumping through him, to see what his grandmother would say. She hadn't said anything, nor had she gone into the forest. What she'd done was to cover his face with a soggy red rash for a full three months. Still, even with a face that brought scores of averted eyes, he'd believed it worth it.

Mawdoor was looking at the men he'd sent to kill the prince. They were all tangled together, one man's leg twisted through another's clasped hands, another man's head sticking between yet another's legs, eye level to his behind, and Mawdoor couldn't stop laughing. And Branneck—just look at Branneck, hanging there, as if by invisible cords from the heavens, screaming his head off, still holding the bloody knife that, Mawdoor hoped, had indeed slain the damned prince of Balanth.

Such a short time ago Mawdoor had been willing to live and let live, a philosophical stance he'd had no choice but to adopt when he realized it wouldn't be at all an easy thing to kill the prince of Balanth.

But all that had changed when he'd seen Brecia, that witch of the oak forest, who with one look made him as hard as the rune diamond that blinked like spun light, and whose symbols meant nothing he knew of.

And he'd found out very quickly that the prince wanted her too.

He wanted the prince dead.

And now Mawdoor knew that Brecia had taken the prince, alive or dead, to her fortress deep in the oak forest, a place he'd never seen. He'd only heard whispered tales about it in the deep of the night.

In hindsight, Mawdoor realized he should have given the men more than just a dash of power. As soon as he thought it, he dismissed it. No, that wouldn't ever be a smart thing to do. Mortals fast became monsters when given even the simplest of powers. All had seen over the years how mortals, given even a dash of a wizard's power, enthusiastically tried to tear the earth apart in a very short amount of time, and each other with it. Mortals were a distrustful, lame lot, worth about as much as demon piss.

Branneck hadn't stopped yelling that he'd stabbed the prince in the chest—killed the arrogant bastard—until Mawdoor had taken that same knife and stuck it cleanly through the man's neck, just to shut him up. And since it wasn't smart to leave people around who very possibly had failed in their mission, he killed the other three men as well.

Before Mawdoor killed him, Branneck had sworn that the prince couldn't have survived the knife stuck in his chest, that Mawdoor's magic poison that Branneck had pierced deep into the prince's chest had to have done the trick. He claimed that damned woman had tangled them all up and hung him in the air as if he were naught but a buzzing fly. And as for the damned women, they'd been no help at all. They'd just stood there pointing and laughing. One of them had even waved her fingers at Brecia, as if in thanks. If he could have, Branneck would have slain all three of them himself.

Had she somehow managed to save the prince? Mawdoor stood there, rubbing his hand over his jaw as he looked at the dead mortals, knowing in his gut that this was a witch's work, not a wizard's.

Mawdoor took the three women to Penwyth and gave them to the old men, who unfortunately had no memory of what to do with the splendid gift, but knew they should be pleased. They'd sighed, knowing there had to be some memory of pleasure in their ancient brains.

By nightfall, the old sots were waiting hand and foot on the women, out of breath with all the demands but relentlessly eager. The old women watched and laughed. The young women preened and demanded endless favors.

As for Mawdoor, he realized he would have to wait to learn if the prince was dead. He couldn't enter the oak forest. He knew in his wizard's bones that very bad things would happen to him if he tried. Everyone knew about the ghosts, the ancient ones who had gone beyond, yet who had elected to remain in the forest. Mawdoor wondered if the ghosts knew what became of those who decided not to remain deep within the forest when their time ran out.

It was said that most ghosts remained because all knew that they drew strength from the soul of the trees that encircled them, drew their haunting songs from the rustle of the oak leaves in a light night breeze, drew their substance from the rays of the moon that speared through the leaves onto the forest floor.

And they protected Brecia, even from a powerful wizard who had wanted her since— it had only been one spring ago, he remembered, at the sacred meeting stones. Odd how it seemed longer. He'd listened to stories of when she'd been just a small witch, unsure of her powers, learning from the ghosts, learning from the very powers that resided in the great stone circle on the plain of southern Britain. And she'd turned a local chieftain who'd murdered a child who happened to wander into his path into a two-headed goat—a female goat who had been milked for the next ten years. All laughed at that story, he as well.

And then he'd seen her. She wasn't a small witch anymore.

He bellowed out several full-bodied curses, and it made him feel better. *The prince.* The bastard had to be dead. He realized he didn't even know the prince's real name. Anyone who spoke of him simply said "prince," and they said it with admiration, with liking, with awe, and with fear. When the prince had been newly born, his mother standing over him, she had said to Mawdoor, "Ah, say hello to my little prince, Mawdoor. Is he not perfect?"

And Mawdoor had looked down at that wizard scrap and hated him to the depths of his soul. Aye, and now the prince was treated with great respect, and that was perhaps the worst of it. It grated in his belly.

Mawdoor of Penwyth—now his was a good name, a solid name, one that would carry on far into the future. Mawdoor, the name given him by his mother, a witch of excellent parts, not his father, who'd been a rank and dangerous demon, he'd been told often by his teachers, a demon whose teeth were always wet with human blood. He himself didn't care for human blood, and truth be told, that relieved him. His father had come to a bad end. Aye, thankfully, he was more like his witch mother—powerful, determined, and patient.

He would wait now. In truth, he could do nothing else. If the prince were indeed dead from Branneck's knife, would Brecia know it was he who had paid the assassins to kill him? If she did know, what would she do? Did she love the prince?

No, he would never accept that, never. Brecia was fated for him and him alone. He had to prepare his fortress for her. Penwyth was waiting to enfold her in its great seamless darkness, and he would keep her here with him, breeding great sons, until time itself rusted with age and collapsed under its own feeble muscle and dissolved into the very air that hung about it. No one would take Brecia away from him once he had her. No one.

As for her powers, he knew she could not compare to him. He found, however, in odd moments, when he prayed to whoever listened to wizards, that this was true, that she would be his and his alone forever.

But the two of them had escaped him before, and that was a worm in his innards. He didn't know how they'd shattered the bubble he'd fashioned, but they'd managed it.

Was the damned prince dead?

The damned prince leaned close to her ear, his breath perhaps warmer than it had been the night before when he'd traced his tongue over that lovely little shell, and made her start singing with the ghosts. She knew even without looking at him that he'd felt the lovely desire that whistled softly through her blood at just the touch of his tongue, the whisper of his breath, the light stroke of his fingers on her flesh. He was smiling, so sure of himself, the damned wizard.

"Say what you will say and don't play with me," she said, drawing away from him, just a bit, just enough to get her brain under control again. How had this happened?

"You love me, Brecia," he said with great satisfaction, still too close to her ear, and she started tapping her foot, to distract herself.

She said, "You have the brain of a toad. You don't know anything."

"I know that you had but to save my life to realize you love me, to recognize it deep within yourself, to surrender to it and to me. When my parents hear that I nearly gave my life to win you, they will be awed by my resolve, by my perseverance. They will believe me remarkable." He frowned at that. "Well, they already believe me remarkable."

"That is not what happened at all, you fool."

He just shook his head at her and looked at her closely. It was difficult, nearly painful, but he continued looking. He said, "You are excessively ugly, Brecia, more ugly than you perhaps had to make yourself. Your head, it looks powerful strange."

"I have disguised the two of us quite well. Mawdoor will not recognize us, you'll see. You think I'm ugly? Ha, if there is a pool of water, look at yourself and fall over dead with horror."

He only smiled as his fingertip traced her ear again, and he felt the jump of her heart as he said, "This adventure I will tell beyond the time of our children's children. How the witch Brecia made herself so remarkably repulsive that it took all the prince's guts to keep him from looking in the opposite direction."

"We are standing outside Penwyth and you are speaking about our grandchildren. You must pay attention, prince. You must stop your play."

He looked to be in pain, then he smiled, this wizard prince who looked like an ancient, gnarly sot, and she wanted him—despite filthy tangled gray hair, lines as thick as a gown's seams dug in his face. It was amazing, this wanting, something no one had ever before explained to her.

He said, "All right. Tell me what you have planned for Mawdoor, Brecia. Is it bloody? So painful that all the ghosts' fires will leap into the air, filling the sky with orange flames?" He sighed. "No, you haven't the finesse. You want me to stomp his wizard's guts into the ground, don't you?"

Slowly Brecia shook her head. "You will see. First things first. Now, look at me, prince. Do you see an old woman who is as decrepit and ugly as you are in your rotted old carcass?"

"Aye, just looking at this old hag makes my guts cramp. Yet I love every black tooth in her ancient mouth. Don't I?"

"The ghosts told me that Mawdoor keeps a very special golden cask that holds his demon father's visions. They told me it is so terrifying that Mawdoor keeps it locked away and hidden."

"I have heard of it, now that I think about it. What else did the ghosts tell you?"

"They said that if the chest is unlocked and opened, Mawdoor will be sucked into old, violent visions conjured up by his father and used eons ago to slaughter his enemies, a loop of very unpleasant visions, visions that even a wizard cannot escape."

"Will he die in the visions?"

"I don't know. The ghosts say that once he's inside, it will hold him forever."

"Well done, Brecia," the prince said, rubbing his bent old hands together. "That would be good for Mawdoor. He has crimes heaped high on his door stoop. He has slain many mortals in gruesome ways, but worse, he believes himself above the common-sense rules and compromise, and the reasonable continuation of the world, and that is more dangerous than I can say."

"I understand. We must find and unlock that chest." Brecia looked up at the old man who stared down at them from Penwyth's wooden ramparts.

She called up in an old woman's querulous voice, "Hear me, gracious keeper, my husband and I seek word with Mawdoor."

"I am Supney. I guard the gates on Fridays. I am the one who decides who will and who will not be allowed to come into Penwyth. It is I who give all the orders. And I say to ye, no words with the master now, old woman. Get ye gone. Just look at ye, old crone, yer face fair to makes my gizzard clamp shut. My lord Mawdoor has no time for someone as old and ugly as ye are."

"My husband is just as ugly. Why don't you remark upon him?"

Supney yelled, "Get ye gone, old woman, and take the ancient old sot with ye."

"We must speak to Lord Mawdoor. We are capable of many things, other things as well. It is these other things, these very special other things, that we wish to speak to my lord Mawdoor about."

"Shut yer jaws. I won't hear more. Go away. There's nothing for ye here. Go away!"

28

Mawdoor's voice, smooth and bored, came from deep within the fortress, echoing all around them, an excellent effect. "What more are you capable of, old crone? What are these very special things?"

"Who speaks?" Brecia jerked around.

"It is the master," Supney said, and he looked around too, even though he had many times heard the master do this. It still scared him to his twisted toes.

Brecia said, her old voice quavery as a feather in a wind, "Is it you, the master of Penwyth? The famous wizard who controls all the lands here about?"

"Aye, it is I," Mawdoor said, his voice not bored now. He suddenly appeared beside old Supney on the wooden ramparts. "What can you do, old woman?"

"I can see things, my lord." She lowered her voice, certain that he would have to strain hard to hear her. "I can see things that others cannot. I can make things happen after I look at them."

There was a hitch in Mawdoor's breath, they heard it, but naturally their ears were very sharp indeed. She had him. Brecia said—more softly because she was speaking now to Mawdoor, not to old Supney on the ramparts, who looked ready to spit on them at any minute—"I served the witch in the sacred oak forest. I heard that you wanted her, but none can enter the sacred oak forest without fear of death. I know how to go deep into the sacred grove without danger. I can see where she is, see what she is doing. I know how to bring her forth." She ended up whispering, her voice so old and so parchment thin, she wondered if even a wizard could hear it.

"How do you do this?"

"The old man here, my husband, he places his hands on either side of my head, and he squeezes. He focuses my sight, and the tighter he squeezes, the more deeply I see and understand clearly what it is I must do to achieve what I want. Don't you think my head looks too narrow—too long for a head? See, it rises straight off my neck and soars upward."

"Aye, you are powerfully ugly, old woman. Your nose juts out."

"By the time I pass to the hereafter, I imagine my head will be only wide enough for one eye, and so long that my nose will not only jut out, it will also look to be a foot long."

Mawdoor laughed at the image the old woman painted. She could bring Brecia out of her oak forest? To him? He came to the edge of the ramparts, began to pace. Old Supney moved quickly out of his way, even though now Mawdoor was moving so quickly he couldn't see him. But he could hear him sure enough.

Then Mawdoor let the old pair see him clearly, every handsome powerful piece of him. He called down, "Tell me, old woman, why do you want to do this for me?"

"Brecia's mother wanted her to wed with you, but the ghosts fought it, sang relentlessly that you were untrustworthy, that you would destroy the forest if you could, that you would lock their mistress into your black tower and hold her there forever."

"I had not thought quite that far ahead," Mawdoor said, and looked interested.

Brecia said, "Aye, the ghosts want the prince of Balanth as Brecia's mate. They trust him, you see, know of the honor of his parents, believe him pure of heart. He has won them with his false smiles. It fair to curdles my innards to see him prance about the oak forest, as if he truly belongs there."

"The prince is very likely dead," Mawdoor said, and muttered prayers that it was true to any god who might be listening and who might believe him worthy.

"He is not dead. Just last night he was eating roasted hedgehog and dancing to a merry song sung by the ghosts. I do not like him. He believes himself blessed by the sarsen stones, believes himself a wizard above all other wizards. I believe he should suffer for his lust for Brecia. He isn't worthy of her. Brecia's mother is right. You should have her, my lord, only you."

"All you say about the prince is true," Mawdoor said. "I have heard that he is so conceited, he spends hours each day staring at himself in silent stands of water.

"As for me, old hag, you are right. I am not what the ghosts think. I am trustworthy, not the prince. It is true that my grandmother ate goat meat before it was even warm over the fire, but withal, she was a witch to admire, just as Brecia is. Aye, with Brecia at my side, we will rule more than the prince could ever dream of ruling, attend great happenings, bend the realms of the world to our will. Now, what do you wish in return, ancient crone, if you bring me Brecia?"

"In return for Brecia, you will send both my husband and me to the plains of Britain to the sacred circle. I wish to commune amongst the great sarsen stones."

Mawdoor said, "You know that stone circle opens itself only to witches and wizards, not to plain folk, even if they might have a bit of magic in their narrow heads."

"Aye, I have heard that, but it doesn't matter. I must see the sarsen stones. I must learn how they came about, those old stones. Something strange happened, but none know what, not even the most powerful wizards. I want to know the secret. If I am there, standing beneath those mighty lintels, in the midst of the trilithon, my husband's fine hands squeezing my head, I know that the answers will flow into me. I know it."

"You're wrong," Mawdoor said. "None will ever know the genesis of the great stone circle. It goes back from before time itself considered forming endless fragments of sod and stone that became the earth. But if that is what you want, then I will send you there, it is nothing to me. But you must accept that you could die, the spirits of the past crushing all your questions in that skinny head of yours."

"Have you been there, my lord?"

Mawdoor looked down at the ugly old woman, at her skinny head, at that nose of hers that was too long indeed. If the ugliness was any indication of what she had accomplished with her husband's head squeezing, then just perhaps she could get Brecia to him.

"I have been there. It is where I first beheld Brecia, and my breath boiled in my body."

"That is where the prince of Balanth first saw her as well. The ghosts say that he was so impressed with her that he stretched out on his side atop one of the lintels, rested his face against his palm, and claimed himself content simply to gaze upon her, to hear the beauty of her bell-like voice."

The old head squeezer wheezed behind his hands. The ancient hag grunted as she smacked him hard between his shoulder blades, nearly knocking him to the ground.

Mawdoor said, "I know nothing about him lying atop a lintel. The prince is dead. He must be dead—the knife went right into his chest, and there was a touch of magic and a bit of special poison on that knife to pierce the wizard's shield."

The ground shuddered beneath the old man's feet.

The old woman lightly squeezed his shoulder.

Mawdoor didn't notice.

The old woman said, "No, he is not dead. My mistress saved him, nearly killing herself in the doing, but she had no choice. He was dying and wretched, all told, and so she saved him. Unless she takes him into grave dislike, she will marry him, if you cannot take her first."

Mawdoor was silent a moment, thinking hard. There was no risk here. It would be nothing to him to send these two ghastly old relics to the sacred stone circle on the plains. They would die, of that he was certain, but it truly didn't matter to him. Finally, he nodded down to the old couple. "Supney will allow you to enter now."

The old woman bowed deeply, grabbed the old sot's hand, and whispered upward, knowing Mawdoor could hear her clearly, "You are a worthy wizard, my lord, the only worthy wizard good enough for Brecia. You will gain all that you deserve."

"I will," Mawdoor said. "Aye, I will."

The big gates swung open. The prince whispered against Brecia's temple as they walked into the courtyard, "I preferred being invisible. Then I could place my hand on your breast and none would see me do it. Even better, I wouldn't have to see that ugly face of yours whilst I fondle you."

Her breathing hitched, and he smiled and looked straight ahead at Mawdoor, who was now standing on the top step of his great hall, hands on hips.

The prince said, all laughter gone from his voice, "You will be careful, Brecia."

"We will both be very careful. Mawdoor will surely sense the magic in us, but he will expect that since I told him about it, and we've cloaked the rest as best we can. Think you, prince, that he will want to squeeze my head and kiss my long, skinny nose?"

The prince turned his laugh into a rheumy old cough and pounded himself on the back, bending his right arm over his shoulder.

Truth be told, Brecia thought, looking around her, the two of them fit in quite well. Only old people were about, shuffling along, their backs bent, their faces so seamed with lines she wondered if they were as old as some of the ghosts. And how did they get this old?

It wasn't until they were in the huge great hall that they saw the three women who'd been with the assassins two days before. They were surrounded by old men, one offering them food, another holding out a bowl of water in gnarly, shaking old hands, and a third reverently covering their legs with soft blankets.

Mawdoor suddenly appeared directly in front of them. A trick to impress them, possibly to frighten them as well, Brecia thought, and smiled, a fearsome sight. He said, shuddering a bit at that smile, "Tell me how long it will take you to bring Brecia out of the oak forest."

"The fact is, my lord, I cannot truly see my path until the full moon shines upon my skinny head. That will be tomorrow night. Then my husband will squeeze my head, and all the secrets I need to bring her forth will flow out of my mouth. I will chew booser berries so my breath will be sweet as the secrets that will pour out of me."

"If the secrets don't fall out of your mouth, old crone, you will die, your husband as well, his hands squeezing your skinny head until there is simple air between his palms. Tomorrow night, under the full moon, no later. In the meantime, you will make yourselves useful. Whilst you are preparing yourselves, your husband flexing his hands to strengthen them for the task ahead, you may clean the fortress." He flicked his fingers in their faces and was gone.

"He likes tricks," the prince said, stretched, and looked about the immense hall. "At least he won't try to seduce you, I am very sure of that. I will not lie to you, Brecia—you are very ugly."

"You are not one to complain of my ugliness, you scrawny old sot. Don't speak too loudly. Look, one of the women might have heard you."

"You're right," the prince said, looked directly into the woman's eyes, wide with questions, and very slowly nodded his head once, then twice. The woman blinked, smiled, and patted the broad head of one of the wolfhounds lolling beside her. "Bring me some ale," she called out. The prince wondered if she was ordering him, but almost immediately another old sot was moving as quickly as he could to get the woman a wooden goblet.

"None of them recognize us," he said to Brecia.

"Your own mother wouldn't recognize you," Brecia said. "Now, let us go to his chamber, to clean it."

"Aye, I want to see what he's created for himself. Do you have any idea where we'll find this vision cask?"

"One old ghost told me that he saw it once, the key in its lock. He said it was a very old chest, no larger than the length of my forearm, as high as my stretched fingers. It is supposedly made of gold and studded with precious gems. It is probably well hidden, so attune yourself to it."

"Hard to hide anything," the prince said, "particularly from such as I," and he followed Brecia up the wooden steps to the upper floor of the fortress.

"Remember to walk slowly and shuffle," she said over her bent old shoulder, her long, narrow nose quivering as she felt a ruffling of the air around her. It was from him, she knew, and smiled. So he wanted her, did he? She added another crooked line to her wrinkled old face, turned, and gave him a fat smile showing her remaining four teeth.

No more thoughts of lust for him, she thought, and smiled.

Suddenly there was a great wrenching sound, as if stones were being jerked from the very walls, as if the mortar binding them together was being gouged out and thrown aside.

Brecia froze on the wide wooden steps, feeling them shudder beneath her feet.

29

Present

Bishop couldn't believe she'd picked up her skirts and run from him. Surely she wasn't afraid of him. He ran out the mouth of the cave, only to have her jump on his back.

She was laughing. Merryn was actually laughing. He felt her kissing his ear, tugging on his hair. His heart was pounding so hard and fast he thought it would burst from his chest. She released him, and he turned to take her in his arms. "I've got to have you." He was panting so hard she could scarce make out his words.

"I know," she said. "I know." Oddly, she understood his urgency, his frenzy. It was the curse, and it was pushing and prodding him. And she really didn't mind it at all. She pressed herself against him. "Bishop," she said, grabbing his face between her palms. "Bishop, I've got to have you, too. Don't rip my clothes. Here." She pulled his tunic over his head, saw his violent, heaving breaths, knew he was trying to control himself. Well, it didn't matter. Merryn leaned forward and kissed his chest. He became still as a rock.

"Come inside the cave."

As he walked her inside, she kept kissing his chest, nipping at his shoulders, breathing in the taste of him, licking his warm flesh.

She realized the air was warmer, softer, even as she pulled down his trousers. His sex was hard, ready. He was in bad shape, she realized that—she, the girl who'd had no experience at all before twenty-four hours ago. It was amazing. There were so many things she didn't yet understand, but none of these things mattered a whit to her now. "It's all right," she said, and watched him kick away his trousers.

"Merryn," he said, and he was on her, pulling her onto her back, jerking up her gown, looking down at her, and then his hands were on the insides of her thighs, stroking her, feeling her flesh, and he closed his eyes, his head back, whilst he felt her, and his fingers went higher and higher, to touch her, and he nearly spilled his seed at the feel of her warm woman's flesh. By all the saints' faint hearts, he hurt, hurt so much that he clenched his teeth against taking her violently. Merryn lay there on her back, smiling up at him, trusting him. He moved his fingers over her, stroking her and soon, so very soon, she lurched up at the intense sing of her blood roaring through her. It was lust, and it was on her as well as on Bishop. How very odd it all was. She let herself sink with the weight of her own need. She raised her hips, let him cup her in his big hands, and she said his name. He came deeply into her.

Knowing he was again inside her body made her want to cry with the wonder of it. Then it made her wild; she accepted it, reveled in it and wanted more. She clasped her legs around his flanks and jerked him down to her.

He was pushing, deep, deeper, then withdrawing. He was in control again, finally, and he looked down at her face and smiled. "This is beyond what a man could imagine. Just a moment, Merryn, just give me another moment," and he was gone from her, his head thrown back, and he yelled to the cave ceiling, and it reverberated off the walls and echoed to the depths of the cave, echoed into time itself.

She felt a humming deep inside her, knew it was something different, apart from her, but she still felt it, that odd humming, and feelings leapt about, stirring her, and she felt an incredible desire to rear up and bite his chin, his earlobe. She began kissing him again, her need suddenly as great as his had been. She shoved upward, taking him off guard, and he fell backward. "No, don't move," she said, her voice as fierce and as mad as his had been. She splayed her hands on his chest as she looked down at him, wanting, wanting, and she brought him even deeper. He was hard again, filling her, just like that, or maybe he had never left her, even for a moment. She grabbed his hand and placed it against her, felt his fingers stroking her, and it was her turn to throw her head back and yell. He was with her, and his cry came together with hers, echoing in the warm air. The strange humming softened inside her, flattened to become nothing but the soft air she was sucking in. She lay there on top of him, hearing the echoes of voices—or maybe they weren't voices at all, but the sound of her heart singing. It didn't matter.

Bishop felt the ground move, shift hard beneath them. It didn't stop, it became more intense. He held Merryn tightly against him. By all the saints' crooked teeth, was the earth was going to break apart with its violent tremors? Then, suddenly, all the shuddering and shaking seemed far away, not really touching them now, even though he knew it was happening.

What?

The soft humming he'd heard in his ear— Merryn humming in her pleasure—stopped. Everything stilled. Merryn settled her face in the crook of his neck, her heart pounding against his. He breathed her in.

When at last she could breathe, when she could at last find words again, Merryn said, "Bishop, this is beyond what should be, isn't it?"

"Yes"—the only word he could get out of his mouth. In truth, he didn't care, but she was right. And here she was, talking. It amazed him. He still wondered if another breath would fill his chest—it was so hard to suck in the air. He stroked his hands over her back, wished her gown were on the floor beside her. He wanted desperately to feel her flesh, to feel her breasts, to feel her heart against his, to give her his mouth.

He managed it, somehow managed to get the gown off her. And then they were together as they were meant to be. "Sleep, Merryn," he said against her ear. "Sleep."

"The humming," she said, her breath warm on his neck. "The humming."

Aye, the humming, her humming against his ear. "It was very fine," he said, kissed her hair, closed his eyes, and slept, his breathing deep, finally slowing.

Sometime Else

The prince laughed. "Did you like that, Brecia? It is my lust that is shaking the very fortress beneath your weathered old feet."

"Stop it, you mad prince. Just behave yourself. We have to find that chest."

"Do you know," he said, looking up at her as the violent quivers settled once again, "I want you even though you are so ugly it makes my eyes burn to look at you."

"You are so ugly I would have to pull a sack over your head to bring myself even to kiss you."

"But how could you kiss me if I had a sack over my head?"

"I could pretend it was a beautiful wizard beneath that sack, and surely that would be more pleasant."

Suddenly there was an old sack over his head and she heard him laughing, muffled. "It's true, Brecia. I want you. Now. Kiss me, witch."

It was a short kiss because Brecia knew they didn't have much time. But then the prince followed that kiss with many more kisses. Soon his hands were everywhere, and he didn't stop.

The afternoon sun was slowly lowering when at last Brecia and the prince stood in the center of Mawdoor's vast chamber. Both of those very ugly old beings were smiling, memories of pleasure still tingling in their blood.

"There isn't much sunlight coming through those windows," she said. "I wonder why."

"Mawdoor is more at ease hovering in the shadows, letting the darkness cover him, don't you think?" He stroked his ancient, sagging jaw. "I can also see him squating under big rocks."

"You're just angry because he wants you dead and he wants to wed me."

"Aye, that is at the bottom of it. I've always known, deep inside, that there would be a final battle between us. It's near, I feel it. Now, let's find that chest."

It wasn't in his big, gloomy chamber, with its brooding shadows that filled the corners and cast dim light onto the old wooden floors, bare and worn. Brecia looked at his bed, a huge thing that was covered with an incredible white cloth. She touched it. It felt just like her white woolen gowns.

"We must work quickly."

"Yes," she said, walked beside him to the door, then turned to look about the chamber. She spoke very quietly, waved her hand in a half circle. The room was still shadowed and dim. She said, "Ah, a wonderful job. The room is clean now, although there wasn't much dirt to begin with to sweep into the courtyard."

Three hours later, they still hadn't found the chest.

"Mayhap it doesn't exist," the prince said, and scratched his armpit. "It could just be a ghost tale."

"But you'd heard of it too."

He nodded.

"The ghosts were very certain about the chest. His demon father gave it to him, told him it was his decision whether or not to accept it. It would give him greater powers, but if he lost it or if it was taken from him, it would suck him in, destroy him."

"So mayhap he decided not to take the risk. Mayhap he destroyed it. Mayhap the ghosts were wrong about him keeping it."

Brecia was shaking her head. "Think about Mawdoor. Think of what he is like. He would scoop up all the power he could get, no matter the risk. Aye, he has the cask, and he's hidden it well, because his very being is bound up in it."

"His very being, Brecia? That makes no sense," the prince said.

"Your father isn't a demon. They are a different matter, prince. Demons hiss and brood and find wrongness in every corner of their world, and this wrongness is all directed at them, and thus to survive, to flourish, they must destroy anything they perceive to be a threat to them. This vision chest or cask, the ghosts also said that it could, if he were careless, draw Mawdoor into it and hold him there forever."

"Yes," the prince said. "You told me that. How to get him into the cask?"

She frowned, and rubbed her very narrow, very long nose. "Maybe if you squeeze my head I'll think of something."

He laughed, said, "By all the gods, you're ugly. I must tell you, Brecia, when we were on the steps before—I had to close my eyes so I could find my pleasure in you. It was difficult, but I wished to prove my constancy to you. Did you realize my eyes were closed? Did you comprehend and appreciate my constancy?"

She laughed. She hadn't laughed as much in the past year as she had in the past two days. "Constancy, from a wizard?"

"Aye, Brecia, from a wizard. You wound me."

"I did notice that your balance wasn't very good since you had your eyes closed. As for me, I had no problem since you had that sack over your head."

Even with the jests, she felt something move deep inside her. Warm and true, those feelings that were filling her now. She touched his ugly old face, smiled. "Let's find that wretched chest."

"I prefer to think of it as a cask."

Late that night, when the fortress slept, all the old people stacked like cords of wood around the great central hall in the fortress, snores filling the air, Brecia pictured the cookhouse in her mind's eye, saw some succulent roasted boar and some well-milled white bread. She brought it to them with one shake of her right fist.

"If we don't find the chest," he said between bites, "then we must have another plan."

"I have one," she said, and sank her teeth into the very nicely roasted boar.

He rolled his eyes. "You're a witch. A witch always has plans for this, for that, but I don't believe many of them work. You know the chest is hidden, well hidden. We've searched the fortress. What is your plan?"

"We must raise our power to find it."

"Aye, and if we do that, Mawdoor will realize something is very wrong. I don't want to escape from his damned bubble again. I don't want your hands burned again. It was bad, Brecia, your pain."

"It was. Now, listen. I saw him take one of the women upstairs, and there were carnal thoughts in the wizard's mind. He is distracted. Soon he will sleep soundly."

"It's good that you don't wish to marry him. He is not worthy of you. He has proven that he has no constancy, taking another woman with you close by."

She laughed, heard an old man jerk away not far away, and smothered the laugh behind her hand. "I also put a sleeping potion in the wine the woman is giving to him. They will sleep like babes until morning."

"Ah, now you smirk with your cleverness. You want me to search this damned fortress all night?"

"You are a wizard. You can go days without resting."

He tore off another bite of boar meat, closed his eyes at the wonderful taste, and leaned back against a wall. "All right, we will meld our powers and prowl the fortress."

It was nearly dawn when Brecia's hand

started vibrating. She was standing near the jakes, where an old man was sitting, his frayed old leggings down around his knees, speaking to another old man who was waiting his turn.

"Aye," the old man was saying, " 'twas I who brought the maid some warm bread dripping with butter and honey. But what is her gratitude? She goes off with Lord Mawdoor, a skip in her walk, the faithless maid."

"If she went off with you, what would you do?"

"I would think of something between journeys to the jakes."

The old men laughed.

She moved her hand a bit to the right and it vibrated more. Then she moved her palm a bit to the left. Her hand vibrated so hard it flew up. "Ah," she said, and smiled. Slowly, very slowly, she moved her fingers over the surface of the wood until she found something that shouldn't be there. It was a small button. She pressed it. The wooden planks slid to the side. Inside was a space not much larger than her head, and shaped just about the same, long and narrow. And there was the vision chest that had belonged to Mawdoor's demon father.

She was suddenly very afraid. She thought what she'd found to the prince, witch's mind to wizard's. In the next instant, he was standing beside her, looking at that strange gold chest.

"There are incredible diamonds here," he said. "Call off your powers, Brecia. No reason to take any more chances now that we've found the chest." He stared down at it, then very slowly, he stretched out his fingers and lightly tapped them against the top of the chest.

It was as cold as an ice floe in the northern seas.

He jerked his hand back.

Brecia touched her fingers to it as well. She blinked as she jerked her hand away from the gleaming metal lid. No, not just metal—it was solid gold.

"The key is in the lock."

"Aye," he said, "just as it should be. Just as the ghosts told you. Once we have the key, once it opens, we will have him."

Suddenly the key jerked out of the lock and vanished in the next heartbeat. "Oh, no," Brecia said, whirling about. "Mawdoor built in a protection. We weren't fast enough."

They heard a mighty roar. They knew it

was Mawdoor and that the key had gone to him, but the noise sounded like a thousand hungry lions, very angry, very hungry lions, and they were loose in the castle, headed for the jakes.

"He can't realize it's us," Brecia said, grabbing the prince's sleeve.

"He would be beyond stupid if he didn't suspect."

The cask began to glow, growing larger and larger until it burst out of the hidey-hole.

"By all the gods' mortal sacrifices, it's a wondrous spell Mawdoor has placed upon it." He raised his wand and yelled at the top of his lungs, "*Sostram Denesici avrat.*"

The damned cask just kept growing larger and larger.

The prince looked shocked.

Brecia shook his sleeve. "Leave it be. Come, quickly." In the next instant, they were pressed against the backs of two very old snoring men. They settled in and began snoring themselves. When the old men jerked up at the awful noise, they jerked up as well.

Mawdoor stood over them. He held his wand in his left hand, and he was raising it high.

30

Present

Bishop closed his eyes a moment, and felt again Merryn's mouth on his mouth, her tongue licking his chest, his belly, until at last she brought him to her mouth and licked him. He'd nearly heaved off the ground. He shuddered, opened his eyes to see her looking at him. He said, "When you ran away from me, it was like a blow to my belly. I couldn't bear it, Merryn. Then you jumped on my back and brought me down."

She laughed. "I jumped on your back because I didn't think you'd catch me, you fool." She touched her fingertips to his mouth and let him nibble. "That was all very exciting, Bishop."

He smiled at her, very pleased that he was Bishop and she was Merryn, not some long ago wizard and witch. They would wed and she would be his wife and bear his children; he would protect her and their children with his life. If they were lucky, life would stretch out an ample number of years and bring them more joy than otherwise.

It was a very nice thought. Bishop was content.

It wasn't long until he became serious. He knew they had to act, and act in just the right way or—he didn't know what would happen. He said, "We must find something to help us break that curse."

She stood up and wiped her hands on her soiled gown. She looked very young, very dirty, and very well loved, given the quite satisfied look in her eyes.

He said, looking over at her, "You are carrying my babe."

She was utterly still for a moment before she said finally, "You said that before. Why do you say it again?"

"It sounds very nice to my ears. Now I

must go back to that black hole. There must be something there, something hidden from us."

She walked beside him until they reached the hole. She said, after she'd stared down into the impenetrable darkness, "You want to go down inside the hole?"

"Aye, if I can figure out a way to do it. I don't have a rope, and even if I did, there isn't anything to tie it to here in the cave. Do you have an idea how I can get down there?"

"Why, yes," she said, and handed him the wand. "It is here for you. Use it, Bishop."

He took it, his eyes never leaving her face. "I don't know what to do with it."

"You will tell it what you want."

Tell a stupid old stick that he wanted to go down in a black hole? Suddenly he felt it growing even warmer in his hand. He wasn't imagining it. The thing was pulsing warmth through him. He swallowed, realizing for the first time that he held something he shouldn't be holding, something that was powerful and beyond what any mortal could or should know.

He closed his eyes for a moment, saw clearly the gleaming wand in the prince's hand, saw the lighter, glowing wand in Brecia's hand, both radiating such power that it made him tremble inside.

And now there was a wand in his own hand.

Bishop said nothing more. He walked to the edge of the black hole and looked down into the pure black pit.

He pointed the wand directly into the hole and said, feeling both foolish and hopeful, "Give me light so that I may see to the bottom of the hole."

To their utter astonishment, the black hole became instantly filled with stark white light. He looked down, blinked, then began to laugh. He turned back to look at Merryn, who was staring into the white light. "I still can't see," he said. "The white is just as strong as the black." Someone, something, was playing tricks on him.

"Let me see to the bottom, damn you!"

He waved the wand into the hole, and instantly the light, the darkness, were no more. The light was perfectly clear now. Bishop knelt beside the edge and looked down. He saw that the hole went down only about twenty feet, not all that deep. And at the bottom he saw something else, something that seemed to shimmer, something small, casting out a golden light that made the very air quiver.

"No, Bishop, don't."

"I must," he said, and poked the wand into the hole. "Take me there."

He was standing at the bottom in an instant, looking up at Merryn's face staring down at him over the side. "Don't fall in."

"Bring me down there with you."

Bishop said as he waved the wand up toward her, "Bring Merryn down here with me."

She was standing right in front of him, breathing hard because she was so excited and so afraid that she was nearly ready to puke with it.

She whispered, her voice sounding like fine dust in the air, "By all the saints' knobbled knees, Bishop, what does this mean?"

"It means," he said, drawing her against him, "that we have found something we were meant to find. At last. And it was the wand that brought us here."

"This is very frightening," she said into his tunic, which smelled of male sweat and thus of him. "Nothing is as it should be. You actually waved that wand at me, and suddenly I was here with you."

"I know," he said. "I know, but it will be all right." Then, as one, with no more words between them, both of them turned to see a gleaming golden cask on the floor. Its surface wasn't dulled or covered with millennium-old dirt. It looked as fresh and clean as it had been when it had been sent here. Sent here by whom?

Bishop studied the cask. It was longer than it was wide, maybe the length from his fingertips to his elbow, and maybe a hand's height high. Its lid looked to be solid gold. It was encrusted with diamonds and rubies and emeralds, on the top and on the sides, some of the gems larger than anything he'd ever seen or heard of.

They went down on their knees. Bishop gently laid the wand on the ground beside him. He reached out his hand and lightly touched his fingertips to the top of the small chest.

He jerked his hand back. The lid was colder to the touch than the ice that had covered London and the Thames the past February.

Merryn frowned, touched it herself. It was

so burning cold that she yelped and fell back on her bottom, holding her fingers.

"This is very curious," she said, crawling back up. "The instant I moved my fingers, the pain was gone."

Bishop pulled Merryn close, took the hem of her gown, and wrapped it round and round his fingers. He drew in a deep breath and touched the cask again. It was icy cold, but he could bear it. He saw the keyhole, felt its outline. He felt the key, tried to turn it. He thought his fingers would freeze off his hands.

He wrapped his fingers even more, and tried to turn the small key. But it didn't move. He sat back on his haunches and stared at the damned thing.

He'd been led here, given the wand, the cask, but—Bishop picked up the wand and aimed it at the cask. "Open the cask."

The key turned and the cask lid flew open. A hellacious noise sprang up, like a thousand maddened animals were all around them, charging, drawing closer and closer until it seemed they were right on top of them, closing over them, suffocating then, wanting to destroy them, swallow them.

Bishop tried to see what was in the cask,

but all he could make out was billowing clouds, the color of gold, turbulent, whipping around and around. The racket was nearly unbearable now. Bishop picked up the wand and yelled over the racket, "Stop it!"

The noise stopped. It was quiet again— no, it was more than quiet, it was as silent as death itself. It was as if all life had been sucked out of this hole.

Bishop raised his hand and laid his palm over Merryn's left breast. He felt her heart.

She said, "I'm still alive, I think. Is your heart beating as well?"

"Aye, it is, thank the saints and all their countless sacred bones."

"I don't like this," Merryn said, and pressed herself closer to Bishop's side. "Look inside the cask, Bishop. All those racing clouds inside. I don't see anything else, no animals, all of them wanting to kill us. This is very frightening, Bishop."

"I know," Bishop said. "What does it have to do with the curse?" He looked at the wand, turned it over and over in his hand. "The cask is open, yet we can't see anything."

Suddenly, with no warning, the cask lid slammed down. Both Bishop and Merryn could have sworn that the key turned itself in the lock.

Merryn straightened, rose to her feet. She looked down at the beautiful, barbaric cask. She felt the dead silence recede, felt the life of air filling her lungs again, filling the hole, making things seem normal again, though, of course, nothing that had happened to them had been normal. All had been strange, beyond strange. She looked at that cask again. "Let me try, Bishop."

He handed her the wand. Merryn felt the precious warmth that pulsed from the wood against her palm. "Open the cask," she said, and pointed the wand at the key hole.

They heard a faint rumbling sound, animals running toward them, wild, out of control, but it was still distant, not right on top of them. Slowly, the rumbling grew louder and louder.

Merryn was ready to yell for it to stop because she could swear that those maddened animals were nearly upon them.

She said again, "Open the cask."

The key turned very slowly. They stared at the cask, watching the lid come open, very slowly.

Sometime Else

The prince breathed out loud, fleshy snores, and his ancient limbs twitched and jerked. Brecia's long, narrow nose pressed hard against his bony shoulder blade.

Mawdoor looked down at the pathetic ancient pair and slowly lowered his wand. He was sure they were the ones who'd found his demon father's chest, but now, just looking at them—how could it be? The miserable ugly sots—just look at the woman's narrow head and the old man's bony chin. By all the gore-hungry gods, if that old crone had ever had any magic to even get near his chest, he would spit up peach pips. It was absurd to believe she could bring Brecia out to him.

He sighed. He would give her a chance, just until midnight tonight, and then he would know whether the old crone would die at the sacred stone circle, dashed down by ancient magic that knew no reason and no end, or die by his hand for her failure.

Slowly, Mawdoor took a step back, then another. He whispered, "Until tonight. If you do not bring her here then you will both die. And I will make them very unpleasant, your deaths."

He sucked in a deep breath, then blew it out. He did this three times. Soon, all the old people asleep in the big room woke up and stared at him, standing there, sucking in great breaths, sucking deeper and deeper. Then he seemed to go round and round until he was moving so fast he was a whipping funnel, faster still, until he was only a blur. He whooshed upward to the very top of the big hall. To everyone's astonishment and fear, he streaked out into the dawn sky through a long, narrow window, a window surely too narrow for a man's body.

Brecia wanted to laugh at the very showy trick he'd just performed, but she didn't want to draw any attention to herself and the prince. She pressed herself harder against the prince's shoulder and whispered against his smelly old shirt, "What did you think of that? He wanted to kill us, but he held off. We have until midnight tonight beneath the full moon. No longer. So, what do you think?"

The prince snored. The damned wizard wasn't pretending sleep, either—his snores were quite real, obnoxious and loud. He'd slept through Mawdoor's performance. Brecia looked up to see one of the young women Mawdoor had brought to Penwyth standing in the middle of the room, staring upward to that narrow window.

She said, "How did he get through that small space?"

"He be a wizard, ye young beautiful maid," said a gravelly old voice. "Have ye not two wits in yer head?"

The young woman slowly shook her head. "I guess I haven't even a single one."

A chorus of ancient voices rose. "Get ye to sleep, young'un! Think ye he will spin ye more of his tricks? Nay, he won't. The master likes his sleep, he does."

Apparently all wizards liked their sleep. Brecia pressed herself against the prince's back again, his twisted old bones rattling with his snores.

Just after dawn on the morning of the full moon, Mawdoor looked at the two ancient, very ugly old people and said, "I trust both of you slept well throughout the night?"

"Oh, aye," Brecia said, stretched and yawned. "We slept like the blue sarsen stones at the sacred circle."

"If you don't bring me Brecia, I will kill you in a manner you won't like. Then I will toss your tattered old bones to my wolfhounds."

The prince, who was busy chewing on some singularly sweet bread, raised his head and said, "Dogs wouldn't touch her bones. Her bones would stick in their throats and kill them dead. Throw them mine."

Mawdoor looked from one to the other, then rose, and shouted, "Maida! Bring me yourself. I have plans for us."

The young woman walked to him, her lovely hair floating over her shoulders and down her back, a wolfhound on either side of her. "My lord?"

"We will go hunting," Mawdoor said.

"Where will we go, my lord?"

"To Spain, I think," Mawdoor said, and in the next instant both of them were gone.

"Why would he want to go to Spain to hunt?" The prince said aloud, then swallowed more sweet bread. "There is nothing to hunt in Spain."

Brecia could only laugh at him.

They didn't have long to find the cask again. Neither of them doubted that it would be as easy to find this time.

"Mawdoor is gone," the prince said. "He isn't here to sense our magic."

"I don't know," Brecia said slowly. "I just don't know. As you said, why would he go hunting in Spain? And take a mortal with him? This doesn't make much sense."

"If it is a trap, we will have to deal with it. We have no choice but to find that damned cask, Brecia. We have no choice but to get rid of Mawdoor. Damned witch, if only he didn't want you so badly."

"I am not a damned witch."

"Aye, you are. A trap, you think? You are probably right, but no matter. We will do what we must."

Brecia said, "Do you think he carries the cask with him now?"

"I think he's afraid of it," the prince said. "Probably too afraid to keep it very close to him."

All day they searched Mawdoor's fortress. They even sent their sight into the cow byre and the chickens' pen, even sifted their hands through the miller's flour. Nothing.

When the fortress bells rang six o'clock, Brecia called to him, "I have found it."

The prince, who'd been searching each crevice in the wooden ramparts, was beside her in an instant.

"Look," Brecia said and pointed down-ward.

The prince came next to her and saw the

cask at the bottom of the fortress well. Only a wizard or a witch would have seen it beneath a good twenty feet of water.

"An excellent hiding place," Brecia said. "I dropped my cup in there and that's when I saw it. I never sensed it. Mawdoor has protected it very well this time."

The prince called up the cask.

The cask didn't move. He sighed and disappeared, only to reappear at the bottom of the well, the cask in his hands. In the well water the cask wasn't cold to the touch.

He waved up at her.

Suddenly, without warning, Mawdoor's laughter filled the courtyard. Brecia had no time to do anything before she was thrown headfirst into the well.

Present

The brilliance of the light that burst out of the cask blinded them. They staggered back, covering their eyes. Then, slowly, still keeping their eyes shaded, Bishop and Merryn stared down into that impenetrable light.

"What is it?"

Bishop just shook his head. "It doesn't look like the billowing clouds anymore, but it doesn't matter. I still can't see through it."

Merryn looked hard, but she couldn't see through it either.

Suddenly they saw something whirling in the middle of the light, something that was going round and round so fast they couldn't make out what it was. But it was small; the brilliant light held it. They watched it hit against the light again and again, but it couldn't free itself.

"It's a prison of light," Merryn said. "What is being held in that light, Bishop?"

"I believe you're right, but I don't know what is in that light." He reached for his wand.

They heard a voice scream, "NO!"

31

Sometime Else

"This isn't good," the prince said, staring through the water into Brecia's eyes.

"We have the cask. We will figure out how to get out of this well."

They drew their wands from their sleeves and pointed them directly overhead. The prince said, "*Dranore narbus.*"

The water trembled about them, bubbled wildly, then settled. Nothing had happened. They weren't free.

"I wonder if this will be more difficult than Mawdoor's damned bubble," the prince said.

Brecia remembered her burning fingers and said, "I hope not. We must think about this, prince." She sat down at the bottom of the well. She said a few words beneath her breath, and both she and the prince looked like themselves again. In that instant she knew the answer. She smiled up at him. "I know," she said. "I know what to do. Don't worry."

She billowed her cloak out about her, wrapped her arms around her bent legs, pressed her cheek against her knee, and held on tightly. She chanted softly, so softly the prince couldn't hear her. Time passed. She chanted until the water seemed to flow along with the cadence of her chant. Suddenly she was gone. She'd told him not to worry, damn her witch's powers. Where had she gone? Then he knew.

"Ah, Brecia. Is it you?"

"My lord Mawdoor. Thank you for bringing me up from the well bottom. I knew that if I spoke directly to you, you would release me."

"It was a difficult decision," Mawdoor said, looking her up and down. "By all the new gods whose power I spit upon, you made yourself into a powerfully ugly old crone. That gives a wizard pause."

"I thought the narrow head was a nice touch."

"It was. I freely admit it. It convinced me not to look beyond that small bit of magic I felt coming from the two of you. The magic was distant, weak, no real power in it at all. Now I have you. Was that not a well-executed trap?"

"Aye, the cask at the bottom of the well—that was very well done of you, Mawdoor. And the key was gone. Do you have it?" He only frowned at her. She hoped he had the key. She knew that Mawdoor didn't realize he hadn't been what brought her out of the well. She'd sent out the thought and he'd snapped it up.

He nodded, smiling. "The prince will remain at the bottom of that well until time itself ceases to go forward and the earth stalls and withers beneath the heavens. The bands of magic that hold him cannot be severed, no matter how strong the wizard. He will spend all of eternity stroking that damned cask. To be in a well with a demon's chest—it's a dreadful thing. It is a quite perfect punishment for the damned wizard. Forget the key."

Brecia said, "I thought you had made the decision to keep the demon cask with you. Does that not mean that you must bear the responsibility of it?"

Mawdoor shrugged. "I suppose the ghosts told you of this. They seem to thrive on tales of lost caskets and magic keys that unlock the secrets to the universe. As to the cask and my responsibility to it, we will see. But the prince will stay there until the day of doom, if such a day ever comes."

Brecia tapped her foot up and down, and stroked her chin with her fingertips. "That makes no sense, Mawdoor. You have me now. Why would you want to kill the prince?"

Mawdoor became a foot taller, towering over her. "The prince must die. I've always wanted him gone from this earth. He had you, didn't he? He was your first lover, wasn't he?"

Slowly, she nodded. "Aye, he was my first."

Mawdoor brought himself back his normal height again. He looked down at his boots for a moment, then said, "I have heard it said that the prince makes his women do unnatural things."

For the moment, she forgot her fear and her plans and perked up. "Hmmm. What sorts of unnatural things?"

"You know what I mean, Brecia."

"No, I truly don't. I was innocent. I think everything he did seemed very normal may-hap even too normal—boring, mayhap, nearly sent me off to sleep, if you know what I mean."

The water in the well heaved and churned.

Mawdoor looked at her, blinked. "You say what he did was so boring it sent you off to sleep? Ah, what, specifically, was boring?"

"Why he rubbed his toes against mine and kept rubbing until I thought my skin would be raw from it. That was boring. Don't you think?"

"He rubbed your toes with his?"

"Aye, for an interminable time. I thought perhaps it was some sort of wizard mating ritual. Do you think that is unnatural?"

Mawdoor shook his head. "No, you're right, that was boring. I wouldn't rub your toes, Brecia. Or if I did, it would just be for a moment."

"What is unnatural, then?"

She was still wet from her stay in the well. Mawdoor lightly touched his fingers to her sleeve. Instantly she was dry, her hair shining beneath the afternoon sun.

He said, eyeing that glorious hair of hers, "Tell me what else he did and I will tell you whether it is natural or unnatural."

"He chewed on the flesh behind my knees."

"Hmmm."

"Is that unnatural?"

"Yes, that is unnatural, if done in excess."

The water in the well bubbled as madly as a boiling cauldron, nearly overflowing.

Brecia shook her head. "No, he did it only about twenty minutes." She paused, frowned. "One candle did burn down, so maybe it was longer."

"He is obviously mad. You are blessed to be rid of him."

Brecia smiled. "There were all the other things he did, Mawdoor." She shuddered delicately.

"What, damn you?"

"I cannot tell you, it embarrasses me."

"It is said that he has his women on their

knees in front of him, and they must see to his needs until they swoon from fatigue."

Brecia nodded slowly. "Aye, I can see how that would be tiring. And your knees would grow sore. He did not have me do that. Would I be praying whilst on my knees in front of him?"

"You stupid witch, you would have his sex in your mouth until your jaws locked and you gagged until you couldn't breathe—if he is of a size, that is, to make you gag."

Her eyes lit up. She said, a wealth of disappointment in her voice, "He didn't show me how to do that. Now that doesn't sound boring. You say he would want me to do that for hours on end?"

"So it is said about the prince, damn him. But now I've got him, and he will dissolve in the water over the endless years ahead."

"It still makes no sense, Mawdoor. Why keep the prince entrapped? Why not let him roam the land alone, without me, contemplating his defeat at your mighty hand? Surely that would be a punishment worse than floating at the bottom of a well, all relaxed, holding your father's cask to his chest."

"I see the deceit in your eyes, Brecia."

Mawdoor clasped her throat in one big hand and tightened his fingers, but Brecia only kept looking at him, so calm she looked bored, cocking her head slightly to the side, which was difficult to do with his hand around her neck.

He said right in her face, "Damn you, you have tried to bring me low, Brecia. All I wanted to do was mate with you, make you my wife, have you birth incredible wizards, but just look at what you and the prince tried to do. What you would still like to do."

His fingers tightened about her throat.

"Kill her, Mawdoor! Kill that ugly bitch!"

"No, I won't kill her," Mawdoor shouted over his shoulder, never looking away from Brecia's face.

"In that case, let her go, and I will kill her!"

Mawdoor slowly turned, taking Brecia with him, to see Maida standing twelve feet away, two of his wolfhounds at her side.

Mawdoor shouted, shaking Brecia's neck, "This doesn't concern you, Maida. Get back inside."

"Last night you told me that you wanted me to stay with you. If that is true, then why do you want this creature?"

Mawdoor yelled at her, "Can't you see I'm choking her?"

"You're doing it with lust in your eyes. Let the wretched woman go, let me kick her in the head."

Mawdoor gave Brecia a good shake, and again yelled at Maida, "She isn't a woman. She's a witch."

"A witch? Aye, she looks like one, doesn't she, the hag? Just looking at her makes me shudder."

Brecia's eyes narrowed. "And just what does that mean? *Make me shudder?* I'll make her shudder."

Maida yelled, "Aye, it's obvious to me now that she is a witch, and you're choking her, but she doesn't feel it at all. She's hanging there and she's laughing at you. Aye, she's making fun of you. My lord, she isn't worthy of you."

Maida went flying backward and landed on her back, the breath knocked out of her.

Mawdoor dropped his hand from Brecia's neck, and she landed lightly on her feet. He said, "You did that, didn't you?"

"Of course," Brecia said, smiling to herself even as she rubbed her neck. "I'm a witch."

"I bedded her," he said. "I enjoyed her. I

will continue to enjoy her after we are wedded."

"I believe she broke her leg when I threw her against the wall, Mawdoor. Maybe I broke her neck as well. Is she gagging, lying there with her arms twisted at such odd angles?"

He turned quickly and ran to where Maida was lying on the ground. Brecia heard the woman screeching, "The witch! Kill the witch!" and Mawdoor saying, "Be quiet, woman. That witch will be my wife. Are you all right? Are you broken?"

Brecia smiled, watching the woman grab his arm and shake him. All his attention was on her. Brecia looked skyward and began chanting. When she stopped, after just two breaths had passed, everything else stopped as well, including Mawdoor—thank the gods.

Time froze.

Only the wind moved, fanning the warm air in her face. She looked toward Mawdoor, locked in the instant that time had stopped. He'd left himself vulnerable by touching the woman, letting her humanness into himself. He was concentrating on her, feeling anger, hate, love—it didn't matter. And thus the spell worked on him as well.

The earth stood still and one very strong wizard as well. But not for long, not for long.

She ran to the well and called down, "Prince, would you like to join me in some unnatural acts?"

She heard his laughter even as she drained the power from the spell. The prince stood beside her, shook himself like a dog, then flicked his head back and he was as dry as she was.

"I am a very clever witch."

The prince looked toward Mawdoor and the mortal woman and nodded. "You have become more clever since I am with you. But Mawdoor isn't mortal, Brecia. We haven't much time, you know that. We must hurry." He lightly touched his fingers to her jaw. "Do you have it?"

"Aye, I have it," she said. Brecia smiled as she brought the golden cask from beneath her gown. She held it in her hands. It wasn't so cold now since Mawdoor was as still and silent as the score of old people huddled together near the pigsty.

"Look at him," the prince said even as he readied himself. He slowly pulled out his wand, gently caressed it with his fingers. "Soon now. It can't hold him much longer. Do you know, Brecia, I was right. He was unfaithful to you, and with a mortal woman who wanted to kick you in the head. Aye, he would have forced you to wed him and taken her as his concubine. That is disgraceful."

She wanted to laugh, but she was too afraid. "He has the key."

"I know. We must find it quickly."

She brought up her wand, held it outstretched, pointing toward Mawdoor.

But there was no time. It happened quickly. The earth began to shake. Maida screamed. The old people tripped over themselves to escape.

Then there was silence. There wasn't a single breath of life for one very long moment.

Mawdoor was standing now, his wand in his right hand, and in his left hand he held a golden sword. "I will kill you with this, prince. I searched far and wide for a sword that would pierce a wizard's heart and freeze it in his chest."

32

"Well, now, Mawdoor," the prince said, legs apart, hands on his hips, "this is all very interesting. You fashioned a special golden sword, just for me?"

"I have always hated your wit, prince. But soon you will speak no more. After I have mated with Brecia, I will burn that oak forest of hers, pile rocks until the trees flatten and the earth beneath them gives way, and let her grieve for all the ghosts who will be no more. Brecia, you brought up the cask, that was devious of you. Once the prince is dead, I will teach you a lesson even a witch won't forget."

Brecia spoke softly, blowing the words at Mawdoor, as she spoke. "Your feet burn, Mawdoor, burn, burn, burn."

He jumped three feet into the air, and his golden sword fell from his hand.

The prince was on him in a minute, moving so quickly he was nearly a blur. Mawdoor's sword was in his hand the next instant, and he yelled as he aimed the brilliant golden point at the prince's chest.

The prince didn't have a sword, but he had a knife. It was in his hand, come up to Mawdoor's throat, when the skies turned utterly black. There were voices, loud voices, all around them, screaming, and the voices were converging on Mawdoor and the prince.

"Kill him!"

The screaming voices suddenly took shape. Hundreds, no, thousands of crows swooped down upon the prince, covering him, their great black wings flapping wildly all around him.

Mawdoor stood back, the tip of his golden sword buried in the ground at his feet, and he was laughing.

Suddenly a dozen of the black crows went flying through the air, landing hard on the ground, dead. More fell away, all dead. The prince was standing there, slapping his hands in a circle around him, a protective circle that shielded him and killed anything that touched it.

Mawdoor roared and came at him again, the golden sword raised.

Brecia saw that the prince was covered with blood from the birds stabbing him with their beaks before he'd gotten the shield into place. She yelled in fury and aimed her wand at Mawdoor. "Bend the golden sword around his neck!"

But the sword kept coming toward the prince.

And now winged creatures swooped down. They were demons—a score of black demons flying straight at him—and at their center was a great red demon, the most powerful, the most dangerous of all demons. They were Mawdoor's kin. He'd alerted them, brought them here.

Brecia shouted as she waved her wand, "Demon blood scorch the earth!"

The red demon drew back and looked at her, and Brecia thought she would die of fear at the malevolence in those red eyes.

Nothing happened. She felt as helpless as a mortal, an awful feeling.

The prince knew he had little time. Demons were the worst, nearly invincible, and there were so many of them. Mawdoor had done things correctly this time.

A demon broke away and came right at him. He felt long claws dig into his face. He couldn't see, couldn't see. He pictured Mawdoor in his mind's eye and flung his knife.

He heard a loud yell but couldn't see where his knife had struck.

Three more demons were on him now, and he couldn't get them away. The pain was hideous, worse than the assassin's sword in his heart. He saw the red demon hovering, waiting for the black demons to hold him. Then it would come in for the kill.

He fought, breaking necks, arms, legs, but there were just too many. He used all his power, but the demons were from another realm, a realm not touched by a wizard's magic, and Mawdoor had brought them here, doubtless a favor for his long-dead father. He felt Brecia's magic slamming against the demons, but nothing helped.

She knew the demons would kill him, rip

him to pieces, and knew he was helpless against them. She had to hurry.

She yelled, "Bring me the key!"

In that instant, the key was her hand. She stuck the small key in the cask lock and turned it. The lid flew open. Brecia raised the cask toward Mawdoor and yelled, "Come inside, Mawdoor, for all eternity! Your demons with you!"

There was a huge whooshing sound. The demons and Mawdoor all came together in a tall funnel. They were whipped together. She saw that Mawdoor's golden sword seemed to be bending around him, holding him prisoner. The whole mess of them hovered over the cask, then whooshed into it. She slammed the lid closed and turned the key.

The prince was on his hands and knees, his head down, panting. He was covered with blood.

She touched him, kissed him, began her chants to heal him. But the demon wounds didn't respond. She said, "Prince, listen to me. I can't heal you. We must use other methods."

"There are no other methods," he said, and knew that very soon he would be dead.

"No, you stupid prince, there must be something!"

He managed to raise his head to look at her. "Brecia, dearest, I am so very sorry that it must end like this. The bastard brought in demons. Who would have imagined that? Mawdoor surprised me. I wonder where my knife hit him."

She was utterly terrified, utterly distracted, and said, "Your knife took off his ear."

"Good. Ah, this was very interesting." And he fell onto his side, his eyes closed, his blood flowing bright and thick onto the ground.

"No!" Brecia raised her head and yelled, "Help me!"

Ghosts filled the air, swirling about the prince, who lay still on the ground. They were nearly transparent, save for their long, shadowy, naked feet. Brecia watched them settle over him, enfolding him in their very being, and they began to chant. Soft, sibilant voices rose to fill the courtyard, to rise into the heavens themselves.

Brecia fell to her knees beside the prince. She felt one of the ghosts gently shove her back. She sat back on her heels and

watched. And she prayed. There was nothing else she could do.

The soft chanting began to fade just as
the ghosts themselves began to thin into the
air itself. Then they were gone, back to the
oak forest.

The prince lay motionless on the ground.
No more blood was on him, but he was so
still. She leaned over him, touching his be-
loved face, stroking her fingers over his
chest, his arms, his legs. "Prince, enough of
this. Come back to me, my lord."

Time passed, endless time. She was
ready to scream her fear, her sorrow when
suddenly his eyes fluttered open. He smiled
up at her.

She leaned down and kissed his mouth.

"Your tears are wetting me, Brecia."

"You mad, mad prince." She kissed him
again and again. "You will be all right." She
continued to kiss his mouth, his nose, his
ears.

But he was so tired, his very being so bat-
tered, that he couldn't even kiss her back,
and surely that was something he hated.

Slowly, strength flowed back into his
body. He drew a deep breath and sat up.
He shook his head. There was no more

blood, no more of the huge wounds the demons had gouged into his body, some of them nearly tearing him in two. He said, "Your ghosts saved me."

"Our ghosts, prince," she said. "Our ghosts."

"You called for the key. That was very smart of you, Brecia. You opened the cask?"

She nodded at the cask, sitting on the ground, unmoving, the key in the lock. "Mawdoor and all the demons are inside, his golden sword wrapped around him."

"All that animal wailing," the prince said, "it was a charming idea." He nodded to the cask and in the next instant, it was in his hands. "What happened?"

"The demons seemed to grab Mawdoor up, all twisting together. They looked like a whirling cyclone, coming straight toward the cask. It was like a huge funnel sinking deeper and deeper into the cask until I couldn't see it anymore—"

"—and you slammed the lid down and locked it."

She nodded.

He held the cask close, frowned. "This is very curious. I know they're in there, but I can't feel them, any of them. I can sense nothing."

She kept her eyes on that cask, still so afraid that it would burst open and the demons would burst out and tear him to shreds and Mawdoor would force her to watch him die. She was tensed, alert, everything in her ready to whisk the both of them off to Spain, perhaps for some hunting, if something happened. She hated that cask, hated the creatures imprisoned inside it.

The prince was rubbing his chin. "I am thinking, Brecia. We must deal with this cask."

Brecia knew it, she just didn't want to deal with it yet. She looked over at Maida, who was lying on the ground, a scream frozen on her mouth. All the other old people were as still as the fortress itself. She couldn't see any animals.

There was no more danger now. Brecia closed her eyes, chanted ancient words that none now understood. The earth righted itself. The old people didn't move much. They were too frightened to do anything but stare. A single chicken squawked. The first thing Maida did was shout, "What did you do to Mawdoor, you foul witch?"

"Mawdoor is no more," Brecia said. "All will be right again."

Maida rose, dusted herself off, and walked to the prince and Brecia. She was frightened, it was clear, but she had guts. "You are magic, just like my lord."

"Yes," the prince said easily. "We are magic, and Mawdoor will no longer terrorize the earth."

Brecia stared at Maida with her thick, fiery hair and her moss-green eyes, and her own green eyes narrowed. She said, "You insulted me, you stupid woman, actually waved your fist at me—"

"Aye, and didn't you just hurl me right against that wall over there? No thanks to you that my leg isn't broken."

"—but I am beginning to think that you would make a great mistress of Penwyth."

Maida said, sneering, "I would be great at anything I did, but let me tell you, miserable witch, I wouldn't have long remained Mawdoor's mistress. He would have strangled you finally, and I would have married him!"

"No, you stupid woman, I didn't mean that you would be great as some man's mistress. I meant that you should run things around here."

Maida's mouth hung open, then her brain came alive. "Ah, and just how will I protect this land? What do you have to say to that, ugly witch?"

"I'm not ugly. I'm beautiful, just ask anyone. Besides—and know that I hate to say this—you and I do look somewhat alike, what with all the red hair and the green eyes."

"Hmmm. The red and green look better on me."

The prince coughed, cleared his throat. "Now, to protect this land, Maida, the first thing to do is get rid of this black fortress." The prince held his wand close and lightly stroked it on his sleeve. In the next instant there was a very normal structure made of wood, wattle, and daub. Even the pigsty went from menacing black to weathered wooden planks lashed together with thick ropes.

The people murmured. The animals yelped.

"Hmmm," Maida said. "How am I to keep Penwyth going with all these wretched old people?"

The prince merely smiled and said, waving his hand in a dramatic wide circle, "To live a very long life at Penwyth will never again be a punishment. Long life will be bestowed upon those who are utterly loyal to Penwyth. Return those ancients to what they were."

Brecia shouted, "Bring youth back to the old people!"

And with that utterance, they became what they'd been years before. They shook themselves, rubbed elbows and knees that no longer hurt, scratched heads with hair on them once again. Three young maids did a dance, kicking up their heels. Several boys yelled and cursed. Young voices filled the courtyard. It was a marvelous sound. Some of the young people just stood there, wondering at what had happened and marveling at it.

Brecia called out, "Mawdoor is no more. Your lives are yours again."

Maida looked around, rubbed her hands together. "Look yon. I believe that beautiful young man standing over there, looking quite surprised and pleased, was old Dorom. Hmmm. What a lovely smile he has."

"He has all his teeth again," Brecia said.

"I think I must see if his breath is sweet

as well," Maida said, and walked to young Dorom.

The prince said, stroking his jaw, "You know, Brecia, I am feeling labyrinthine. Yes, the workings of my brain even exceed my normal complexity. I wish to protect Penwyth and all Maida's descendants—"

"Given what she is like, I imagine her heirs will hold Penwyth close for a very long time. Now what is this, prince? You wish to cast some sort of spell on Penwyth?"

"No, I want a curse." He stroked his jaw three more times, looked quite pleased with himself, and raised the cask high in his hands for all to see. "Listen, all. If a man ever takes this land by force, let him die."

He smiled at Brecia. "There. It is done."

"For a labyrinthine mind," Maida said, tossing her lovely red hair, "you didn't have much to say." The prince nearly threw the cask at her. He was ready to take back his splendid curse when Brecia said, her voice carrying just as far as the prince's had, "If the Penwyth maid has red hair, if she has green eyes, then she will be saved."

The prince guffawed. "That miserable offering is so much better than my straightforward, clearly proclaimed curse? You merely protect anyone who looks like you and Maida."

Brecia shook her fist at him. "You're just angry because you didn't think to do it." She paused a moment, watching Maida give all the young people orders. She said, "You know, Maida would have made a great witch. Penwyth is now protected, Maida now has people to help her, and now"—she sucked in her breath "—now we must deal with the cask." She looked at it, shuddered just a bit. "What shall we do with it?"

"It must go to my cave. But first, Brecia, you must realize that a day will come when the curse must end. Do you know, I believe I have another labyrinthine thought."

He grabbed her. Brecia was so startled that she dropped the cask. But the prince snapped it up even as he kissed her ear. "Yes," he said, laughing and kissing her, "one day, long in the future, the curse will no longer help. It will hurt. It will have to be lifted, and thus I have decided to tie Mawdoor to the curse."

"Mawdoor? Are you mad?"

"No, listen. I will tie the curse to the cask, and since Mawdoor is inside, he must be a part of it. Trust me. You know, Mawdoor doesn't really deserve to remain forever with demons. No one is that rotten. It is too much." The prince opened his voice so that it could be heard in the very depths of a demon's mind and said, his mouth close to the cask, "Mawdoor, you now have only one ear, since I sent my knife through the other one, so you must listen carefully. You can free yourself in the future by breaking my curse and swearing to leave your demons in their realm. You will swear to become a wizard all can trust."

The cask shook in his hands. The prince leaned close, nodded, then straightened and smiled. "He is very, very angry, but how long can that last? Yes, I see it all clearly now. The time will come when the curse must be broken. A man will come, a man with a brain, perhaps a man with just a touch of magic. I will direct him, and all will be well." He closed his eyes, murmured words she couldn't hear, then said, smiling, "It is done."

She said, "This man will lose his magic and become completely mortal again?"

He looked down at her. "I don't know if I would go that far." He snapped his fingers.

"Don't forget, just a touch of magic. This man will find the cask."

"Mortals always find things, no matter how well you hide them. With magic, this man will walk right to the cask and kick it. I certainly would. Will this man look like you, prince?"

"Since I am such a splendid specimen, what more could a man ask?"

She touched her wand to his nose, and he felt it kiss him. She was laughing as she said, "There must needs be a woman, to guide him, to make him laugh, to love him, to save his life countless times."

Brecia could have sworn that his chest puffed out larger than it should. He said, "And will she look like you?"

"Why not? Then they will be well matched. You know, I will give our man a little nudge as well. Let us hope he will deal well with Mawdoor."

"He will be my man. He will deal well with everyone. Perhaps he will have a bit of trouble with the woman, if she is too much like you. But he will win her over. He will tame her and she will worship him."

"Your arrogance," she said, kissing his chin, "charms me."

She saw that all the people were talking

about them but were too afraid to come close. "Let us leave them with a tale to tell over their winter fires." She took his hand and cried, "Home!"

And they vanished.

The staring people heard a woman's voice, as if from the very air above them, "Come, show me unnatural things, prince. Will you really ask me to be on my knees for hours at a time?"

A great laugh rumbled through the sky.

33

Present

When the voice screamed "NO!" Merryn thought her heart would stop and she would collapse and die in this wretched hole twenty feet under a cave floor.

Bishop was still, not moving even a finger, staring into the cask.

The earsplitting noise of wild animals charging toward them slowly fell away, until it became nothing more than a sound that, oddly, soothed the mind and the ear, like the smooth breaking of waves against a shore.

"There is something in there," he said.

She grabbed his hand. "No, don't reach into that thing. We don't know what will happen."

"That's true, we don't. But we must know." She was so afraid, she'd locked her teeth together. She didn't want to watch, but she did. Her eyes followed his hand as it sank slowly into the cask.

The cask wasn't deep, no more than six inches at the most, but his hand kept going down, down, down even further, until he was up to his elbow.

He was on his knees, leaning over the cask now, his entire arm in the cask, his fingers outstretched.

He looked at her. "I don't feel anything, nothing hot, nothing cold."

A voice said clearly, "I am Mawdoor, keeper of the curse, prisoner in this damned cask for longer than a wizard should exist. Release me, mortal."

Bishop said without hesitation, his voice deep, "Will you swear that you will be the most trustworthy wizard in this world?"

There was a deep rumbling sound, then, "Yes, I swear it."

"You will return the demons to their realm?"

"Yes, it will be done."

"When?"

"Immediately. Release me!"

Bishop sat back on his haunches, staring into the cask. He nodded slowly. "It is done." He picked up the wand and pointed it into the cask. "The curse is done."

There was utter silence. Then there was singing—many voices raised in a beautiful harmony, singing, chanting—and then silence again.

The cask began to shake. Bishop and Merryn backed away from it.

It exploded into brilliant colors—reds, blues, oranges, greens—and those colors flew upward and outward, cracking and popping, like myriad small explosions of noise and color, and the noise became louder and louder until they both clapped their hands over their ears.

Then the incredible noise, all the colors, the cracking and popping, the cask, all were gone. Simply gone.

They were alone in the hole.

"Do you know something, Merryn?"

She cocked her head to one side.

"It just occurred to me that I should very

much like to see you on your knees in front of me."

Her head remained cocked. "Whyever for, Bishop? You wish me to worship you?"

His eyes nearly crossed. He could see her, dammit, see her on her knees, see her touching him, see her taking him in her mouth. He shuddered. They were in the bottom of a hole, by all the saints' wayward children, with no way out, and he suddenly wanted her to take him in her mouth?

He was mad.

And what had happened was madness. They were trying to ignore it, to focus only on the present, on what was real, on what they could see and touch. A good thing, he thought, the present. He knew neither of them wanted to think about the strange cask and the wizard Mawdoor and the demons, all gone now, thank God. It was all just too much.

Suddenly Bishop heard laughter. It was the same laugh he'd heard when he'd first leaned over the mouth of the hole. The same laugh as when a hand had slapped his face. The laughter was becoming louder and louder.

He looked at Merryn. She was waiting for him to speak, but he couldn't, just couldn't.

He realized that she didn't hear the laughter.

Suddenly he smiled. "No, being on your knees in front of me, it's not at all about worship. I'll tell you all about it later. Let's get out of this hole now, Merryn. Give me your hand."

She didn't question him, just gave him her hand.

He clasped her fingers, pulled her close and wrapped his arms tightly around her. The laughter was soft now, right in his ears, filling him, and he knew there wouldn't be a hand to slap him this time. And he wondered, *Is that you, prince? You want me out of this wretched hole, don't you? You want me out of your cave.*

Bishop smiled as he closed his eyes. When he opened them, he saw a rope ladder going up the side of the hole.

"Where did that come from?" Merryn said, and there was no fear in her voice, just wonder. "It wasn't there before, was it, Bishop?"

"No, it wasn't."

He said no more. After all, what could he say? That the prince had put the rope ladder there? He supposed they were both beyond fear now, beyond what they couldn't begin to explain, to understand. Bishop said, "Mayhap the ladder was there all the time, and we just didn't see it." Aye, it had been invisible. Was that true? He had no idea. But he'd known, known all the way to the soles of his dirty feet, that it would be there when he opened his eyes.

He knew when he stepped out of the hole onto the cave floor that he wouldn't hear the laughter anymore. Whatever it was, or whoever it had been, the prince or perhaps even Brecia, had again disappeared—only the thing was, they hadn't ever appeared. He looked back down into the hole, not at all surprised to see that the rope ladder was gone.

Whatever had happened, whatever he'd imagined or dreamed, or whipped up in his maddened brain, Bishop knew it was over. The curse was gone. The cask and Mawdoor—where had they gone? Into past time? Future time? He had no idea. Perhaps the cask was floating about in the ether, just overhead. Who could possibly know? Or was it waiting for another to come who could be used to replay an ancient story?

He said to Merryn, who was straightening her filthy gown, "The curse is lifted." He said it with firmness, with absolute conviction. He knew both of them had to believe it.

"Aye," she said, smiling up at him, "I think you're right. It was tied to that golden cask. I do wonder where that cask came from. How ever did it keep getting deeper and deeper? That was scary, Bishop. And who put it at the bottom of that hole in this particular cave?" She paused. She saw something on his face, something that made every question die in her throat. It was just as well, she thought. *Leave all of it alone, leave all the questions here in this cave.* It was over and they were alive and the curse was no more. It was enough. She said, "Shall we go home to Penwyth?"

"Home?"

"Aye, it is home to both of us now. I shan't have to worry that you will topple over dead in your roasted pheasant at our wedding feast."

"No, it wasn't one of my favorite thoughts, either. Merryn, we should wed as quickly as possible. You're carrying my babe."

He saw her hands cover her stomach, an instinctive gesture. "Mayhap you're right,"

she said. "Finally, I will bear my fifth husband a child."

He threw back his head and laughed.

When they stepped out of the cave, Fearless raised his head and whinnied at them.
Merryn breathed in the sea air, content.

And Bishop thought, *Not only is the curse
gone, all of them are gone—the prince, Brecia, Mawdoor.* Ah, what happened to Maida?
Merryn, with her red hair and green eyes—
was she descended from Maida? Or Brecia? There was no understanding of it, and
it really didn't matter what he understood or
didn't understand, now, did it?

He smiled, reached out his hand. "Let's go
home, Merryn."

St. Erth
Two days later

Dienwald said as he tossed Bishop an apple
from the St. Erth orchard, "We know only
that a young man named Fioral of Grandere
Glen has taken Penwyth. This was some
four or five days ago. It is said he has about
twenty men with him. It's said he plans to

wait for Merryn to return. Then he will wed her."

Philippa said, "We were hopeful, but evidently the curse hasn't killed him."

"That's because I wasn't there to marry," Merryn said, and bit into her apple.

"Also, the curse is no more," Bishop said.

"We thought you would lift it." Dienwald took a bite of his own apple. "My damned father-in-law—aye, the wretched king must continually rub my nose in it—sent us a message, telling me to help you as much as I could, but he said, regardless, you would lift the damned curse. He wrote there was just something about you that made things happen." Dienwald tossed his apple core to one of the wolfhounds. "I suppose when Philippa and I next visit Windsor, he will go on and on about your shrewdness, your damnable cunning, your ability to see to the depths of things." Dienwald sighed, laced his fingers over his flat belly. "Then he will lament loudly to everyone at Windsor that he wishes you were my sweet Philippa's husband, not I, the poor fool who will have so many babes that my farmers will surely wither away because they will have to work so hard to feed all of us."

Philippa gave her husband a kiss and patted his shoulder. She smiled at Merryn and Bishop. "He frets."

"Oh, no, Philippa, he is jesting," Merryn said. "No one at St. Erth is in danger of starving."

Philippa said, even as she stroked her long fingers through her husband's hair, "No, it's not that. He frets because there's a small band of thieves not far from St. Erth and he wanted to go after them, but our sons held his legs, pleaded with him, begged him not to go, told him the king— their grandfather—wouldn't be pleased if he did."

Bishop laughed. "Edward and Nicholas are only eight months old. Even they couldn't be strong enough to beg with their father and hold him here."

Philippa said, "Actually, Crooky spoke for them, didn't you?"

The fool straightened to his full height, which didn't quite bring him to Merryn's armpit, and sang, head thrown back, to the high hall ceiling,

"The king has spoken, his will is done.
No more will my lord catch thieves for fun.

*He's here to sleep, and then
before he sleeps, he will—"*

Crooky fell over onto his back, pounded his head with his fists, and howled. "I ruined it. I wanted to sing about how the master makes the mistress yell her head off when he pleasures her, but I ruined it because I didn't follow my vision. Ah, but now that you know what I should have sung, it wasn't so very bad, now, was it?"

"No, Crooky," Philippa said, "it wasn't so very bad. I do not yell my head off, you fool."

"Ha," said Dienwald, "you yell so loudly poor Prinn the porter believes St. Erth is being attacked. What you sang, Crooky, it was a worthless truth, all those ridiculous notions tied together. You must scratch your lousy head and come up with something better. We have guests, after all, worthy guests." And Dienwald rose, kicked the fool and sent him rolling into the rushes.

34

Dienwald said to Bishop, "My men are excited, flexing their muscles, bragging about their prowess. They haven't had any villains for a good fortnight. They're ready to gullet the soldiers holding Penwyth. I hope you have a good plan."

"Aye," Bishop said, looking into the distance at Penwyth, "I have a plan." And he smiled. Dienwald didn't push him. Bishop would tell him when it was time.

Bishop was thinking how very odd it was that everything was green—the fields, the bushes, the trees. The earth was rich and dark with life and moisture, wildflowers dotted the landscape. There was no more drought at Penwyth. But why had it happened in the first place? The prince hadn't told him. Bishop blinked. Somehow, it had been tied to the curse, mayhap even tied to his coming. He remembered the cloud of despair that had hung over the dying earth and felt relief fill his soul.

Bishop and Dienwald rode at the fore of their group. Behind them, beside Merryn, rode Gorkel, a man who could crush three men's heads at the same time.

Dienwald looked briefly over his shoulder, then said, "Merryn shouldn't be with us, Bishop. This could be highly dangerous."

"Actually, I couldn't carry out the plan if she weren't with me. She's very necessary. There's really no choice in the matter. I will see that no harm comes to her. But you know, Dienwald, I should like to know how you managed to keep Philippa at home."

Dienwald grimaced. "The truth is I had to bribe the wench."

Bishop raised a dark brow.

"I told her I would I would speak to Graelam about a marriage contract between little Harry and my Eleanor."

"An excellent match," Bishop said, "but I

still cannot believe Philippa agreed to re-main at Sr. Erth for that paltry bribe, since I imagine you would have made a match with de Moreton in any case."

"I would have. Since you are soon to wed Merryn, Bishop, let me give you a hint about dealing with a stubborn wife—never hesitate to lie to gain your ends. I spent hours yelling and swearing that I would never be allied to de Moreton's family." Dienwald grinned. "I was really quite good. Then I let her beat me about the head, yell at me, claim I was an idiot. Aye, my dearest wench sees this as a remarkable victory." He began whis-tling, very pleased with himself.

They heard Gorkel the Hideous laugh be-hind them. It was a terrifying sound.

Dienwald swiveled in his saddle. "Merryn made Gorkel laugh. It is amazing how much the girl pleases him. You are a lucky man, Bishop. Now, enough about future wed-dings. Tell me your plan and what you wish me to do."

Inside Penwyth, Fioral of Grandere Glen, twenty-two years old, convinced that he was invincible and more clever than most men who inhabited the earth, rose from Lord Vel-

Ian's chair, where he'd sat himself in comfort and authority for nearly the past sennight, and said to his master-at-arms, Dolan, "This waiting grows monotonous. We need some entertainment. Bring in one of the old relics."

Dolan brought in the old man Crispin, simply because Crispin told him to. Crispin didn't want his men to be tortured by this mad whelp. He'd been their leader for so many years he couldn't begin to remember when it had all started. As for Dolan, he was weary to his bones because he was so worried, nay, he was downright afraid. He knew something bad was going to happen. He realized well enough that since his young master hadn't died of the curse, and still looked healthy as a stoat, he thought he'd won. In fact, Fioral seemed happier, more content, than Dolan had ever seen him. But now this. Dolan cursed under his breath. What did he want to do to Crispin, a harmless old man who was close to becoming his friend, but who would, naturally, stick a knife through Fioral's heart if given the chance.

It was obvious that the curse wouldn't work unless and until a man married the granddaughter, Merryn de Gay. As far as Dolan was concerned, if he and the men managed to leave this place with most of their hides intact, he would feel blessed. He rather hoped that Fioral would wed Merryn de Gay. Then he just might topple over, and good riddance to him. It had become very clear over the past days that Fioral wasn't nearly as astute as he believed himself to be.

As for Crispin, he knew well enough that the young man was bored, knew Fioral was probably going to torment him. Would he kill him? Crispin didn't know. Like Lord Vellan and Lady Madelyn, he was very worried about Merryn and Sir Bishop. Where were they? What was happening to them? Oh, God, there was simply nothing to know save that this young dolt was sitting in his master's chair, lording it all over everybody, and now the fool was bored, looking for sport, and Crispin knew he was the sport. At least Fioral had kept his promise. He hadn't killed anyone. Yet.

Dolan gently pushed the old man, Crispin, in front of Fioral. He was worried what Fioral would do. A bored warrior could be more potent than a real curse. Ah, the damned curse. Fioral was convinced that the curse was all a lie, despite all Lord Vellan's endless tales, told in great, horrific detail, all about the deaths of the first four husbands, each recounting gorier than the last.

Fioral was thinking about the third husband's death as he rubbed the back of his head. The sore hadn't gotten any better. It felt larger, as a matter of fact. Fioral forced his hand away from his neck and looked at the old man who stood beside Dolan.

"Your name is Crispin and you are Lord Vellan's master-at-arms."

"Aye, for many years more than you've been walking this earth, young thief."

Fioral got up from Lord Vellan's chair, went to the old man, raised his fist, and slammed it into Crispin's jaw. The old man would have collapsed to the rushes had Dolan not held him up. Dolan, because he realized another blow was likely, gently eased the old man down onto the rushes and lightly pressed his hand against Crispin's shoulder to keep him down.

Fioral stood over Crispin, tapping his foot, his arms crossed over his chest. "How many years would that be, old man?"

Crispin felt his old bones shudder and heave from the force of the blow. The rushes felt good. He wasn't about to move.

"I was the master-at-arms at Penwyth before your father was born."

"Do you believe in the curse?"

"Aye, certainly. Only a stupid man would disbelieve the deaths of four husbands."

Fioral leaned down to strike Crispin again, but Dolan grabbed his arm. "Nay, my lord, leave the old man be. Remain above his insults. Realize that all who live here at Penwyth are a superstitious lot, and since it looks like all the people have lived here since the dawn of time, it's obvious that they would become only more superstitious as time went on."

"Ah, so it is all that clear to you, then, Dolan?"

Dolan nodded. He heard the softness in the master's voice and it curdled his belly.

Fioral grew still. The sore on the back of his neck throbbed and dug deeper. He wanted to rub it. "You dare to lay your hand on me, Dolan?"

He'd been a fool, Dolan thought as he felt the hand of fear drawing close. In that hand would likely be a knife, his master's favored weapon, and that knife could slide so easily into his chest. He held himself very still. "I meant no insult. It is just that all the old folk are just that, old and thus no threat to us. There is no reason to kill them."

"He's right, you young fool. Leave Crispin alone. He's a good soldier, a solid man, and he's done naught to you."

Fioral jerked around to see Lord Vellan stride into the great hall, with perhaps not as much vigor as he once had, but he was still impressive, that old man, particularly wearing his beautiful ermine-trimmed tunic, just finished for him, he'd heard one of servants mention, by Lady Madelyn. Fioral couldn't believe the mad old crone could still make such fine stitches, her fingers were so knotted and gnarled. He wanted that tunic. It was fit for a king, not this doddering old fool who should have been sent to hell years before.

Fioral said, "You will answer for your man's rudeness, my lord?"

"Oh, aye, that I will. Tell me, Fioral, what did Crispin do to so enrage you? Did he attack you? Threaten to run his sword through you?"

Fioral spit, not more than an inch from Crispin's head. "I would prefer to kill you, old man, and then it would all be over."

Vellan said, "Nothing would be over, you idiot. Sir Bishop will return soon, and he will draw your fingernails off your hands, one by one, and I will laugh when each one drops to the ground and your howls resonate from the keep walls."

Fioral couldn't help it. He looked down at his hands, his fingernails, blunt, short, dirty, and strong. He looked up. "This Bishop of Lythe is probably dead, my lord, and you know it as well as I do. He just up and left and took Lady Merryn with him. What do you think happened to them? They went perhaps to London to see the king? I don't think so, and neither do you. They're dead, killed by bandits. I would have killed them had I seen them before arriving here at Penwyth."

No one said anything because no one wanted to die. Lord Vellan just continued looking at him as if he were a bug to be trod upon. Fioral paused a moment, then said, "No, let us say that there is a curse here at Penwyth. This Bishop took Lady Merryn away from Penwyth and forced her to wed him, believing the curse wouldn't touch him. But it did. What do you think of that, my lord? Bishop of Lythe is dead because this curse of yours can act anywhere, anytime."

"All right," Vellan said. "If the curse killed Bishop, then where is my granddaughter?"

"She is on her way back to Penwyth. She will come back to me, to wed me, her rightful husband."

"You have no right here, Fioral," Lord Vellan said. "You will die for your impudence. All your bragging, it is nothing."

Fioral walked to Lord Vellan, drew back his fist, and would have slammed it into the old man's jaw, but in that instant the sore on Fioral's neck seemed to explode. He felt his skin tearing, pus spewing out, disease pouring through him, eating him alive. By all the saints' blessed sins, he felt fear tear through his belly. He clapped his hand over the sore and ran out of the great hall.

Slowly, Crispin stood up. He brushed the rushes from his trousers, raised his head, and said to Dolan, "Something is very wrong with your master. Other than his madness."

"Aye, it's a sore on his neck that doesn't heal. I will go see to him."

Lord Vellan was laughing, then yelled after the young warrior, "The Penwyth curse is many-faceted, is it not, Fioral? Just look at you, rotting from the inside. How does it feel knowing that you will soon die and nothing you can do will stop it?"

Vellan laughed and laughed as he

watched Fioral disappear up the winding stone staircase, Dolan at his heels. Then he began hiccuping, and even that felt very good. He said to Crispin after he'd swallowed some warm ale, "So where do you think Bishop is?"

"I pray he is close, my lord."

"Aye, me, too, Crispin. Me, too."

Not more than an hour later, when the afternoon was sinking over the hillocks into the western horizon, Dolan came into the great hall. He stopped in front of Fioral, who now had a bandage on his neck and was sitting again in Lord Vellan's chair, holding himself quiet as a stone. "We have visitors, my lord. An old man and an old woman, asking to be allowed to see you. They say they barely escaped bandits. They beg for protection."

"Tell them to go elsewhere or we'll slit their scrawny throats. Penwyth needs no more ancient varmints."

"They said that they can tell you about the whereabouts of Lady Merryn de Gay."

Fioral rubbed his jaw. The sooner he got his hands on the girl, the sooner he'd be the lord of Penwyth. And then the dreadful sore on his neck would heal. He was sure of it.

He nodded. "All right, then, bring them here. Dear God, are there nothing but crumbling old bones littering this miserable place?"

When the old man and woman shuffled into the great hall, Fioral knew he'd never seen two uglier specimens. The old woman looked hideous, all scrawny, hairs sticking out from three warts on her face, a face that could sour a man's belly with but a look.

The old man was just as bad, bent and hunchbacked, dirty gray hair hanging over his face and down his back, his teeth black.

Fioral said, lounging back in the chair, "I allowed you into my keep. You will tell me now what you know of Lady Merryn de Gay or I will slit your withered old throats."

35

The old man took a faltering step forward. He bowed, holding his back as he righted himself again, and said in an ancient, croaking voice that sounded to Fioral as though it was filled with the echoes of time, "My wife is a seer, my lord. On the night of the full moon—tomorrow night—she will be able to tell you exactly where the lady is."

"This old hag, a seer? If that is true, then why must she wait for a full moon?"

The old man shrugged, and it looked painful, that shrug. "I know not the answer to that, good lord, but it is true. Nothing happens if there isn't a full moon. Then I will press my hands against her head. While I'm squeezing her head, the full moon must be shining down on her head, and she sees clearly."

"Aye, it is the way," the old woman said, stepping up, "of the Witches of Byrne. When the old man dies, then my powers will die also because it must be his hands to press against my head. No others will do. It is our bond and it works well. Will you protect us, my lord?"

The sore on Fioral's neck pulsed hot.

Lord Vellan walked into the great hall at that moment and started when he saw the doddering old man and woman. Fioral called out, "The old hag claims to be a seer, my lord. She claims she can tell me where your precious Merryn is at this moment."

"She can, can she? Hmmm." Lord Vellan walked up to the pair and looked them up and down.

"Ah, I see. She has the witch's eye. I can see it now that I look at her closely. Is my granddaughter all right, old witch?"

"Aye, she is, for the moment, my lord. So is Sir Bishop of Lythe, who is with her. I will show the young master here where she is so that he may fetch her and kill the bounder who has her."

Vellan took a step back, a shaft of fear knifing through him. "How do you know his name, old woman? What is this? Where do you come from?"

Suddenly the old woman stiffened, stared hard at Fioral. "You are ill," she said. "What is wrong with you?"

Fioral touched his fingers to the bandage on the back of his neck. "You can see this, can you? For one so ancient, your eyes work remarkably well. It is nothing, just a small sore that annoys me."

"It's not nothing, my lord," she said, and somehow she knew that it truly was bad. "It's snaking into you, making your innards rot, that's what it's doing."

"What is this? Come, old woman, can you heal the sore?"

The old woman's eyelids fluttered, closed. She threw her head back and said in a loud, too deep voice that sounded from one end of the great hall to the other and made everyone shudder with fear, "There is evil in that sore, and it is eating its way through you. It seems to me that the sore is retribution. What have you done to deserve this?"

Fioral didn't like this at all. "Damn you, answer me. Are you a healer, old woman?"

"Nay, my husband here is the healer. I see the evil in you; he can remove it."

Fioral was on his feet in an instant. "Old man, come here."

The old man shuffled to Fioral and stood right in front of him. He was looking at the strip of white wool tied around Fioral's neck. "My wife must know what evil you have done before I can help you."

Fioral gnawed on his lower lip, said nothing.

Lord Vellan strode forward, stood right in the old man's face. "This young thief has come into Penwyth like four others before him, demanding to wed my granddaughter, demanding to lay his boot upon our necks. Is that evil enough, old man? Will that sore on his neck kill him? It should, for he is worth nothing at all. I beg you, don't heal him. He isn't worthy."

Fioral, enraged, jerked his stiletto out of his tunic sleeve, ready to spear the sharp point through Lord Vellan's heart.

The old witch shouted, "You kill him and

that sore will spread until your whole head spouts pus!"

Fioral stopped. He was breathing hard. "What is this? The sore isn't from the damned Penwyth curse. I had it before we came. It has merely gotten a bit worse." He clapped his hand to his neck, and yelled. It was so hot he could not even press his palm against the wool bandage. Oh, God, what was wrong? "Heal me, old man. Heal me now or I will kill both you and your miserable wife."

"All right," he said, and stepped directly in front of him. He moved Fioral's hand away from the bandage, then lightly touched his fingertips to it. The old man closed his eyes, said a few words, then bowed his head for two minutes, eyes still shut, his lips moving. There wasn't a single sound in the great hall. All were staring at the old man, staring at his hand on Fioral's neck.

"It is done," he said as he raised his head. His fingers still touched the white wool. "If the evil you have committed is repented, if you commit no more evil acts, then the sore will disappear. Do you repent your past evil, my lord?"

"Oh, aye, I do."

"And any future evil? Will you cease what you are doing here at Penwyth and take your leave?"

When he said nothing, the old man moved his fingers away, took a step back. The sore throbbed and burned and itched. What to do? Fioral threw back his head and yelled, "I am doing no evil. I am here at Penwyth to wed the heiress, to become Lord Vellan's heir. What evil is there in that? I am young, I am able, I am a fine warrior and will serve King Edward well. He would have sent me here if he'd only known me."

The old man said, "But the king doesn't know you, Fioral of Grandere Glen. He sent Sir Bishop of Lythe here. You are an interloper. You are no better than a thief, like the other four who came here to steal what wasn't theirs, and thus to die."

"No, I'm not a thief! I just wish to make my way as so many second sons must do. Penwyth is a fat plum, and I have plucked it. It is to be expected that a well-trained, brave knight could do that."

"I see no brave knight here," the old man said. "I see only a puling young lout who will die of the evil poisoning him from the inside out."

"But I have done nothing wrong!"

The old man said, "Very well, if that is what you believe to your very soul."

"Aye, it is."

The old man said, his voice as gentle as a summer breeze ruffling through water reeds, "You will fight me, my lord. If you can kill me, then the cursed sore will slide off your neck."

Fioral couldn't believe what he was hearing. He shook his head to clear it. Was the sore making him hear words that hadn't really been said?

"Will you fight me, young thief?"

Fioral said with absolute astonishment, "You want *me* to fight *you*? You're so old that you can barely stand upright. Look at you, all hunched over as if your body is drawing you inside yourself. You can't even hold a sword, can you? By all the saints' runny innards, I could blow on you and you would fall over. I could then press my foot against your chest and your old heart would burst with the pressure. What is this, you old fool? A lame jest? Just heal me and be done with it."

The old man said, "What I said is true. If you fight me, if you beat me, the sore on your neck will heal. Cease your insults, young Fioral. Will you fight me?"

Fioral didn't know what to do. He wanted to know where Merryn was, but he imagined that if he killed the old man, then the old witch wouldn't be able to see Merryn since her husband wouldn't be alive to press his palms against her head. What to do?

Lord Vellan stepped forward. "Listen, old man, he is right. He would quickly dispatch you." He threw back his head and said contemptuously, "This thief will fight me."

Fioral fell back, laughing. The more he laughed, the more his neck burned and itched and thudded like a pounded drum all the way to his bones. He knew in that moment that he couldn't wait, he had to kill the old man or the sore would kill him, and he wasn't about to let that happen. He said, "Lord Vellan, it is not for you to fight me, it is for him. Old man, Dolan will give you a sword. We will fight to the death. In the inner bailey."

The old man gave him a slight bow, shook off his wife's hand that clutched at his sleeve.

The old man said, "Prepare yourself to die, deceitful varmint."

Fioral rolled his eyes, laughed, spit into the rushes. "In which lifetime do you predict that, old man?"

"In the next thirty minutes, Fioral, you will be dead. Your men will leave Penwyth, carting your body away with them. Will you do that, Dolan, so there is no remaining evil to befoul the air here?"

Dolan blinked, unable to take this all in. It was unbelievable, a play written by a madman, but he found himself nodding. "Aye, I will take the master's body away."

"Will you give Fioral a decent burial?"

Fioral smashed his fist against Lord Vellan's chair arm. "Enough of this! Shut up, old man. You are trying to weave fear in my mind."

"Will you put a stone marker on his grave, Dolan?"

"Aye, I will have a man inscribe a marker with his name, and it will be set well atop his grave."

"STOP IT!"

The old man turned again to Fioral. "I will accept a sword from Dolan. He is a good man. I will see you outside, Fioral."

The old man turned on his very ancient heel and shuffled out of the great hall, one foot lagging a bit behind the other, paying no attention at all to the staring people, many of them as old as he was, a handful mayhap even older.

Fioral knew this was ridiculous, but it didn't seem he had any choice but to kill the wheezing old fool. Damnation, this was not going well at all. The sore on his neck seemed to swell. Oh, God, he had to cure that damned sore.

He cursed and ran out of the great hall, jerking his sword out of his scabbard, holding it firmly in his hand.

The old witch looked at Lord Vellan, waved her hands about her, and said, "All this is very strange, is it not, sir?" She cackled loud and long, her ancient old head thrown back on her neck.

Vellan came up close to her, lightly touched her face, and said, "Your nose is falling off."

She grabbed her nose to keep it from sliding to the right. She said as she patted it back into place, "And your nose, sir, is too ugly to fall off."

Lord Vellan grabbed his nose, twisted it a bit, then patted the tip. "My nose is not at all ugly. It is a warrior's nose, one of ancient lineage. But your nose, now, I have never seen a nose so ill-fashioned on a face."

She sighed. "I am relieved that it didn't happen sooner."

Vellan laughed behind his hand, said low, "I am as well, Merryn. It is a fine performance you and Bishop have provided us. I am pleased to see that you and Bishop are closer than you were when he took you away from here. Where have you been?"

"I have been more places than I wished ever to visit, Grandfather. Hurry, we must go to the inner bailey. Bishop might need me."

Vellan raised an old brow.

They heard an animal roar, but it came from a man.

Merryn lifted her skirts and ran. "By all the saints' holy dreams, what has Bishop done now?"

36

Bishop yelled, "Come along, young puppy, let me see if you have any skill, any strength, any cunning."

Bishop was very pleased. A straightforward, simple fight, something he was good at, something that made his blood hot and his young heart pump fast and hard.

He looked back to see Merryn coming down the stone stairs to the great hall, just ahead of Lord Vellan.

So Merryn's grandfather had finally figured out who they were. That was all right. Lady Madelyn then appeared behind her husband, and Bishop saw him turn to speak quietly to her. She nodded slowly, smiled, sent a small wave to him.

Bishop took the sword from Dolan. "Thank you. You are a good man. Do you wish to stay here after your master is buried?"

Dolan stared at him, then slowly nodded. "Aye, my men as well."

He yelled again, "Well, Fioral? Have your bowels turned to water with fright?"

Suddenly Crispin stepped into the circle formed by all the people in the inner bailey.

He laid his hand on Bishop's sleeve. "Listen, sir, I cannot allow this. It is vicious murder. You cannot protect yourself from him. No, I will not allow it. Give me the sword, old man, and go take your rest yon beneath the apple tree."

He then whirled about and yelled, "*I* will fight you, Fioral—not this old man who's never done you any harm!"

Now this was unexpected. Bishop raised his hand and laid it on Crispin's shoulder. He said low, "There is no need for your valor, Crispin. It is I, Bishop of Lythe, here to claim what is mine."

Crispin nearly tripped over his boots, he was so surprised. "My lord," he said at last. "It is difficult to believe. By all the saints' wedded mothers, I have never in my life seen such a fine performance. It is quite remarkable. You look older than I do."

And that was quite an accomplishment, Bishop knew. "I thank you, Crispin. For myself, I thought that Merryn's performance was even better."

"By all the saints' colored rosary beads, that old hag who makes my belly lurch just to look at her is my lady Merryn?"

"Aye. Now take your ease, Crispin. Let me deal with our poacher."

Fioral's men were ranged behind him. Bishop saw him speaking to a smallish man who looked as tough as a chicken that had survived many a fox. What was that about?

Then Fioral, a big smile on his mouth, strode into the center of the circle, slashing his sword to and fro, so quickly, with such force, that the air seemed to vibrate.

"Well, old man, do you wish to lay your head on that rock by Dolan's foot? I will lop it off so quickly you will feel scarce anything at all. What say you?"

"After I have stuck my sword through your guts, Fioral, I will then smash your head with the rock. What say you to that?"

Fioral gave a mighty roar of laughter and

came running, sword held in both hands, drawn high over his head. It would be a mighty blow when that sword came down. Bishop smiled, at his ease, and watched him come. Fioral was strong, his eyes were sharp, no doubt about that, but Fioral believed him harmless, and thus his attention wasn't focused on him, and that was a very big mistake. Bishop smiled, waited. It wasn't, after all, Mawdoor coming at him with a golden wizard's sword.

"Well, old man, will you huddle there shaking inside your old bones until one of my men fetches you out? You see your death coming toward you? Come on, you worthless old braggart, fight me, damn you!"

"All right," Bishop said. Just as Fioral ran the three final feet to reach him, his sword ready to cleave his head in two, Bishop slid quickly to the side and stuck out his booted foot. Fioral went crashing to the ground just beyond where Bishop had been standing. He was up in an instant, breathing hard, so furious, so surprised, that he couldn't think of anything to say. Ah, Bishop saw, that had gained his full attention. He knew, too, that he'd moved too fast for an old man. Would Fioral realize it?

Fioral realized that the old man was spry. More than that, he was lucky, but there would be no more luck for him. Fioral didn't run at him this time, he slashed his sword up and down, then back and forth, all the while walking steadily toward his ancient prey, who was standing there, leaning lightly on his own sword.

"What's the matter, old man? You stand there like a jousting dummy. You're too weak to lift that sword, aren't you? Come, bend your neck over that rock. I'll make it fast."

"Come and see how weak I am, sweet lad," Bishop said, his voice as smooth as newly churned butter. "My, aren't you a brave young fool, so sure of yourself now. Yet weren't you just on the ground, bested by a man older than the mortar in the castle walls? Aye, I stuck out my foot and you landed right on your face."

Fioral quickened his pace, anger pouring off him in waves. "You will die slowly now, old man."

Bishop knew Merryn was coming closer, not because he saw her but because he knew her that well. And he felt her.

Bishop concentrated on Fioral, raised his

sword at the last moment and brought it down. The two heavy blades clashed hard, ringing loud enough for the sheep grazing beyond the ramparts to hear.

Fioral, surprised, released and pushed back. He didn't wait an instant, came again to pound Bishop's sword. Bishop once again met the blow, twisting his wrist at the last moment, nearly knocking the sword from Fioral's hand.

Fioral couldn't believe this, wouldn't believe it. He was panting, by the saints. The miserable old man had made him—a fine, strong warrior—pant. He yelled, "You bastard, what is this? Aye, I see it now, you have magic in you, don't you, old man? You have evil magic, and you're here to ruin my chances. Damn you, I won't let you! Start praying your way into heaven, you foul old relic!" He sliced his sword down, hard, with great precision, missing Bishop's shoulder by a scant inch.

Bishop knew he was preening, showing off, showing all of them how skilled he was. The result of his arrogance was that he'd nearly gotten Fioral's sword through his heart.

Bishop stood straight now, drawing his

shoulders back, and it was he who now ran at Fioral, sword high.

"What is this?" Fioral had only time to speak the words before the old man was on him, a man who wasn't old at all, rather a man as young as he, as skilled as he was.

Their swords clashed loud and hard, making their hands shudder and burn. Bishop came close to Fioral's face, and he was smiling, all his straight white teeth now gleaming in the sun. "You will die because you tried to take what was mine."

Fioral knew in that instant that it was Bishop of Lythe, knew that he'd been fooled completely, but it hadn't been his fault. Surely there'd been foul magic at play here brought on by the wretched curse. And that wretched sore on his neck—aye, evil had ground that sore into his flesh. He shouted to the heavens and began to fight with all his might. Bishop pulled back, letting Fioral come to him this time, and he did, screaming, swinging his sword wildly.

Bishop waited until the very last moment. When Fioral raised his sword high, Bishop turned quickly to the side. As the huge sword came down, he slipped his own sword deep into Fioral's chest. The sword went deep, deeper, sliding through his chest and out his back.

Fioral didn't make a sound. He looked at Bishop, then slowly, very slowly, he staggered back, finally falling on his back, the force of it sending the tip of the sword back through his body and nearly dislodging it from his chest.

Bishop heard the people shouting in shock, some in anger, others now cheering wildly.

He was turning toward Merryn, relief pouring through him, when that small man Fioral had spoken to came forward and smiled even as he stabbed Bishop in the chest.

Dolan was on the man in an instant, clamping his arm around his neck, stabbing him and slitting his throat. He threw him to the ground.

"Merryn," Bishop said, looked down at that knife that was now a part of him, weaved a moment, then very slowly fell to his back onto the ground.

"NO!"

Time seemed to stop. Merryn wasn't aware of anyone else as she ran to him. She had to get to him. The men parted for her. She threw herself onto her knees beside him, saw the blood snaking down his chest, the knife stuck obscenely into his flesh. She didn't hesitate. She pulled out the knife, then slammed both palms on the wound. Blood quickly seeped through her fingers.

She had to press down hard, yes, she could do that, and she did, with all her strength. But she knew deep down that it was no good, no good at all.

Tears streaked down her face, and she was swallowing, sobbing, aware that people were closing in because she saw their shadows, heard their movement, their words. Oh, God, she had to do something.

She yelled in his face, "You won't die, you miserable sot! You hear me? How dare you get yourself stabbed! I will surely kill you for this."

She still heard voices, but they were faint and made no sense. Someone was trying to pull her off him, and she yelled, a mad yell that sent the man back.

Suddenly, it was very clear to her what she had to do. She didn't question—she stretched out over him, her heart against his heart, her arms stretched against his arms, her fingertips touching his wrists, her legs against his legs. She felt his blood seeping through her gown, felt it wet her breast. She felt his heartbeat, so faint, growing fainter by the moment.

She pressed her cheek against Bishop's, and felt his blood pumping out his heart.

Old Sarno, leaning over the ramparts, looked down to see the old woman lying flat atop the old man, arms and legs stretched wide to cover him, and there was blood everywhere. It was odd, but in that moment, they didn't look old. They looked very young and somehow different. He shook his head. The sunlight was bright, making him see things. He would later swear that he saw more than just Sir Bishop and Lady Merryn atop him. There were shadows there, hovering over them, sinking into them, becoming one with them. But surely that couldn't be possible, could it?

Bishop opened his eyes, saw her above him. "No," he said, so dizzy his vision blurred. He could feel the pull of death, hated it, but he wasn't about to let her continue what she was doing. "Get off me, you stupid brave witch. You will not die for me. Get off me, damn you!"

But she didn't, of course. She pressed harder against him. With all his remaining strength, Bishop managed to lurch up and shove her off him. She rolled onto her back on the ground, stared up at the clear sky, the clouds so white above her.

He fell onto his back again. Merryn saw people coming close now, and when a hand touched her arm, she yelled, "Get away from me, you damned fool! Get away!"

She threw herself on top of him again, her heart against his heart, her fingers tightening their grip on his wrists, her belly flat against his, and in the next instant, she felt his pain flow into her; she welcomed it, knew in some shuttered part of her exactly what was happening. She wondered if she would die. His heartbeat—oh, God, it was fainter, slower.

"Bishop," she said against his throat, and bit him hard, "don't you dare die, damn you." And she said it over and over. "Do you hear me, you damned brave fool? You will not die." He was quiet, so very quiet, too quiet.

Suddenly awful pain smashed through her. She didn't think she could bear it, but there was no choice, she had to bear it or he would die. She gritted her teeth and didn't move. Oh, God, he was so still, she couldn't feel his heart, just his blood, so much blood she was drowning in it, and it was her blood too.

Then, suddenly, Bishop opened his eyes, looked up at her. "You will bear my babe alone. I'm sorry, Merryn, so very sorry. We should have wed. I'm sorry." His eyes closed.

She closed her mouth over his mouth, breathed in his breath. "You will not die," she said into his mouth. "Do you hear me, you stupid mortal? You will not die. You are part of me, can't you feel it?"

She felt the brunt of the dreadful pain now pulsing into her, coming from the deepest part of his heart where the knife had entered and lodged. It had hurt before, but not like this. She closed her eyes, seamed her lips together so she wouldn't scream with it. She began shaking as the pain grew and grew. Oh, God, she felt his blood, her blood, and they were one now, and it was too much, simply too much.

He was trying to push her off him again, but he was too weak to manage it. She knew, despite the grinding pain, that she wouldn't let him push her off this time.

Then, amazingly, the pain began to lessen. No, she was dreaming that it was so.

It didn't matter, the pain was receding, slowly, it was leaving her. She sighed softly, kissed his mouth, laid her cheek against his.

They lay together as if dead.

"Make room," Lord Vellan said. "Get away from them. Move back, all of you."

Lady Madelyn stood over them, wringing her old hands. "What is she doing? What is happening?"

"I don't know," Vellan said. "But I do know that we must keep away from them."

Crispin and Dolan were on the other side, staring down at the two young people who looked older than the ancient oak forest that the Witches of Byrne claimed to have stood thick and deep so very close to Penwyth.

No one moved.

It was the strangest feeling, Bishop thought. He felt so tired he wanted to sink into the earth and just lie quietly, the sun shining down on his face. No, he felt beyond tired, felt as if his body could float, there was just so little of him now. But the really strange thing was that there wasn't any more pain. Merryn had taken his pain; she'd taken his wound.

No, that wasn't possible. But it had happened before.

"Merryn?"

Slowly, so slowly he thought he would die of the fear of it, he felt her eyelashes flutter against his flesh.

"Merryn?"

She raised herself above him at that whisper of her name, shook her head, blinked. "What happened?"

He said slowly, eyes still closed, his lips barely moving, "I was stabbed. You came over me. Why did you do that?"

She managed a smile. She was exhausted, felt as though a hundred fists had struck her. "I don't know," she said, and kissed his chin. "I just knew it was the thing to do." She stared down at him a moment, not seeing the ancient old man, but Bishop, the man she loved, the man who wasn't going to die, ever. "I just knew that my heart had to be against your heart, my body against your body. The pain, it was awful, Bishop. But we survived, somehow we survived."

Lord Vellan's hands were on her, raising her, but she grabbed Bishop's shoulders and wouldn't let go.

She looked up over her shoulder at her grandfather. "We are all right. Give us some more time, just another moment. I swear to you that we are all right."

"But that isn't possible, my sweet girl, it just isn't. I'm very sorry, but Bishop was stabbed in the chest. He's dead now. He has to be."

"No, he isn't dead, Grandfather. Indeed, he just spoke to me. I promise you it's the truth."

"If he isn't dead now, he will be in but another instant of time. Come, Merryn, you must leave him. You must let us attend to him."

She looked at her grandfather's old hand, held out to her. Slowly, she shook her head. She leaned down and kissed Bishop's mouth. Then she threw back her head and said, "Bishop, it is time for you to rise up and tell everyone that you will wed me this day."

No one moved. Everyone heard the old woman, who wasn't old at all, speak to Bishop of Lythe, who was dead, perforce had to be dead, or soon would be.

Bishop opened his eyes. He even smiled at her. "Aye, I will do that."

Merryn took her grandfather's hand and let him lift her up. There was a huge circle of blood on the front of her gown. She stared numbly down at it. She heard people all around her, speaking now, saying, "It is the Lady Merryn!"

". . . Why isn't he dead? He should be dead."

". . . Why did she throw herself on top of him?"

On and on it went. He rose to his feet, shook himself like a dog after a storm.

Like her, his chest was covered with blood. But it was drying now, that blood, looking blacker than a thief's heart, stiffening the tunic.

There was utter silence. One chicken squawked. A breeze lifted Bishop's hair off his forehead. He felt only a bit weak now. He touched his hand to his chest. He was whole.

"He isn't dead, he isn't dead, he isn't dead." The shock made the voices all blend together, until they sounded nearly one voice in his head.

It was impossible, all knew it was impossible. Then someone said, "I understand now. It was just a prick of the knife, the sort that causes a lot of bleeding, but withal the knife struck nothing vital, nothing to kill Sir Bishop."

"Aye, that's it."

Bishop could feel the people's relief that they could now understand that nothing had happened that would make them hear dark wings flapping over their heads in the deep of the night. He said nothing, just took Merryn's hand, looked down into her ugly old face. "Will you wed me in an hour's time?"

"Aye, just as soon as we clean the blood off ourselves and I can let this nose fall off."

She vaguely heard cheering. She felt her grandfather hug her, her grandmother's busy hands patting her here and there.

37

There was no wound in his chest, no sign that a knife had ever sunk through his flesh into his heart. There was nothing save mayhap a bit of soreness, but perhaps that was because Merryn had pounded her fist so hard against him and laid herself so heavily on top of him.

That made him smile. He leaned back in the tub and closed his eyes. She would come to him soon, a sponge in her hand, and she would bathe him. Then, he thought, he would bathe her, although he knew she'd already been bathed by all her hovering women.

He wondered if there was any mark on her breast, any bruise or mark to prove that something had happened.

He felt energy pulse through him, perhaps more energy than he'd had before the fight with Fioral. Now, that was odd.

Merryn came into the chamber, the sponge in her hand. She was smiling, her blood-soaked gown gone. She was wearing a simple robe, one he knew she would change when they were wed this evening. She stood over him, laid her hand on his shoulder. "How do you feel?"

He only nodded. "Show me your breast."

Slowly she laid down the sponge, took a step back and opened her robe. She pulled it wide. He stared at her breast, the soft white flesh, but—and then he saw the faint white line and knew it was right over her beating heart. He swallowed. "I don't have even a mark."

"I'm glad. This, it's nothing." She closed her robe. "I am here to bathe you, my soon-to-be husband. I wish you to lean back, be at ease, and let me attend you. I would say that you have had a hard day."

Bishop did just that, laughed. "Aye, I have. Do you love me, Merryn?"

She said without hesitation, without even slowing the smooth stroking of the sponge, "Aye, I love you. I love you more than I did just a minute ago. Soon I will have such love for you I will feel knocked about the head with it."

He opened his eyes and smiled up at her. He lightly closed his hand over hers. "I know that feeling exactly."

There came a knock on the chamber door.

Merryn called out, "Who is it? Who wishes to behold the bridegroom in his bath?"

"It is I, Crispin, my lady."

"Come, Crispin," Bishop called out.

Crispin came into the chamber, not looking at the two young people who'd so recently been older than his father, mayhap even older than his grandfather, but down at the strange stick he held in his hands. He thrust it out toward Bishop.

"My lord, one of the children found this, said that when you stood up, the stick dropped from the sleeve of your tunic. It's just a stick, only it's not, if you know what I mean."

Bishop took the wand. "Thank you, Crispin. I thought it was gone." And he wondered how it had gotten into his sleeve. No, he didn't want to know.

After Crispin closed the door after him, Merryn took a very deep breath. "It fell out of your sleeve? I thought it disappeared back at the cave near Tintagel."

"It did. But it's here now." They looked at each other. Merryn whispered, "We're both alive. Something happened, Bishop. Did the wand help it happen?"

He said nothing, merely held the wand, feeling its soft warmth against his palm. There was so much flooding through his brain, making his breathing hitch when he thought too deeply about what had happened.

"It's the same wand, isn't it?"

"Aye, it's the same." He sat forward and she soaped his back with the sponge. He looked closely at the wand, and then he stiffened straight as an arrow. He jerked about, splashing water onto the floor, onto Merryn as well.

"What is it? Are you still hurt? Bishop, speak to me."

"Look, Merryn. Look."

He held the wand up, his thumb pressing against an indentation in the wood. She knelt next to the big wooden tub, laid her finger atop his thumb.

"Feel." He moved his thumb and her finger traced the indentations. "Let me hold it to the light," she said, took the wand from him, and stood. He watched her walk over to the window with it, hold it to the afternoon sunlight.

She read slowly, " 'Ambrosius.' " She looked back over at him. " 'Ambrosius?' What does that mean?"

Bishop stilled. "Is that all you see? Is there another name, another word?"

Merryn turned the wand slowly in her hands, examining each inch of it. "Here, wait. It says 'Merlin. Merlin Ambrosius.' Do you know what that means? Is it a name, Bishop?"

Bishop said slowly, "When I was wounded once several years ago, Benedictine monks took me in and healed me. One old monk loved to read the tales written by Geoffrey of Monmouth, who lived more than a hundred years ago. He wrote about an advisor to Uther Pendragon—the father of King Arthur."

"Merlin," Merryn said. "Aye, I remember now. He was a magician, wasn't he?"

"Aye, and he was more than that. He was a wizard, so it was written," Bishop said. "A wizard," he said again, more slowly.

"I don't understand this, Bishop."

He didn't either. He didn't think he wanted to. The wand had belonged to Merlin? It was more than a mortal could bear.

A mortal. Aye, he was a mortal, but the prince and Brecia, they hadn't been mortals. And the prince had made Brecia pregnant in their first wild mating, just as he knew he'd made Merryn pregnant.

In that moment, Bishop sensed something. He knew he felt the prince close to him, heard the prince's voice, and he was laughing, softly, and then, suddenly, he was gone, and there was only the sweet warm air and Merryn at his side.

"Come here and kiss me, Merryn."

"We've been married for a full five days now and I am still very much alive."

"Aye, you are, husband. Have you written to King Edward?"

"Aye, and a messenger should be with him soon. Dienwald and Philippa and their children will be arriving tomorrow. Vellan and Madelyn wish to meet them."

Bishop rose and tapped his knife handle several times against a goblet from the Rhineland, one of Lord Vellan's prized possessions.

He waited until there was complete silence in the great hall, all faces turned toward him. He raised the goblet. "Here is to the end of the Penwyth curse. It is over and gone."

There was wild cheering and everyone drank.

Bishop smiled down at his wife. "I am the fifth and final husband!"

There was more wild cheering.

Merryn rose to stand beside Bishop. Everyone fell silent again. "No more curses to haunt Penwyth!"

Bishop said after they'd quieted a bit, "All have wondered why people live so very long here at Penwyth. I will tell you. It is because anyone who loves Penwyth, who is utterly loyal, deserves a long life. And so it is."

"—I can't lift my sword but I am alive, aye!"

"—All of us deserve long life!"

Everyone was cheering and laughing and talking about the four husbands who'd all toppled over dead so quickly after their marriage to Merryn.

"No more curse!"

"No more curse!"

"Long life to those who love Penwyth!"

Lady Madelyn said, "I wonder if there truly was a curse. One that came from the ancient Druids? From the Witches of Byrne? No, I don't think there ever was a curse."

"Of course there was, Grandmother," Merryn said. "Bishop and I broke the curse."

Lady Madelyn just shook her head.

Vellan looked at his wife of so many years he would need more fingers and toes to count than were in the great hall, and said, his voice thick with disbelief, dread, and a dab of pleasure, "What do you mean, Madelyn?"

"I poisoned Arlan de Frome, that's what I mean. Then I prayed that the others would die as well since I couldn't manage to poison them. My prayers worked."

Epilogue

Sometime Else

The prince stood beside Brecia, his hand lightly touching her shoulder, pointing. "See, yon, my love, is where we will live when we are not in your fortress in the oak forest."

They'd just stepped out of the prince's cave and were looking toward a promontory in the distance. On its very edge stood a large white structure that soared toward the heavens. It was like nothing Brecia had ever seen before. He said, "My parents wanted it like this. You see, my father said that an ancient people called the Greeks built many beautiful structures like this for their gods and goddesses. Now we have one as well."

"It is beautiful."

"Our son will grow up here. He will learn who and what he is within these walls," the prince said.

Brecia turned to rest her cheek against his shoulder. "What will we name our son?"

He kissed her beautiful red hair, pulled her closer. "We will see," he said, his voice a whisper of sound against her temple, his breath warm and sweet as the incredible scent of the blossom he'd just plucked for her and woven into her hair. "He will be known forever, that I do know. We will select a name to fit him."

"Thank you for coming to me in the oak forest," Brecia said.

He remembered for a blinding instant lying there on his back, evidently sleeping just outside her forest, Callas standing over him, and he'd had no idea how or why he was there. But maybe he had known and just forgotten. Whatever had happened, it didn't matter. He smiled, stroked his fingertips over her smooth cheek. "Aye, I came for you. Thank you for saving my miserable wizard's life."

She laid her hand over his, both lightly set against her belly, now swollen with their son. They looked toward the beautiful white fortress that wasn't really a fortress at all, and felt the sunlight warm them.

His hand stilled. "I can feel that all is well," he said, and smiled. "In all times." He looked back at his cave, and his smile widened. Then his full attention was on her. "Do you know, I feel like making you yell to the heavens." He leaned over, pushed Brecia's heavy hair away, and nibbled on her ear.

She turned quickly, laughing, and grabbed him. "This is madness, prince. It's magic, what you make me feel so quickly."

"No," he said, his mouth against hers, "it's us. Just us."

She laughed as she squeezed him tightly against her. "Then why can I streak my fingers through a cloud?"

Present
Penwyth Castle

Bishop felt a bolt of lust so great he nearly fell out of his chair. He didn't understand, but he didn't care, not a whit. He lifted Merryn's hair away and nibbled her earlobe. She turned, laughing. "What is this, my lord?"

In the next breath, she was looking at his mouth, breathing hard, and pushing out of her chair to get closer to him. Her eyes were nearly crossed, she was trying so hard to kiss him anywhere she could reach.

It didn't matter that the great hall was filled with people, that conversations were slowing, stopping, as their people stared toward the dais. Nothing mattered but that they have each other. Fast.

Bishop couldn't stand it, couldn't wait another second. He leapt up from his chair, grabbed his wife, who he happily saw was in as bad shape as he was, and dragged her across the great hall, but only for a couple of steps. She was soon running beside him. The racket of so many voices raised in laughter didn't really touch them. *All is well,* Bishop thought as he raced up the stairs to their bedchamber, Merryn breathing hard beside him. *Aye, all is well everywhere.*

And in every time.